WHAT HIDES BEHIND THE WALLS

Sherri Stewart

Chapter One

"You will find it is necessary to let things go, simply for the reason
that they are too heavy."
~ Corrie ten Boom

Tamar Feldman stared up at the curtained bedroom
window that used to be hers a lifetime ago. She checked her pocket
for the screwdriver. Should she chance entering the house?

She swallowed hard. Was it only five years since she'd been on
the other side of that window, searching the sidewalk for her
brother's handsome friend, Daniel? One good thing had come out of
the past few tumultuous years—her brother's friend now was her
husband. Yes, beauty had come out of the ashes of war, as Daniel
had promised her. Was it worth it now, risking arrest, breaking into
the house the Nazis had ripped away? How else could she open the
upstairs grate to retrieve what her parents had hidden behind it?

Before they'd been driven away, her father had called Seth and
her into the hall and showed them the grate. Said he'd tucked
important documents and small family heirlooms behind it. Maybe
he'd hidden the deed to the house there.

Daniel would definitely tell her to walk away. He'd argue that
nothing good could come from dwelling on what couldn't be
changed. Easy for him to say.

Tamar kicked an empty cigarette pack with her toe. Garbage

everywhere. The war had decimated the face of Haarlem—the very spirit of Haarlem. And now, in 1949, the town was a scarred, wrinkled version of its former visage.

No, she would not accept the decline of the Netherlands or live as though it didn't matter … because it did.

Was it a crime to break into a thief's house, anyway?

A casual glance up and down the *Barteljorisstraat*—her old street—showed no one with suspicious eyes. Bicycles whizzed past in both directions. Boys with book bags hugging their shoulders jostled each other on their way to school. The aroma of freshly baked bread and pastries emanated from the bakery across the street.

Tamar inhaled deeply. Sumptuous memories filled her of waking up every morning to the same scents coming from the Betzes' bakery. But the Betzes were gone. Dachau and Vught had seen to that. They'd be happy to know their shop was still blessing the neighborhood with the aroma of baked bread and sugary treats.

Tamar checked her watch. Hadassah could only watch the twins for the next hour. She should heed the warnings tugging inside her to let the past rest. But someone was living in her family home. Someone was benefiting from the house sitting empty after her parents were taken to the camps. Where was the justice? Didn't she owe it to her parents' memory to enter the house and see if anything remained of her family's?

Tamar ambled to the front of the four-storied home, to her parents' jewelry store on the first floor. She shielded her eyes and peeked in the front windows. The jewelry store was gone, replaced by a dry-cleaning business. With the shortage of food and high unemployment, how could anyone afford dry cleaning? But the rotating racks showed paper-covered garments waiting to be picked up.

Gone were the mahogany counters in which her parents had displayed jewelry. Gone were the clocks on the walls. The crystal stemware and silver. Now it just looked drab. Plain. Soulless.

So many memories tumbled over each other. Of helping in the shop, feather dusting the bracelets, rings, and necklaces. Even as a teen, she liked to imagine herself slipping on those rings and necklaces someday to accentuate the beautiful designer gowns she'd wear to post-opera parties.

The sign on the door read, *Be back in a few minutes.* This was her chance. If she thought too hard about it, the opportunity would be gone.

Tamar took in the whole street. When she saw no one, she returned to the side steps that led to the third floor. After another glimpse of the sidewalk, she tugged on the door.

Locked. Now what? Time was not her friend. She needed to get in and out before the owner returned. Her eyes landed on the third brick from the ground. A spare key used to hide behind it, but that was five years ago. Five years of hiding out at Neelie's house, imprisoned at two labor camps, drifting through life in England for three years, then back to Haarlem. How could the key still be there after all those events? She knelt and worried the brick loose. With a little effort, it gave way, revealing the key—rusted and covered with dirt. With a sigh of relief, Tamar pulled it out and inserted it into the keyhole. It turned.

With another glance at the street, she waited, turning her back on two women dressed in long black dresses who carried shopping baskets. Once the road was empty, she stuffed the key in her pocket, hurried inside, and climbed to the third floor, the stairs creaking much more than she remembered. With each echoing footstep, she winced. Despite the sign on the store, it didn't mean the occupants were gone. What if the proprietor was eating a late breakfast in her former kitchen?

When she reached the top, memories returned—heavy ones. The familiar hall that opened into the three bedrooms and a bathroom didn't smell the same—in fact, it smelled old, as if it had sat dormant for the past five years. Gone was the aroma of her mother's soup and roasts which wafted up from the second floor and seemed to linger for days. Gone was the scent of her mother's cologne and the lemon polish on cleaning days that preceded *Shabbat*.

The portraits of aunts, uncles, and grandparents had vanished from the wallpapered walls, replaced by framed artwork—so many portraits and paintings and still lifes that the hall looked cluttered. The heavy, dark credenza still sat against the wall, now stacked with knickknacks, statuettes, and silverware. It reminded her of the antique shop down the street, as if the stacks were there temporarily until they could find permanent homes.

Her mother would have hated the clutter. She always

maintained that a home wasn't about possessions but people. Whoever lived here now didn't share her viewpoint.

The chimes of a clock brought her back to the task at hand. Time was running out. Who knew how long that sign had been in the window? She pushed the credenza a few centimeters to the right, but it was so full of glassware and ceramic bowls, she feared they would crash to the floor. Her eyes squeezed shut with every effort.

Down on her knees, she took the screwdriver from her jacket pocket. If only Daniel was with her, he'd be able to open the grate in a flash, but working with tools wasn't her forte. She lined up the edge with the straight groove of the screw on the left. It didn't fit. The groove was too narrow. She'd need to return with a smaller screwdriver.

A rustling came from the first floor, but maybe it was her imagination. Tamar peered at the staircase, then back at the grate. Through the holes, she squinted to see behind the grooves, but it was too dark.

Climbing to her feet, she surveyed the hall. Pushing the credenza back would make too much noise, so she'd have to leave it, hoping the piles of paintings leaning against the wall would mask the two-centimeter shift to the right. With her toe, she swiped against the stripes on the floor, then moved toward the stairs but stopped, turned, and studied the doors.

If she was quiet, what would be the risk of grabbing one quick glimpse of the bedrooms on her way out? This might be her only chance. She tiptoed toward her parents' door and inched it open. Holding her breath, Tamar recognized her parents' bedspread and the dark oak armoire in the corner. The bureau with its twin mirrors stood against the wall, but now it was covered with candlesticks, stacks of paintings, and statuettes. More paintings covered every millimeter of the walls. It reminded her of one of the small rooms at the Rijksmuseum in Amsterdam.

She slipped the door shut and moved to Seth's bedroom next. It seemed odd that all the doors were closed. Throughout her twenty-two years of life in this house, the doors were always open—that is, until her brother had become sullen and stayed to himself all the time. She'd thought he'd been jilted by a girlfriend—as if it were only a girlfriend that caused him to age a decade.

Tamar wriggled Seth's doorknob, but it refused to budge. Her face puckered. Why was it locked? Who lived here, anyway? Surely, a dry-cleaning business couldn't be so profitable that its owner could afford to buy what looked like expensive paintings, especially after the war.

Tamar steeled her nerves for the only room left. She slowly opened her bedroom door and froze. What appeared wrenched her heart. Gone was her bed, her posters of Sonja Henie, Clarke Gable, and opera singer Iva Pacetti, whose face she used to stare at whenever she needed motivation to keep up her *solfeggio*. Where her bed once stood was a crib. A rocking chair had replaced her desk, and a dozen paintings covered the walls.

One picture caught her attention, and her jaw dropped. The violin girl? How could—? Why was it—?

The painting had shown up twice in her life before, and it always merited a second look. On the first occasion, she'd been on her way home from school when she was twelve and stopped to peer through the windows of the Hamels' art gallery. Tamar always delighted in seeing the new monthly display of pictures. The girl with the violin had caught her eye, and she'd found herself stopping every day to see the painting.

While she and the girl in the picture were not the same age, Tamar felt a kinship with her. They had the same blond hair and blue eyes, although she was quite sure the young girl wasn't a Jew as she was. But there was something that went deeper than mere physical appearance. Maybe it was because the girl in the picture looked lonely, as if the violin in her hand prevented her from living a normal life. It was the same for Tamar. From the time she was eight, and the rabbi's wife had discovered Tamar could sing, her parents had enrolled her in private bi-weekly singing lessons. Ever the taskmaster, her brother made her practice scales and intervals until she was hoarse.

At first it was fun, but soon Tamar lost herself in the music. At nine, her life became a series of running from practice to lessons to homework to bed. Tamar read the same mixture of determination tinged with a bit of sadness she'd experienced in the girl's eyes.

She walked slowly toward the picture, then glided her fingers over the frame.

She'd been surprised later to encounter the Hamels, the owners of the gallery, as "guests" hiding at Neelie's house from the Nazis.

A sigh erupted, unannounced or invited. What had happened to the Hamels after she and Daniel had been taken to the labor camp? They were such a sweet couple and reminded her of her parents.

The second time she'd seen the violin girl was stuffed into a closed drawer in her mind. Now the drawer opened, emitting a fresh wave of humiliation. The painting of the girl had hung on the wall of the concert room where she'd been forced to sing for the Führer's birthday at Westerbork labor camp.

Now here it was in her bedroom. Coincidence? Was this what Daniel and Neelie always called 'God moments'? From the Hamels' gallery to a concentration camp to her bedroom wall? Maybe she was meant to find it.

A single chime of a distant clock brought her back to the present. Time to leave before the owners of the house returned. She'd been here at least twenty minutes.

With another glance at the picture, she headed to the door, then turned to look at the painting once more. Should she just take it? Was it wrong to steal from the thieves who lived in this house? Following that line of reasoning, it would be all right to kill a murderer. Her own murderous thoughts had played in her mind at the camps and even more so for a certain Nazi officer. But God said revenge didn't belong to her, so she'd swiped those thoughts from her mind. But like uninvited guests, they returned every once in a while.

She'd have to give the moral dilemma of stealing from a thief some more thought—maybe even ask Daniel for his opinion— hypothetically, of course. And next time, she'd bring the right size screwdriver.

The door to the stairs from the dry cleaner creaked. Her breath caught. That same creak had been a harbinger that her mother had finished work and was coming up the stairs to begin dinner. But the person on the stairs wasn't her mother. She needed to get out of here now, but her feet refused to move.

The rustle of a bag below and a woman's humming brought memories back of her mother returning from buying groceries at Albert Heijn's market. She'd hum as she came up the stairs—songs from *Shul.*

Tamar put her ear close to the door, then opened it a few millimeters. The voice sounded familiar. A soprano with a large range and perfect pitch. Could it be? No, the last time Tamar had seen Margot was at the same place she'd seen the violin girl painting. Another coincidence … or a God moment?

If she didn't leave right now, the humming woman would catch her. And if it were Margot coming up the stairs, she would certainly call the police. With one more glance at the blond girl and her instrument, she tiptoed toward the back stairs, wincing with each creak, then scrambled down the steps.

Inching the door open, she slipped out. Hopefully, the woman wouldn't look out the kitchen window. She fished the key out of her pocket, and after scanning the area for the curious eyes of people living in neighboring houses, Tamar eased the brick from its place and hid the key behind it.

She'd be back. Tamar looked both ways up and down the Barteljorisstraat, and when the sidewalk emptied of pedestrians, she headed for home. A glance at her watch made her step up her pace. Peri and Zari could become ornery before naptime and foisting the twins on Hadassah would test the limits of their in-law relationship if she didn't hurry home.

Tamar held her nose and stepped around an overflowing trashcan. How Haarlem had changed since the Nazi occupation. A depressing pall added to the gray skies, as if nature knew the country wasn't ready to celebrate yet. Bridges remained impassable, making it difficult to cross the canal unless one walked an extra kilometer out of their way. Potholes and rubble marred the road, uncared for since the start of the occupation.

The physical appearance wasn't the only change in Haarlem. People had changed as well. No longer did they stop to chat with their friends on the sidewalks as they went about their morning errands. Now the quiet was deafening. The lack of trust that started during the occupation years hadn't dissipated once the Nazis were gone. It wasn't just distrust, Tamar mused as she sprang to the side to avoid tripping over a divot in the sidewalk. It was guilt. So many of her fellow Nederlanders had turned on their Jewish neighbors, either by disclosing their location to the Nazis or refusing to offer them help when they needed it.

Guilt weighed on her shoulders, although both Daniel and Neelie told her it wasn't her fault she had survived when most other Netherlands Jews hadn't returned from the camps, including her parents, her friends, and her neighbors.

She hurried through the market square under the shadow of St. Bavo's cathedral. This had always been such a joyful place. The market with the pungent aroma of gouda and edam. The bustle of shoppers browsing the aisles full of kiosks on Shabbat. Sometimes she'd sneak out of the house by climbing out the upstairs window to leaf through the racks of clothes, sample the offered cheese and breads, and enjoy the music of the bands.

A woman with eyes blackened with kohl that made her look like a raccoon leaned over a balcony and waved a handkerchief at a man who stood on the sidewalk. A red scarf covered most of her hair, but the short spikes peeking out identified her as one of the shaved ones. Hadassah had told Tamar the women who had collaborated with the Nazis were shunned. Even four years later, their heads were still shaven.

With time running out before Hadassah had to leave for work, Tamar scrambled up the four floors to her apartment, stopped at the entrance across from hers, and knocked.

Hadassah flung the door open. "Look, Peri, your *Eema* is here." She stepped aside to let Tamar enter the small parlor and hurried to the closet to grab her coat. "How did it go? Wish I didn't have to run. Did you find any of your parents' things?" She held up her ebony hair as she donned her overcoat, then let her long tresses fall over her shoulders. "I was so worried you'd get caught. You didn't, did you?"

Tamar bent down to plant a kiss on Peri's chubby cheeks. He lifted both arms to be picked up. She hoisted him onto her hip and joined her sister-in-law at the door. "I have a lot to tell you, but you have to go." She surveyed the toys that littered the floor. "I'll make sure everything is back in its place. Thank you so much for covering for me."

"No problem. I always enjoy watching my niece and nephew. Zari colored the whole time you were gone. She's going to be an artist, that one. So, quick, did you find anything at the house?"

With a glance at her studious little girl, she turned to her best friend. "Not behind the grate. I brought the wrong size screwdriver. Did you know there were different sizes? The house is so old, it was probably some kind of ancient tool they don't even make anymore."

A furrow appeared between Hadassah's eyebrows. "So what are

you going to do? Are you going to tell Daniel?"

She squirmed. "I don't like to keep secrets from him. We made a pact early on that we would never lie to one another. I'll think about it. But there's much more to tell you—"

Hadassah placed a hand on her arm. "We'll talk tomorrow. *Dag.*" She rushed out and clamored down the stairs.

Tamar closed the door, pivoted to face the untidy job ahead of her, and set her son down. "Time to go home, kids. Zari and Peri, would you each pick up five things?" She'd learned giving them a number made it more like a game.

Zari jumped up from where she sat on the floor. "Five plus five is"—her face scrunched up— "ten. How many will you pick up, Eema?"

"Well, if I pick up the same number as you two, how many in all?"

She shrugged. "A lot?"

She bent down to her daughter's level. "Yes, twenty is a lot, but that should make *Tante* Hadassah happy." Her eyes landed on Peri, who careened around the room and tripped over Zari's favorite doll. Zari was taking after her father—serious, determined, but kind. Peri was his own person.

Thoughts of Daniel ran through her mind as she watched the twins compete for the toys on the floor. Tamar had never kept secrets from her husband. Not after their conversation years before on Neelie's balcony when she'd told him about the Nazi officer's interest in furthering her singing career. Daniel was troubled, but he allayed her fears and promised to be with her. From that day on, she'd never kept anything from him. Until now.

Two Jews in the midst of dozens of drunken Nazi officers could have ended so badly, but God was with them. She didn't know it then, but she knew it now. Would God be with her if she broke the law by breaking into that house even if it used to be hers?

At any rate, Daniel would be opposed to the idea. In the years since the war, her husband had changed from wanting to tell the world about their experiences to merely surviving each day. Neelie had urged Daniel to come to the rehabilitation center in Amsterdam where she worked, but he always declined, saying he had too much work to do at St. Elizabeth's Gasthuis, the hospital where he treated burn victims.

Tamar roused herself. Zari was jumping up and down, asking her mother to count the items in her arms and dropping a few with every leap. "Good job, Zari. Put them in the basket in the corner." Peri was whirling around with a toy in each hand. She hurried over to stop him before he knocked over a lamp. "I bet I can pick up more than you."

The three-year-old stopped, his competitive spirit ignited. Soon the room was tidy, and the children were vying for the doorknob. Everything was a contest for these two.

Tamar grabbed the basket of toys and headed across the hall to the only other apartment on the fourth floor. How lucky she was to have her brother, Seth, and Hadassah right across the hall, not just for caring for the twins but also for companionship for herself since Daniel worked such long hours at the hospital. Since her hands were full, Tamar propped up the basket with her knee, turned the doorknob, and spilled through the door behind the twins.

"*Abba!*" Zari dashed to her father, who sat in the worn armchair, snoring lightly, his head twisted at an uncomfortable angle. Even now, Tamar's heart sped up as it always did when she saw him. He'd warned her that their next couple years together would be like passing ships, but someday, when they'd saved enough from his earnings at the hospital to buy a house, he'd open his own practice and simply climb the stairs to come home after work. She liked that dream—it had been what helped them endure the long days at Neelie's house.

Peri followed close behind his sister, and both climbed onto Daniel's lap. He woke with a start and glanced around as if he'd landed in some foreign place. A smile spread across his face, and he tickled the twins, causing them to arch their backs and giggle.

His lovely brown eyes sparkled in her direction. It was all she could see with Peri's blond head covering his face. "Hi, love of my life. Where have you been?"

A hint of guilt poked at Tamar. Somehow, she knew her lie would build a wall between them. But was not telling him the same as lying? "We were at Hadassah's until she left for work. I didn't expect you home until late tonight."

Daniel rested his head against the chair back, a satisfied smile covering his face. "They have enough residents to cover for me. I'm on call, but the attending sent me home. I have tomorrow off as well." He set the twins on the floor, stood and stretched his long arms, and yawned. "You know what I'm going to do? I'm going to sleep as long as I can." Stepping over the twins, Daniel grabbed her and twirled her around. "Hey, beautiful, what do you say we go on a real date tomorrow? Maybe we can persuade Hadassah to watch the kids and—"

She swallowed the lump that always filled her throat when she was nervous, but if she didn't tell him, it would stand between them. "First, I have to tell you something. You might want to sit down."

"If I do, don't be surprised if I start snoring. Although I don't."

Tamar rolled her eyes. "Peri, does your abba snore?"

The three-year-old's chubby arms flew up, and he gleefully roared, "Yes," echoed by his twin sister. "Can we play horse, Papa?"

"All right," he moaned and slowly lowered himself to the floor on all fours. "Climb on. But this will be a slow ride." He glanced up at Tamar. "Can we talk now, or do you need my undivided attention?"

Hm. Good question. If she told him now, he might be less reactive—not that he was ever anything but a gentleman. She cleared her throat, then thought better of unloading her guilt in front of the twins. "I'll wait."

Tamar headed to the kitchen to put on the kettle for tea. While the kids bucked and squealed, she filled a tray with teacups, cream, and sugar. Then she added a small plate of cookies. Sugar always made bad news more palatable.

Five minutes later, while the tea was steeping, she heard Daniel say, "All right, this horsey is sleepy, and you don't want to fall off a sleeping horse. Why don't you go play in your room? See what you can do with the dominoes."

Once the twins had tried to outrun each other to their room, Tamar brought out the tray, placed it on the coffee table, then sat down on the sofa. Daniel claimed the seat next to her and grabbed a cookie. "These look good. Did you make them?" Then he slapped his knee and laughed.

"Stop it," she said. "I'll try making cookies when I'm good and ready. Hadassah made them." She poured him a cup and added a bit of cream and one sugar cube, just the way he liked it.

"Thank you. Now tell me what's bothering you."

She didn't pour herself a cup. Her stomach was too queasy.

"Well, I … uh … went to my old house and found the key I used to hide behind a brick. No one was there at the time, and—"

His wide eyes met hers. "You did what?"

She breathed deeply. This wasn't going to end well. "I went into the house to check that grate by the bedrooms. Remember, I told you my father had hidden some personal papers and valuables behind it?"

Daniel frowned at his teacup. She wrapped her arms around her waist. When his eyes met hers, he was the epitome of reserved. "Okay, tell me everything." His jaw tightened to the point that taut lines appeared around his mouth.

"That house belonged to my parents, and it has occurred to me, as you know, that the people squatting there may not know about what is behind the grate. So I took a screwdriver with me just in case, and I tried to open the grate, but the screwdriver didn't fit."

He shook his head slowly. "Don't you realize how much trouble you could have gotten into? It's not your house now. I know it's not fair, but you can't go breaking into other people's houses."

She patted his arm. "I know … but listen. The place is full of art and sculptures. You should see it. The house looks like a museum—no, more like a storehouse for a museum." His interest was piqued. "Every room upstairs was bursting with tapestries and statues and—"

"That makes that place even more dangerous for you, Tamar. It sounds like it's a repository for stolen art. What if they'd caught you? I couldn't stand to lose you—"

The fear in his eyes made her regret telling him, but at least the truth was out. "There's more. I went into my bedroom, and now it's a baby's room with a crib and a rocking chair." She bit on her lip to stop its quiver. "And you know what I saw? That painting of the violin girl was there, hanging on the wall. I told you about it. The first time I saw it was at the Hamels' gallery when I was ten or eleven. I always felt the girl in the picture and I were kindred spirits."

Daniel pulled her toward him, smoothing stray strands of hair from her face. She must look a fright. Normally, she would have cleaned up before he came home from work.

"It was just the imagination of a young girl, but I felt as if the girl in the picture and I had given up part of our childhood for music—hers for the violin and mine for my singing. Does that make sense?"

"Sure it does." He kissed her temple, which sent shivers through her body.

She rested her head in the crook of his neck. "Did I ever tell you that I saw that same painting at Westerbork when I had to sing for the Führer's birthday?"

He straightened and turned to face her. "You didn't tell me. Now it's in your bedroom? It could be just a coincidence—the new owners could have bought it at an auction, but whoever is living there is obviously profiting from the looting of Jewish stores and houses. Still, it is concerning. What are the chances you would see the same picture in three places?"

"I know. You often say that with God, nothing is an accident. Do you think I was meant to find that picture?"

He rolled his eyes and chuckled. "I see what you're doing. You're trying to justify the fact that you broke into someone's house."

She pushed him away. "You make it sound so bad. Don't you understand why I had to go? And now we know there's stolen art there. From the Jews—our own people's collections. We have to do something."

Daniel gripped one of her hands and rubbed it against his cheek. "I couldn't stand it if anything happened to you. Can't you let it go?" He must have read the regret and determination in her eyes and the set of her mouth. "You're going to go, anyway, aren't you?" A smirk crossed his lips, and he shook his head.

"Will you go with me? Please? You can open that grate a lot more quickly than I can, and I want you to be a witness to what's being held there." Her hand went to her lips. "Another thing. I'm pretty sure Margot is the one living in my house."

"Margot, the soprano? The one who called us vermin when she saw our yellow stars?"

She nodded. "Not to mention, she was on the arm of a Nazi officer when she said it."

His Adam's apple rose and fell as it often did when he was considering the pros and cons. He took in a deep breath. "Okay. I'm going to regret this so much." Daniel held up his index finger. "One time. I'll go with you to open the grate, and that's it. But you must promise never ever to go back."

Relief filled her. "I promise."

He squeezed her hand. "Please note that I'll be grumbling the whole way to the house."

Chapter Two

"When I try, I fail. When I trust, he succeeds."
~ Corrie ten Boom

Neelie Visser took a fortifying breath before entering her old house. Layers of memories, good and bad, piled heavily on her shoulders, as they always did whenever she stepped into the foyer. The art deco cabinet still sat there, battered and dusty. The one that had held the repaired violin of Nazi Captain Bergman. She'd been so busy cleaning up after her guests, she'd left the door that connected the foyer to the kitchen stairs open. That's when Bergman had heard Tamar singing while she mopped the kitchen floor and insisted upon meeting her.

How naïve Neelie had been. Bergman had probably known all along that she was hiding Jews. Bringing in the violin for repair was just an excuse.

Enough of such maudlin memories, even those that had proven life-changing. Perhaps Bergman had been thrown into prison after the Nuremburg Trials, but he was as wily as a red fox. The man was probably sipping a cocktail on the beach of some exotic island. *Drink up, Officer. God will bring justice in His own time.*

She smoothed back errant gray hairs and climbed the stairs to the kitchen. The intervening years had made it a more arduous task, and she had to stop to catch her breath. Five years had made her a soft forty-seven-year-old.

Neelie waved a hand in front of her nose. Jan's dishes overtook the countertops. Her son was a wonderful young man, but tidiness was not his forte. Of course, law school kept him busy, and he was also handling a clerkship of some kind. While she was here, she'd give the kitchen a good polish.

She donned an apron and made quick work of the dishes, then grabbed the mop and started on the floor. Soon the place smelled like pine trees, as it had when Neelie and her seven adult guests lived here, thanks to Tamar's constant scrubbing. A glance at the rooster clock above the sink showed her son was already a few minutes late.

He'd asked her to meet with him here. Said he had something to tell her. Maybe there was a new girlfriend. Wouldn't that be something? She headed to the sink to fill the kettle and opened the cupboard to take out two cups and plates. Fortunately, Jan hadn't moved everything around. She'd lived in this house all of her married life. It had been in Frans's family for at least a century— one of the '*grandes dames*' on the canal.

At least Jan had made sure to stay in the house after she and the guests were sent away. As a result of him not being Jewish, the Nazis hadn't taken over the house and its furnishings as they had so many of the homes in Haarlem.

Still, she couldn't blame the Nazis for her reluctance to move back here after the war. Even before they made her neighborhood a ghetto, Neelie hadn't liked staying in this five-story house after Frans passed away. The walls echoed her solitude. Back then, every creak of the house magnified in her mind, and she was sure someone had taken residence in the attic. That made the move to Amsterdam an easy choice, and she'd settled into her new position at the rehabilitation center for Jews returning from the camps. So few returned, and those who did needed so much help—broken human beings who'd lost their families, their health, their reason to live.

Just like Daniel and Tamar. Both drifted through life as if busyness could sweep away the demons of the camps. Daniel with his work with burn victims and Tamar with the twins. Neelie read their faces—the vacant eyes, the resignation, the lethargy. All survivors needed to talk and vent and pray and finally forgive. The last step was the hardest even for her.

The back door creaked its age. Neelie caught her breath, reliving the urge to tell everyone to hide. Instead, she turned on the kettle and unwrapped the cinnamon-banana *brood* she'd made the night before. Jan didn't usually phone her to come to Haarlem unless it was important. She steeled herself for bad news.

Her son's deep voice came from the foyer. "Mam, are you here? It smells piney." Quick steps to the kitchen, and Jan's winsome smile was the first thing she saw.

How she loved her Jan. He was such a godsend since Frans had been promoted to his maker's house. She rose and stood on tiptoes to hug her son, whom she saw too infrequently since they lived in different towns and had their own lives. "You've grown a half a meter. How are you?"

"Too busy. Thanks for cleaning up the kitchen. When I'm home, I'm always studying for my classes or working on research for Jacob Kohn, so the dishes pile up, as does the garbage." He sniffed, then took a seat at the table. "It smells like evergreen trees with a touch of cinnamon."

Neelie poured some tea into his cup, offered him a small pitcher of cream, then served a piece of banana bread on a plate. "So tell me, what kind of work are you doing for this Jacob Kohn?" She took a sip of the brew to make sure it was strong enough.

"Jacob is an art-restitution lawyer. His whole practice is devoted to returning paintings and sculptures to their original owners." He took a bite of the bread and closed his eyes as he chewed. "This is so good."

"Thank you. Returning art to its owner should be a given, yes?" Neelie peered over her teacup at her son.

"It's complicated because we have to determine who actually owns the art. Museums bought stolen pieces at auction, so they have a legal claim if they paid in good faith. Though most of the time, they bought the art at drastically reduced prices, which makes 'good faith' something Jacob has to prove in court. In other cases, the original owners sold the paintings for a pittance to keep from starving. Now they want justice."

She finished swallowing a bite of the bread. "It's not right for museums to profit from art stolen by the Nazis."

"That's what Jacob wants to prevent. I'm working with a widow named Sarah Klein, whose Kandinsky painting was sold by her first husband for a few coins in 1940, although it was hers originally. Now *Painting with Houses* sits in the Stedelijk Museum in Amsterdam."

"And the rich get richer. That makes me so mad." She jostled her cup, tea spilling onto the table. "Sorry."

"I feel the same way," Jan said. "I know art isn't life and health, but when a family has been ripped apart, it's comforting to have something to remember them by."

Neelie patted his hand. "You've always had a strong sense of justice, even as a young boy. Now what did you want to tell me? Does it have something to do with a young lady?" She waggled her eyebrows. It would irk him, but she couldn't help herself.

Jan frowned. "Hm? No, well, Isabelle isn't a young lady by any means. I think she's your age."

Neelie gasped, and her hand went to her chest. "What are you saying? Who is this Isabelle?" She looked at the ceiling. "Frans, your son—listen to him."

Jan covered his mouth, but a guffaw came out, anyway. "Isabelle LeClair. She's French. You should see your face."

"French? I know those people have a different idea of what's proper, but—" She shook her head and stood. "I don't understand you young ones."

"No, Isabelle LeClair is the curator at the Jeu de Paume Museum in Paris. During the war, Hitler's right-hand man, Hermann Göring, chose paintings from the museum for his own collection and had them shipped to certain hiding places. Apparently, he liked modern art—even what Hitler considered degenerate art. Paintings by the likes of Picasso, Renoir, and Van Gogh were chosen for his collection."

She breathed a dramatic sigh, sat back down, and took a sip of her tea. "Well, I'm happy for you but not so happy for our country. It just gets worse and worse."

"Yes, but what Göring didn't know was that although LeClair was French, she spoke fluent German and could understand where he was sending the pictures. She kept good notes and has spent the last few years in Germany hunting down the stolen pictures to reclaim for France."

Neelie studied her son. "That's a God thing, you know. So what does this woman have to do with you?"

He scratched at his neck, leaving a track in his nails' wake, as he often did when he was nervous. "Jacob wants me to move to Paris for a few months to work with Isabelle and the museum's attorney to learn more about what's happened there, so I can help with art-restitution cases here."

She sat back and fanned herself with her napkin. "Paris is a long way from here, but it sounds like a good opportunity for you. But what does this mean for law school? What about exams?"

He stood and took their dishes to the sink. "I don't have to leave until June, and my exams are in May. Jacob has agreed to be my *patroon*, along with the attorney representing the Jeu de Paume."

"Patroon? What is that?" She joined Jan at the sink and filled it with sudsy water, then wrapped the remaining brood in a tea cloth.

He washed a plate and passed it to her. "A patroon oversees an apprentice. I still have to take classes, but Jacob's my advisor, so I'll be learning on the job."

"But will they pay you?" She wiped the plate and put it in the cupboard, clucking at the leaning stack of dishes behind its doors.

Jan passed her a cup. "No, but most law students don't get paid for clerking."

She studied her son out of the corner of her eye. "Are you sure this is the area of law you want to work in? It seems like a narrow field. Didn't you want to fight for the underdog?"

He shrugged. "I've prayed about it a lot. I went to law school because I wanted to seek justice for those who've been damaged by the war. Think about it. The survivors of the Holocaust can never get their loved ones back, but art restitution is one small way to right a wrong."

Neelie wrapped her wet arms around her son's neck, which made him grab a tea towel. "I am proud of you. Your father would be too. I'll miss you, but you have my blessing."

He wiped off his neck. "Thanks, Mam. Now come to the table. We have to talk about this house."

The house. Her eyes took in the whole kitchen. It was still hard for her to be here, with everything that had happened. The hall still held the scars where Captain Bergman and his men had bashed in the walls with their axes, searching for the babies she'd hidden. She sat, steeling herself for what Jan had to say. Would he urge her to put the place up for sale? How could she, even if she didn't want to live here?

He sat across from her. "Mam, we can't let this place sit empty while I'm gone. You know what's happened to our neighbors' houses. Nazi collaborators live in all of them—all those

Nederlanders who turned in their Jewish neighbors. They'd take over our place and squat. Especially a house like this on the canal. It's hard to evict squatters through legal means."

"What about renting it? I'd move back, but my work is in Amsterdam, and it's too difficult to take the train to and from Haarlem. You know how often the trains go on strike. And you'll only be gone for a few months." She paused at her son's intake of breath. "What?"

"It may be longer than a few months." A shoulder lifted. "It's a challenge to find good renters who will keep the place in good repair. Still, I can't imagine selling this house. So many memories, and they don't make houses like this one anymore. Plus, with the economy the way it is, we wouldn't receive near what it's worth."

Neelie placed her hand over her son's. "Whenever a situation seems unsolvable, God gives a third option, so let's pray about it." She grabbed her Bible from her book bag and set it on the table. A small paper peeked out of the top, one she'd put there for some reason, now forgotten, so she opened to the page and took it out. "Oh, I'd written a section of Genesis to show Tamar. You know how sensitive she is about her name."

Jan's head tilted. "I didn't know. What's wrong with her name?"

"Kids used to make fun of Tamar when she was a young girl because she shared the name with a woman in one of the spicier stories in Genesis. Tamar wasn't familiar with the story—as I see you aren't, either—so I told her about her namesake." She glanced up at her son. Now was not the time. "Anyway, I put this note in here as a reminder to tell her something I'd learned about the original Tamar." Neelie closed the book. "Let's talk about something else, shall we?"

They sat in comfortable silence for a few moments, each deeply entrenched in their own thoughts, then she glanced up. Jan was nodding at her, and a grin spread from dimple to dimple. "Are you thinking what I'm thinking, Mam?"

Her mouth fell open. "Why, of course. We have our third option, and that took, what? Five minutes? Tamar, Daniel, and the twins can move in here. Is that what you were thinking?"

"Absolutely. It makes perfect sense. We know they can be trusted to take good care of the place, and you'll have a room to stay in whenever you come and visit your 'grandkids.'"

She hugged her hands to her chest. "And they live in such cramped quarters in a fourth-floor apartment. I shudder every time I have to climb those stairs. So narrow and slanted. Daniel will be close to the hospital, and Tamar will be within walking distance of the opera, if it ever should open again. And there's the park just up the street—"

Jan took her hand. "What is it?"

"What happens when you come back? We can't offer our home to them and then make them leave. And knowing you, you'd stay away just so you wouldn't put them in that position."

He grinned. "I'm a big boy now. It's time to cut the apron strings. I'll be fine. Not to worry. Chances are, I'll be moving to Amsterdam, anyway, since that's where most of the restitution cases are handled."

Neelie pushed to her feet. "That's double good news. I'll have my favorite people close to me in Haarlem and in Amsterdam. Would it be all right to tell them? I can't wait to see the looks on their faces. I might as well visit them now while I'm in town."

"Of course, but remember, I'm not moving until June." He walked her to the door.

She turned and gave him a hug. "One more thing. Promise me you won't meet some pretty little French girl and stay in Paris."

Jan rolled his eyes. "I wouldn't think of it. Plus, I'll be too busy with dusty old paintings to think about a social life."

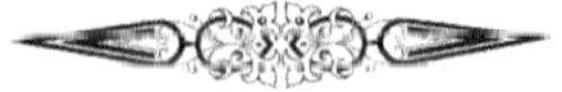

Neelie stopped to catch her breath and peered up at the last set of stairs to the fourth floor of the forbidding, red-stoned building. She had what should be good news to share, and she couldn't let a possible leg fracture stop her. She straightened her shoulders and counted each step.

The odor of cabbage and the children's giggles met her at the landing when she stopped again to recapture her breath, then tapped on the door. Galloping steps and the twins' voices arguing who could reach the doorknob first preceded the door opening wide.

"Oma!" the two tousled-headed three-year-olds shrieked.

Neelie bent down to hug them. It was always so remarkable that these two precious children had such different temperaments but were so alike in many ways.

"How are my favorite twins?" She kissed them both on their curly blond locks.

"*Goed*," they said in unison.

Zari held out a picture book to her. "I read the first page all by myself. It's about a little bunny. Will you read the rest of the story to me?"

Neelie took it and followed them into the small apartment. "It would be my pleasure."

"Plea…sure," Zari repeated, always the student.

Peri zoomed his pretend car in circles. Neelie caught the little packet of energy in her arms and blew a raspberry on his stomach. He responded with a belly laugh.

"Where are your eema and abba?" Neelie used their Hebrew monikers in deference to the twins' parents who were trying hard to bring them up proud of their heritage.

"In the kitchen," Peri said and squirmed out of her arms.

Neelie glanced up to see Tamar and Daniel standing by the kitchen table. The tiny apartment only had two small bedrooms, a galley kitchen, and a small living room with a sofa, armchair, and coffee table piled high with books, toys, and a radio. They shared the only bathroom on the floor with their neighbors. Yes, God had certainly led her to make the right decision.

Daniel joined her at the door, brushed her cheek with a kiss, then took her coat and hat. "You must be winded after that journey up the stairs. Come and sit on the sofa." He picked up one child in each arm and deposited them on the floor by their toy box.

Tamar linked arms with Neelie and led her to the couch. Her eyes sparkled in a way Neelie hadn't seen in years.

"What's happened to make you so happy?" Neelie asked while Peri dismantled her purse. She winced and swooped down upon the floor, handed him his toy car, and deftly stuffed everything back into her purse. Neelie resumed her seat on the sofa and smoothed her skirt. "Redirection still works with little ones. Now I have a proposition for you and Daniel. Sit, please, both of you." She swallowed. Daniel and Tamar would have misgivings, as Neelie did whenever she entered her former house. The fear that came with each knock of the door. The catch of her breath whenever one of the orphans cried. Sometimes she imagined she still heard the babies crying.

"What is it, Tante?" Tamar's blue eyes widened with expectation, while Daniel's were a bit more guarded.

"Keep an open mind, as they say, although I'm not sure how one does that. Maybe you as a doctor can explain it to us, Daniel." Neelie chuckled and cleared her throat. "Jan is moving to Paris for a few months starting in June to intern with a woman named Isabelle and an art-restitution lawyer—" She shook her head and stood. Pacing always helped. "You don't need to know all that. Anyway, the house will be sitting empty after he leaves, and we both would like you to consider moving in." She hazarded a glimpse of their reaction. Furrows formed between their brows. "You'd be doing us a big favor. If the house sits empty, squatters will be sure to move in, and Jan says it's impossible to evict them once they're … squatting." She wrung her hands and took a seat. "Please say yes."

They looked at each other, and the silence grew lengthy and uncomfortable. As she always did, Neelie filled it with chatter. "You'd have a lot more space, and the park is close by, and—"

Daniel interrupted. "Sorry, Tante, but I have a few misgivings. First of all, as much as I appreciate your offer, moving to a new place for just a few months while Jan's away would mean we'd have to move again. Finding a place is hard nowadays in Haarlem, and—"

"Not to worry. Jan doesn't anticipate moving back to the house even when he returns to Haarlem. He says, 'it's time to cut the apron strings'—his words. So you can stay for as long as you like. Forever, even."

Tamar grasped Daniel's hand. "Think about it, Daniel. We'd have our own bathroom, and the kids would have their own bedrooms. As they get older, they'll want that. And you'd still be close to the hospital."

He squeezed Tamar's hand, the concern apparent in his eyes. "We appreciate your offer, but that house will…bring it all back. The isolation, the fear, that last day. I don't know if I can handle—"

"Daniel, it's over. We have to—no, we *must* move on with our lives, or Bergman will have won. We can't let that happen. Sure, the memories will be there at first, but it's a step in the right direction.

Please." Tamar begged him with her eyes, as did Neelie when he looked her way.

He took in a breath, stood, and walked to the window.

Tamar shrugged and shook her head. "Please, Daniel? It will be good for us. Once we triumph over the demons of the past, things will get better."

Daniel turned, his shoulders slumped, and he held up a palm. "Okay, I can't fight both of you. If it's what you really want, Tamar, we will accept your kind offer, Tante."

Tamar rushed over and wrapped her arms around his neck. Neelie clapped her hands, sending a thank you upward. This was a huge step for all of them.

Chapter Three

"Discernment is God's call to intercession, never to faultfinding."
~ Corrie ten Boom

Throughout the meal of chicken soup along with the fresh bread Tamar had picked up at the bakery, she hadn't mentioned the move to Neelie's again, although she wanted to. From Daniel's pursed lips, she knew it was best to avoid the subject. Instead, they chatted about Neelie's work at the rehabilitation center in Amsterdam. Neelie described the dozen men and women who'd lived there since the war had ended.

Neelie took a sip of her tea and dabbed her napkin at the crumbs circling Peri's lips. "At first, we dealt with the survivors' physical needs. Most were suffering from malnutrition, so we slowly introduced hearty food to put some weight on their skeletal bodies. Some were so weak they refused to get out of bed. It took a long time before they'd sit at the table for a meal or join in conversation. They were dealing with so many things—survivor's guilt, grief, bitterness, hopelessness, depression. Did you know that a greater percentage of Nederland's Jews died in the war than any other country in Western Europe? And there's that 'conspiracy of silence' that Nederland Jews adhere to. That if they don't talk about what happened, the past will go away." She eyed Daniel not so subtly.

Tamar tucked her chin on the palm of her hand. "Why would anyone want to hold to a 'conspiracy of silence'?"

Neelie lifted a shoulder. "The survivors were stripped of everything. The one thing they own is their voice—to use it or to refuse to use it. They choose silence. But their silence is slowing their recovery."

"So how do you help them?" Tamar asked while refilling Neelie's and Daniel's tea.

"We try to provide them with a safe, pleasant environment. Sometimes we bring in entertainment—musicians, artists, even comedians. If we can convince the residents to join the others, we give them tasks to do. By doing so, they shift their attention from their own problems to other people."

"It's important work you're doing. Wish I could help." Tamar glanced at Daniel. "Perhaps I could bring the twins and maybe even … sing?"

He shrugged and studied the floor.

"I'd love for you to come sing for the residents. And, yes, you could bring the twins. Children have a natural ability to cut through the residents' hardened shells." Neelie eyed Daniel over her glasses. "And Daniel, if you'd be willing, the residents would have many medical questions for you. Would you consider coming?"

His jaw tightened. Neelie had hit a nerve—the same one Tamar had pressed on many times. Whoa, it dawned on her that Daniel was the perfect example of a conspirator of silence.

He shrugged. "Maybe sometime when I can break away from work."

Sometime.

"Great." Neelie stood. "Well, I'd better return to Amsterdam before it becomes dark, so I'll be leaving now." Daniel retrieved her coat and helped her put it on. She flashed him a smile. "I'm so glad you agreed to live in the house. It has great bones, and I hate for it to sit empty. All the house needs is the laughter of children to drive away the ugly memories. Those two will bring that to the house."

Daniel went to the bedroom door. "Peri, Zari, come and say goodbye to your *bubbe.*"

Peri tripped over untied shoelaces but quickly caught up with Zari, who presented Neelie with a picture she'd drawn.

"How lovely and look how tall I am." Neelie chuckled.

Tamar joined her at the door, kissed Neelie's cheek, and thanked her for her offer of the house. "And you must stay with us whenever you come to town." Just as Neelie opened the door, Tamar touched her sleeve. "Do you know what ever happened to Job and

Carina Hamel? I'd like to visit them, but I don't know where they went after we were taken to the camps."

"I heard they moved to Amsterdam to one of those senior neighborhoods with a *hofje*—a courtyard—like the ones here in Haarlem. I hope they're happy. You know they lost everything when they lost their art gallery. They didn't have children."

"The gallery is what I want to talk to them about." Tamar redirected Peri who was busy untying Neelie's shoes. "Sorry about this one's new favorite hobby."

"Such a little scamp." Neelie's head tilted to one side. "Pardon my nosiness, but why do you want to talk to them about the gallery?"

Tamar cut a glance at Daniel, who was gathering toys from the floor. She lowered her voice. "There was a painting in their gallery of a girl with a violin. I used to stop and look at it on my way home from school. I always felt an affinity with the girl in the picture because of our music. Anyway, all that to say that—" Tamar cast another glance in Daniel's direction. "I saw the picture this week."

"Really? Where did you see it? So much of our art vanished when those Nazis—" Neelie pretended to spit over her shoulder. "I'm sorry. I should be a better role model for my adopted grandchildren."

"She saw it when she broke into her parents' house." Daniel joined them and wrapped his arms around Tamar's shoulders, causing an intake of breath, as if she'd been caught with her hand in the *koekje* jar.

Neelie unbuttoned her coat and quickly returned to the living room. "Okay, I can't leave until I hear the whole story, Tamar, sit." She patted the sofa seat next to her.

Tamar swallowed hard. "Kids, would you go play in the bedroom, please?" The twins glanced at her, then stumbled over each other to reach the bedroom door first. If only Daniel would join them instead of staring at her with those appraising eyes. How to explain to Neelie what she'd been feeling in just a few words?

Neelie patted Tamar's leg. That's what she appreciated about her tante. She never judged her, even when Tamar had voiced her doubts that a good God would allow such atrocities to occur to her people during the war.

"Tell me, dear, what happened. I can see it's bothering you," Neelie urged.

"It's just that every time I—"

Daniel interrupted. "Every time she goes past her family's house, Tamar becomes angry that someone is living in there."

A sigh emitted, and she nodded. "But it's more than that. My father hid some important family papers and heirlooms behind a grate in the hall outside the bedrooms. The present owners—residents—probably don't even know about them. They're *my* treasures … and Seth's. So I went to extract them, but I took the wrong size screwdriver."

Neelie's eyebrows lifted. "It must be hard to see the place where you grew up taken over by strangers or profiteers."

Could she truly understand? She still had her own home.

Her tante continued, lips firming. "But, sweetie, you could have been arrested or worse. I would hate if anything happened to you—" Tamar opened her mouth to respond, but Neelie lifted a hand. "But I completely understand why you did it."

"Thank you, Tante." Tamar stood and paced the small room. She cut a glance at Daniel in time to see him roll his eyes. Daniel didn't know what it was like. He'd also lost his family in the war, but since he'd grown up in another town, he didn't have to face the past every single day. And really, he wasn't handling things so well himself, darting from the past at every turn with work and silence. Indignation was spiraling up. She tamped it down, refocusing. "Let me tell you what I saw in the house." She described what she'd witnessed on the third floor.

Neelie covered her lips with her knuckles. "Stolen art. That's what Jan is interning in. It's called art restitution."

Tamar clasped her tante's arm. "Do you think Jan would know what we should do? Should we go to the police? Or an art expert? And what would God say about Daniel and me sneaking into the house to take evidence?"

Daniel sprang up from his seat. "I never agreed to sneaking into the house to take evidence. Tamar!"

She cast a sideways, somewhat apologetic glance at him. "I was being dramatic." And hopeful.

"So many questions. If you want, I'll have a chat with Jan and ask him what you should do, but in the meantime, don't even think of breaking into that house. It may be your and Seth's house now, but if the residents are collecting stolen art, you don't want to deal with them."

Her shoulders slumped a centimeter. It was ironic. Here Daniel had served in the Dutch Resistance and Neelie had opened her house to fleeing Jews, but Tamar was the one who was willing to take risks to reclaim what belonged to her parents. "The reason I asked you about the whereabouts of Job and Carina Hamel is because I saw that painting hanging on my bedroom wall, of all places. A crib had replaced my bed, so the current occupants must have a child, and the walls were covered with what looked like valuable paintings of children and clowns and animals."

Neelie shook her head. "You could have been hurt or worse—"

Tamar winced and held up a palm. "This is what I want to know. Who owns that painting? Would the Hamels own it? Or the artist who painted it? Or the people in that house? Maybe they bought it at an auction."

"That's a question for Jan. As to the Hamels, what about a field trip to Amsterdam for your family and me? I can check and see if the telephone operator has their number."

Tamar peered at Daniel. "How about a field trip?" she mouthed.

"I have to work," he said.

She rolled her eyes and turned back to Neelie. "There's more about the painting." Tamar picked up Peri, who'd wandered into the room rubbing his eyes. "I saw the violin girl painting at Westerbork when I sang for the Führer's birthday. Since the audience was made up of Nazi officers and their lady friends, perhaps one of them took the painting from the Hamels' gallery."

"That is a logical conclusion," Neelie said.

"And, Neelie, I saw Officer Bergman there. He was waiting for me in a room off the stage, but I dashed out as fast as I could. It wouldn't surprise me if Bergman stole the painting from the Hamels."

A visible shudder passed down Neelie's body. "He had the most evil smile—and that tic by his lower lip. You might be right about him taking the picture. Bergman probably helped himself to a lot of our neighbors' art after he sent them to concentration camps." She pushed to her feet and shouldered her purse. "I'm not sure I want to walk to the train station now after thinking about him. You've given me a lot to ponder. I think I'll stay at the house and leave early in the morning."

Daniel met her at the door. "How about I walk you home?"

Neelie nodded and patted his arm. Tamar caught her aunt's wink. Undoubtedly, she'd use the opportunity to try to persuade Daniel to come to her rehab center for some much-needed counsel. If anyone could get through to Daniel, it was her tante.

The streetlamps cast long shadows across the sidewalks but failed to illuminate the whole street. Since leaving the labor camp, Neelie always tensed when she walked home in the dark from the rehabilitation center, but Daniel's presence made the difference tonight. She actually enjoyed peering around at familiar places in Haarlem. "So much around here brings back memories—good and bad." A bicycle flew past mere centimeters from the sidewalk. She edged closer to Daniel, who pulled her away from the curb. "Was it difficult to come back to Haarlem for you?" Her attempt to make small talk wouldn't fool Daniel, but she had to try.

"At first, but I try not to think about it." He let go of her arm. "I know what you're trying to do, Neelie. Not everyone needs to go into therapy to get over what happened, and Tamar and I are doing fine. We must live our lives as we find them, and the past will fade in time."

She linked arms with him as she sidestepped a crack in the sidewalk. The night air smelled a bit fetid. "Maybe, maybe not. Engulfing yourself in your career may work for you, but Tamar seems to be drifting. What would you think about her returning to the opera? It might help her handle her obsession with that house."

He shrugged. "The twins take up most of her time. Perhaps when they are a few years older and going to school. She'll be fine as long as she stays away from it."

Their footsteps were the only sound for a few minutes. Neelie took a breath to take another stab at it. "What about that dream of yours to tell the world about what you experienced? People still don't know, or they refuse to face what happened. You could start with the Jewish people I deal with at the center. They would listen to you more than they do me. You share their religion and have been there—"

He stopped. "Neelie, I'm doing the best I can, working and being there for my family. My burn patients need me right now. That's where my focus is. I can't save the world." He slipped his hands in his pockets and headed toward the canal bridge.

Neelie had to step up her pace to catch up. Marine smells and the lapping of the waves against the boats that lined the canal brought her some comfort, even if this conversation didn't.

"Almost home." She removed the key from her purse. "Would you like to come in for a cup of tea? There's some more banana bread unless Jan ate it." Perhaps the simple act of entering the house would be a first step in handling any misgivings he might have about moving here.

"Thanks, but no thanks." He stuffed his hands in his pockets and strode away.

She inserted the key. *Physician, heal yourself.* If he didn't, he'd be hurting more than himself—his marriage would suffer.

Chapter Four

"Hold everything in your hands lightly, otherwise it hurts when
God pries your fingers open."
~ Corrie ten Boom.

As the tulips and showers of April gave way to the warm
breezes and sweet-smelling blossoms of May, Tamar couldn't wait
to leave the confines of the apartment and take the twins for a walk
in the park. Restless to return to the house she'd grown up in, she
found herself taking a detour down the Barteljorisstraat to glance in
the windows of the dry cleaner as she passed by. Never was anyone
working, and more times than not, the *be back in a few minutes* sign
hung on the door, making her wonder if the shop was ever open.
With as much art as the house held, maybe the dry-cleaning business
was just a front for more nefarious dealings.

Although Daniel had promised to accompany her to retrieve
what waited behind the grate upstairs, he was always too busy at
work, and his jaw tightened whenever she brought it up. Maybe she
should just go by herself. With the right tool, she could be in and out
in mere minutes, and Daniel didn't need to lose his position at the
hospital if they got caught.

Her conscience warned her to wait for Daniel, but Tamar's
impatience was winning the battle over her common sense. What if
the art and statues were only kept there temporarily? The way they
were crammed onto every inch of horizontal surface was not how an
owner would display such items.

Well, no good could come from lingering in front of the house, so she headed to the nearest park where the twins could swing and slide, and she'd packed a picnic lunch for them to enjoy before heading home for their naps. How she loved the way the sun dappled through the lofty branches overhead and the ducks waddled nearby, hoping to catch a crumb that fell under the benches of the picnic tables.

The warm spring weather had brought a generous crowd to the park, and the music of children's laughter filled her with joy. She found an empty bench to sit on and placed their lunch basket under it, then helped the children out of their stroller. "Now, you two can go down the slide a few times, and then we'll have some sandwiches." They took each other's hands and scampered toward the slide.

"Tamar, is that you?"

Hearing her name, she swiveled to the female voice. The woman stood mere meters away, but Tamar didn't recognize her at first. Short bleached hair peeked from under a pink polka-dot bandana. A cigarette hung from full red lips. Sunglasses hid her eyes. A pretty summer dress clung to wide hips, the outfit incongruous with the garb of the other parents in the park.

"Don't you recognize me? C'mon. It's Margot."

Tamar's hand slapped over her mouth, and she stood. Margot in a park? "Of course. Forgive me. The sunglasses made it hard to see your face. How are you, Margot?"

The woman removed her glasses, showing heavy wings of eyeliner and bright blue shadow on her lids. She held the hand of a little boy, not more than two years old, with curly brown hair and a soiled shirt. He rubbed his eyes and begged to be picked up, but Margot's eyes fixed on Tamar. "I'm doing well." The child pulled on her dress, finally capturing her attention. She slapped at his hand. "Karl, go play on the swing. I'll just be a minute." His face turned a petulant color of red, and he gripped her dress even tighter.

"Is Karl your son?" Tamar fought to keep the incredulity from her tone.

Margot had never seemed to be the maternal type. In fact, when Neelie had brought a child to rehearsal because she couldn't find a babysitter, Margot had demanded she be fired. And how old was Margot, anyway? She'd been a well-known soprano as far back as

Tamar could remember. A poster of Margot had hung on her bedroom wall when Tamar was a young teenager.

"Yes, Karl is my son. He just turned two."

Tamar did the math in her head. They'd moved back to Haarlem in the spring of 1947 when Daniel was hired at the hospital and the twins were still babies. Now it was two years later, and her kids were three. Her calculations would have to wait. Margot was waiting for an answer.

Tamar took two steps toward the child, who seemed ready to throw a tantrum, and knelt beside him. "Good morning, Karl. I'm happy to meet you." She held out her hand, but the little boy stuck his thumb into his mouth and backed up, stepping on his mother's shoe.

Margot released a slew of curses. "Look what you did to my hose. Do you know how hard it is to keep them clean? If I have a run, you'll be sorry. Go…Play…Now!"

Tamar rose, brushing off her skirt. This was not going well. Why was it that every time she met up with Margot, bad things happened? "It's my fault. I probably scared him."

For once, Margot didn't appear to blame her. She even offered her a smile. "I don't know what's wrong with him. He's probably ready for another nap. I bring him here almost every day to tire him out." She shrugged and peered at Tamar's stroller. "So do you have children?"

"Yes, twins. Peri and Zari. They're three. They were born in London…" Her voice trailed off. Too much information. Zari was watching her, probably wondering whom she was talking to. Tamar motioned for her, and her daughter trotted over and grabbed her hand, staring up at the stranger with the little boy. Tamar shifted her daughter around and placed her arms around her. "Zari, this is…*Mevrouw*…I'm sorry, I don't know your last name."

"I've kept my professional name. Won't be long before I'm back on the stage. No sense in confusing my fans. Van Ormer, of course." She brushed a short strand of hair away from her face. "Mevrouw Van Ormer." Margot smiled at Zari.

"Of course. Zari, say hello, dear."

Zari held her hand out as she'd been taught to do. "Pleased to meet you, Me…vrouw. I'm Zari."

"Aren't you the cutest little girl?" Margot took her hand and gave it a little shake. "Wish I could instill some manners into my son. Maybe when he's a little older." She gently pushed her son toward Zari. "Would you mind taking him with you, dear?"

Zari took his hand and led him to her brother, who was inspecting something in the grass.

"So you're going back to work here in Haarlem?" Tamar hadn't heard that the opera was functional again.

Margot lifted a shoulder. "I'm working with a vocal coach. My voice isn't what it used to be. That filthy war—what a waste of time." She uttered an exhausted sigh. "But my husband has assured me that things will return to normal soon, and Haarlem's opera will be full of patrons again." She reached into her pocket and extracted a cigarette and some matches. "This isn't helping, but it calms my nerves. My singing coach doesn't need to know. But how about you? Is motherhood enough, or are you ready to return to the chorus?"

Of course, Margot would only think of her as a chorus member. It had been a long time since she'd sung anything but nursery rhymes. "My voice is rusty. These twins keep me busy, but someday—perhaps when they're in school—I'd like to return to the opera." Tamar watched Peri struggle to climb up the slide instead of the stairs. "It seems like so long ago. Another life, really." Then she remembered Margot's first question. "But I love being a mother." She chuckled. "You want to know a secret? When we were doing *La Traviata*, I used to pray for angst because I didn't think I'd experienced enough hard times in my life at that point to play Violetta—" Her eyes widened. "I mean, play your understudy." Nerves were making her prattle on.

Margot waved a dismissive hand. "Angst? Ever since the war ended, I've had enough angst to fill every seat in the opera house. Just because I went out with a German officer or two, the people of this town branded me a collaborator—some of them my very own fans. Can you believe that? What was I supposed to do with my time? It was so tiresome." Her chin shot up. "I know you didn't have it easy, either—being a Jew and all, but you weren't the only ones that suffered. It was tough on us all—the ration cards, the opera closing. I wasn't a collaborator. I just wanted my life to go back to normal for a little while. The officers made me feel like I was somebody…again." Her eyes locked on Tamar's, begging for sympathy.

Tamar had none to give. She averted her gaze toward her children. Her piece of normal. Daniel and the twins held her feet steady when everything around her distorted her balance. Like this conversation. And the Lord helped steady her. Daniel's Messiah—hers now—had indeed given her a sense of peace, a sense of stability. Their new *shul*—not the synagogue she'd grown up in—offered the opportunity to meet new friends. Most of her parents' friends were gone now. A sigh trickled out. Margot must have heard it because she filled the momentary gap with more words.

"Well, it's over, and we have to move on with our lives—" Just then, Karl screeched when a larger child bumped into him, causing him to fall. The little boy righted himself, toddled over to his mother, and lifted his arms to be picked up. "Oh, look what you did to your knee. It's bleeding all over your new pants." Margot glanced at Tamar with savage eyes. "How do you manage with two?"

The child was still crying, begging for his mother to pick him up. Tamar knelt down and took the boy in her arms. "There, there." His tears and running nose created a wet spot on her blouse. She didn't mind. Her kids had done the same to so many of her shirts. Tamar patted his back. The boy rubbed his eyes, then sucked his thumb. "He's a tired little boy."

Margot's eyes widened. "Well, you must have the magic touch. I can never convince Karl to stop crying." A smile slowly crept across her face. "I have a proposal to make." Instead of taking her son, she headed over to the bench and patted the seat beside her.

Tamar checked on her children. Zari now held hands with a girl about her size in a pastel dress, and they twirled around faster than they should. Peri sat by himself, zooming a stone back and forth in the dirt. Talk about dirty pants. Carrying Karl, she took the seat next to Margot, the two-year-old's warm cheek against Tamar's neck, his breath coming at even intervals. Amazing. "Karl's already asleep."

"Good." Margot fanned herself with a brochure she'd removed from her pocket. "Like I said, you have a way with kids—something I don't. The boy's father and I run a business, which takes a lot of my time. My singing coach insists that I practice for hours every day. And then there are social engagements at night. As you can imagine, I don't have any free time." She inclined her head toward Tamar. "What would you say to watching Karl for me a few times a week? Of course, you can bring your children. They'd be good for Karl. He doesn't have any friends to play with." She tapped Tamar's leg. "And it would be good for your children as well. I'd pay you."

Tamar worked to keep herself from appearing too excited, although Daniel's warning came to mind. She tamped it down. Here was the answer to her dilemma. Neelie used to talk about God adding a third solution to a choice between two bad ones. Karl's crib was the one in her old bedroom. The girl with the violin was in the same room. She didn't have to worry about being arrested. Taking care of Karl would afford her the opportunity to catalogue all the art. Daniel could legally enter the house and open the grate. The list of benefits went on and on.

Margot was waiting for a response. She swallowed. "I'd be happy to watch Karl. But I should check with my husband first."

"Wonderful. Guess I should check with Klaus as well. He's my husband. I'm sure he'll be fine with it, though." Margot looked as though she'd been sprung from a birdcage. "I'm so glad we bumped into each other today. Karl seems taken with you." She stood and reached for her child. "Well, I should be on my way. Hopefully, he'll sleep through my practice today." She rolled her eyes. "Motherhood is so much work sometimes. How about we meet back here tomorrow after we've talked to our husbands?"

Tamar pushed to her feet. "All right. It was good to see you as well." She picked up the picnic basket from under the bench. The kids could eat their lunch at home. She headed toward the playground, where Zari's little legs tried unsuccessfully to pump her swing into an arc, but she hadn't figured out timing yet.

"Eema, will you push me, please?" Her little face puckered with each unsuccessful effort.

"In a moment. I'll brush off your brother first and bring him over." She hurried over to her son and knelt beside him. He didn't even glance up, so intent was he on the back-and-forth movement of his 'truck.' With practiced fingers, she brushed back sandy blond curls from his face and dabbed at the smattering of dirt on his nose. "How would you like to swing, dear?"

He glanced up, suddenly aware of her presence, and jumped to his feet, sand spilling from his trousers. How he'd gotten sand all over him was beyond her. Since Tamar was the younger of two children, Seth being almost a decade older, she'd had no experience taking care of a little brother. At Neelie's house, she'd quickly learned how to take care of the three young orphan girls, but that had been during three months of hiding within the confines of the house. Keeping such an active boy both occupied and safe in the wider world was another challenge entirely.

Tamar led him over to the swing next to her daughter's and set him on the wooden seat, making sure that his fists held tight to the chains. "Now don't jump off like you did last time. Your father almost had to stitch up your lip." She pushed him gently, his little legs pumping double time. By standing at an equal distance behind the twins, she could push them at the same time.

The rhythmic creak of the swings brought a wide-mouthed yawn and desire for a nap. Maybe she'd indulge in one while the twins took theirs. Twins and another child. What had she gotten herself into? Knowing Margot, she'd probably expect Tamar to take care of Karl every day. People like her expected others to wait on them. Margot van Ormer was the quintessential definition of a diva. What was that saying their American uncle used when he visited from New York—a big herring in a goldfish bowl? The image of it turned her yawn into a giggle.

Just then Peri thrust his hands off the swing chains to jump down. He lost his balance and plummeted face-first into the dirt below. Howls erupted—the kind that meant he was tired. Time to go home. With a gentle grip, she stopped Zari's swing and helped her down. The little girl hurried over to her brother and attempted to brush off the sand, making clucking sounds all the while, which sounded very much like Tamar's own mutterings.

The twins refused to climb into the stroller, so they inched along the three blocks to their apartment, the kids intermittently squatting to pick up an interesting pebble or weed. Tamar didn't mind. It gave her time to think.

First, she'd have to discuss the offer to be a *kindermeisje* for Margot's son with Daniel. He wouldn't like it, but she'd make him see the benefit of her being a babysitter rather than a trespasser. Maybe they could also meet with Neelie's son, Jan, who'd tell her what to look for in the house.

A twinge of guilt hovered over each thought. This was Margot's son, Margot's house. Maybe she and her husband had bought the house legally. Or perhaps Margot and her family were indeed squatters. What then? She'd learned a bit about squatters from Seth. According to her brother, the Supreme Court required only the presence of a table, a chair, and a bed for a squatter to prove ownership. Well, Margot had a lot more possessions than that. Did she ever!

But Tamar's need for justice knocked the twinge aside. Her parents had bought that house and had lived and worked in it for at least three decades before it was ripped away from them when the Nazis forced them into a labor camp. Her skin bristled at the thought that the government would keep her from what was rightfully hers. Hopefully, the deed to the property hid behind the grate.

Justice also reminded her of the many times Margot had been unkind to her. The time when Margot, on the arm of a Nazi, had sniffed at Tamar and Daniel as if they smelled bad because of the yellow stars on their lapels. The time when she'd announced to everyone who would listen that Tamar was a Jew, as if it was a dirty word. No, Margot didn't deserve to live in *her* house.

Buoyed with a renewed sense of righteous indignation, Tamar climbed the stairs to her apartment, stopping every few steps to help Peri and Zari, who scrambled up the stairs on their knees. As soon as Daniel came home, she'd broach the subject with him and make him see things her way.

Tamar was drinking a cup of tea, relaxing in the quiet. The kids were happily ensconced in their bedroom—Zari with her picture book and Peri with his "zoom-zoom." As the remnants of sunshine disappeared, the room darkened, but Tamar didn't care. The dark and quiet relaxed her.

Familiar footsteps echoed in the hall staircase. Daniel would be coming through the door any moment. She hurried to the lamp to turn it on. Her heart still did a somersault every time Daniel came home. Her skin still quivered at his touch, just as it had when their love was young and fresh.

The door opened, and Daniel ducked so as not to bump his head. He smiled when he saw her, his dark eyes crinkling the way she loved. Good, he appeared happy. So often of late, he fell asleep the minute he reached the sofa. The last few years had added mature lines to his face—the visible parts above his beard. A few gray hairs peeked through his mustache. Though he was only thirty, the strain of his job and the past were taking a toll on him. Whenever she caught him pulling them out, she told him the gray added a layer of elegance to his handsome face.

Tamar hurried to wrap her arms around his neck and kiss him with a renewed passion that fatigue tamped down so many nights after watching the twins all day. His eyes sparkled, and she gloried in them.

"Guess what," they said at the same time. "Great minds," they said in unison and laughed.

She backed up, took his hand, and hurried him over to the sofa. "You first." Her news could wait.

He shifted so their knees touched, and he took her hands between his. Daniel stared at her, not saying anything at first, which meant his news might not be to her liking. She steeled herself and locked eyes with his.

"You know how you've been talking about returning to the opera someday when the twins are in school?"

"Yes," she murmured. What was this all about?

"Well—" His Adam's apple bobbed. "What would you say to singing for the patients in the burn ward?" His last few words tumbled over each other, as if he were trying to push them out quickly. He held up his palm. "Before you answer, let me tell you a bit about some of our guests." He always liked to call the patients 'guests.' Said it humanized them. Another thing she loved about him.

She nodded for him to continue.

"We have about eight guests who've been with us for a long time. They don't seem to be improving, so one of the nurses had heard that you were a singer and suggested that it might help them start the healing process from within." He swallowed. "One is a child whose parents were killed in an apartment fire. He's about ten, and we can't convince him to do anything other than stare out the window. There's one man who was transferred from Amsterdam a month ago. He hasn't spoken a word since he arrived. His face and upper torso are covered with bandages. The man just sits there all day. They all do."

"What happened to him?" She inclined her head. Daniel didn't often speak about his work. Something to do with doctor-patient privilege.

He lifted a shoulder. "His records say there was explosion at a warehouse in Amsterdam. The man was in an induced coma when the ambulance brought him in. We still don't know his identity because he had no papers with him. He doesn't speak. Doesn't react. I would say he's trying to die. Then there's an elderly couple who were burned in one of the camps. It's taking a long time to heal, but at least they have each other. And one of the Nazi collaborators suffered acid burns to his arms and face during a shame parade." His sigh held a tremble. "It's hard. We're trying our best to keep them alive." Daniel stared at her, his eyes begging her. "I know you haven't sung in a while, but this could be a start for you, and it might give them hope. They need hope."

She brought his hand to her lips, kissed each knuckle. For the first time, she understood why he didn't want to talk about his day when he came home. Why he looked so tired, almost defeated at times. "I'd be honored to sing for your guests. Can't promise I'll sound very good, but I'll practice. When?"

"Soon, either before or after lunch. Then the patients are in the same room. I was going to suggest tomorrow, but if you need some time to practice, how about Thursday? That gives you a few days."

"Of course." Tamar patted his wrist and rose. "I'll go put dinner on the table." She longed to tell him about her encounter with Margot and her request to care for her little boy, but the time wasn't right. Her news could wait.

She filled a basket with bread and took it to the table. A warm glow filled her that her husband had something so important to do in life, even if it wasn't their original plan to tell the world what happened behind the barbed wire of the concentration camps. But now here in Haarlem, people were tired of hearing about the war. Maybe Daniel's work at the burn unit was his way to heal.

"I'll help. What can I do?" He'd crept up behind her at the stove, breathed against her hair, which sent a shiver down her spine. She leaned back against his tall frame, enjoying the feel of his strong arms on her shoulders, the spearmint of his gum meshed with the antiseptic of his uniform.

"You can set the table," she murmured, "or just hold me. We

don't need to eat."

"As nice as this is, I'm starved," he whispered in her ear, which tickled, sending another shiver through her. She took his hand and led him to the cupboard.

"I have some roast lamb left over from the weekend's dinner, and it's warming in the oven with some vegetables for a stew. How does that sound?"

"'Delicious,' my stomach says." Whistling, Daniel took out silverware, cups, two adult plates, and two smaller ones for the twins.

Good. Whistling meant his spirits had lifted. While she made a roux to mix with the drippings from the meat, she planned what she would say once the kids had finished their meal. She put on a fresh pot of coffee, which she'd serve with some cookies Hadassah had left on their doorstep this afternoon.

The meal passed happily, except for the usual cup of spilled milk. Zari gushed about how high she'd swung at the park. Meanwhile, Peri had pulled his toy truck out of his pocket and was zooming it through the remnants of gravy.

"See, Abba? My car is swimming through the mud."

Daniel covered his mouth, but his shoulders gave him away. Tamar threw him an exaggerated frown, but instead of scolding their son, she removed the truck from Peri's hand and replaced it with a spoon. "So you think my stew tastes like mud?"

He swiped up some of the sauce and plunged it into his mouth. "I love mud."

His sister giggled at Peri's antics. "Eema makes good mud."

Tamar rolled her eyes, rose, and lifted her son from the table. "I think we're finished here. Go play in your room." She washed off his hands, arms, face, and neck and handed him his truck. "I'll be in after the dishes are done to give you both a bath." As she wiped her daughter's mouth and set her on her feet, Daniel started to get up. She glanced over her shoulder. "Please, stay for a few minutes. I'll bring us coffee and dessert. I need to tell you something."

Daniel took the dishes to the sink and rinsed them off. She grabbed a dishcloth and washed off the table, then poured two cups of coffee, placed a few *pindakoeken* on a small plate, and took them to the table.

His eyes were saucers. "Did you bake…cookies?"

She waved a dismissive hand. "Are you joking? Hadassah made these."

"Always, my dream's deferred."

"Yes, your dream. When you open your own practice on the first floor of our house, I'll make cookies."

"And I'll kiss the crumbs off your face." He leaned over and brushed her nose with his lips. "Who knows? Maybe I'll open my practice at Neelie's house."

She hadn't thought about that. "Hmm. It might work. Frans's grandfather and father had medical offices on the first floor." Buoying her nerves, she took a sip of the warm brew. "Guess who I saw at the park today?" Tamar told him about Margot and her little boy. "She seems to be flummoxed on how to mother the child and for once sought my advice."

Daniel stirred sugar into his cup. "So what did you tell her?"

"Nothing, really. Karl was rubbing his eyes and whimpering, so I picked him up. He fell asleep on my shoulder. A sweet little boy." She circled the rim of her cup with her finger. "Here's what I wanted to talk to you about. Margot is singing again. Said the opera is going to be opening soon and wants her voice to be ready. She's working with a coach, and she asked me if I'd be willing to care for her son while she's…out." Tamar emphasized the last word.

Their eyes met, lingered. He knew, but the smile she waited for wasn't forthcoming. Daniel still had his doubts. He'd become too careful, too afraid. No, her husband wasn't afraid. *Weary* was a better word. Tired of hiding and running and looking over his shoulder. Tired of being one of "those people." Years of being God's chosen people but treated like wads of gum on the pavement.

She understood. Still, she longed to see that spark in his eyes again. To have him risk something—anything. Tamar wanted her Daniel back.

"What if you get caught?" He studied her from under furrowed eyebrows, his hands folded in front of him on the table. "What about the twins?"

She gulped past the lump in her throat. "I'll take them with me. It would probably be just a few hours a couple times a week. Karl needs other children in his life. He seems to be a little lost boy. Zari and Peri would be good for him—"

"But that's not your motivation, is it? You want to use this opportunity to check out the house. Catalogue the paintings you saw there. Steal the violin picture, even. Am I right?"

She nodded, her lips pressed tight. "And why shouldn't I? It's my house. Or it was. I wouldn't do anything stupid, though." She leaned forward on her own folded arms. "It's better than breaking into the house and…trespassing, as you call it. Now I'd be there by invitation."

He leaned back, his head tilting to one side as if he was examining her. "Your invitation, as you call it, is for caring for her son."

"Daniel! I'd only look around when the kids were napping." She sprang to her feet and paced the small space around the table. "When did you become so careful? Margot doesn't even know it was my home. I will be careful. Yes, I'll look around. Something's going on there—"

"Something criminal. When it was just me and you, we did what we had to in order to survive, but now we're parents. You'd be taking the twins into a situation that could put them in danger. What if you get caught?"

She stopped. "Daniel, I would never put them or Karl in any danger. Think about it. Margot has asked me to care for her son. I want to do that."

Lines formed on his forehead. "After everything she did to you? Where's all this good will coming from? She treated you like you were worthless because of our religion. I saw it myself in the wrinkle of her nose." His lips quivered. Her husband—Daniel—was fighting back tears. She'd never seen emotion like this. Ever.

She found her own lips quivering. This was something she hadn't expected. Tamar circled the table and wrapped her arms around his neck. Gone was the wall that had slowly grown higher and higher since the war. This was raw Daniel.

They stared at each other, so close she could see her reflection in his irises, though it swayed in the tears that brimmed in his eyes. She swiped a gentle hand over the side of his face, felt the slight shudder of this man she loved so much.

His hands cupped her cheeks, brought her closer, and kissed her with such an impact that it took the breath from her lungs. This was what she wanted. What she'd been waiting for. A breakthrough. He moved back and placed his hands on her shoulders. "Sorry. I lost it.

Think I'm just tired, and all the possibilities of what could happen at that house overwhelmed me." He sniffed. "All right. You're smart, and you wouldn't put our children in danger."

She ran light fingers down his face. "I wouldn't ever do that. But I don't want to do anything without your backing. And I was also thinking of that little boy, Karl. He's starving for affection. Margot seemed to ignore him."

"How old is the child?"

"Karl's small for his age. He just turned two, but he'll probably follow Peri around like a shadow." Should she broach the subject while they were in a good spot? She didn't want to ruin the moment, yet her weak filter wouldn't let her wait. "Would it be wrong to check on my parents' stuff behind the grate? While the children are asleep?"

He didn't answer right away. The red-rimmed clock's tick sounded like a clang in her ear.

"Didn't you say it was behind a…a… what did you call it?"

"A credenza. A really heavy credenza." She saw it in his eyes. Daniel was joining her side. The Justice side.

With a dramatic, audible sigh, he lifted both hands. "Since you're not going to give up on this idea, I'll do it." He directed a palm at her. "But it will have to wait until my day off, and only if you can assure me there will be enough time to get in and out without Margot coming home."

Tamar resisted the urge to jump up and down. Instead, she leaned over, pulled him toward her, and hugged him hard. "Thank you," she whispered. "Thank you."

He drew back. "That's it, though. I can read you pretty easy. We're not in the Resistance any more. We're respectable citizens of Haarlem, or trying to be. But since you're doing me the favor of singing for my patients, I will return the favor."

Chapter Five

"In order to realize the worth of the anchor, we need to feel the stress of the storm."
~ Corrie Ten Boom

The antiseptic smell of the hospital almost bowled Tamar over as they entered St. Elizabeth Gasthuis by a side door. Her eyes watered, and she gripped Daniel's arm and pursed her lips to prevent the odor from traveling down to her lungs.

He grinned at her. "You'll get used to it. It's stronger here than on the floor. The custodian must have just mopped."

She heaved a shudder. "It brought back memories of the bleach water at Vught. The hours I spent washing cups and rags at the infirmary. My hands were raw by the end of the shift."

"I remember them well—not your hands, your lips. I'd steal a kiss until the guard shouted for me to hurry up." Daniel held the door open to a staircase. "Okay, let me tell you what to expect. It's upsetting at first to see the scars. Just remember these are real people who are dealing with their new bodies. Look them in the eye. See beyond the scars to the real person."

"Thanks," she whispered, her breath coming fast as they reached the third floor. "So what should I do?"

His hand lightly pressed her back. "Just be you. I'll introduce you to the patients one by one. Shake their hands. Smile. And there will be a lectern you can stand behind—I always like to lean on something when I have to address a group—and then you can begin."

They'd reached the burn-unit doors, a *no admittance* sign in big red letters. Suddenly, nerves took over. She grabbed his arm. "Wait." He stopped and gave her a quizzical look. "How many songs should I sing? Will there be any accompaniment?"

He pulled her into a hug, his warm lips touching her forehead. "How about three or four songs? There's a piano in the corner, and I've asked one of the nurses to accompany you, but I don't know how well she plays."

She linked arms with his as she always did when she was nervous. "What do you think of me singing *'Het Wihelmus'*? People always loved singing our national anthem when the Nazis were forcing their anthem on us, but what about now that the war is over?"

"That might be a good choice to end with. Remember how it brought people together at Neelie's?"

She kept her grip on his arm. "But this is a different time. People are more…more jaded now."

He shrugged. "It will be a big hit. What else are you going to sing?"

She ran her finger against the pocked, painted wall. The green of it defied identity. No wonder the burn victims were depressed. "Well, I thought I'd sing a children's song for the kids in the ward, *'Opa Bakkebaard.'* Maybe they'll sing along once they feel comfortable."

"Okay, so now we have music for the children and the patriots. What about a modern love song? Or one of your opera songs?"

She lifted a shoulder and her face scrunched. "I'm too rusty to sing opera, but I could sing *'Diep in Mijn Hart.'* That elderly couple might like it."

"Good choice. Well, here's the door. May the party begin."

Tamar fortified herself with a gulp before entering. The camps had trained her senses not to see what was around her. She had a feeling she'd need to do the same here.

A different odor whooshed at her as Daniel opened the door. Antiseptic and decay mixed together into a pungent blend. Her lips tightened, and she held her breath.

He winked at her. "You'll get used to it. Follow me." Daniel led her into a rotunda-like room with windows looking out onto the street three floors below.

Flowerboxes hung from each window, adding some color to the otherwise institutional-green room. A half a dozen patients sat at small tables or in wheelchairs in a horseshoe pattern facing the center, where a small table stood next to a scuffed piano.

A nurse in her twenties dressed in a habit rolled in a patient no more than ten years old whose arms were bandaged from shoulder to fingertip. The nurse's face brightened when she saw Daniel, and she nodded toward Tamar. She adjusted her wimple and smiled. "*Goedemorgen*, Doctor Feldman. Everyone is looking forward to your singing, Mrs. Feldman." She pulled her passenger's wheelchair up to a table and flipped on the brakes, then pulled some paper and crayons out of her pocket. "Here, Luuk, this will give you something to do until the songs begin." She gently patted his head and hurried over to them.

Daniel pressed his arms around Tamar's waist. "Are you ready for this, Sister? May I present my wife, Tamar Feldman, and this is Sister Griet."

Not sure of the protocol with a nun, Tamar nodded and smiled. "Nice to meet you."

The nurse, all smiles, offered her hand, which Tamar took. "As I said, the patients have been looking forward to your performance." She wagged her head. "They need music more than anything."

Tamar surveyed the room that was filling up with wheelchairs and bandaged patients sitting in plastic chairs that matched the walls. What was missing was the noise. They didn't talk or move, except for the little boy, Luuk, who tried without success to hold a crayon between his bandaged finger and thumb.

Several of the nurses brought cups of water and set them on the tables nearest the patients. When they spoke, it was in hushed terms. The silence wasn't helping her nerves. Tamar wished for noise. Anything to make her voice less of an intrusion.

Daniel motioned toward the lectern. Sister Griet moved toward the piano. Tamar hadn't gone over the songs with the sister yet. What if she wasn't familiar with them? She hurried over to join the nurse on the scarred wooden piano bench.

"Sister, are you familiar with 'Opa Bakkebaard'? I thought I'd sing that for Luuk."

"Of course, that's a wonderful choice. What else?" She flexed and unflexed her fingers.

"Well, first I thought I'd sing, 'Diep in Mijn Hart,' and the national anthem. Do you know how to play them?"

"Sure, some of the notes may be off on this piano. It's sorely in need of a tuning." She leaned so close that her wimple almost touched Tamar's forehead. "These people need God. Do you have a worship song you could sing?"

Tamar tapped a finger on her cheek for a few moments. "How about '*Esa Einai*'? It's been a long time since I've sung it." It *had* been a long time. Caring for the twins had drained her of time with the Lord, whom she'd met—really met—after Daniel taught her about the Messiah, and she'd hung on every word. His eyes sparkled when he talked of his Messiah. She'd been brought up in a strict Jewish family, but Daniel told her there was more to God than the traditions of men, religion, following rules spoken of in the Talmud. There was relationship—and after her father and mother had perished, how she craved such a relationship with the Lord. So she'd knelt by the bed and invited Yeshua Hamashiach—Jesus—to be the Lord of her life. Such a simple prayer, but it changed everything.

And then the twins came. A twinge hit her with such a force it made her gasp.

Sister Griet glanced at her. "Are you all right?"

"Yes, I'm fine. Just a bit nervous. I haven't sung in public in years."

"Well, I know that song. It's perfect."

Sister Griet didn't need to know that she was having a momentary epiphany. It wasn't the twins. Something else was blocking her desire to sing for the Lord. But now was not the time to examine her recent past. She was here to serve, and serve she would.

Daniel came up behind and touched her elbow. "Before we start, I'd like to introduce you to our guests, though we're still missing one or two." He glanced at the door, then appeared to rally himself. "Let's begin on the left." They stopped at the first table where a couple sat so close their knees touched. "May I present Eduard and Tonij Meijers. Mr. Meijers was a jurist before the war. He worked on the Dutch civil code. This is my wife, who will be sharing a few songs with us today, Tamar Feldman."

The man's eyes held the pain Tamar had come to recognize in the survivors of the camps. Knowing eyes. Eyes that had seen more than God ever intended, yet Eduard nodded and patted his wife's hand. "You remind me of our youngest daughter," he said. "Tonij, doesn't she look like Hedy?"

Mrs. Meijer's eyes brightened, but she didn't say anything.

Next, they moved on to a fragile-looking woman with large eyes, who but for the scar that swept across her cheek was beautiful enough to be a model. "Tamar, this is Ida Simons. Do you recognize her?"

Tamar tried to see beyond the shriveled skin to the woman behind. She did look fam— "Ida…you were a pianist. We worked together." She started giggling and enveloped the thin woman in a hug. This connection with her past—it took her breath away.

The woman smiled, and half of it filled her face. "Yes, of course. You played Violetta that one night when Margot up and quit. I remember it well. You did a magnificent job." She reached over and weakly squeezed Tamar's hand.

Uninvited tears formed in her eyes. Not here. Not now. "What happened, Ida?"

"Spoils of the war. Spoiled by the war," she said under her breath.

Just then, a nurse rammed against Tamar, causing her to stumble forward. Daniel broke her fall before she tumbled into Ida's lap.

"I am so sorry," a short, hefty nun in a blue-and-white habit exclaimed, maneuvering a wheelchair around so it faced the center. "It's just I was in a hurry to bring our guest out here before you started." She placed the patient's mummified arms on the wheelchair's armrests. The man's head and upper torso were covered in bandages, except for small holes for his eyes, nostrils, mouth, and ears. "There you go, sir."

"It's quite all right, Sister Anna," Daniel said. Sister Griet came up to Daniel and whispered in his ear. He nodded and turned to Tamar. "We have to begin now, or schedules will be disrupted. If there's time, I can introduce you to the rest later."

"What happened to the man who just arrived?" she whispered.

"He's the one I told you about who was in an explosion in Amsterdam. We don't know who he is. He's been in a coma for weeks. Hasn't spoken. Hasn't reacted." He nodded toward the lectern.

Gripping the wooden edges of the stand, Tamar faced the small circle of patients. Her heart went out to them. If the pain of the war hadn't been enough, these folks had to suffer more recent injuries. She was the biggest baby. Hadn't she burned her finger on the gas burner last week and howled? A sudden rush of fear swept over her, and she wanted to flee. She wasn't worthy to be here. No, this was for Daniel. He deserved her best efforts.

Daniel gave her an encouraging nod.

She swallowed past the lump lodged in her throat. "Hello. If I haven't met you yet, I'm Tamar, Dr. Feldman's wife, and I'm happy to be here…with you. Before Haarlem's opera closed, I sang in the chorus, but that was a lifetime ago. To tell you the truth, I haven't sung in a long time—except for nursery rhymes with my twins." A few of the guests chuckled, which buoyed her confidence. "I'd like to start with my parents' favorite tune. 'Diep in Mijn Hart.'" She nodded toward Sister Griet.

The piano certainly needed a tune-up, as did her voice, which sounded as rusty as an old pipe, but the song was an easy one to start with. It reminded her of those American crooners on the radio—Bing Crosby and Gene Autry. When she reached the second chorus, Tamar ventured a glance around the room and was amazed. All the guests, except for the man who hadn't yet spoken, and both nurses were swaying to the music. Her heart soared. She motioned for them to join her in singing the chorus, and they did for the next song as well—"Opa Bakkebaard," a familiar song to every Nederlander. These people were hungry for music.

The man sitting by himself hadn't even tapped his bandaged fingers. If only music could bring him back. Maybe the Dutch national anthem would be the song to reach him. It had changed the whole atmosphere of the refugee house she and Daniel had visited when they were in the Resistance. She stood tall and began to sing it. A few of the guests rose to their feet, their voices joining hers. The nurse in blue brushed tears from her eyes.

When they finished the song, everyone except the man clapped. "Encore," Luuk called out, and the others echoed his request. It was hard to tell, but at least two of the "guests" were Jewish—the couple who'd been sent to the camps. When the Nazis occupied Haarlem, Jews weren't allowed in St. Elisabeth's Gasthuis. Even Daniel had lost his residency at this hospital. But things were different now. She started "Esa Einai," a Psalm they'd sung at shul. Its uplifting melody brought everyone to their feet once again. When Luuk demanded an encore, laughing and clapping as he repeated his new favorite word, Tamar sang it again.

Tamar bowed, then clapped toward Sister Griet, who'd done a remarkable job despite a few piano keys that didn't work. The nurse stood, bowed, then made her way over to stand behind Luuk.

Tamar was just about to join Daniel when a raspy voice came from the corner from the man who hadn't spoken since arriving.

All eyes turned toward the mummy who sat with outstretched bandaged arms. Daniel strode over to him, knelt down, and examined his eyes with a small flashlight. "Welcome back, buddy. What did you say?"

A voice more like a croak came from the slit covering his mouth. "Day ma."

"I'm sorry. I didn't understand what you said. Say it again."

He lifted his chin toward where Tamar stood. "Day mar."

"Yes." Daniel flashed a smile. "That's my wife, Tamar. Very good."

He shook his head. "Day mar. Si…Bab…bi…no." The man took a loud intake of breath, "Ca…ca…ro."

Daniel turned to her, confusion etching lines on his forehead. "Do you know what he—"

Rooted to the spot, Tamar covered her mouth. Her whole body trembled. It couldn't be. She gripped the edges of the lectern to keep from falling. Her worst fear. Her worst nightmare.

In four steps, Daniel caught her. "What is it? You're as green as…this room. What?"

She spat the word out. "B…b…Bergman."

He led her to a chair next to the piano bench and helped her down. "That's impossible. Why do you think it's him?"

"He said my name." Spots formed in front of her eyes. The kind that came before she'd passed out one other time when she'd stayed at Neelie's house.

"Darling, everyone knows your name here. You introduced yourself."

The room grew silent. She looked up to see everyone staring at her, concern on their faces. How she hated being the center of attention. Tamar struggled to her feet. "I'm fine. I'm not a flower. Let me up." She stepped to the lectern and thanked the group for coming.

The two nurses and the guests clapped one more time. Tamar pasted on a poor excuse for a smile.

Daniel pulled her to the side away from the others. "Okay, what just happened? Why would you think that poor man is Officer Bergman?"

"I know it's him. When I was at Neelie's, mopping the floor, that was the song I was singing when he heard me and demanded she introduce me. '*Babbino Caro*.' That's what that man said."

He turned to stare at his patient, who sat as stiff and immobile as a mummy, then Daniel swiveled to her. "You must be mistaken. No Nazi would dare to live in this country. Bergman's probably been dead for a long time."

She peered over Daniel's shoulder. "He's watching me. I can feel his eyes on me," she said under her breath.

And he was because at that moment when their eyes locked, he said her name again, this time more clearly. Despite the chatter of voices and the squeak of wheelchairs as the nurses pushed patients to the door, everyone turned toward his voice.

Daniel's mouth stood agape for a moment. "I don't see how this could have happened. This man has been in a coma for weeks. Could it be your singing brought him out of the coma? And he's fixated on your name?"

She looked away. Couldn't stand to look at that mask with the dark holes that kept staring at her. "No, Daniel. I don't know why or how, but I know it's Bergman. I can even hear the slight clip of a German accent. I'd know that voice anywhere. It's been part of every nightmare."

Here he sat in his plaster cage—a spectacle, a curiosity. Erich would have laughed if it didn't hurt so much. The doctors—those receptacles of higher education—what did they know? They thought he was comatose. Well, let them think that. Then they wouldn't bother him with a barrage of questions of who he was and what had happened.

And then that voice.

In a matter of a few seconds, the voice that had played in Erich's head night and day broke through the fog of drugs or whatever they were feeding him. That tentative yet perfect-pitched soprano voice was better than any drug. And he couldn't help himself—he blurted out her name, said it time after time until the other people in the room started focusing on him as if he were an insect in a petri dish. *They* were the insects. Everyone in the Netherlands were insects. But here he sat, unable to spew an invective or call on his lackeys to arrest them.

The beauty of that voice and then the doctor's words hit him like the debris at the warehouse after the explosion. Tamar Visser was married to the Jew? He'd always figured once Tamar had spent time with him, when she discovered that Erich shared her love of music, she would break it off with the doctor. Had she converted to Judaism?

How could the love of his life adulterate herself? If it weren't for that voice that played in the background of every thought, every dream, he'd have found a way to end his life long ago.

But it was her fault that he was imprisoned in this poor excuse of a hospital. Nothing as scientifically advanced as the German ones. If it wasn't for her, he would have left this godforsaken country right after the war. His longing for Tamar and love for her voice had him making foolish choices. Now she was married to that tall reed of a man who called himself a doctor.

"Sir?" A female voice. Not hers. Too harsh. Too common.

Erich shifted slightly to see who was interrupting his thoughts. That's all he had now was his stream of thoughts. It was the nurse. Short, squat, eyes like a hawk. "Yes?"

"Sir, welcome back to the world. We're so glad you've joined us. Would you tell us your name?"

They still didn't know his name? What an utterly infantile establishment this was. If the Germans did one thing well, it was keep excellent records. Apparently, the Netherlands did not. Yet it had worked to his benefit with the art. At least he'd unloaded most of it before the explosion. If he ever got out of this plaster prison, he'd be a very rich man indeed. And one thing he'd learned—everyone had a price, even little Miss Tamar.

Chapter Six

"Forgiveness is an act of the will, and the will can function
regardless of the temperature of the heart."
~ Corrie Ten Boom

Tamar stood at the door to the dry cleaner and straightened her collar before she knocked. It seemed bizarre to stand outside a business and not just enter, but a peek in the window showed a dark room. Did anyone work here? Yes, the hanging bags of clothes meant there were customers. Or was it all a front?

"C'mon, Eema, it's starting to sprinkle." Zari knelt to swipe drops from her yellow boots.

"Yeah, we go in now." Peri echoed his sister's whining.

Tamar knocked on the door, waiting a minute before knocking again. The sprinkles quickly turned into a full-fledged downpour. Zari stared up at her with stormy eyes. She cracked the door open, careful not to drip on the polished wood floor. *Her* family's polished wood floor.

"Margot? Is anyone here? It's Tamar—"

Footsteps pounded down the stairs. Wearing a kerchief and a silk dress, Margot scrambled to meet them at the door. "Sorry, I didn't hear you. These stairs will be the death of me. I've asked Klaus to put a lift in this house. All the grand homes in Amsterdam have them." She checked the clock above the door. "Oh, I'm wasting time. I have to be at my lesson in twenty minutes, and it's a kilometer away." Margot whipped around. "Come. I'll show you where everything is."

Not a *hello* or a *how are you.*

Tamar took her children's hands and followed Margot up the stairs. Familiar stairs, which led to the kitchen. How many times had she raced up the stairs, stopping halfway up to savor the scent of her mother's roast beef dinner? She probably knew more about the rooms upstairs than Margot did. But it would be better to keep her reactions to herself.

They reached the top step. She squeezed Zari's and Peri's hands, for no other reason than to buoy her own nettle of nerves, then stepped into the kitchen. And her lower lip dropped. A dozen or more pictures covered the walls.

"Eema, it's like that museum near Oma's house in Amsdam," Zari said, her gaze darting from one gilded-framed picture to another.

"Amsterdam. Yes, lots of paintings."

Margot grinned. "What do you think?"

Tamar's attention spanned the cluttered kitchen that smelled like an attic full of old books. Peri tugged on her skirt with one hand and pointed at a large painting of a fox ready to bite into a farm fowl—a graphic picture for young eyes. "Mama, rooster."

"That's right, and there's another rooster over the sink." Her mother's rooster clock was still there, its ticking evoking too many memories. She swallowed back the lump and said the obvious. "You have a lot of paintings."

"Yes, it's become a hobby, although we're running out of space. We go to auctions whenever we can. Klaus says art is a good investment right now. You can buy paintings, sculptures, jewelry— you name it—for next to nothing."

Tamar should smile her agreement, but she couldn't.

Margot noticed. "I know what you're thinking. Well, the owners are long gone now. They're not coming back. Why shouldn't we take advantage of a deal? That's what good business is all about. Besides, if we don't, someone else will." Margot glanced at the clock. "Oh, look at the time. I'm going to be late. I should be back early in the afternoon. If you don't mind, I'd like to stop by the Albert Heijn to pick up a few groceries on the way back from singing practice. Help yourself to food in the refrigerator. Give Karl a bottle when he starts getting fussy and put him in his crib after lunch. He should sleep until I come home. If you're lucky." She lightly pushed Karl, who toddled toward Tamar. "Karly, go play with the kids."

Tamar had so many questions. How many days a week would Margot need her to take care of Karl? Could Tamar take the children to the park? But Margot had grabbed an umbrella and was quickly tying the belt of her raincoat, mumbling about nerves making her voice shallow. In seconds, she clamored down the steps.

Karl careened against her leg and begged to be picked up. She propped him on her hip and fished a handkerchief out of her pocket to wipe the goop off his cheeks.

Zari tugged on her dress. "Eema, where are the toys?"

"Sweetie, I don't know. I've never been…" No, she wouldn't lie to her daughter. "Karl, where are your toys?"

The child didn't respond but instead pointed at a pacifier on the floor. She bent to retrieve it and handed it to him, which he immediately stuffed in his mouth.

"Let's go find them." The breakfast dishes sat in the sink. If she had time today, she'd give the kitchen a good cleaning—a way to assuage her conscience. "Peri, don't eat food off the floor." She bent down and grabbed his hand before he stuffed what looked like a raisin into his mouth. "Let's go into the parlor. Come along, Zari." She summoned more strength to face yet another room full of memories.

They passed the stairs that led to the third-floor bedrooms and single bath and stood at the arched entrance to the room where Tamar's family had spent time together every evening—her father reading parts of the newspaper out loud to her mother while she knitted another scarf for the coming winter months.

Tamar caught her breath at the sight—at the blight. Paintings, candlesticks, statuettes, and large books filled every centimeter of space. The piano still stood in the corner, though it, too, was covered with everything from tapestries to tea sets. She remembered standing next to the piano bench with rigid posture, Seth tapping her lower back with a meter stick if she slouched.

She resented her brother back then, but now Tamar wished she could thank him. He'd taught her not to settle for average, to practice until it hurt. Maybe sometime soon when Hadassah and Daniel weren't present, she'd find a way to thank her brother. It was because of Seth's work with her that Tamar was chosen to be Margot's understudy before the Nazis closed down the opera.

Peri had climbed onto the sofa and was jumping up and down.

Amazing how children—even at three—pushed the boundaries. "Enough, Peri. Let's find some toys for you to play with."

Zari was leading little Karl around by the hand like a big sister, pointing at various things in the room and asking, "What is that?"

She picked up Peri and meandered into the dining room. Newspapers and magazines covered her parents' mahogany-leafed table and each of the eight brocaded chairs. Her eyes took in the stack of newspapers, including *Haarlem Dagblad*, a Nazi-friendly newspaper. She'd thought the Nazis were a thing of the past. Maybe she was wrong.

A shudder zipped down her spine as memories of Officer Bergman came to mind. His mummified face leering at her from behind the bandages, reminding her of Lon Chaney in that American film from the twenties—*The Phantom of the Opera*. The way his disfigured face looked like a skeleton. Bergman's face probably looked the same.

"Mam, there's nothing to do in here," Zari whined. Her daughter was right. Tamar didn't have time to think about Bergman now. She was here for a purpose.

"Come on, kids. Let's go upstairs and see if Karl has any toys in his room." It surprised her that the child had nothing to play with down here except a soother. "Karl, could you show us your room?"

He looked up at her, and his whole face spread into a smile. "Up," he said.

Tamar lowered Peri to the floor and picked Karl up.

Peri raced his twin sister to see who could reach the banister first.

Tamar inhaled deeply but couldn't stave off the tears when she reached the top of the stairs. This house—this storehouse of memories—was too hard. It took every bit of reserve she had to tamp down her tears. Zari and Peri didn't know the history of this house, that the grandparents they'd never met had lived here and would have loved them so much. Someday, she'd tell them—but not now.

She leaned over to set Karl on the floor. Peri was already running up and down the small hall, his energy needing release, or he'd never settle down. Zari's eyes ping-ponged from one wall to the other, her mouth hanging open as Tamar's had the first time she'd set eyes on this warehouse of sorts.

"Eema, what is all this stuff? Is this an attic?"

Tamar scraped the toe of her shoe over the strip she'd caused by moving the credenza. Why hadn't she thought to bring the screwdriver? "Karl's mother and father collect art and other valuable things."

"Why?" The three-year-old's face scrunched up at the musty smell.

"Why?" *Greed. Profiting from people's misfortune.* "It's like collecting dolls, like your friend Saskia does. Her grandmother sends her a new doll every birthday and Christmas."

Karl was lifting his arms toward his bedroom door and whimpering a single word, "Mam…"

Zari scampered behind him to open the door, apparently not realizing the boy was leaning against it. "Here you go, Karl." As he fell inside, she stopped at the threshold, peered wide-eyed at the walls, and covered her mouth with both hands. "Wow!"

Peri echoed her reaction, even placing his hand over his mouth.

Karl scurried under his bed and dragged out a straw basket full of toys. The children hurried to join him. Peri lifted up a colorful wooden train, claimed a piece of the floor, and zoomed the vehicle over his stretch of property, already ensconced in his own little world. Zari pulled out some loose crayons and pages ripped from a coloring book. She handed one of each to Karl and showed him what to do.

Tamar surveyed her former bedroom and the hall at a more leisurely pace. It was the clutter that bothered her, and the cloying smell of used diapers mixed with talcum powder. The myriad of artwork on the bedroom walls depicting clowns and puppies and children. Old paintings in ostentatious frames. She couldn't tell if they were masterpieces or fakes.

Gone were the posters of her favorite sopranos—Mary Martin, Elly Ameling, Elisabeth Schumann. Those same women had inspired her to give her best when she remained in the chorus, passed over once again when the producer insisted on bringing in a substitute singer from Amsterdam. She was always the understudy but never the lead, except for rehearsals when Margot threw another one of her tantrums.

A poster of Margot's Violetta had graced the wall with the other sopranos until Margot had treated Tamar as if it were her fault that the Haarlem opera closed because of her religion. The poster had ended up in the trash later that night.

And now, four years later, in the place where Margot's poster had peered down at her was the girl with the violin.

With the children otherwise engaged, Tamar approached each painting, touched the rifts and edges of the paint, checked for a familiar artist's name, and inhaled the smell of oil paint and turpentine.

Her eyes returned to the girl with the violin time and again. The girl hadn't aged as she had. Tamar had always wondered what happened to a person's age when they died, when they went to be with Yeshua. If she lived another twenty years before she died, would her mother and she be the same age? Would Mrs. Betz, the elderly baker who'd lived across the street before dying at Vught, still be bent over, or would everyone return to the age when they were at their best?

Up close, shades of red and orange streaked the girl's blond hair, a spray of freckles swept over her nose, and her eyes held a plaintive look—as if she was unhappy with her lot. There was something so familiar about her. They'd surely known each other at shul or school. Somewhere.

"Eema, is that Bubbe?" Her daughter stood next to her, little arms folded across her chest, as if she was a knowledgeable appraiser of fine art.

"Tante Neelie? What makes you say that?"

"She has a gui..tar?"

"That's not a guitar. That's a violin. Your Bubbe Neelie plays the violin. But you're almost right. They are both stringed instruments. Neelie was very good, and she was my best friend at the opera."

Zari lifted her arms to be picked up. "I want to see it up close."

"*Oke.*" With her daughter on her hip, they moved as close as they could. Zari was right. It wasn't just the violin. It was as if they were looking at a young version of Neelie. The long face, those eyes that didn't miss a beat, those wide lips that couldn't hide what she was feeling. Taken apart, the puzzle pieces didn't quite fit right. But put together, that same sympathetic expression that made Tamar want to share all her secrets was there before them in the young girl's face. Those probing eyes saw too much but never judged. Just like Neelie's.

"It does look like Tante Neelie. I wish I could show her this picture. She'd like it very much," Tamar said, tilting her head to the side. "You know, Zari, I've seen this picture before. It used to be at the art gallery just a few blocks from here. I used to pass it on my way home from school."

Zari tilted her head like her mother's. "Someday, I want to learn how to play the violin. Do you think Bubbe would teach me how when she comes to visit?"

It didn't surprise her Zari would be drawn to play the violin. She was interested in everything she saw, and no matter what she was doing, Zari hummed incessantly. "Of course, I'm sure Neelie would be delighted to teach you how to play."

"*Delighted.* I like that word." Zari touched the girl's cheek. "She doesn't look happy. Did something bad happen to her?"

"I don't know. I always thought she looked trapped. As though she would rather be at the park than practicing. I used to be like that when I was young. Your Uncle Seth would make me practice singing when I wanted to be out in the sunshine."

Zari shifted to face her and traced her finger down Tamar's nose. "Did you throw a tamper tentrum?"

"Temper tantrum? Maybe once or twice if I really, really wanted to go outside." She giggled. "But I'm glad I listened to your uncle. He helped me become a better singer." Tamar leaned forward and whispered in her daughter's ear. "Don't tell your uncle I said that, okay?"

"Okay."

She kissed Zari on the cheek and set her down. Something was missing. What was it? Studying the wall, she chuckled. The newspaper picture her mother had cut out and framed of Tamar singing Violetta. Of course, Margot would have taken that picture down—probably stomped on it until the glass broke. Did Margot wonder why Tamar's picture was on the wall in that bedroom? Did it ever cross her mind that Tamar's family owned this house?

The kids were becoming restless and probably hungry. She touched the face of the violin girl one more time. What if she took it today? It wouldn't fit in her knapsack, but if she took it out of the frame? No, the space on the wall in the midst of the clutter would draw Margot's eyes. But what she could do when the time was right was move around a few of the pictures. When a person had hundreds of expensive pieces of artwork, they'd hardly miss one, right?

"C'mon, children, let's go have lunch."

"Yay," Zari sang out, echoed by Peri, then Karl.

Tamar smiled. It hadn't taken long for the little boy to join her kids. Before she closed the bedroom door, she took one more glimpse of the picture. She knew one thing for sure. One of these days when she came to this house to care for Karl, she would be prepared with a means of spiriting away the picture. It couldn't be a sin to steal a picture if she were to return it to its rightful owner.

Chapter Seven

"And so I discovered that it is not on our forgiveness any more
than on our goodness
that the world's healing hinges, but on his."
~ Corrie ten Boom

When Daniel's footsteps sounded from the stairs, Tamar set the casserole dish to dry on the counter and hurried to the door. How she longed for adult conversation. Circling her arms around his neck, she giggled at the suds clinging to his ear. "Sorry, I didn't wipe off my hands." She sniffed. "You smell good. Antiseptic and peppermint, and is that nicotine? When did you start smoking?"

Daniel laughed. "I can account for the first two, but the third must have come from the doctor's lounge where we met to discuss a patient." He sniffed her neck. "Asparagus and soap and lemon polish. An interesting combination."

The brush of his beard against her skin sent shivers through her, and they stood locked together until Peri chose that moment to march into the room as if he were Sousa himself. "Zari, Papa's home."

Both children scampered to the door and hugged his legs. As always, he walked stiff legged in a circle, the children squealing.

"Okay, that's enough. Give your father some room." Tamar took his hand and led him to the table. "I saved you some dinner, though our Peri is developing a wholesome appetite for *stamppot*." She gently pushed him into the chair, then hurried to retrieve his plate from the cooling oven. After she placed the plate and a glass of milk in front of him, he pulled her into the chair next to him and said a blessing on the meal.

"Now tell me about your day, love. How did it go with Margot today?"

His eyes lingered on her and made her want to tell him everything, and she would in time. "Well, Karl enjoyed the kids. In just a few hours, he was following Peri around like a puppy. Mostly, they sat next to each other zooming cars." Her smile faded.

"It was hard, wasn't it?" He covered her hand with his.

Tamar nodded. "Harder than I thought. My family's furniture is still in the living room, though it's covered with artwork and antiques. They keep Karl's toys in my old bedroom, so while the kids were playing, I checked things out—" She held out her palm. "I didn't take anything." *Yet.*

"But you're planning on it."

Tamar didn't respond at first, then she nodded. "That picture of the violin girl is compelling. Zari even noticed. She said it reminded her of Neelie. Of course, Neelie's the only one she knows who plays the violin, but it was more than that. It did look like Neelie at a young age."

With his finger, he turned her chin to face him. "Don't do it. You don't know who you're dealing with."

Time to change the subject. "How are your patients?"

He rolled his eyes. "Funny you should ask. Tomorrow we're going to unwrap the bandages from the comatose man. The one you thought said your name?"

"Bergman. He did say my name." A snake of a shiver slithered up her spine. She'd somehow tamped down all thoughts about that encounter. "Has he said anything else?"

Daniel blew out a breath. "We don't know what to do with him. He refuses to talk, although he's no longer comatose. Seems to be alert, but he won't answer our questions."

Her hands clenched involuntarily. "It's Officer Bergman. Can't you tell? Same build, same mannerisms, same voice. He clearly thinks he's better than everyone else."

"Tamar—"

"If it *is* him, why do you think he's here?"

Daniel's lingering stare answered that question. He raised an eyebrow.

"You truly think he's here because of me or my voice?" Tamar started rubbing her arms at a quick pace. "I always said my singing is a blessing and a curse. But surely, life isn't safe for a Nazi officer in this country. He should be in prison."

Daniel gently took her hand. "You're going to hurt yourself. It is a mystery. All we know is, he came from Amsterdam in an ambulance. So there's a good possibility he never intended to be here in Haarlem. I'll know more tomorrow about the man. We'll see if you're right."

Daniel hurried through his rounds, although he spent some extra time with Luuk, whose restlessness increased with the late spring temperatures outside. What a shame that the ten-year-old had to suffer through long periods of idleness, interspersed only with physiotherapy and meals. He should be out riding his bike or playing in the park.

Daniel also spent extra time with a new patient, Hanni van Halen, a young scientist who'd burned her hands in a flash fire in the hospital laboratory. The pain was always unbearable at first, but she was more concerned with deformity than discomfort.

"Doctor, I'm getting married in July—that's less than two months away. What if my scarred hands aren't healed by then?"

He adjusted her pillow and sat on the edge of her bed. "They should almost be healed by your wedding. We'll keep them bandaged for the next few weeks to prevent germs from getting at them. There will be some small amount of discoloration, but I wouldn't worry. You will be fine."

Once he'd checked her vitals, Daniel headed to the operating room where Sister Griet, Sister Anna, and he would meet to remove the bandages of Mr. X—the name Sister Anna had given the patient. He hadn't reacted negatively, so the name stuck. Usually, they did this procedure in the patient's room, but because of the question marks regarding what awaited them, he'd decided to remove the man from the curious eyes of his roommates.

The two nurses and the patient were waiting for him when he

entered the sterile room that contained nothing but a chair in the middle and a table with surgical instruments. He dimmed the lights because the man's eyes would take time to acclimate.

Normally, this was an anxious time for the patient, but also a highly anticipated one. They couldn't wait to remove the bandages, not only to see the scars for the first time, but also to remove the source of the scratchy irritation that accompanied healing burns. With young patients, a heightened atmosphere prevailed with the parents hovering closer with each rotation of the gauze.

But there were no hovering parents in this room. Mr. X had received no visitors in the weeks he'd been on the wing. How did a person remain in a coma for weeks without the slightest bit of interest from relatives? Why had the ambulance brought this man all the way from Amsterdam to Haarlem? He'd stopped at the administrator's office to ask, but they had no information.

"Well, let's begin." Daniel rallied the two nuns.

Sister Anna slid the tray of surgical tools close to the raised chair where the patient sat. They'd start with the man's hands, then remove the bandages from his head. Hopefully, once there was a face, they'd have some answers.

After Daniel scrubbed his hands, Sister Griet helped him into a sterile surgical gown, gloves, and a mask. The possibility of infection was high with burn victims, so the personnel took extra precautions to keep the rooms as sterile as possible.

Normally, Sisters Griet and Anna were full of good cheer on these days, but not today. The ambience reminded him of the large room at the medical school in England where he'd taken his final medical exams, stiff, tense, serious. Daniel cracked a smile at his two assistants, although his mask covered it. In surgery, he was used to reading smiling eyes. The nuns' eyes weren't.

Daniel addressed his patient. "Good afternoon, sir." He waited for a response but didn't expect one. "We're going to take off your bandages today. How's that? I'll bet you're eager to have them removed."

Daniel nodded to Sister Griet to pass him thumb forceps. He gently teased the bandages around and around until the man's right hand appeared. Yellowed from the iodine, it was covered with flaky, dead skin which Sister Griet would slough off, and the remnants of some deep burn blisters. They'd heal in time. The left hand was in even better shape.

Mr. X didn't audibly react, but his head inclined a bit as if he was interested in his hands' appearance. Good. That meant he was responding.

"Well, sir, they look pretty good. Sister Griet will clean them up, and if you keep them sterile, they'll heal with little scarring."

No reaction.

Daniel nodded to Sister Anna to give him fresh forceps and a sponge for his brow. For some reason, he was sweating, which was surprising since they kept the temperature at thirteen degrees Celsius. What if Tamar was right? It seemed ludicrous to think that a Nazi officer—one that had deported their neighbors into concentration camps—would step foot in Haarlem or anywhere in the Netherlands.

So few of Haarlem's Jews had returned. He wouldn't be standing here right now if he and Tamar hadn't escaped from Vught. Daniel studied the man sitting in front of him. They hadn't put him under because they needed his reactions. The man was aware of everything even if he wasn't responding. Mr. X had the same wiry body structure as Bergman—shorter than most Nederlanders. He released a deep exhale into his mask. "Let's begin. Thumb forceps, please."

Sister Griet handed him the tool, and he began gently parsing and teasing the bandage from this man's face. They'd cleaned him up as best they could when he first arrived, though Daniel hadn't been on call that night, so this would be the first time to see the injuries the man had sustained. Sister Griet helped hold his head up, and Daniel cut through the layers of gauze and tape until they reached the last row. "Sister Anna, would you lower the lights to the lowest setting, please?"

After Sister Anna returned to the patient, all eyes were on the man, whose own remained closed as Daniel removed the last bit of bandages.

It wasn't Bergman. He blew out a breath into his mask that sent a vapor to his glasses. The patient had sustained minimal scarring to the left side of his face, but other than that, he wouldn't need a lot of painful skin-graft operations. In fact, he was in remarkable shape. Daniel would estimate the man's age to be in the mid-forties. A narrow nose, prominent cheekbones, a few wrinkles but no freckles or marks. Tamar would be relieved to hear it wasn't the Nazi officer, but there *was* something familiar about him. Where had he seen him before? Probably in one of the camps—one of the guards, perhaps.

"Oh, he looks very, very good, doesn't he, Doctor?" Sister Griet said, always sensitive to the patient's greatest fear—that they'd look like a monster for the rest of their life.

"Yes, Sister, he does look good. Not a lot of scarring at all." Daniel picked up his ophthalmoscope. "Sir, you can open your eyes now, but do so gradually. The light might hurt at first, but it will improve with time."

Mr. X slowly opened his eyes to a squint, then lifted his arm to shield them. He examined his hand by bringing it close to his eyes. Meanwhile, the two sisters gently dabbed at his face to remove any dead skin or remnants of the bandages. All the while, they assured him that God had taken good care of his face and that he was a blessed man. He still hadn't uttered a syllable, but a frown furrowed his brow at the sisters' words.

Daniel smiled when the man's eyes finally met his. "Good morning, sir. You're a lucky man. What do you see? I assume everything is a bit blurry." The man didn't smile back, but after what he'd endured, it would probably be a while. "How does your face feel? I can assure you, it is healing nicely."

"How long must I stay in here?"

The nurses stopped at the gravelly voice, glanced at each other, at Daniel, then back at the man.

"Well, you speak. It is good to hear you. What is your name, sir?" The voice had a bit of an accent, although it was hard to distinguish from his succinct question.

Three parallel lines formed between his brows, and he shifted his body as if uncomfortable.

The man was not making this easy. Daniel tried again. "If you will give us your name, we'll let you rest. I'm sure you're tired." With a finger, he turned the man's chin to get a better look at each part of his face in the mirror Sister Griet held. It was hard to believe this man had been in an explosion. Except for a few blisters and rough spots, the epidermis was clear—like a baby's bum—as his mother used to say.

Now that he could see the man's face, he needed information. "You were brought here to Haarlem in an ambulance from

Amsterdam. The medics said you'd been in an explosion. Do you remember?"

No reaction, not even the move of the Adam's apple or a tightening of the jawline.

"Once we have a better picture of what happened to you, we'll be able to make an assessment and set a date for your release."

The man began coughing uncontrollably. Sister Anna brought him a glass of water, from which he drank greedily, and she wiped off his forehead. Once he calmed down, Daniel told the nurse to take him back to his room.

"There you be," Sister Anna said as she and Sister Griet helped the man into the wheelchair. "Doctor Feldman is right. We've seen a lot of burned faces. Yours is one of the best we've ever seen. It's almost as if—"

Daniel squeezed her arm. Something was wrong here. From a distance, it was as if he were looking at a mask.

Good. The damage was minimal. The plastic surgeon would be elated to know his handiwork had withstood the explosion.

Erich hadn't planned on talking. Didn't want them hearing his accent. He'd made his first mistake when he'd called out Tamar's name. Heard that beautiful voice and couldn't help himself. He'd learned how to suppress those uninvited thoughts—those moments of remorse for letting his need for revenge cloud his judgment. If he'd learned anything during the occupation, he'd learned that thoughts must be constrained. The Führer hadn't followed his own advice and look what happened to him.

The moment the nurse wheeled him into his room, his hand swept to shield his eyes from the blinding light. Peasants! Couldn't they have thought ahead to pull down the shades? The nurse called for help and bustled to the window. "I wonder who put these up. We need it dark in here. So let's leave them down, okay, roommates?"

Roommates. He'd forgotten about them. The last thing he needed was curious conversation, a lot of questions. He'd pretend to sleep, and soon they'd forget he was even there. Although these people thought they'd won the war, they were dead wrong. The

Reich would rise again, stronger next time, and he'd be part of it. The art had financed his new face. The Amsterdam doctor had done a remarkable job. Erich had studied every crag that added ten years to his appearance. If it hadn't been for the explosion, he'd be weeks ahead in his plan, but that blip of misfortune had set him back.

The sound of footsteps, and the gravelly voice of the other nurse said, "You needed something?"

"Yes, could you help me lift him into bed?"

"Certainly."

The nurses moved to either side of the bed. He went somewhat limp, enough that they'd think he was unconscious again. As long as they thought he was out of it, he'd have time to regroup. Erich suppressed a laugh. How fortuitous to be brought to Haarlem, of all places. When Feldman had introduced himself back when the bandages hid him, he couldn't believe his luck.

He'd heard from Sneider that Tamar and her fiancé had escaped to Switzerland or England. Now, apparently, they'd moved back to Haarlem. Everything was falling into place. Tamar was here in Haarlem, and most of the art he'd confiscated—the masterpieces he'd gathered over the last few years—were sitting in Klaus Sneider's house, although some minor art had probably been destroyed in the warehouse blast.

Erich had enough on Sneider to ruin the man if he didn't turn the stash over to him, although he'd throw him a few bones for his trouble. Sneider was scared. If the government found out he'd collaborated with the Nazis, he'd be a persona non grata, so Sneider had played along.

The nurse left, saying she'd return with fresh water. Good riddance.

Sneider still had his uses. He could procure a new identity card, traveling papers—whatever Erich needed to make a fresh start. The man could be bought. His desire to start the opera in Amsterdam was the carrot Erich would use to ensure his compliance. He'd offer Klaus enough money to establish himself here in Haarlem, with the hopes that its success would lead to bigger and better things in the capital.

And when the time was right, when the room was dark and the halls were empty, he'd take his leave. Tamar was alive and probably living close by. She was his weakness—his carrot. But he'd capture his prey through logic, planning, and determination. He'd bide his time, and when the opportunity presented itself, he'd find her. He'd rescue her, and they'd be together forever.

Chapter Eight

"The measure of a life, after all, is not its duration, but its donation."
~ Corrie ten Boom

May had somehow slid by, and she didn't even see it pass. When it was just the twins and her—and sometimes Daniel—life went as slowly as it had when Tamar was a child, when each day lasted forever. But now with little Karl, time was racing by as quickly as a passing bike.

Two or three days a week of caring for the child had turned into five days, including a weekend when Margot and her husband went to Amsterdam to see about the opera situation in their bigger neighbor. They'd invited Karl to stay at their apartment, and Margot had brought her son to the downstairs door, yelling up that she wasn't wearing the right shoes to travel to the fourth floor with Karl and his suitcase in tow. Fortunately, Karl was a compliant child and played well with Tamar's children.

Today, the twenty-seventh of May, was a beautiful one, and as soon as Margot left for her singing lesson, Tamar would take the children to the park. She had a lot of thinking to do, and she could do it better when a warm breeze and the fragrance of lilac trees hovered nearby.

The twins raced each other up the steps that led to the kitchen, giggling all the way. She loved their joy at the simplest things. The minute Tamar reached the top step, she froze. It had been years since she'd seen this man. At the table, smoking a pipe and peering at the paper, sat Klaus Sneider.

He must have felt her shock because he glanced up, then a smile spread across his face. Without taking his eyes off her, he rose from his chair and walked toward her as if in a trance. "Tamar? Is that you?"

She swallowed the ball in her throat, coughed twice, and fought to keep her composure. Life here in Haarlem since their return from England had been safe until now. Tamar tightened up when he hugged her, then he grabbed her arms and straightened them to look at her. She read astonishment in his eyes—the same startled expression as the last time she'd seen him where she'd been forced to sing at the Führer's birthday at Westerbork. Was Klaus Margot's husband? Margot hadn't said his last name.

"I cannot believe my eyes. You look wonderful. And who are these two little scamps? Ah, Margot told me that the woman who was taking care of Karl brought her own children, but she never mentioned it was you."

The years hadn't been kind to Klaus Sneider. Although his suit was as immaculate as always and his pomade-polished hair reflected the light from the kitchen window, now strands of gray wove among the shiny black ones, and his face appeared more gaunt than elegant. Still, he carried himself with the same dignity as he had at the Führer's birthday party. He was waiting for an answer. She was beyond words, so she burbled out the first thing that came to mind.

"We met at the park in April."

"Ah, yes." His eyes locked on hers as if she were a medical specimen, his head tilting from one side to the other, his brows angled. "Are you still singing? I have so many questions. I thought you were—"

The missing word hung in the air. *Dead*? Almost, many times, no thanks to him and his wife. "I'm concentrating on my twins right now." *And retrieving whatever I can from the life you stole from me.* But that wasn't true, and she knew it. Although he'd collaborated with the Nazis, he'd been nothing but kind to her. He'd even promised her that when the war was over, he wanted to help further her career as a soprano.

"That is a shame. Your voice, your pitch, your phrasing… It's our country's loss." He still studied her. "You know, if you ever want to pursue a singing career again, it would be my honor to help direct your path. The opera is opening all over the Netherlands.

People are hungry for music. Investors are starting to come forward."

"I don't think so, Mr. Sneider. My twins are still young, and they must be my top priority." Tamar winced at her words. In truth, she'd meant to disparage Margot, but her barbs failed to hit their mark.

"As they should, but it wouldn't hurt to take a few singing lessons. Surely, you could carve out a few minutes to practice your solfeggio every day, yes?"

Yes, how she wanted to return to that life she'd tasted before the opera house closed. To sing *La Traviata*, even if it was just the "*Brindisi*" in the chorus. But that was a long time ago. Her voice had been a blessing, but it had also been a curse. People had died because of her voice—because she'd been careless at Neelie's, and Bergman had heard her sing, then taken some of the guests to the camps, Lars and Bram not returning. She didn't deserve to sing again.

He touched her arm—a gentle touch, and she had to force herself not to jerk away. "You have been through a lot. Everyone has. But I would wager that the years have added benefit to your voice. Do you ever sing?"

She shrugged. "At shul when they ask, and of course, with my children." Tamar's eyes widened. She'd just announced to a former collaborator that she was a Jew. No, she would *not* be silent. Her chin lifted. "Yes, Mr. Sneider, I am a Jewess."

As if on cue, Margot bustled into the room, her arms full of hat boxes and a mink jacket. "Which one should I wear today, Klaus?" She plopped the boxes on the kitchen table and draped the mink over a chair. Without a glance at Karl, who lifted his arms toward his mother, she opened a hexagonal box, took out a smart hat with a veil, and gently placed it on her head, then did a twirl. "What do you think?" She moved to the mirror just outside the kitchen.

"It looks lovely, dear. However, the weather is too warm for a fur coat." Klaus walked up behind her and stayed her hand from primping in front of the mirror. "Sweetheart, we have guests." He pulled her into the room. "You didn't tell me Tamar was taking care of Karl."

Margot glanced over her shoulder. "Oh, I didn't realize you knew my former understudy." She threw a smile toward Tamar.

"Yes, dear. I met her twice, actually. Berg…a German officer had asked me for my opinion of her voice in Amsterdam at the Silveren Spiegel. I have to admit, I was duly impressed."

She whirled toward Tamar, the smile gone. "And when was the second time?"

Tamar tightened her arms around her waist. She didn't like the implications coloring Margot's voice.

"At Westerbork for the Führer's birthday celebration." His eyes narrowed. "You were there, dear, remember?"

She tsked, then opened another hatbox. "What I remember is a very gaunt singer in a very dreary place. And I also remember a commotion which seemed to cast a pall over the event."

There it was. Would her past ever evaporate? Daniel had said it would, but he was wrong. Yes, a drunken officer sitting next to her had keeled over into her lap, dead. Another case where her singing had caused her to be at the wrong place at the wrong time.

Klaus brushed at his lapel as if he were sweeping away a bad memory. "I'd forgotten about that, but you'll remember that it was hardly Miss Visser's fault. The officer died of a heart attack and probably too much drink."

Margot snorted. "Visser? That's not her name. She's a Kaplan." She raised her chin to her husband as if challenging him.

A furrow formed between his brows. "I must be mistaken about her maiden name." Klaus studied her for a few moments.

Tamar could easily explain, but a verse Neelie used to quote from time to time popped into her mind. *Do not throw* your *pearls before swine*. Tamar whispered the words in her heart to buoy her strength.

"I suggested that Tamar take some voice lessons, practice some scales. It won't be long before we'll be holding auditions at Haarlem's opera."

"Phff." Margot whipped around, her lip curled up in a sneer, but she must have thought better of what she was going to say and spun toward the mirror to check how the second hat looked. "I'm going to be late if I don't leave now." With one glance at her husband, she clamored down the stairs.

Klaus stared in her wake for a few awkward moments, then focused on Tamar. "I am sorry. She tends to become high-strung when it comes to her music." He was studying her again. "How about a lesson right now?" He gestured his palm toward the living room.

She backed up a step and caused Karl to tumble. "Oh, I'm sorry, honey." She reached down and picked up the little boy, then peered at his father. "I don't think that would be a good idea. I'm here to watch this little guy. That part of my life—my music—is over, at least for the present." Tamar's gaze darted to the stairs. "And I don't think—"

"Margot would approve? It's not her decision. It's mine. I'm trying to reestablish the Haarlem Opera. We need beauty in our lives again. And this would bring much-needed income to so many people." He gestured again. "Please?"

"Zari, Peri, come with me into the living room. You can color in there." Tamar carried Karl like a shield and followed Klaus to the baby grand piano, which was covered with clutter. She set the boy down and led him by the hand to the area on the floor where Zari was setting up her coloring books and crayons like a little teacher. Peri sat next to Karl and helped him choose a color.

"How old are your children?" came from behind her. Klaus motioned to the piano bench. He was asking more than this one question.

"They're three. I'm sorry I didn't introduce them. My daughter is Zari, and my son's name is Perez."

"Ah. I recognize that name from my youth. Perez was in David's line, isn't that right?"

A Nazi sympathizer knew about the Bible—especially an uncommon name?

His mouth held a wry grin. "Yes, Tamar. I grew up in a family that belonged to the Dutch Reformed Church. My father and mother read the Bible every night before dinner. This surprises you?"

She didn't know how to answer. How did someone who organized a celebratory birthday show for Hitler and whose house was filled with stolen paintings believe in the same Lord she did?

He must have read her thoughts. "My family's house was destroyed in the Rotterdam Blitz, May fourteenth, 1940. Everyone died. Those Bible stories didn't mean as much after that."

"I'm sorry. I lost my family…and house…as well." She straightened her jumper. "What would you like me to sing?"

After several rounds of solfeggio, the strength of her voice slowly began to return. And she had to admit, it invigorated her to sing with someone who understood the intricacies of voice training. Yet her mind kept traveling to Sneider's past. How could someone who was raised with the rich stories of the Bible from godly parents throw it all to the wind when the enemy destroyed everything? She was just starting to dwell on this train of thought when Sneider interrupted.

"Focus, Tamar. You're not hitting the notes."

She glanced down. "I'm sorry." Her apology was not only for her shoddy performance but also for her judgmental attitude. How dare she judge him? Hadn't she done the same when her parents were taken? Hadn't she questioned God's presence and care when her life turned inside out? Tamar stopped mid-scale and held up her palm. "I am sorry, but I should take care of the children. That is why I am here. It is time for lunch, and I promised the twins I'd take them to the park."

Sneider rose from the piano bench, pulled down the keyboard cover, and took out a handkerchief and wiped his hands. "I understand. However, I will have some free time later this afternoon around two. Would you have some time to practice again while Karl is taking his nap?"

She could feel lines forming between her brows. "Why are you doing this? Surely, you have more important things to do than waste time on your son's caregiver."

He reached for her arm. She backed up a step. "Tamar, I mean no harm. It's just that I want Haarlem's opera to be the best it can be. You have so much potential, and I want to help you reach it. And selfishly, I would like you to be part of the ensemble when it opens again. There's something I need to confess—I heard your Violetta the night you took my wife's place."

Unconsciously, she backed up again.

"Yes, I was there in the audience. And when I heard your voice at the Silveren Spiegel in Amsterdam, well, it didn't take me long to figure how who you were. Margot was there that night as well. It wasn't a good time for her, and she'd had one too many cocktails. As you've probably guessed, when the opera closed, it upended her life. She's made some…poor choices." He brushed off his jacket. "Well, I've taken enough of your time. Please, would you do me the honor of meeting me here at two for a short time of practice?"

"Yes, sir," she blurted before thinking and scurried over to the children, who were busy biting the paper wrapping off the crayons. "It's time for lunch." She knelt beside Peri, took him onto her lap, and handed him the opened tin box where they kept the crayons. "Let's count as we put them in the box."

They made quick work of tidying the floor, yet her thoughts strayed to those dark places from her past, playing and replaying them as she grabbed the fixings for sandwiches—a tomato, some leftover lamb from the dinner the night before, and two pieces of hearty bread that she'd brought from home, not feeling comfortable rummaging through Margot's icebox. Though Tamar had cared for Karl numerous times, she still felt like she walked on broken glass in this house. Ironic, since the last time she and Daniel had entered this house together, it had been over broken glass.

Apparently, the paper surrounding the crayons hadn't filled the children's tummies because they finished off every crumb of their sandwiches. Karl's cheeks held a healthy glow, and he'd gained some weight since she and the twins had spent their days with him. The child laughed more readily. Of course, it could just be because he was growing up, and the sunny skies of May had added the color to his cheeks. Margot hadn't complained yet, but Tamar always figured it was coming.

As they walked to the park, Karl trailing behind the twins who were hopping from crack to crack, she fingered the screwdriver in her pocket. Today was the day she had planned to open the grate in the hall, but it would have to wait until Margot's husband wasn't home. Another day wouldn't make any difference. Why had she agreed to sing for him? Somehow, it seemed wrong, as if she were sneaking behind Margot's back. Singing lessons could add a level of complication that could thwart her plans.

When they arrived at the park, the children ran to the swings, insisting that she push them. Tamar helped them onto the three adjacent ones, pushing harder against Zari's and Peri's backs and more gently against Karl's.

"More, more," all three children chanted, until she said, "That's high enough. How about going to the slides? You'll have them to yourselves." That's all it took to convince Peri. Karl echoed his demands, and soon the two boys ran to the slides. Tamar positioned herself between the slides and the swing where Zari had finally mastered the art of pumping her legs at the right time to maintain her pendulum.

She glanced at her Grönefeld watch—actually, Daniel's watch that he'd received from a grateful patient. One-thirty. If she were to meet Mr. Sneider, they would need to leave now, so she'd have time to put the kids down for a nap. "Time to leave."

Their grumbles made it clear they weren't happy about leaving, but they complied when she promised them stroopwafels if they took a nap when they returned. What a fraud she was—bribing the children and carrying a screwdriver in her pocket and practicing with Margot's husband.

It was almost two when they clamored up the stairs to her bedroom—Karl's bedroom. A half-full bottle of milk sat in his crib. A sniff of it ruffled Tamar's nose, but he grabbed it out of her hand. The twins slid under the crib, happy to take a nap in their tent-like enclosure. Tamar took a light blanket out of her rucksack, bent down, and placed it over their shoulders.

"Story, Eema," Zari said, echoed by Peri, then followed by Karl, who probably didn't know what it meant.

"Not this time. Eema has to go practice her singing."

"Then sing loud so we can hear you, oke?" Zari lifted her head from her makeshift pillow.

"That would hardly help you fall asleep." Tamar threw a kiss. "Now go to sleep, and sweet dreams." She rose to her full height, her eyes landing on the girl and her instrument. With the blanket, she could cover it and keep it safe. If she just moved the clown to the left and covered its empty spot with one of the paintings from over the rocking chair, Margot wouldn't miss the girl or her violin. Now she had mere minutes before she had to be downstairs, and the children would wonder what she was doing.

Next time, while the kids were downstairs, she'd sneak up and take it. For some reason, Tamar felt an urgency—that if she didn't take it soon, she never would. Was that because she'd lose her nerve, or because Margot would tire of their arrangement and fire her?

Straightening her frock, she hurried down the stairs, stopping long enough to put the children's sandwich plates and glasses in the sink, then she grabbed a cloth to wipe off the table, counter, and high chair. Calming herself, she entered the living room.

Klaus wasn't there yet, so she meandered around the room, straightening the throw pillows on the sofa and picking up small slivers of paper from the floor that the kids hadn't digested. The paintings stacked on a pie-crust table drew her attention. Did she dare look at the pictures?

On top was a painting of a portly elderly man in a black robe with a white pleated ruffle around his neck. Was this a Frans Hals painting? It couldn't be. Like Rembrandt and Vermeer, Fans Hals belonged to Nederlands. He actually belonged to Haarlem. Every young student in this town took a field trip at least every few years to the artist's museum. He was the father of the portrait. He was the father of the smile. Tamar searched for the signature. Was this a stolen picture? Surely, it must be worth thousands of guilders or more. But it couldn't be. It must be a fake.

"What are you looking at?" The voice behind her jolted her heart. She whipped around and clasped her hands behind her as if she concealed a stolen cookie.

"Oh, I was just waiting…and this painting. It's stunning. Where—" Tamar constrained herself in time. There were two—no, many more issues going on here—that she didn't understand. Why was this family living in her house, and did they know it had been hers? And while her parents' jewelry store was now a dry cleaner, why was this family not manning it? Was the business below a cover? And why did all this art sit in careless stacks on tables as if it were discarded newspapers? Her suspicions must show in her eyes. Tamar averted them.

"You're asking where I obtained the painting?"

"That's none of my business." She inched toward the piano. "The children won't sleep long. We'd better get started."

Without words, Sneider sat at the piano and leafed through some sheet music. The air hung heavy between them. Something had changed, although Tamar had felt constricted since she'd arrived. Her mother had once told her as a teenager it wasn't proper for a young woman to be alone in a room with a man. This seemed wrong.

"How about a Verdi, and then we'll move to a Rossini?"

After a few stops and starts, she released her nerves to the music, and her voice came more squarely, and then she lost herself in its ebbs and folds and flows.

Sneider stopped and turned to face her from the piano bench. "Good. Your voice is returning. Much better than at first. Well done." He riffled through the scores of music from the pile on the floor next to the piano, then stopped. "Here it is. Would you sing '*Addio del passato*'? I know it's a lot to ask, but you've sung it before. Remember, this is Violetta's farewell to Alberto before she dies. Of course, I don't expect you to convey the emotions the song requires, but give it your best."

Tamar blew out a breath. She pursed her lips. Here she was in Margot's house with Margot's husband, singing Margot's song. It was wrong, but what could she say? Closing her eyes, she remembered how sick Violetta had been when she sang this song— her heart breaking, her body wasting away. Tamar had lived this at Vught, at Westerbork, wasting away on a tepid bowl of broth with gristle floating on its surface and a hard piece of flavorless bread. Her voice erupted, a bit strained as it should be. And she sang for her mother and father who never returned, for Mrs. Betz who would never make another loaf of bread, for Hannie whose generosity belied her rough exterior.

Never had she sung with so much pathos. Yes, it was time to return to the opera. It held her heart, but so did her kids and so did Daniel.

"What is this?"

Tamar whipped around, her hands going behind her back again.

Margot appeared, her eyes stormy. Those eyes that used to make Tamar stutter and back up whenever Margot was having a prima-donna outburst. "What is going on in my house?" She glanced at Sneider, who rose to his feet, but slower than Tamar had reacted.

"Margot, the children are sleeping, so let's lower our voices," he said with a bemused expression on his face.

His paternal tone made Margot step forward, hands on hips, lips twitching as if she couldn't suppress the rage. She looked as though she wanted to spit. "Lower *our* voices? I could hear her from outside. What are you doing singing at my piano with my husband when you're supposed to be watching my son?" Every pronoun was enunciated with more and more vigor.

This was not her battle, so Tamar wouldn't enter it. In the past, when Margot's tumultuous screaming over a hemline or the dust or a baby's cry made rehearsals come to a standstill, Tamar would gather her courage and defend the victim from being fired.

Sneider was assuaging Margot with quiet words, and Tamar had missed most of them. "Margot, you will always be the best singer, but we need an outstanding ensemble to draw the crowds back to the opera. Tamar would be a tremendous boon to our program."

What? He wasn't going to clear the innuendo from the heavy tension in the room? Enough of this. She had a mind to leave and not came back. How dare this woman insinuate that there was anything untoward going on between Tamar and that patent-leather-haired man who'd vanish if he turned sideways?

She lifted her chin. "If you will excuse me, I'll gather my children." Tamar barely edged past Margot, who blocked the doorway. Her footsteps clattered up the stairs while the rising voices of the couple were sure to wake up the dead.

The moment she entered the bedroom, Zari's voice chirped from under the crib. "You sounded beautiful, Eema. That last song was sad."

"Yes, it was, sweetie." She knelt down, squeezed under the crib, and joined the twins, which evoked giggles from both kids.

"Is Mevrouw mad at you?"

"I don't know, sweetheart. Maybe we shouldn't come here anymore."

"But what about Karl? He'll be lonely. We're his friends."

On cue, Karl began to whimper above them. She hadn't thought that her children were invested in this almost daily job of hers. Well, she'd think about it later, but now it was time to leave before she burned a bridge.

"C'mon, kids." She shimmied out from under the crib and pushed to her feet. With raised arms, Karl whined to be released from his bed. Lifting him out, she felt his diaper, which needed changing. "Zari, put your coloring books and crayon box in my bag by the door. Peri, grab your trucks. As soon as I change this fellow's nappy, we'll head home."

A heavy grayness weighed on her shoulders. Why hadn't she listened to that tiny voice? She shouldn't have agreed to sing. Daniel wouldn't be happy when he heard that she was considering returning to the opera—not now when her children needed her.

Once Karl was diapered, she lowered him to the floor and scanned the room for anything that was out of place. "Let's go home." With one last glance at the violin girl, she zipped up her backpack and rose to her feet—but froze.

Margot blocked the door, her arms across her chest. Tamar held her breath. Perhaps a simple apology would suffice. Singing while the kids napped was outside her job here.

"I'm sorry. It won't happen again. We'll be on our way."

Margot didn't respond right away, yet her eyes remained on her, studying her.

Tamar stepped toward the door, but Margot remained leaning against the doorjamb.

"My husband is eager to get the opera back on its feet, and he thinks you have talent. There will be auditions soon, and he wants you to be there." Her eyes narrowed. "But hear me well. What my husband doesn't realize is that the Haarlem opera belongs to me. Therefore, my fans will return only if I return. Do you understand what I'm saying?"

Tamar shifted her bag to the other hand and took the clammy hand of Peri, who was whining to leave. No, she would not kowtow to this woman as so many had. "I am a mother to these children. They are my first concern, but if God opens up a door for me to sing at your—the opera—then I will audition to the best of my abilities." Her chin lifted of its own accord. "Now we will be leaving. Dag."

Zari wriggled out of the door, echoing her mother's goodbye. Margot moved enough to allow them to leave.

As they hurried down the backstairs, Margot's voice stopped them. "Wait."

Tamar turned midway down. What now? She steeled herself for Margot's cutting retort.

"Your husband is a doctor, is he not?"

What? What did Daniel have to do with anything? Was Margot going to tell him what she'd done while the kids slept, adding innuendo to create division between her and her husband?

Margot's hand went to her neck. "My throat has been bothering me of late. Especially after I've been working with my voice coach. I was wondering if your husband would be willing perhaps to make a house call?"

Relief shrouded her. "I could ask him. He works most days and many evenings at the hospital. But Daniel works with burn patients."

Margot peered around her. "I don't want Klaus to know. Is that understood? This is between you and me."

Chapter Nine

"In this dark world, the Lord Jesus gave us the task of passing on
His love."
~ Corrie ten Boom

The sound of the doorknob brought Tamar out of the kitchen
while untying the bow of her apron. Finally, her prince was home.
She flung the door open to greet him, and her hand went to her chest.
Daniel stood there with a bouquet of daisies in his hand. Even after
a long workday at the hospital, he had thought to surprise her.

"For you, my love." He held them out with a flourish and a bow.

"Daisies? They're lovely." She pulled him into the room.
"What's the occasion? Did I forget my birthday or our anniversary?"

"Let me put my bag down and take off my tie, then I'll tell you."
He opened the closet door.

"I'll go put the flowers in water." Hurrying into the kitchen,
Tamar grabbed a pickle jar from the cupboard, filled it with water,
and one by one, she strategically arranged each flower. Lifting the
jar to her nose, she sniffed the blossoms. "Come, sit. I have your
supper ready." Tamar placed the flowers in the center of the small
table.

Daniel rolled up his sleeves and joined her, taking a seat across
from her. "It smells delicious. What are we having?"

"I made your favorite soup—lentil with lamb, some crusty
bread to sop it up with, and some strong Gouda."

"When did you have time to make soup? You were at Margot's
all day." He glanced around, then raised one eyebrow. "The house

is awfully quiet. What have you done with my children?"

She batted his arm. "Silly. They've already eaten and are playing dominoes in their room. They'll want you to come in later and flick the first one."

Tamar brought a tureen to the table and served him a bowl, then placed a basket of fresh bread by the flowers. After praying, Daniel picked up his spoon. "Aren't you eating?"

She lifted a shoulder. "I'm not hungry."

"Oh, c'mon. I don't want to eat alone." He pushed the basket toward her, stood, and grabbed a small plate from the counter. "You can at least have a piece of bread and some cheese."

Tamar leaned on her elbows. "All right. I'll have a nibble of bread, but you have to tell me what we're celebrating."

The excitement on his face reminded her of Peri's when he shifted from foot to foot for the warm cake she was cutting and placing on a plate for him to enjoy. "Today we took the bandages off Mr. X's arms and head."

"Mr. X?"

"Yes, the man you thought was Officer Bergman."

How could she forget? He'd interfered with her thoughts every day since she'd sung three long weeks ago. "Well?"

Daniel took a drink of his milk, seeming to enjoy her rapt attention. Then he slowly swabbed a piece of bread with butter.

"All right. You're baiting me. Was it him or not?" She grabbed a piece of bread and stuffed it into her mouth, her eyes remaining on him.

"Minimal scarring to his arms and face. He'll heal quickly. But….but he's not Officer Bergman. This man is older. Different bone structure. His hair is graying and the nose is wider, as are his lips." He took a drink of his milk. "So you can relax. I know it's been bothering you."

"Whew. You have no idea." She shook her head and frowned. "Was I just imagining it? That voice? The fact that he mentioned the song I'd sung that day at Neelie's, and he said my name. Am I going crazy?"

He patted her hand. "It's not Bergman. But there was something familiar about him. Maybe he was one of the guards at Westerbork. We couldn't get any information out of him. He wouldn't tell us his name or how he ended up in Haarlem. But—"

"Did he have that tic? The way Bergman's lip drooped at certain times?"

"As I said, he didn't talk. We'll be releasing him soon. There's no reason to keep him, but I'll keep my eye out for that tic. Again, it's not Bergman, okay?"

"Okay." Why did she still have doubts? "All right. This is good news. Now I can concentrate on packing for our move to Neelie's house. Two weeks. Can you believe it? We won't have to traipse up four floors anymore."

"Except one of the twins will have to sleep on the fourth floor if we want to give them separate bedrooms. We can give Zari Neelie's old bedroom on the fourth. Peri's probably not ready to be a floor away from us yet. He'd climb out of his crib and we'd find him toddling into the canal."

She nodded. "Maybe we'll keep them in the same room for the time being. Ease them into separate rooms. I'm not sure I'm ready to visit that floor yet. It's too close to the attic."

He took her hand and kissed her palm. "How will we get to our special meeting place on the roof if you won't go near the attic?"

Each touch of his lips against her knuckles brought a shiver. "That was the only good thing about our stay there. I fell in love with you in that alcove. You won me over with your dreams about us living in our future house with your office on the first floor." Tamar pulled her hand away. "Daniel, the kids will come out any minute."

"And they'll rejoice that their parents are still in love with each other."

When he'd finished his dinner, she carried his dishes to the sink. "Would you like some coffee or tea before knocking over the twins' dominoes?"

He sat back, massaging his temples. "Tea would be nice, nicer if you join me."

She put the kettle on to heat and measured tea leaves into the strainer, then took the creamer out of the icebox. Now was the time to tell Daniel about her day at Margot's. All of it this time. She put a small platter of stroopwafels in the center of the table along with the cream, sugar, and two cups. Then she sat. "May I tell you about my day before you spend time with the kids?"

"Of course. I'm all ears." He fanned them like an elephant. "I'm sorry I didn't ask."

"That's okay. You had big news, and so do I." She told him about Klaus being in the kitchen when she arrived.

Daniel's eyes widened. "Why was he at Margot's house—pardon me, your former house?"

"They're married. He's Karl's father. Can you imagine?" She stood and filled the teapot and brought it and a cozy to the table, then poured him and herself a cup.

He folded his arms across his chest and sat back. "It's actually not surprising. We met him at that Nazi restaurant you sang at, and wasn't he with Margot that night at Westerbork when you sang for the birthday? Whoa." He brought his knuckles to his lips. "So Margot and Klaus Sneider are living in your house with all that art. That can't be good for you or the kids."

She held up a palm. "I don't feel as though we are in any danger. Margot simply wants me to watch her child. But there is a chink in the saw."

He smirked. "You're mixing your metaphors. But before you tell me about the chink, I want you to know that your safety is more important than anything, so we're not done discussing your job there."

She fortified her resolve with a deep breath. "Klaus wants me to audition for the opera…eventually, when it opens. In the meantime, he wants me to practice singing."

Daniel stared at her for a while—too long without saying anything. The longer the quiet, the more she wished she hadn't said anything. "Do you want to?"

"Want to what?"

"Audition for the opera," he said, circling the rim of his teacup with his finger faster each time.

"I'm…I'm considering it, but of course, you and the children have to agree to it, and we'd have to find a babysitter for the twins when I go to practice. I'd only want to work part-time." The groove between his brows deepened. "Haarlem's opera won't open for months, perhaps even years."

He leaned forward on his elbows, studying her as if reading between what she wasn't saying. "Did you talk to Sneider?"

"Yes, he was surprised to see me. Apparently, Margot hadn't told him I was watching Karl." Tamar swallowed beyond the bread that was sitting in her esophagus. She gulped the hot tea to force it down. "Klaus…Mr. Sneider…asked me to sing for him at the piano in the living room."

He didn't react the way she wanted, so she continued. "Margot had left for her voice lesson, so I agreed to sing for him. He had me do some scales and some short songs, and then he asked me to sing some opera pieces, including Violetta's aria from *La Traviata*. Said I should keep practicing because he wanted me to try out when Haarlem's opera finally opens." She winced.

"And you said?"

"Nothing. Margot came home and heard me singing. Huffed and asked me where the kids were, insinuating that I was more interested in singing for her husband than taking care of her child."

"And were you?"

She swatted at his arm. "How can you say that? You know me. You're just like Margot with the innuendos. The kids were taking their naps. I can't believe you said that." Her lip started to quiver.

He clasped her hand and spoke just above a whisper in his calming voice. "I'm not implying anything. It's just that you've seemed so restless lately. Obsessed with that house. Maybe you want to go back to work. It meant a lot to you, and maybe we're holding you back."

Her head shook at a fast pace. "You're not. I would never do anything to put you or the twins second to a career, and I can't imagine leaving the twins with a babysitter twice a day five days a week. Plus, with the move to Neelie's, I'll have my hands full."

Her words seemed to appease him. "So what did you mean when you said, 'Margot's innuendos'?"

"I might have just imagined it, but she was so angry. Whether it was because I was singing, and she doesn't want any competition, or if it was because her husband was coaching me. I'm pretty sure it wasn't because of the children that she was mad. All I knew at the time was that I needed to grab the kids and get out of there before she fired me and told me never to enter the house again."

"And then you wouldn't be able to snoop." His lips curled into a smirk.

He was making fun of her. "I'm not a snoop. I just want my parents' stuff back." She stuck her nose in the air to accentuate her point, then cut him a sideways glance to see if her point was taken.

"Since my time may be limited at the house, when can you come with the screwdriver and help me open that grate?"

He leaned his cheek on his fist. "Obviously, it's up to you. It will have to be when you're there and the Sneiders are not."

She sighed. "Well, I seem to be there every other day from late morning to mid-afternoon. So Monday, Wednesday, or Friday? Could you come on your lunch break? I could leave my hair ribbon tied to the back door if it's not a good time."

He thought a minute. "All right. I usually take my lunch about twelve-thirty to one-fifteen, but if I'm called to an emergency, I don't take a lunch." He traced a circle on her knuckles with his finger. "So we can't really set an exact time."

"Emergency." She covered her mouth. "I forgot. Margot asked if you could make a house call. She's having trouble with her throat."

"A sore throat?"

"Not really. It hurts after she's been singing for a while. I told her you worked primarily with burn victims, but she still wanted to know if you could come and check it out." Tamar stood and took the dishes to the sink. "Would you like some more tea?"

He was mumbling, low enough so she couldn't understand what he was saying. "What was that?" She peered over at him.

He glanced up, a storm brewing between his brows. "Nothing," he spat.

Nothing, huh? She slid into the seat next to him and massaged the tight muscle in his shoulder. "What is nothing?"

Daniel expelled a breath in a huff. "I think of the way Margot looked at us as if we were polluting her with our presence, like we were the barnacles on the side of rotting wood. Like—" He glanced at her, saw her suppressed smile. His eyebrows drew together. "What's so funny?"

Tamar suppressed a giggle with her knuckles. "Now you know how I've been feeling when it comes to my house. Like Margot's the queen bee, and she's entitled to everything inside. And I'm always the understudy or the servant or the babysitter. But knowing that my parents' papers are hidden in that grate gives me a bit of entitlement." Tamar lifted her chin like a peacock.

"Hope we don't have a roof leak, or you'll drown with your nose in the air like that." His lips pursed together.

She stuck out her tongue at him—it was the best she could do on a moment's notice.

Daniel rolled his eyes. "We're a pair, aren't we?" His shoulders lifted. "All right, my Hippocratic Oath tells me to treat the ill to the best of my ability, so that I shall do with your friend, Margot." He winked and backed away before she swatted him. "When should I make this house call?"

"I'm sure she'll want you to come as soon as you are able—especially if it's bothering her. How about the day after tomorrow? You've never been introduced, so I'd like to be there. Margot did say that she didn't want Klaus to know."

"Oh, so it's Klaus now," he said with a playful smile.

"I didn't call him that in person, but I do in my head. She's probably afraid that her throat problem will affect her singing future, and that would be devastating for her. Margot lives to sing."

His lips tightened the way they did when he was making a decision he didn't want to. "All right. I'll be there the day after tomorrow at noon." He stood and stretched his long arms. "Well, the kids have probably configured a path of dominoes to the street by now. I should go and spend some time with them."

With a contented sigh, she filled the narrow sink with sudsy water and placed the dishes in it. How nice it would be to have Neelie's full-sized kitchen rather than this mere dip in the wall. Everything would be bigger there. And they wouldn't have to share a bathroom anymore with Seth and Hadassah, but she'd miss them.

A muffled voice shouted her name from one of the floors below. Tamar opened the door and called down to the woman who served as concierge on the first floor of the apartment building, "What is it, Roos?"

"It's the hospital for your Daniel. Tell him to hurry. I'm expecting a call any minute now."

Roos van Pelt's footsteps stomped into her flat. It was hard for four floors of tenants to share a single phone, and she felt bad whenever a call from St. Elisabeth interfered with Roos's cooking or embroidery or radio programs. Soon they'd be able to install their own phone. Maybe Jan Visser had already done so. Tamar dashed to the bedroom where Daniel was sitting cross-legged on the floor with one twin on each leg. Concentric circles of dominoes surrounded them.

"Are you ready?" He helped Peri prepare to flick his finger near the first domino. "Let's count to five. *Een, twee, drie, vier, vijf.*" Then Peri flicked his pointer finger. One toppled into another. Peri sprang to his feet and jumped up and down, clapping and laughing as little black rectangles toppled over one at a time.

Tamar touched her husband's arm. "Phone call. Hurry. Roos is expecting a call."

He set Zari on the floor next to him and stood. "I'll be right back."

Once the dominoes were spent, Tamar knelt down and stacked the dotted tiles in the box. Peri protested, whining that he wanted to keep playing.

"It's late, sweetie. We can do this again tomorrow, and maybe you could teach Karl how to play dominoes."

When her son's lower lip protruded, she said, "If you'll help me put these away, I'll tell you a secret about the dominoes, okay? Now that you're older, I can teach you another way to play."

His eyes brightened and his lip receded. Soon his head was bobbing as he picked up one at a time and set it in the box. At this rate, he'd still be at it at midnight, provided he didn't keel over from the effort. Zari's hand went to her hip as she observed her brother, then she pushed him aside and gathered a handful. This made Peri's red face turn redder.

Time to intercede. "Watch me." Tamar closed her eyes. "I'm going to pick a domino and tell you how many spots are on it. Your job is to pick that number of dominos up. Understand?"

Zari's face puckered. "Is this the secret?" She didn't appear too enthused.

"No," Tamar said, "but it will help us get used to the pips."

"Pips? That's a funny word."

Peri bolted to his feet, hopped around, and said 'pips' over and over, then emitted a belly laugh at himself.

"Silly bear, the pips are the little spots." Tamar held one up. "How many pips does this one have?"

Peri stopped, squinted, held up four fingers, and said, "Five."

Tamar checked the domino in her hand. Did he need glasses? "Almost. Your fingers were right. It has four." She picked up another. "Zari, how many does this one have?"

"Six." Zari glanced sideways at her brother.

"That's correct. All right, you two. Pick up all the sixes you can find."

The twins made quick work of the dominoes while Tamar reached for errant tiles that had somehow ended up under the bed and bureau.

"I have to go."

She whipped around at the low voice, noting the twins had abandoned her. Daniel's face was devoid of color. "What happened?"

"That patient—Mr. X—"

"Did he die?"

Daniel's Adam's apple bobbed. "He's disappeared."

"What do you mean, 'disappeared'?"

"I don't know the details. That's why I have to go. The nurse just said he's not in his bed. Only one of his roommates was in the room, and when he woke up, Mr. X's bed was empty. I'm leaving now. We have to find him." The door shut behind him.

A shiver traveled down her spine. It was probably nothing. Maybe he was simply taking a walk or had gotten lost in one of the serpentine corridors of St. Elisabeth's. But no amount of self-talk helped her assuage the bad feelings growing inside. Despite what Daniel had said about the man not being Officer Bergman, she knew. She knew that voice. He'd said her name, said the name of the song she'd sung at Neelie's, and he had the same wiry build of the Nazi officer. Maybe he'd changed his appearance in some way, dyed his hair. It had been over four years since she'd had a good look at his face. A person could change a lot in four years.

Tamar blew out a breath. They wouldn't find him. He was too smart. Officer Bergman was in Haarlem, and he was here for one reason.

He knocked on the door once again. They were home, and he knew it. The light was illuminated on the second floor. Probably a kitchen. Why wasn't Sneider or his floozy of a wife answering? It would cost them.

Giggles came from the sidewalk. He backed up into the

shadows of the house's wall, near the door that most likely led to a staircase, as in most Dutch houses. He'd had his fill of those stairs when he and his lackeys clamored up them searching for hidden Jews, hidden ration cards—whatever they could find to evacuate the house and take over its inventory.

The shadows hid the lab coat he'd swiped from the doctor who was too busy reading a chart to notice what was going on around him. A simple smash of his head against the doorjamb and the doctor's head scrambled. Idiot eggheads, all of them. He could have been a doctor—always wanted to, but then the führer drew him in, and here he was hiding in the shadows of the house that held all the art he'd paid Sneider to hold for him. Maybe that's why they weren't answering the door. Someone must have alerted them about his escape from the hospital.

A walk around to the front of the building showed dark display windows of a dry-cleaning business. So this was Sneider's cover? Somehow, he couldn't picture Sneider's wife, Margot, lifting her finger to do something so plebian as waiting on customers or handling soiled clothes. It might chip a fingernail.

Ah, a doorbell—he'd almost missed it. He pushed it once, then again and again. If that didn't bring them to the door, nothing would.

Wearing this lab coat made him stand out. People would remember seeing him if he didn't find a place to hide. Sneider owed him big time. If he didn't answer in five minutes, he'd break in. Find a rock and smash it through the window. There were no windows in the back, or he'd break in there.

The pain was getting to him. Meds were wearing off. Why now? He didn't need this extra aggravation. Pain was a sign of weakness—at least, that's what he'd always told the whimpering jellyfish that begged for their lives.

Mind over matter, the führer had taught them. He had pounded the message into them. "Keep your mind on the two goals, to acquire *lebenstraum*—to reclaim living space from those who don't belong—and the Jewish reckoning." Make them pay for what they'd taken from the Germans. His lip curled at the thought, the movement of which sent a strike of pain through his face.

He circled slowly, maintaining an impassive, forgettable demeanor as he searched for something hard enough to break a window. With hands behind his back, he strolled to the corner of the house. There he found a cinder block. Big enough to do some damage, though loud enough to alert curious onlookers. With a glance around for snoops and snitches but seeing none, he bent down too quickly to pick up the block.

Stars streamed past his line of vision. He backed up until he made contact with a tree—something to hold onto until the dizzying stream and the pain passed. Okay, maybe it wasn't such a good idea to leave the hospital just yet. But he'd had enough of the curious stares of his roommates and the incessant questions about his identity from the staff.

Buoying up his strength, he slowly lowered to pick up the cinder block by bending his knees and expelling regular breaths through his nose, careful to look straight ahead. This time, the stars stayed back, and he rose to a standing position. The weight in his hands caused the burns on his arms to scream—like the skin was ripping apart.

Without wasting anymore time, he stepped toward the entry, raised the block in both hands while gritting his teeth, and prepared to hurl it through the windowpane in the door. What a weakling he'd become. Had this been five years ago, he would have been sent to pasture if he were lucky.

Just then, the door swung open. The floozy stood there, a hand over her ample chest, her mouth hanging open like a broken hinge.

"Let me in."

Sneider's wife maintained her position at the door. A young child sucking his fingers peeked out from behind her skirt. "Who are you?" She glanced down at the cement block in his hands. "What are you—"

He used the block to push her inside until he could close the door. She screamed. The boy started crying for his mother. The noise in his head was killing him. "Quiet!" He had to make it stop. Even now, his mother's admonitions to be polite rang in his head. "Please!" He set the block on the floor.

Her knuckles went to her mouth, but she quieted, although the child still whimpered. He'd always been good with kids. With a smile that pulled at his tight cheeks, he said, "Calm down, child."

She moved the boy behind her. "Who are you? What do you want?"

So she didn't recognize him. Maybe that was a good thing.

They'd met a few times at social events, but again, he'd forgotten his face had changed. Should he tell her? She was never one to trust. In fact, it had surprised him that Sneider would marry a diva like Margot. "Where's Sneider?"

She clenched the counter, her knuckles whitening. "You haven't answered my questions. Are you Tamar's husband?"

What? Tamar's husband? *If there was a God.* But he'd eschewed God's existence the moment he'd realized the heights man could reach on his own without the help of religion. "I have no idea what you're talking about, Madame. Is Sneider here?"

"Maybe, but he doesn't need to be here while you examine my throat. In fact, I'd rather this visit remain between you and me. Is that understood?" Her face scrunched into a frown.

"What?" He didn't have time for this. That cinder block could come in handy with this chatterbox. His head was splitting, and the burns were sizzling like bratwurst on a grill.

She lifted a shoulder. "I just thought Tamar's husband would look different. Taller. Darker. Jewisher."

The thought finally seeped through the pain. The lab coat. This woman thought he was Dr. Feldman. Which also meant that she knew Tamar. But of course she would. They were both sopranos from Haarlem. Somehow, he hadn't put Tamar in the same category—in the same breath—with the trollop standing before him. "It doesn't matter, does it? Let's move upstairs and begin the examination."

Her eyes narrowed. "What were you going to do with that cement block?" Her arms folded across her chest. "You don't look so good."

The room started a slow spin. He forced his eyes wide open past the pain to make it stop. "I could use a drink. I'm not feeling so good." He pressed his temples. "Could you get me a drink? Then I'll have a look at your throat. When is your…your husband coming back?"

Margot studied him as though he was a derelict. She pushed from the counter, almost tripping over the boy. "Follow me. A good shot of whiskey will do the trick. Then we're even. You tell me what's wrong with my throat, and I won't tell the hospital about your drinking problem."

Erich followed her up the stairs, gripping the railing to keep from falling. He probably should have given it another day before leaving the hospital.

She pointed at a chair in the kitchen, the yellow color of the walls making his head spin like a ride at a park.

He fought the urge to lower his head to the table, to close his eyes for a few moments. But he must have done so because the sound of the glass making contact with the table next to his ear jarred him to a sitting position, which brought a new wave of vertigo.

"Drink up." She looked around. "Don't most doctors carry medical bags?"

"Do you want me to check your throat or continue to argue? Maybe that's the problem." He winced. This wasn't working out the way he'd planned. Still, these were the cards played. "If you have a penlight or a flashlight and a spoon, I'll get to work." After downing his drink, he closed his eyes to wait for the alcohol to do its job. What he wouldn't do for some pain meds. Another poor decision. Had he been thinking ahead of his escape, he could have weaned himself to half a dose, saving the rest for times like this.

"Here you are." The diva's jarring voice made him cringe. She sat across from him, pointing at the impromptu medical devices with a painted talon.

He slowly pushed to his feet and faced her. "What seems to be the problem?"

"Didn't your wife tell you? My throat feels aggravated, raw. Especially after an hour of singing. So I need to know what I can do to make it feel better."

Stop singing? "Open your mouth." He made a show of shining the penlight around her mouth, of examining her throat from all angles. It was red, especially the upper ridges. "You can close it now." His fingers made little circles around her glands, although he was not sure what he was feeling. "Why don't you want your husband to know about this problem?"

Her eyes widened. "You're not going to tell him, are you?" Her eyes narrowed. "I should have known. None of your kind can be trusted." Margot sat up, her lips pursed. "If you must know, the opera will be opening soon, and I need to prepare for the lead as always, but the years since its closure haven't been kind." She sniffed. "So what's the problem with my throat?"

"It's a little red around the edges." He searched his memory bank for past sore throats. Memories of his mother giving him aspirin and soothing foods and drinks came to mind. "Tea with honey or something cold like ice water will make it feel better. But maybe you should consider taking a bit of a break from singing."

Her fist slammed down on the table. "That will never happen. Singing the lead requires hours of practice daily. Can't you give me something for my throat? A pill of some sort?"

His head reeled from her strident voice. If there was anywhere else he could go, he'd be out of here, but Sneider had his art, and he wasn't leaving without it. He massaged his temples. "Try the tea with honey. Some frozen juice will certainly feel good. I didn't bring any medications, but I'm sure you can go to the pharmacy and buy some aspirin."

She nodded, mollified for the moment.

"If the symptoms don't go away in a few days, you'll need to make an appointment with a doctor to do some tests, which I can't do here." There, he'd given her the same type of advice his mother had. It was sound advice. "Now, when will Sneider be home? We have business to discuss."

"Why would you have business with my husband? How do you even know him?"

She had him there. Playing two roles without any rehearsals was wreaking havoc with his mind. "I'm here to discuss art with your husband. He is your husband, isn't he?" What had compelled Sneider to marry her? Ah, yes, the lad. "I met Sneider at a restaurant in Amsterdam years ago." She didn't need to know any more details.

Her painted eyebrows lifted. He didn't blame her. The story didn't sound logical to him, but it was the best he could do through the pain.

"I don't know when he'll be home. You should go and come back another day. And don't forget. You didn't examine my throat." She fumbled in her pockets, took out a cigarette, and lit it with a match sitting on the stove, then grabbed an ashtray already filled with butts.

"You shouldn't be smoking. It will make your throat worse."

She heaved a dramatic sigh and snuffed out the cigarette. "The sacrifices I make for my singing. Wonder if it's even worth it."

A loud cry came from another room. The child. Margot shoved the ashtray across the table. "He's fallen again. How did I create such a clumsy boy?" She started for the room but cast a glance at him over her shoulder. "You can let yourself out the back way. Remember, not a word to my husband."

Erich headed toward the stairs, his head pounding to the beat of his footsteps. Where could he go? He had nobody in Haarlem—not a single associate. Except Sneider, and their relationship was tenuous at best. The hospital staff was no doubt hunting for him, had probably already called the police. It wasn't safe or smart to leave this house.

He stopped at the landing. Down meant danger, risk, and who knew when he'd gain access to the art that was his ticket out of here? Erich looked up. All these old houses had attics on the top floor. How many had he and the other soldiers scavenged through to find hidden Jews and treasures? Whimpers from the child and scolding words came from the other room. Did he dare? He hurried back into the kitchen, opened the icebox, and nabbed a piece of cheese and a bottle of wine, and crept up the stairs.

The air smelled musty, as if the windows hadn't been opened in a long time. After being cooped up in a hospital room for months, he craved the scent of a fresh breeze. The first door opened to the child's room—a crib, a table, and pictures of animals and children all over the walls. Margot obviously hadn't learned that less was more. Some of those pictures were his. Surely, she knew they were here only temporarily. The painting of the girl with the violin was the one that had ignited his interest in art. It had reminded him of a young Tamar. He'd planned on giving it to her on their first date.

The second door led to the master bedroom—art all over the walls and lying in piles on tables. Sneider would be in so much trouble if the frames were scratched or the art damaged from negligent handling. He shut the door too hard, then winced. With any luck, Margot would think it was the back door slamming shut.

A small staircase led upward, probably to the attic. Should he go up there where it would be safer?

He checked the bathroom first. Almost fell over when he saw his yellow face in the mirror. No wonder Margot reacted so harshly when she saw him. Looking closer, he rubbed at his cheek. Iodine— that's what it was. And his eyes were puffy and red—as if he'd been crying or drinking. Pills. That's what he needed. He opened one drawer, then another. A bottle of aspirin and an apothecary bottle, but the writing on the label was too faded to read. It didn't matter. He emptied half the bottle of aspirin into his mouth and took a swig of wine, then put the prescription bottle in his lab-coat pocket.

Footsteps were coming up the stairs. Margot's voice. "C'mon, Karl. Don't dawdle. It's time for your nap. Maybe Tamar will bring the children over later today. Wouldn't that be nice? Can't believe that man was her husband. For some reason, I thought he was taller. A lot taller. I must be going crazy. But why would Klaus be dealing with a Jew?"

She had reached the landing. *Don't come into the bathroom.* The child was whining for her to pick him up. He'd wait.

More footsteps. "Now you get some sleep."

"Sing a song, Mama."

"Okay, a short one." Margot's voice rang out a soprano, slightly raspy version of "*Slaap, Kinderje, Slaap.*" Too many cigarettes had combined with age to limit the former diva's range. If the lullaby was any indication of her future in opera, it didn't look promising.

Erich took advantage of the song to sneak to the staircase at the end of the hall. With any hope, the attic door was unlocked. Ten steps up ended with a closed door, which opened with a creak to a large, dusty room. Suppressing a cough, he blinked against a cobweb that blanketed his face. He went to swipe it away from his cheek and almost howled in pain from the contact.

As his eyes acclimated to the darkness, he noted a shaft of light coming from a window covered with shutters. Disarray was too generous of a description of the attic. It was hard to believe that Klaus Sneider with his perfectly coiffed hair and dapper suits would allow such a mess.

He stepped over piles of detritus to reach the single window. If this was to be his home for the next few hours or days, he needed to be able to see. The semi-open window didn't improve the ambiance. Stacked against the four walls a dozen deep leaned paintings— Impressionist landscapes and other degenerate art, probably copies of the masters by their apprentices back in the day. Unlike Göring, he didn't share a love for squiggly lines and points, but he liked the money they'd bring him in secret auctions, even if they were copies.

Sneider was such a snob but didn't understand a thing about business. Didn't he realize these were good copies? That's why Erich had chosen them. They'd fetch a good price with the nouveau riche who fancied themselves art connoisseurs. Even the best eye would be hard-pressed to distinguish the fakes from the masterpieces, but they wouldn't sell with all the dents and scratches caused by stacking them like this.

The pain was getting to him. What he needed was a nap. Then he'd be able to think clearly and make a plan. Mind over matter. Finding a meter of empty space along one of the walls, he slid down and closed his eyes.

As Erich waited for sleep to descend, he reviewed the facts. One, pain medication. The effect of the aspirin wouldn't last, so he'd have to make a trip to the nearest apothecary. The lab coat would help convince the pharmacist to give him something. Maybe he could ask for samples. Two, he could never meet Sneider's wife again because she'd know he wasn't the doctor he'd led her to believe he was. Three, he had to stay here until he regained his health for two reasons—he didn't want to run into Dr. Feldman or any of the nurses. And more importantly, his whole future was tied up with the art in this house, which he'd bought at great risk to himself.

So he'd stay put, and when he'd regained his strength, he'd make sure Klaus turned over the whole cache, the size of which would require a truck, which his host would have to provide. If truth be told, Erich didn't care about the art, but he did care about the money it would bring in, which would allow him to achieve what he really wanted—Tamar Kaplan, any way he could get her.

He opened his eyes past heavy eyelids and stared at the piles of stuff in the middle of the room. So familiar—so like the dozens of attics he and his soldiers had left in shambles in their search for anything that would bring a good price.

His gaze landed on a lapin—a stuffed rabbit, probably belonging to the whiner downstairs. Next to the stuffed animal was a portrait that pulled Erich to his knees, making him forget his pain and his plight for the moment. A young blond girl of twelve or thirteen stood behind a microphone, her eyes closed, her lips parted perhaps in a song, and her hand placed over her chest. Could it be? What was a photograph of Tamar Visser doing in this attic?

Erich winced against the pain and climbed over boxes to get a better look. This was definitely a young version of Tamar. He'd recognize her anywhere. Bringing the picture close to his lips, he kissed it, then gently touched the cold surface to his cheek. This must have been where Tamar Visser grew up. Other photographs lay behind this one. He fingered through one of a boy, one of an old couple, then one of a family.

His breath caught in his throat. Not because of the pulsing pain. The sepia-tinted picture was of a family of four. A mother and a father, a teenaged boy and the same blond girl as the one in the picture but a few years younger. So Tamar had an older brother—a gangly, solemn-looking fellow with dark blond hair. The mother was petite and blond as Tamar was. A pretty woman, as Tamar would be at her age. He leaned forward to get a closer look, then almost dropped the picture. Could it be? Both the father and the son wore yarmulkes.

Jews.

This changed everything. Tamar wasn't Neelie Visser's niece. She was hiding out at Neelie's house along with the doctor and the orphans because they were all Jews. How blind his love for her had made him. She was a Jewess now married to another Jew.

And to think about everything he'd done for her—all the art he'd collected, the plans he'd made, the new face he'd adopted—it was all for her. What a fool he'd been! He was just about to throw the family photograph against the wall when he remembered where he was.

No one made a fool of him. He'd follow through with his plan, and he'd take her, and he'd make her pay.

Chapter Ten

"Any concern too small to be turned into a prayer is too small to be made into a burden."
~ Corrie ten Boom

Her foot tapped more out of anxious expectation than impatience. Margot was still upstairs, singing scales before she left for practice. She should save her voice for her lesson because it sounded an octave lower than normal. Tamar had reminded her that Daniel would be here at noon to examine her throat. Margot had given her a strange look, then said that he'd better hurry because she didn't have all day.

The nerve of Margot. Here Daniel was doing her a favor— giving up time from his busy schedule to run over here to see her in secret—and she was acting as though he was her servant. But it would be just as well if Margot left before he arrived. Hopefully, Daniel would remember to bring an assortment of screwdrivers to open the grate. And today, Tamar had brought a portfolio case to carry the picture of the violin girl. She'd need Daniel's tools as well.

With all the happenings, it was no wonder Tamar couldn't make herself stop fidgeting. The children were more placid than she. Zari was circling the boys, who were coloring on the kitchen floor, stopping ever so often to remind them with her pointy finger to stay within the lines.

A knock downstairs caught Tamar's attention. "I'll be right back." She hurried down the steps and through the dry cleaner, which was as dark as usual. Tamar opened the door and pulled

Daniel in, then wrapped her arms around his shoulders. She couldn't get enough of this man.

"Hello to you. Everything okay?"

She backed up and rested her palm on her chest. "Yes, did you bring the tools?"

"I did, reluctantly."

She rolled her eyes. "Put your conscience away. Whatever is behind that grate belongs to my parents." Grasping his free hand, his other one carrying a medical bag, she led him to the stairs.

"Whoa, this is tough," he said. "The last time I was here, this place looked a lot different."

Tamar glanced back. "Although this used to be a lovely jewelry store, now it just looks…industrial. And I have never seen a single customer in here. Can you believe that?"

"Must be a front. Which puts you—"

"I know what you're going to say." She led him up the stairs but whispered over her shoulder. "Leave the tools with me, and I'll bring them home." When she reached the top, she opened the door to the kitchen.

"Papa," Zari and Peri cried and ran over and wrapped their arms around a leg each.

"Hello, kids." His eyes took in the disarray of crayons and paper scattered over the floor. "It looks as though you're having a good time. Maybe you should clean up before someone trips on a crayon and breaks a leg. How would you like a plaster cast on your leg?"

"I want a plaster cast," Peri said, echoed by Karl, then Zari.

Daniel glanced at Tamar and winked. "I remember this—"

Just then, Margot entered the kitchen, her heavily made-up eyes wider than usual. "Who do we have here?"

"This is Daniel, my husband. Daniel, this is Margot."

He walked like Frankenstein's monster to shake her hand, the kids chortling with each step. "Pleased to meet you. Where would you like me to examine you?"

Her eyebrows formed a deep angle. "I don't understand." She eyed Tamar. "Who is this man?"

"Doctor Daniel Feldman, my husband. You asked him to examine your throat. He took time from his busy schedule to do so." Was she daft? Tamar's voice was shaking. How dare she treat him as if he were a piece of lint? If it weren't for that grate and picture in Karl's bedroom, she'd flounce out of here right now.

Margot's hand went to her chest. "A man claiming to be you came to the door yesterday. I thought it was strange he didn't have a doctor's bag. He seemed almost…sickly." Her eyes narrowed. "He was probably an addict. I let him in because I thought he was you. Even left him alone in here while I went in search of an aspirin." With a swift intake of breath, she shook her head slowly, then glanced at Daniel. "My apologies. He told me to drink tea and honey, and it has helped a bit, but I'd like a real doctor's opinion. Let's move into the parlor, but I have to hurry. I have a lesson in twenty-five minutes." With a frown at the crayons strewn across the kitchen floor, she sauntered out of the room.

Tamar tried to hear their conversation as she helped the children gather their things, but the dining room table was on the other side of the parlor, and she'd be eavesdropping if she came any closer. Since it was after twelve, she took some bread, Gouda, and juice from the almost-empty icebox to make sandwiches for the children. The cheese was past old, but she cut off the moldy parts and slipped the remnants between buttered bread. She'd brought an apple to munch on, but her stomach was doing somersaults, so she cut the apple into small pieces for the three children.

They were finishing their lunches when Margot strode through the kitchen. "I'm going to be so late. Dag." She threw a kiss in Karl's direction, then hurried down the stairs.

Daniel appeared in the entryway, carrying his medical bag.

"How did it go?" Tamar casually glanced in his direction.

"Fine. I gave her a prescription for penicillin in case it's an infection, but since it's lingered so long, I told her that it might be her tonsils which will need to be removed."

Tamar backed up a step. "Ew. Bet she didn't want to hear that."

"Nope, she did not." He checked his watch. "I'm going to have to leave soon. Patient rounds at one-fifteen. You said there was something upstairs you wanted me to look at?" He pointed at his medical bag.

With a quick glimpse at the children who were busy imitating each other gnawing off the skin of their apples, she said, "Follow me." Tamar hurried up the stairs with Daniel on her heels. Once they were out of earshot of the little ones, she said, "I know this is the last thing you want to do." She pointed at the grate. "We don't have much time."

Together, they pushed the credenza far enough so Daniel could remove the grate. He bent down to examine the size of the screws holding it in place. "This ought to be fast." Opening his bag, he pulled out a flashlight and a screwdriver. "Hold the flashlight so I can see what I'm doing." And with little effort, he removed the screws and then the grate to reveal a dark hole filled with cobwebs. Daniel covered his nose and mouth and leaned as far as he could into the hole.

Tamar aimed the light in different directions, but she couldn't see over Daniel's frame. She'd lost so much already. *Please, Lord. May there be something to remember them by—even if it's just a picture. Anything.*

"Think I found something."

Giggles emanated from the floor below. Tamar glanced at the stairs. "We'd better hurry, or Peri will lead an insurrection."

"Shine the light on the left side. It's a long reach…but…I think I…got it." Daniel backed up a few centimeters, holding a small pile of papers. "There's more." He wiped sweat from his forehead and plunged his arm into the abyss. "A miniature velvet box and a larger one, and I think that's all there is. These were on a narrow ledge." He quickly swiveled around and joined her on the floor.

Tears splashed down her cheeks. She swiped at them with the back of her hand. Her gaze fixed on a legal document. Slowly, she lifted her eyes to his, then handed him the papers. "It's a deed to the place. My father's name is on it. My mother's isn't, but I don't think women could own property back then." She blinked back fresh tears.

He scanned the papers. "From the dates, it looks as though this house belonged to your grandparents on your father's side, and they deeded the property to your father, probably as a wedding gift. That's what families did."

Tamar leaned her head against Daniel's shoulder, and soon sobs shook her body. "He knew something was going to happen. It took him a while because Germany had protected Haarlem during the Great War. But he left Seth a place to live and raise a family." She sniffed and rubbed her knuckles under her nose. "It's Seth's. Not the Sneiders'."

Daniel took her hand, opened her fingers one by one, and placed the two boxes in her palm.

She glanced up, smiling through her tears. She tugged the larger box open, then covered a gasp.

"What is it?"

"It's my father's loupe. My grandfather gave it to him when he retired. My abba always said it was so strong and precise, he could see every imperfection. People trusted his appraisals because of this loupe." She handed it to Daniel. "It meant a lot to him. Guess he thought the jewelry could be replaced if the Nazis broke into the shop below, but this would allow the business to continue when the war was over." A sigh tumbled out of its own accord. "I'm glad he didn't get to see what became of the business."

"Open the second box," Daniel said, hardly above a whisper.

She gulped beyond the lump in her throat and opened the tiny blue box. A ring box or earrings—too small for anything else. "Oh." Her hand went to her chest.

"What is it?" he touched her arm.

"It's my mother's wedding ring. It was my grandmother's and my great-grandmother's wedding ring before that." Tears slid down her cheeks. "My mother must have known something was going to happen. They wanted us to have these things." She looked at her husband. "If they had lived, they would have given this ring to you to give to me. It passes down the maternal line. Then I would give it to Zari."

He took it out of the box and gently slipped it onto her ring finger. "It's lovely. Reminds me of a winding branch of sapphires and diamonds. Looks like it's found its perfect home."

She held up her hand. "First, we have to get the papers and the valuables out of this house. You take the deed and the loupe." She widened her eyes. "You'd better hurry. Leave your tools with me, and I'll bring them home." Tamar stood and pulled him to his feet. "But before you leave, I want to show you my bedroom." Without releasing his hand, she led him to her room and opened the door.

He took in a swift breath. "I only was in this room once—when you asked me to bring the suitcase from your brother's closet so you could pack a few things before the Nazis came back. You were in a daze. Your parents were gone. I couldn't convince you to hurry." Daniel pulled her to him. "I understand now. This must be so hard for you." Tears brimmed in his eyes. He kissed her forehead.

Tamar tugged him over to the picture by the crib. "This is the one I was telling you about. *The Violin Girl*. That's my name for this picture. Do you remember the painting?"

He shook his head but moved closer. "Who painted it?"

"I don't know. There's a blurred spot where the signature might have been. It's almost as if someone tried to blot it out."

He lifted her chin with his finger. "I can see it in your eyes. Don't do anything you'll regret."

She couldn't respond.

Daniel kissed her cheek, whispered a quick "I love you," and hurried down the stairs. The kids' voices were getting louder. Her time was limited to take the picture, but if she didn't do it now, there'd be no other opportunity because the children would be taking their naps in the room. And who knew when Margot would return.

It was now or never. What she could do was remove the picture from the room, put another picture in its place, then once the kids were taking their naps, she could slip it into the portfolio case she'd brought. Zari had noticed the case and asked why she was carrying it instead of the usual rucksack. Preferring not to lie to her daughter, she'd pointed at a squirrel that flitted across the street.

Zari. Nothing much passed that girl's attention. Would she notice the rearrangement of the pictures? This was not a good plan, but what could she do? The picture had become a principle—a symbol of taking her life back.

Tamar hurried into the room. Glanced around for a replacement. It had to be a picture of a girl. There were dozens of pictures of kittens and puppies and clowns, but there was no painting that could replace the girl with the violin. She was running out of time. Hoping against hope that Seth's old bedroom was unlocked and had more art, she hurried to his door, opened it with a gush of relief, and scanned the walls. Nothing. She fingered through the piles that leaned against the walls until she found it. A painting of a girl and her nurse. It looked remarkably familiar. A Frans Hals—no doubt, a much older painting than the violin girl.

If this was an authentic Hals portrait, then no doubt, the Sneiders were involved in illegal activities. Her heart went out to poor Karl. But more likely, this painting and all the others were mere copies, painted by apprentices. Yes, that worked to assuage her conscience. Tamar wasn't stealing a real masterpiece. She was taking a very good copy of a masterpiece that had probably been stolen.

"Eema, when are you going to read us a story?" Zari's voice drifted up from the floor below. Tamar grabbed the picture and called out, "I'll be right down, then I'll read you any book you like."

"Any book?" Giggles followed. With her luck, her daughter would have her read the dictionary. Anything to avoid taking a nap.

"Within reason," she answered. "Give me five minutes."

She dashed into her old bedroom, carefully removed the violin girl from the wall, and replaced it with the Hals painting. Stepping back, Tamar frowned. It wasn't going to fool anyone. The painting was too dark for the room. Too noticeable. Now what? She could either move several of the paintings around and put the Hals in a less conspicuous place, or she could return to Seth's room and find another painting.

Noting the dimensions of the violin girl, she found a picture of a giraffe about the same size and moved it to the spot by the crib, then she moved the Hals to take the giraffe's place. It was the best she could do. With a minute to spare, she ran into the hall, tugged the painting into her portfolio case, and hurried down the back stairs. There she hid the case in the space underneath the stairs where she used to put her bicycle, roller skates, and herself when she was playing hide 'n' seek.

Steeling herself for the condition of the kitchen, she bounded up the stairs. When Peri was tired or restless or bored, the food went flying. And she deserved it today. But when Tamar reached the entry into the kitchen, she froze.

There sat three little angels in a row on the kitchen floor, Zari sitting between them reading them a page from a cookbook. How she wished she had a camera to catch this moment. Of course, her daughter couldn't read but sure sounded as though she could. Both boys rested their heads against her shoulders, eyes closed.

Tamar mouthed, "Thank you," to her daughter, picked up Karl, and carried him into the parlor and laid him on the rug. When she returned, she picked up Peri. "How about we take a parlor nap today? I'll go upstairs and grab some blankets and a book—a really big book. How does that sound?"

"Will you read *The Princess with Twenty Petticoats*?" Zari said through a yawn as she followed her into the parlor.

"The book's at home. How about I tell you the story now, then when we get home, I'll read it to you?" Zari nodded, probably too tired to remind her of their deal. The kitchen would be easy to clean, so Tamar joined the children on the floor. The twins rested against her shoulders, and Karl used her thigh as a pillow, his thumb firmly planted in his mouth. "Once upon a time…" She couldn't stop yawning, but she made it through the first part of the story….

"Hello?"

A raspy voice from the kitchen made Tamar startle. She opened her eyes and shook her head to get rid of the haze. What time was it? The kids were still sleeping.

"In here."

Margot poked her head into the parlor. "What's going on in here? The kitchen looks like a monsoon hit it."

Tamar wiped her scratchy eyes. Some of the dust from the grate upstairs must have irritated them. Sleeping hadn't helped. "I must have fallen asleep telling the kids a fairy tale. Guess it wasn't that interesting of a story. I'll clean up the kitchen before I leave."

"Please do. We have a busy schedule tonight."

"C'mon, kids. Wake up. Time to go home." Her arms were tingling from her children's heads pressing on them. "Karl? Time to get up."

When she was free of bodies, she hurried into the kitchen to clean up the lunch dishes. It could have been a lot worse. Once everything was tidy, she called the twins to join her. "Time to go. We'll leave by the back stairs."

"Why, Eema?" Peri said.

She almost said, "Because I said so," but caught herself in time. It wasn't easy to be a thief with a curious son. "It's closer to our apartment." Lame even to her ears. "Come along." Hoisting Daniel's medical bag over her shoulder, Tamar hurried down the stairs, stopping long enough to grab the portfolio case before she opened the door for the kids.

"What's in that big bag?" Zari asked.

And there it was. "It's called a portfolio. It belongs to your papa. He used it to carry projects that didn't fit in his rucksack."

"Well, why do you—"

"How would you kids like to stop at the park for just a few minutes?"

It didn't take Erich long to figure out who owned what in this mess of an attic. He surmised by quietly going through the piles of throwaways that the objects closest to the attic door were the Sneiders' belongings. But the more remote piles had been there for decades. Hanukkah decorations and other Judaica informed him of Tamar's family. Photos scattered willy-nilly, piles of clothes hanging out of almost-empty boxes, and beautiful keepsakes in disarray bespoke of his own soldiers ravaging the place. There'd been so many attics, it was hard to remember if it had been those under his commission. But this had been his area of the ghetto.

His conscience pricked at the sight of the damage, of the disregard. War was hard. But he liked *objets d'art*—beautiful things, and it hurt his sense of…well, it wasn't conscience. That was a man-made idea to coerce people to do what those above wanted. Still. Going through the objects brought some remote feeling of remorse.

Then Erich heard her voice. Tamar's voice. She must have been one floor below, and she was telling someone that she'd be right there. What was she doing on the third floor? It almost sounded as though she was talking to children. Was she babysitting for Klaus Sneider's son? This was better than a gift. If he'd believed in a god, he would have thanked him.

His days in the attic had not been futile. When the family was home, Erich kept a low profile—slept, read from the many books in storage, even carefully exercised his limbs, which had been idle much too long. But when the family was away, he explored. And one of the things he'd discovered was an air vent on the far side of the attic that let him listen—even see—what happened on the floor below.

He crept to the vent, careful not to make any sound. There she was below him. Tamar. His Tamar. She was trying to fit a painting into a large bag. That little thief. It made her even more delightful. No, it made her vulnerable. If this was her childhood home, what was she doing here now stealing art? Stealing his paintings? Could it be Sneider didn't know this was Tamar's former house? Ah, the plot was taking a delectable turn.

Erich ping-ponged between hating her and loving her, but now another thing tied him to her—her love of art. Her beauty, her sweet voice—perhaps there was still a future for them. He'd convince her that life would be fuller with him. There'd be concerts and balls and trips. He would wait until they were all alone and whisk her away. And if she was reluctant to leave that husband of hers, the painting she stole could prove to be invaluable.

He shifted to the right for a better view of the painting. Ah yes, the blond girl with the violin. One of his favorites. That violin had reminded him of his own childhood. Those many hours of practicing under the keen eye of his father. How he hoped that his own son, Dieter, would share his love of music. Had Erich been back in Hamburg during his formative years, he would have made sure Dieter had taken up the instrument. But he couldn't go back. And now his son would be almost thirteen. Almost a man.

Enough reminiscing. It evoked senseless emotions. What couldn't be changed needed to be forgotten. He'd put his efforts into what could be achieved.

Now Tamar's footsteps were hurrying down the back stairs— the same ones he used when he needed to grab some fresh air when the family was gone. Logic told him she was stashing the painting at the bottom of the stairs. There was guilt. He'd use it if necessary.

Chapter Eleven

"The purpose of being guilty is to bring us close to Jesus. Once we are there, its purpose is finished. If we continue to make ourselves guilty to blame ourselves, then that is sin itself."
~ Corrie ten Boom

Tamar couldn't look at the painting. It sat in the portfolio in the bedroom closet behind her winter boots. If that wasn't a sign of guilt, what was? She couldn't tell Daniel. It would just make him worry, and he had a lot on his mind, especially since his patient had vanished. Every time she babysat for Karl, she cringed at the sight of the replacement picture. Margot had said nothing to her, but Zari had noticed and pointed at the painting. Tamar had redirected her. The lies were tumbling over each other.

She sat on her bed and opened her *Tanakh* to that day's reading. Daniel had given her a complete Bible in Dutch, but she liked to read her people's story in Hebrew. In yesterday's section, the Amalekites had attacked Ziklag, burned the settlement, and taken captive the wives and children of David and his soldiers. *But David found strength in the Lord, his God*, I Samuel 30:6. Tamar identified with David and his men, having lost her family too. She was eager to read the next installment, but first, she prayed.

With a glance at the closet door, she fell to her knees next to the bed. How could she expect God to answer the prayer of a liar? Tamar prayed for forgiveness, for wisdom, and she kept praying until she had an answer. She came to the place where if God told her to return the painting, she would do so. And she would tell Daniel what she'd done before she went to sleep. If he told her to return it, she would. After all, it was not up to her to save the painting. She brought the painting out of hiding and laid it on the bed.

The reading for the day was the remaining words of I Samuel 30. Her breath caught as she read. God told David through the ephod that he would overtake the Amalekites and rescue the captives. Then she came to verse 26. *When David reached Ziklag, he sent some of the plunder to the elders of Judah, who were his friends, saying, "Here is a gift for you from the plunder of the LORD's enemies."* Was she reading this right? Was the painting plunder? Was her house considered plunder?

Tamar thought back to the last month. Had God put the desire in her heart to go into her house and see all the stored art, the painting of the girl with the violin? Had he arranged for her to meet Margot in the park? Was this all part of a bigger plan? She was beginning to sound like Neelie and Daniel, who saw God in every event of the day.

Neelie. She needed to talk to her mentor, but first, she had to straighten out things with Daniel. It wasn't just his work at the hospital that separated them. The secret in the closet had erected an invisible wall between them. She could feel it. Today the wall would come down.

He looked tired. Lines framed his eyes—lines that shouldn't be on a thirty-year-old's face. Tamar couldn't keep from tracing her finger on the lines. "You're working much too hard."

"It's not any busier than before. What's bothering me is that patient who vanished. It's been two weeks, and nothing's turned up. He must be in pain. It's all my fault. I should've done a better job of finding out his story."

"Maybe he didn't want you to know. Perhaps he's a spy. Didn't he show up mysteriously and vanish in the same way? Sounds like a spy to me." Thoughts of Bergman resurfaced. The man's voice was unmistakably his.

"He hit one of the residents in the head and stole his coat, but the police haven't come up with anything."

Tamar led him from the door past the kitchen table to their

bedroom. If she didn't tell him right away, she'd lose her nerve. "I have something to show you," she said below her breath.

"What's going on? I'm—" Then he saw it. "You didn't."

"I did." Tamar lowered him onto the spot next to the picture and sat next to him. "I will tell you why, and then if you want me to take it back, I will." She reminded him of having seen the picture three times, its significance to her, and the fact that she wanted to return it to the Hamels. Then she told him about her time with the Lord and what she had read about David returning the plunder to its rightful owners. "Don't you see how everything is converging? Is this what you and Neelie call a God-ordained moment?"

He sat there for a while, staring at his hands, then wrapped her in a hug, and they both fell back. "You're right. I'm wrong and you're right. I used to have that zeal. That sense of indignation at the injustice around me. But work and family made me forget, and I became careful. Careful is a dangerous thing, isn't it? It's made me lose my zeal." He turned to look at her and brushed loose hairs away from her face. "And I almost forced you to lose your zeal as well. Forgive me. I should have listened to what you were saying. To what you weren't saying."

Of all the reactions she anticipated, this wasn't one of them. "So I don't have to return the picture?" Tamar told him about the wall she imagined coming between them, all because she wasn't telling him the whole truth. She took his hand and kissed it. "It started with me reaching the point where our love was more important than the picture, even the house. It was hard, but I told God that I would tell you everything if that's what He wanted. Then I read today's selection, and it was as if the words came off the page and hit me in the middle of the forehead."

He squinted, rubbing light fingers over her eyebrows. "I don't see anything."

She hit his arm. "First Samuel 30. Where David's wife and children and the other soldiers' families were abducted by the Amalekites while they were away fighting. His troops were so devastated they were ready to stone David, but he sought strength from the Lord. God told him to fight the Amalekites, that David and his men would prevail. And they did. And this is the verse that hit me in the forehead. Verse 26. David sent some of the plunder to

Judah's elders, saying, 'Here is a gift for you from the plunder of the Lord's enemies.' So you see, when the enemy steals from us, it is not a sin to steal back what was taken—" She put a finger to his lips as he started to say something. "But it has to be God's way. Not my way. And that's why I had to tell you."

He enveloped her in his arms and kissed her with a hunger that she matched. When they parted, she fell back on the bed.

"Wow. I should make up more stuff to tell you."

Daniel spewed out a snort, which made her laugh. He propped up on one elbow and faced her. "What will Margot say when she notices it's missing?"

"I moved around some of the pictures, and she hasn't said anything. Will you help me find the Hamels?"

"Tomorrow's Sunday. Neelie is coming to our going-away party and bringing the rental papers to sign. If anybody knows what happened to the Hamels, it's Neelie."

Tamar removed her apron and scanned the kitchen table, teeming with three different cakes she had baked during the day. She sniffed the sweet aroma of nutmeg and vanilla. Tonight would be a festive one, a celebration where she would thank Hadassah and Seth for babysitting the twins, although her brother was gone most the time helping others make *Aliyah*, and soon Seth and Hadassah themselves would emigrate to Israel.

This would be a celebration of new beginnings. Neelie and her son, Jan, would be here to give them the keys and have them sign the lease. Although Neelie didn't think a lease was necessary, Tamar didn't trust developers, who would think nothing of forcing them out absent a legal document to prove they had a right to be there. Houses on the canal were so valuable. Businesses were clamoring to buy them in order to open shops that catered to those travelling by boats.

Tonight she would tell her guests about stealing the picture from their home and present Seth with the deed to the house. She'd only told him she was babysitting for Margot but hadn't told him where.

Everything was ready. The twins were dressed in cute little matching outfits, though Peri was eyeing the table, which meant if she turned her back, he'd probably pull the dishes onto the floor. She put a Cees Verschoor saxophone album on the record player.

Daniel came out of the bedroom just in time, looking dapper in his suit and tie. He twirled her around to the music and dipped her like Fred Astaire. "You look divine, my love," he said with a kiss to the tip of her nose when he righted her. Just then, Peri careened into the two of them, then screamed when he bit his tongue. Zari stood shaking her head. Tamar knelt down to comfort him.

Mass chaos, and the door opened. Neelie and Jan stood there, eyes wide at the sight. "What's going on?" Neelie said.

Tamar came over and gave Neelie and Jan the customary kiss on the cheek, then returned to her son. "This boy. Let me see your tongue, Peri."

His nose running, Peri stuck out his tongue, showing a tiny cut with a trace of blood.

"I'll bring him a cold compress to put on it," she said and hurried into the kitchen. While she searched for a cloth and wet it, Seth's booming, sardonic voice commented on all the noise. This party was not starting the way she'd planned. Returning to the main room, Tamar placed the wet cloth on Peri's tongue, then pecked her brother's cheek. "Your time's coming," then Tamar winked at Hadassah, who swayed Zari on her hip.

Soon order returned. Jan and Seth stood by the window, probably talking about politics. Tamar carried a tray of coffee, tea, and *boterkoeken* to them. Daniel had whisked the twins into the bedroom, so Tamar took Neelie's jacket and asked the two ladies to join her in the kitchen while she poured hot beverages and set out more butter cake.

"Delicious, Tamar. I trained you well, did I not?" Neelie licked her fingers after biting into the moist, warm cake.

Hadassah stirred three sugar cubes into her coffee and nibbled on the bread. "I'll miss these treats when you leave."

"Thank you. I still haven't mastered cookies, as they call them in America. And you know I'm only moving a few blocks away. Maybe my boterkoeken will keep you from moving to Palestine?"

Hadassah dabbed at her mouth. "From your lips." She pointed

up. "Talk to your brother. He's the zealous one in this marriage."

Neelie touched Tamar's arm. "Daniel doesn't look so good. He's lost weight. What's happening?"

Of course, Neelie would notice. She knew them so well. "One of his patients went missing a week or two ago. Just up and walked out. Daniel is worried about the man. He wasn't anywhere near ready to be released. In fact—" Tamar leaned closer to both ladies. "The man reminded me of Officer Bergman. He had the same build, the same mannerisms, and although he was bandaged up, I heard him say my name, and he also mentioned the song I was singing in your kitchen that day, Neelie."

"You must be mistaken. Every Nazi is either in prison or has been put to death," Neelie said. "Why was he in the hospital? The burn unit, right?"

"Yes, no one knows why. An ambulance from Amsterdam brought him in and had no paperwork on him. The only thing the driver said was that they found him in a burning warehouse halfway between Haarlem and Amsterdam. He came in the middle of the night, so Daniel wasn't there at the time."

Neelie's hand went to her heart. "Oh, the very thought of that man here in our town—loose. What does Daniel think?"

She shook her head. "Daniel thinks I'm crazy. He took off the man's bandages and said it definitely wasn't him. The man was older than Bergman—maybe in his forties."

"Didn't the man talk?"

"No, he'd been in a coma for a few weeks, and the only time he said anything was when I was singing for the patients in the burn unit. But Daniel said I was imagining things. What if Bergman—"

Neelie brought her finger to her lips. Daniel had walked into the room.

He clapped his hands. "Thank you for joining us for this celebration. Let's call it a going-away party for Jan and a moving-away party for us. How about we clear the legal stuff out of the way while Peri is still occupied? Otherwise, I can't keep the lease from being covered with jam or chocolate."

Neelie smirked. "I don't see why we need a lease between close friends—"

Jan stayed his mother's hand. "It's the right thing to do. A lease will protect them from anyone claiming to have a prior right to the house."

"Who would that be? All of Frans's family have passed away. It's just you and I, Jan," Neelie said.

He lifted a shoulder. "There are a lot of cases before the court concerning deeds and leases. Sometimes the judges take the easy path and hand over the property to the person who yells the loudest. I want to make sure that doesn't happen to Tamar and Daniel even if the house has been in our family for almost a century." Jan placed the lease in front of Daniel, who sat in a chair next to the sofa, and showed him where to sign.

Tamar's ears had perked up when Jan mentioned deeds. Was it the right time to mention it? Yes, while Jan who was almost a lawyer was here, she had to tell him. She cleared her throat. "Jan, I have a legal question…or two." Daniel cut her a wondering glance. *Trust me*, she mouthed.

All eyes focused on her. Confession was cathartic. With a hard swallow, she began. "Seth, remember when Abba showed us the hidden documents in the upstairs grate in our old house?"

He looked at her beneath furrowed brows. "What did you do?"

"You know I've been babysitting for Margot's little boy. They're living in our house."

Her brother's eyes opened wide.

Tamar nodded. "I was curious about those papers and…opened it up…" She chanced a glance at Daniel to gauge his reaction, just in case she needed to involve him. A frown covered his face. "And I found the deed to the house." She fumbled through her rucksack, removed the manila envelope, and handed it to her brother, since the house was his by rights.

"I can't believe this." Seth removed the deed from the envelope, scanned it, then handed it to Jan. "I'm not good at reading wills and deeds and the like. Is it possible the house still belongs to us?"

Jan ran his finger down the yellowing pages of small print. Some of the edges had disintegrated, almost appearing as if they'd been burned off. He looked up. "I'm no expert on deeds, but everything looks legitimate. I could have one of the associates have a look at it. See if you have a legal claim to the property. May I keep it?"

Seth's eyes darted from Jan to Hadassah and back. Mixed emotions showed on his face—the desire for justice, the stronger need to move to Israel. Money from the sale of the house would finance his trip. While Tamar would have liked to keep the house in the family, at least there'd be justice, which she craved, if the deed was legal.

Since she was confessing, she said, "I have one other thing to show you." She glanced at Jan. Was he bound by the law to turn her in if she was indeed a thief? "I'll be right back." Tamar hurried into her bedroom and pulled the portfolio from its hiding place in the back of her closet. This wasn't the smartest thing she'd done, but these were her friends, so she returned to the living room.

"There's something else I took from our house, and this definitely doesn't belong to our family." She carefully propped the portfolio next to her leg.

Daniel was holding his breath—she could tell by the way his lips pursed. "Are you sure you want to do this?"

Was she? Up to now, it was her justice to find, but what might this mean to her family? She stared hard at Daniel. "I don't know. Maybe I need expiation. And as I told you, I will take it back if you tell me to."

Seth interrupted. "All right. You have us all on tenterhooks. What is in that portfolio?"

Tamar stood, set it on her seat, and paced. "Let me ask you a legal question, Jan. If someone were…let's say…squatting in my parents' house, and there were…stolen objects in the house, what would be Seth's and my duty if the deed turns out to be legal?" She pivoted to see all eyes on her—rapt eyes.

"You have our attention, sister," Seth said. "Do tell—"

Jan interrupted. "That kind of scenario is happening all over the Netherlands since so many people didn't return from the camps. But I'd need to hear more."

"You're making my head spin with all these random questions." Seth framed his head with his hands.

Neelie pulled on Tamar's arm as she walked past. "Come, sit down. What's this all about?"

She obliged her, retrieved the portfolio, and sat with a sigh. "Did you find out where the Hamels live?"

Neelie's brows furrowed. "I heard they're living in a hofje in the Jordaan district of Amsterdam, but there are so many almshouses in the area. Now tell us about what's in this portfolio."

"When I was about ten or so, I used to look in the windows of the Hamels' art gallery on my way home from school. And there was one painting in particular that caught my attention. It was a portrait of a girl—younger than I was at that time—with a violin. I always felt a kinship with that girl because we both were…trapped by our music. For me, it was incessant voice lessons when I'd rather be out playing with my friends. For weeks, I'd always stop and look at that painting. I even mentioned it to the Hamels when I discovered they were the owners of the gallery."

"So show us the painting already," her brother huffed.

She wiped moist hands on her skirt. "There's more. I saw the painting again at the labor camp, Westerbork, when I had to sing for the führer's birthday. It was on the wall. So much happened that night, I forgot about seeing it. It bothered me that the Nazis had it when it belonged to the Hamels. They must have stolen it when they closed down their business."

Hadassah took her hand. "I can't imagine what that must have been like—to have to sing for those brutes and then to see the painting."

"Here's the interesting part. That same painting was on the wall of my bedroom."

Collective gasps filled the air.

"So you took it," Neelie said. Her hands framed Tamar's face. "What if—?"

"It doesn't belong to you." Seth's eyes stormed. "You could be arrested. Couldn't she be arrested, Jan?"

Everyone started talking at once. She should have expected this reaction. They were just worried about her, but it still hurt that they were questioning her judgment.

Daniel bolted to his feet. "That's enough. I saw the house. It's brimming with stolen art. I'm no expert, but there are enough paintings and statues to fill a gallery. In Tamar's defense, she needs justice. It's what's driving her."

Her knight. She'd never been prouder. No, that wasn't true. Daniel had been her hero since the moment he showed up in her dressing room at the opera. She swallowed past the lump and continued. "I moved around the paintings in Karl's bedroom so Margot wouldn't notice. She doesn't spend much time in that room, and she's so intent on reclaiming her singing career, she's probably not even aware of any of the art in that house."

Daniel chuckled. "How could she not? It's a veritable storehouse."

Tamar stood and paced again. "I forgot to tell you, Seth, that Abba's jewelry store has been replaced by a dry-cleaning business, but I've never seen a single customer in it—"

"That's happening all over our country as well," Jan interjected. "Nazi sympathizers or opportunists set up business as fronts for more nefarious-type dealings that usually involve stolen items from houses ransacked during the war."

"What can be done?" Neelie said. "The patients at the center where I work feel a lot like Tamar. As though their lives and possessions and property have been stripped away from them and nobody seems to care." She glanced at her son. "Jan, you know about art. What should Tamar do?"

He shrugged. "It's complicated in this case. If Tamar entered the house with the intent to take the picture, she could be charged with burglary, which is a felony."

"But it's our house!" Seth insisted. "If that deed holds any legal clout."

"That's a question for the courts. Do squatters have greater rights than the owners? Did Margot and her husband buy the house in good faith even if there was a problem with the deed? However, since the house is full of what appears to be stolen art, chances are the court would find in favor of you and Tamar."

She huffed. "And although I intended to take the picture, I was in the house with Margot's permission since I was babysitting, so maybe I wouldn't be considered a burglar?"

Jan's lips pursed, and he nodded. "Now you're thinking like a lawyer. I'll have a hypothetical conversation with one of the attorneys at the firm. But here's the issue—it's all about provenance."

"What in the world is provenance?" Neelie and Tamar said at the same time, eyed each other, and giggled.

"It's following the chain of ownership to determine who owns the painting because it's only the owner who has a legal claim to the picture. I'll be working with art experts in Paris, so I'll learn a lot about provenance."

Seth leaned against the wall with his hands in his pockets.

"Well, it seems obvious to me if the Nazis stole the painting from the Hamels' gallery, the Hamels own it—"

Hadassah interrupted him. "Don't galleries receive paintings on consignment? They don't actually own the art they display, do they?"

"You're right," Jan said. "And sometimes museums are involved and generations of families. Not to mention the people who bought artwork at Nazi auctions. Of course, there's that old adage, 'possession is nine-tenths of the law.'"

"Papa." Peri came running into the room with Zari on his heels. Zari stopped near her mother and wrapped her arms around Tamar's legs, while Peri did the same to his father. "We're hungry," Peri whined.

"There's that school folio you took to Karl's house." Zari pointed at the black folder that leaned against the sofa. "I want to see what's inside." She dashed over to the portfolio and tried to detach the buckle, but her little fingers couldn't do it.

"Here, let me help you." Neelie glanced up at Tamar, ostensibly for permission, which Tamar gave with a lift of her shoulder. Together, Zari and Neelie opened the folder, pulled the painting out, and removed the towel that covered it.

Collective gasps. Neelie's hand went to her lips. Peri ran over to it to see what he was missing.

"It's beautiful," said Hadassah.

"I can see why you liked it," Jan said.

Zari's eyes were saucers. "The girl from Karl's bedroom."

"That's Oma," exclaimed Peri and pointed at Neelie.

"You're right. That's me," Neelie said.

Chapter Twelve

"Forgiveness is the key that unlocks the door of resentment and the
handcuffs of hatred. It is a power that breaks the chains of
bitterness and the shackles of selfishness."
~ Corrie ten Boom

Neelie's shaky fist covered her mouth as she stared at the
wraith from her past. The last time she'd seen the painting was on
the wall of her parents' house. It was also the day she'd stuffed its
memory into the back of her mind, into an abyss where only bottom-
feeders could touch it, and if they swallowed it whole, it was fine
with her.

Tamar's eyes darted from the picture to her aunt. "What do you
mean, Tante? What do you mean, it's you in the picture?"

She didn't answer right away. She couldn't. Too many
questions circled like random billiard balls, colliding off one
another. Sublimated memories rose to the surface. Neelie hadn't
thought about *him* in months—almost a year. At her age, it shouldn't
hurt so much, but the painting pulled the scab off, and there was
nothing she could do but pick at it.

All eyes were on her. Even the twins were waiting for her to say
something. Their eyes reflected confusion. Neelie never drew
attention to herself. She preferred it that way, but they deserved an
explanation. Summoning a breath, she began. "My father painted
that picture of me when I was about nine or ten. I remember trying
so hard not to move a millimeter, but it was an impossible feat for
an active child." Neelie swung Peri into her arms and tousled his

head. "Can you imagine this one sitting still for hour after hour?"

She hazarded a glimpse of her son. A vertical furrow dented the space between Jan's eyebrows. Yes, she owed him a more specific explanation about his grandfather. Up until now, she'd satisfied his curiosity with partial answers and evasion. With the children here, she'd give them just enough information to buy herself some time so she could process this phantom from her past.

"Are you sure this is you?" Jan bent over to examine it closer. "The signature is impossible to read."

Neelie brushed fingers over the blur on the corner of the painting. Had her father signed it? She couldn't recall. Oh, if it were even a possibility his fingers had touched this very spot.

"How…how did it end up…" Daniel began, asking the question they all were thinking.

"It's…it's not something I want to talk about right now." She gestured toward the children.

Hadassah came close and knelt down next to the twins. "How would you two like to go for a walk? Get some fresh air." Thank the Good Lord for this perceptive woman. Peri jumped up and down, almost knocking over a drink on the table next to the sofa. Hadassah grabbed their jackets and ushered them out of the room.

Still, Neelie didn't want to revisit that place in front of all these people. "This celebration is not about me. It's about Daniel and Tamar."

Tamar patted her hand. "You don't have to talk about anything if you don't wish to." She glanced at the tableau. "But it's such a coincidence."

Neelie squeezed her hands to stop their twitching, as they often did when the past rose up without invitation. "No, you'll remember, Tamar, what you call a coincidence, I call God's doing." She swallowed deep. "Jan, you might want to take a seat. It's time." He lowered his long frame into a kitchen chair, then she began the history of her life. "My parents weren't the happiest couple in the world, though they tried to hide it from me as a child. My mother, a hardworking, Dutch-Reformed woman, ruled the roost at home and at the church. It's from her I inherited these thick ankles." She had to giggle at the thought. "But she was a good woman, though somewhat stern, and she taught me about her two greatest loves in the world—her Lord and her violin."

Daniel grinned. "And I would say she taught you well, Tante—and your ankles are just fine."

"Thank you, Daniel. You're sweet. On to my father—your grandfather, Jan. His name was Willem, and he was a dashing man. He had an exuberance for life. My father would come home from work—he was a pharmacist—and he always looked so sad. But then he'd see me, and his eyes would brighten, and he'd twirl me around until I couldn't keep my balance."

"Why did he look sad, Mam?" Jan asked.

"Well, I wasn't sure at the time. My mother later told me he felt he was wasting his life working at the apothecary. What he really wanted to do was be an artist. And he was good." She inclined her head toward the painting. "I remember studying his face when he was painting that picture. The lines on his face smoothed and his lips softened, and I would have sat there for hours just to see him like that."

"But he had to work long hours to support the family," Seth ventured.

Neelie nodded. "He'd say, 'Neelie, you have the makings of a great violinist, but do you love it? Because if you don't love it, it will show.' He probably noticed my restlessness. Anyway, moving forward three years, one day I came home from school to find my mother crying. She never cried, so it made my world go a-kilter. Through sobs, she pointed up at the wall above the piano. I looked up to see the painting of me…gone."

"'Was it stolen?' I asked." She shook her head. "Mam didn't go into much detail, but later, when she composed herself, she told me Papa had left a note to say he'd gone to Paris before it was too late."

Jan leaned forward, elbows on his knees. "What did he mean by that?"

Neelie tilted her head to the side. For some reason, it was heavier than usual. "To become the artist he always wanted to be. To put his whole life into it. He asked for her forbearance for one year, and if it didn't work out, he'd come home." Her eyes filled. *Not now. Not with every one staring at me.* "But he never did." She wiped her nose with a knuckle.

The room was eerily silent except for her sniffles. Seth stood and tried to pace, but the small room curbed his efforts, and he sat back down. "You mean, he didn't write? How did your mother pay the bills?"

"Mam had been putting away money to refurbish the house. We lived off that for a while, then she went to work at the church—secretarial work, and at night she gave violin lessons. We got by. I don't ever remember feeling we lacked for anything…but I missed him. I wanted to talk to her about him—ask when he was coming back, ask why we weren't enough. But even at a young age, I knew it would hurt her to talk about him, so I didn't." Neelie lifted a shoulder as if it didn't matter, but it did.

Daniel knelt by her knees to study the painting. He looked up. "So how did this painting end up in the Hamels' art gallery when Tamar was eleven? Do you think your father returned to Haarlem?"

Neelie's head popped up. Her eyes widened. Was it possible? Had her father been living in their small town, maybe mere kilometers from her, and he'd never made an effort to get in touch with her? The pang of betrayal and loss was so palpable that the hurt drilled through her. "I…I don't know."

She did quick calculations in her head. If Tamar saw the painting when she was about eleven, then that would have been in the early thirties—say, 1933. And that meant Neelie had been about thirty-three years old. Married to Frans, with nine-year-old Jan, and living in the house on the canal. Her mother had died when Neelie was thirty, never having seen her father again. "By the time Tamar saw that painting, my mother had passed away, and I was married and living in your future house. We'd sold my family's house by then. Perhaps my father couldn't find us." But even she knew that was a far-fetched thought. It wasn't as though Haarlem was the size of Amsterdam.

Tamar brushed her thumb over Neelie's palm. "I'm so sorry. It must have been rough not knowing." She paused a moment. "Do you want to know, Tante?"

"I've imagined all kinds of things. He became a famous artist or a spy or a Resistance worker, and as much as he wanted to come find my mother and me, something noble always stopped him." She cut a rueful smile at her son. What he must be thinking.

Jan scratched at the cleft in his chin, just as Frans used to do when he was considering multiple possibilities. He finally spoke. "As I said, whenever we take on a new client, we follow the provenance of the painting. The Hamels' gallery would be part of that trail. What say you try to get in touch with them?"

Tamar squeezed her hand. "Let's do it. I'll come with you. Wouldn't it be fun to see Job and Carina again?"

Seeing the excited expressions on everyone's faces, what could she do but say yes? But *they* didn't have to deal with the truth. No, it was time to move forward—face the jumble of emotions in that locked abyss. "Okay, I'd like to see them too. Daniel and Jan? Would you like to come along? You knew them."

"Too many people might be overwhelming for the Hamels. Those hofjes are pretty small," Daniel said. "Why don't you two go and take the twins? Remember how good Carina was with the orphans at the house?"

Neelie peered at Jan.

"I'm working a lot of hours for the firm—you know how they work us interns—but I'll see what I can dig up about this painting. However, I think you should take it with you, Mam. It may jog their memories to see it."

From where Tamar pushed the stroller, each narrow Amsterdam street looked like the one before, punctuated only by different-colored doors on the tall buildings. Bicycles lined both sides of the sidewalk. The only sound on this summer morning, besides Peri's burbles, was the distant clip-clop of a horse-drawn carriage.

Zari pressed her arms tight against her own chest, silently voicing her disapproval of having to be wheeled around.

Tamar hoisted the portfolio containing the painting onto her other shoulder. "Stop whining, Zari. We'll let you out once we reach the next hofje." She felt like whining herself as she swiped back tendrils of hair the wind blew in her face. "Tuck that lip back in. If I didn't have the stroller, you'd be pouting about having to walk so far." The Jordaan district had proven to be quite large.

"I'm sorry, kiddo. I'd pick you up, but my shoes are killing me. Either they're getting smaller or my feet are growing." Neelie chuckled, punctuated by a wince.

"You sit and I'll walk," Zari said, peering up at her oma.

She let out a laugh. "Thanks for your generous offer, but no, I'd have to sit on Peri. Would you like that?" Neelie tousled the boy's head. He whisked her hand away.

Tamar's feet hurt as well, and the kids' whining wasn't making things better. She turned to Neelie. "What does your map say? Where's the next hofje?"

Neelie pulled the folded, dog-eared map from her pocket. "Let's see. We've been to the two almshouses on Prinsengracht and the one on Boomstraat. So Raepenhofje is the third, and it's just two blocks past the canal. Kids, we'll need your help. Remember, we'll be looking for a red door, a turnip, and Noah's ark. That's how we'll find the place."

The request for help mollified Zari's rancor. The arms uncrossed, and the lip retracted.

Tamar gave her Tante Neelie a grateful smile. "Who knew there were so many of these hofjes all over Amsterdam? They're all hidden like beautiful little gems."

"Most were built in the 1700s to house elderly widows from the church, but now anybody can live in them if they qualify. They can't earn above a certain amount of money," Neelie said as she consulted her map and indicated with her finger that they needed to turn at the next corner. "It's like a treasure hunt. When you can find that hidden entrance, you walk into a world of calm and greenery. I love it."

Tamar dodged a puddle in the middle of the sidewalk. "I love the way the little houses face the inner courtyard. And they're all different. I can't wait to see the next one." She grabbed Peri before he toppled over the side of the stroller. "And I can't wait to show the Hamels this painting. How did you discover where they lived?"

"One of the residents at the rehab center mentioned he knew the Hamels. They'd gone to the same underground synagogue after the war. And the Hamels had held a weekly prayer meeting in their house. Mr. Rand couldn't remember the name of the hofje, but he did recall that it was in the Jordaan district."

Tamar nodded. "And the other three clues." The slight rise of a bridge appeared mere meters ahead. "There's the canal. Isn't this exciting, kids? Don't you just love a mystery?" Both the kids cheered and clapped their hands, trying to outdo each other in volume and intensity. From the highest point of the bridge, Tamar caught a glimpse of red on the right side of the street a block away. "Heads up, Zari and Peri."

Peri bolted out of his seat and almost toppled to the ground, but Neelie caught him midair. "What are we looking for?"

"Noah's ark," Peri exclaimed. "Easy to see because it's so big."

"Well, this won't be as big as the real one. What else?" Neelie queried.

"A red door and a vegetable. I don't get it," Zari groused, then climbed to her feet and pointed at an arched red door that didn't look tall enough for the average adult to enter. "There it is."

Peri rubbed his eyes. "I saw it first."

"No, you didn't. I did."

Neelie rested a hand on Peri's shoulder. "You're both great little detectives, but we have to be sure it's the right door, or we might be entering someone's private home instead of an entry into a courtyard. That would be embarrassing, wouldn't it?"

As they drew up before the tomato-red door, Peri pointed above it. "What's that?"

Tamar squinted to read the print over the stone carving about a half a meter above the top of the arch. "Well, sweetie, you found the turnip."

"Yay." Peri climbed over the side of the stroller, then helped Zari out. Tamar eyed Neelie and suppressed a giggle. The young boy was growing into his father.

"I see it over the door." Zari grinned. "It looks like a carrot with a long ponytail."

Neelie chuckled. "That it does. The name of the man who built this group of houses in 1648 was Raep, which means—"

"Turnip!" The twins screamed in unison.

"But where's Noah's ark?" Zari frowned. "Maybe it's the wrong house."

"I think this is the right place because of the first two clues. Maybe the ark is inside." Neelie pushed lightly on the door, saying "hello," in case they were entering someone's house.

The door opened to a dark passageway. Tamar placed the portfolio in the stroller while Neelie took the twins by the hand and said, "Now we must whisper because we don't want to disturb the people who live here. Be as a quiet as you can, okay?"

The dark passageway opened to a pastoral symphony of chirping birds and a bubbling fountain. A dozen shades of green interspersed with a gentle variety of pastel-colored chairs and benches. Four sides of six attached little homes framed a beautiful courtyard. The hofje was well maintained, and although the houses were centuries old and identical, each door was a different pastel color.

"It's so pretty," Zari whispered and sniffed. "Smells like honey. Do children live here? The houses are so little they probably do."

"That's honeysuckle," Neelie said. "No, sweetie. Only omas and opas live here. That's why we have to be quiet. Now, Tamar, how are we going to find out where the Hamels live?"

Tamar shielded her eyes from the sun and peered around. On the far side of the courtyard, a woman wearing a straw hat was watering flowers under the picture window of a house with a yellow door. "Let's go ask the lady with the watering can." Aware of the twins' bursting energy, she whispered. "If you two will talk with your quiet voices, maybe you can ask the lady where Noah's ark is."

"Okay," they both whispered, sharing conspiratorial glances at each other. Of course, the children's whispers were loud enough to cause the woman to turn. White hair pulled back into a neat bun, the woman was slight of stature. Her lined face broke into a smile when she saw the children skipping toward her. "Who do we have here?"

"I'm Zari, and this is my brother, Peri. We're twins but not idont...ident...what is it, Mam?"

"Identical." Tamar had to smile. She extended her hand toward the woman's gloved one. "Hello, we're looking for a couple who lives here. Their last name is Hamel. Would you know where they live?"

"And where is Noah's ark?" chimed in Peri.

The woman's eyes crinkled, and she bent down to Peri's level. "You will find it in the middle of the courtyard." She glanced up at Tamar. "I hope I haven't overstepped myself, but I'm sure the children will enjoy searching for it, and I have warm cookies I just took out of the oven. We receive so few visitors here, you know. My name is Sora Rifke."

"Of course. I'm Tamar Feldman and this is Neelie Visser. You've already been introduced to Zari and Peri." She turned to the bouncing twins. "Remember to be quiet and come right back when you find the ark." But Tamar talked to the wind because the kids were already trying to outrun each other to the courtyard center.

The woman dragged a chair from the adjacent house to her

porch. "Please, ladies, have a seat. Lenore won't mind if I borrow her chair." She shuffled over to the house on the other side of hers and tugged the chair over the grass to meet the other two.

Neelie gave Tamar a knowing glance and nodded slightly. Tamar understood what Neelie didn't say. A few minutes with this hospitable but seemingly lonely woman wouldn't delay them too much. She disappeared into the house and came out moments later with a plate of cookies and placed them on a small bench. A slight scent of cinnamon wafted in the air.

Mrs. Rifke pulled a few folded cloth napkins from the pocket of her apron. "Here we are. I knew there was a reason I had the sudden inspiration to make cookies. He knew."

"Who knew?" Tamar said.

"Why, God did." She handed a napkin and the plate of cookies to her.

"Thank you. They look scrumptious." Tamar took the smallest one and placed it on the proffered napkin, then waited until Neelie held a cookie. "This is such a quaint and calm place. I love the colored doors. Do you know which door belongs to the Hamels? They used to live in Haarlem and owned an art gallery." Hopefully, she wasn't being too forward, but the twins' attention span only lasted so long. A glance toward bobbing heads at the center of the courtyard assured her they were still searching for the ark.

The woman took a seat but didn't take a cookie. "You're referring to Carina Hamel, I assume. She's been a widow for a few years. Carina keeps to herself. I think she hasn't yet overcome her grief. It took me years as well." She offered a rueful smile and pointed toward a lavender door. "That's her place."

"Oh, poor Carina. I wish I'd known. I could have visited her." Neelie shook her head slowly. "Will the effects of this war ever end?"

Tamar sighed for her. "It just goes on and on. I remember how close Carina and Job were. Do you remember, Neelie? They'd sit so close together it was as if they were one person."

"But she came out of her shell and was a big help with the babies and with cooking."

"Both of them were so wise. I remember—"

"We found it!" Zari skipped toward them with Peri on her heels.

"Where is it?' Neelie asked, rising to her feet.

Tamar got the message and stood.

"Yeah, it was on a big flower vase," Peri said. "Could we have a cookie now?" He glanced at his mother. "Please?"

"Of course." Mrs. Rifke held the plate toward the twins. "You must be very diligent to be able to find such a small drawing."

Peri crammed half of his cookie into his mouth and mumbled through the crumbs, "Does it mean I have big eyes?"

The woman chuckled. "No, it means that you don't give up. And that's a very good thing." She leaned forward to remove a leaf intertwined in his blond curls.

"I was diligent, too," Zari said between bites. "'Cuz I didn't give up."

"Well, it was a pleasure to meet both of you. We don't have a lot of little ones visit, so twins are a double treat."

"Say 'thank you,' kids. We should be going. Thank you for your hospitality and your delightful cookies." Once the twins had offered their hands to their hostess, Tamar said, "I have another mystery for you. We need to find the purple door, but remember, good detectives walk very quietly." With the kids occupied for a minute at least, Tamar carried the two chairs back to Mrs. Rifke's neighbors' front stoops, then joined Neelie, who was thanking the elderly woman.

Now they knew. Job had passed away. At a camp? Remembering how shy Carina was when they were first introduced at Neelie's house, she couldn't imagine the diminutive woman living independently. Her eyes took in the enclave. This was the perfect place for such a person.

Gleeful shouts arose from the left side. So much for furtive detectives. Tamar gestured to Neelie that she was heading toward the clamor. Her gaze landed on the open purple door. A stooped woman stood in the threshold with her hand on her chest as the twins bobbed up and down in front of her.

"Carina Hamel? I'm so sorry." Tamar hurried to join them, Neelie's footsteps not far behind.

The old woman, hardly recognizable, glanced up, her eyes widening at the sight of them. "Tamar? Neelie? Am I dreaming?" A smile etched across her face, slowly, as if unused to the sensation. Her hair had whitened, crags framed her cheeks, and she was barely taller than the children.

Neelie clasped Carina's hands and pulled her into a hug while

Tamar gathered the stroller, painting, and twins with whatever appendages she could muster. Then she waited her turn to hug Carina, who appeared like one of those artifacts that might disintegrate if handled too tightly.

"Oh, it is good to see you two after all these years," she said and placed her hands on the children's shoulders. "And who are these two? They're too young to be the orphans at your house, so I must surmise that they belong to a certain doctor and his bride?"

"Yes, this is Zari, named after Zerah from the Bible, and this is Peri, short for Perez. Zerah and Perez were Judah's and Tamar's twins. And yes, Daniel is their father and my husband," she said.

"I'd heard that you and Daniel had escaped to England. I was so happy for you." Carina brushed away tears. "Sorry, it's just that you two added so much spice to our lives at Neelie's house. From your audition with the Nazi officer to your beautiful singing." She turned to Neelie. "And how can I ever repay your goodness to Job and me—taking us in when you hardly knew us? The risk you took to hide us." She shook her head. "Where are my manners? Please come in. I just made cookies this morning. They should be still warm, but I am so spellbound I'm not thinking straight." She gestured toward the door.

The kids pulled on Tamar's skirt. "Mam, we want to show you Noah's ark."

Tamar peered down at Carina. "The twins and I will be in shortly."

Neelie entered to piles upon piles of magazines and newspapers covering every horizontal surface of the small living room. Carina scurried over and cleared away a space on a loveseat and a folding chair. "Here, please sit." Her eyes darted around the room, and she sighed. "I'm sorry for the clutter. It's just that I can't seem to part with them." She gestured with her head toward a pile. "My Job was a newspaper reader. After we lost the gallery, he seemed to need a minute-by-minute source of news."

Neelie pulled her into the vacant chair beside her and wrapped her arm around the woman's thin shoulders. "How did he die,

Carina? I'm so sorry I didn't find a way to stay in touch with you after the war. He was a very good man."

"He was. After your son freed us from the attic room at your house, we scattered. I don't know what happened to anyone. Jan took the babies from us, then vanished into the shadows. For a while, we kept to the alleys until Job suggested it would be easier to hide in Amsterdam because it was bigger. So we walked. Found this place hidden from view. Everyone kept to themselves, not knowing whom they could trust. We did likewise. But soon, Job became sick. I couldn't take him to the doctor or the hospital. There was no money for medications. So I fed him hot tea and honey until he almost floated in it."

"Did he get better?"

"For a day or two, and then he refused food and drink and withered away. Typhus, someone said. We buried him right out there on the square. You'd be surprised at how many people are buried there in unmarked graves."

She patted Carina's hand. "Typhus killed so many in the camps. Tamar's parents died of the disease."

"Yes. What a shame." She stood. "I'll put some of the cookies on a plate. I'm sure the twins are hungry."

Neelie started to tell her cookies weren't necessary, but the little sparrow had already flitted into the kitchen. It would be rude to refuse her offer of hospitality. Good Nederlanders didn't do that. The children's voices clamored outside the door, followed by Tamar's admonition to quiet down. Neelie didn't mind the noise. Sometimes a place could be too quiet.

The door flung open, and the twins flew in at the same time Carina returned with a plate of *pindakoeken*. The twins stopped at the piles of newspapers, their eyes as round as the cookies on the plate. Neelie's knuckle went to her lips. *Please, Lord. Keep their lips closed.*

"Oma, look at all the hiding places. Can we play hide 'n' seek?"
Thank you, Lord. "Just be very quiet."

Tamar joined them, her eyes locking on Neelie's. Unsaid words flowed between them—they were on borrowed time with regard to the twins. Neelie took a fortifying breath and began. "Our visit is not an accident, Carina, although now that I know where you live, I'll visit more regularly. Did you know I work two kilometers from here at a rehabilitation center? It was one of our residents that remembered meeting you and Job at a prayer meeting."

The woman's eyes crinkled. "Ah, the prayer meetings. They were such a source of comfort for us early on. A lot of different people came once or twice—we were a transitive bunch after the war—so I don't remember faces or names. So tell me…why have you delighted me with this visit?"

Neelie glanced at Tamar, who took the cue. She opened the portfolio and carefully removed the painting.

"When I was a young girl—I think I told you this story before—I used to stop at your art gallery on my way home from school. There was a painting you displayed in the window that I just loved. Years later, after we were taken to Westerbork, that same painting was on the wall at the camp. Of course, I figured it had been stolen from your shop."

Carina moved to the edge of the chair. "Let me see it, please?" Tamar flipped it around, visibly holding her breath. A frown furrowed the elderly woman's brow as she studied the picture. "Ah, yes. I remember this one well. A lot of people wanted to buy it, but for some reason, the sales never went through, and secretly, I was always relieved because I loved this picture as well."

"There's more to the story." Tamar glanced at her, and Neelie nodded for her to continue. "A few months ago, I sneaked into my parents' house. Others were living in it, but I had an overwhelming urge to see what it looked like. This painting was hanging in my old bedroom. Can you imagine?"

"That's a God moment." Carina peered at Neelie. "I learned that from you. You taught me to see events not so much as random coincidences but events God designed—"

Neelie interrupted. "Well, let me add another God moment to the list. That little girl happens to be me, and the artist who painted her was my father."

Carina's hands flew to her face. "Chills are going down my back. I had no idea."

"Nor did I. The last time I saw this painting, I was thirteen. The next day, my father left us, taking the painting with him." She tilted her head. "So that girl with the violin fills me with a mixture of confusing emotions."

Carina removed a pair of glasses from her apron pocket and

leaned forward to examine the painting. "I don't see a signature."

"I can't remember if there ever was one. That blur might have been his signature at one time. Carina, the reason we're here is to see if we can jar your memory as to who sent you this painting. Tamar wants—no, needs—to know who owns the painting. If it was stolen from your gallery, do you own it? Or does the government? Or the people squatting in Tamar's old house?"

"Much as I'd love to claim ownership of this beauty, I do remember it was sent to us from Paris on consignment. I don't remember the woman's name we dealt with. Job would have known. Of course, we don't have any paperwork to prove anything since the gallery was ransacked. It was about 1933 when we received it. The name of the consigner was French. She was a widow who had taken over running her husband's gallery. We often did business with him and later, with her."

Tamar gave a defeated sigh. "There could be hundreds of Paris galleries."

A groove formed between Carina's eyebrows. "No, wait. It's coming back to me. The reason they did business with us was because the woman's assistant hailed from Haarlem, so he could write up the paperwork in Dutch." She closed her eyes. "I don't remember the name of the woman, but I do remember…the address. 20 Rue Royale. Now where did that come from?" Her eyes opened wide. "That must have come from God."

Neelie blew out a breath. Could the man who sent the painting to the Hamels be her father?

As much as she'd like to own this picture, she'd give it up in an instant if she could spend ten minutes with him. Yes, she harbored some bitterness at being abandoned. Yes, she'd watched her mother languish after he left. But more than anything, she needed answers. To hear his voice, to see that magnanimous smile that stretched from one ear to the other, to catch a whiff of his shaving powder. Was there a chance that she'd finally get to see her father?

Unlike the trip to Carina's hofje, the trip back was quiet. The twins had settled into the stroller and were sleeping. Tamar had found a way to lodge the painting across the handles so it wasn't banging against her back. And they walked slowly because Neelie's shoes were digging into her heels.

"What do you think, Tante?"

Neelie didn't answer right away.

"Tante?"

Neelie circled her temples. "Sorry. So many thoughts are swirling through my head. My father sent the painting of me to the gallery not far from our house, and that same painting ended up in your bedroom. What does all this mean?"

It was a lot to take in for both of them. "Well, let's talk about what we do know. One, the painting was on consignment from a gallery in Paris, the address of which we now know. The man who brokered the deal was a Nederlander. So perhaps the gallery in Paris owns it or knows who does." Tamar stopped pushing the stroller. "Neelie, it may not be your father, and a lot of time has passed since the painting first showed up at the gallery—"

Neelie waved a dismissive hand. "How's your French?"

"My what?"

"Listen, sweet girl. We both have questions that won't go away simply by ignoring them. You need to find out who owns this picture. I need to find out if the man who dealt with Karina and Job is my father. Sure, we could make a few phone calls, but I think a little trip to Paris is in order." Her eyes sparkled. "What do you think?"

They'd reached a crosswalk and stopped mere blocks from Neelie's flat. Tamar glanced at her aunt, then down at the sleeping children, whose arms linked around each other's shoulders. Like two peas when they were asleep. "I don't know. I've never been out of the country besides England, but that doesn't count because I was too shell-shocked to notice. Who would watch the children? And what about Daniel? Shouldn't he come along too?"

They crossed the street once the traffic had diminished. Neelie pointed at a bench along the canal, and they sat. The breeze and the shade combined with the lapping of the canal's water to present a most relaxing spring ambiance. The sweet smell of the linden trees had Tamar wiping her eyes.

"I'm sorry. I didn't mean to sadden you." Neelie leaned closer and brushed a strand of Tamar's hair behind her ear.

"No, I'm allergic to linden trees, but I love the smell."

"Tamar, has Daniel ever taken time off from work in the years since you've been here?"

"The day last week when we moved into your house was the first one. He's not the type to take time off. Sometimes I feel as though he's missing so much of the twins' stages of growth, but he gives us his full attention when he's home," Tamar said.

Neelie took Tamar's hand in hers. "How about the three of us take the train to Paris just for a day or two? Perhaps we can ask Hadassah to babysit the twins. If not, I have friends at church who would be happy to take care of them. I'll talk to Jan and see if he can give us any art or legal suggestions, or maybe he can go with us if his law firm will let him."

She turned to face Neelie. "I've always dreamed of going to Paris, but how could we manage it?"

"Tamar, you worked for the Resistance. You escaped from Vught. Where did your sense of adventure go?"

She sighed out loud. "It seems I've graduated from the world of dreams to the world of practicality. I want to be a good wife to Daniel and a good mother to these little ones."

"And you are, but I sense a restlessness in you. You need answers to what's bothering you, and I need to find out if that man in Paris is my father. Who knows how old he is now? He has to be past seventy if I'm forty-eight. If there's any chance he's still alive, I have to find him. You see, I need to hear his story, and I need to forgive him, for his good and for mine."

"Oh, Neelie, I never thought…I mean, of course, I'll go with you to Paris to find your father. Remember, my mother was Belgian. She insisted we speak French when Seth and I were young. I haven't used it in a long time, but hopefully, it will come back to help us navigate the city. And maybe we'll even find out who really owns this painting."

***

If he wasn't in so much pain, he'd laugh. Erich scratched against the rash forming on the nape of his neck from the itchy material. The suit which he'd found in an attic trunk swam on his thin frame, but it was of good quality. It smelled of must, and it was too short for Klaus, so it must have belonged to the previous owner of the house.

The irony almost brought a smile. Little did Klaus know he'd been hiding a Nazi in his attic. Now he stood face-to-face with Klaus on the doorstep of his dry cleaner. But Erich didn't smile. It took too much energy, and it stretched the skin around his mouth.

"Erich, I hardly recognized you. How have you been? I heard you left the hospital abruptly. I'm amazed at the change in your face." Klaus leaned forward, squinting at him as if he were a bug in a petri dish.

Erich waved a dismissive hand. "I'm better. The doctors were asking too many questions, so it was time to leave. And I'm eager to reclaim the art you've been holding for me. By the way, how is the opening of the opera coming?" Small talk always irritated him, but perhaps he could apply some pressure—use his cache to get what he wanted. And he needed to find out why Tamar hadn't shown up to take care of the boy.

Klaus's eyes brightened and finally left Erich's face. "It couldn't be better. People are hungry for culture. We're hoping to open in September with *The Barber of Seville* and *La Bohème* in January. That will give us three months to rehearse."

"No Mozart?"

Klaus lifted a shoulder. "It's not the right time. By this time next year, folks will have forgotten about the war."

"Have you selected the troupe yet?"

"No, money's tight. A few promises of funding haven't come through, but as they do—"

This was proceeding too slowly, and his eye was starting to twitch. It was always about money. "How much capital do you need to get started?"

An immediate glint sparked in Sneider's eye. Of course, it did. "With the orchestra, cast, and staff, I could probably manage at seventy thousand guilders. In no time, we'll make a profit. I'm serious. The crowds are clamoring to dress up and be entertained."

Erich suppressed the desire to smile. He'd expected more, but he'd play this close to the chest. A few paintings would easily bring in that much on the black market, even in the present economy. Then he'd go in for the kill. "So who do you have in mind to play Susan?"

Sneider coughed, avoiding meeting Erich's eyes. "Margot—my wife—has been practicing for the role for months. Her voice is getting stronger, but even more important—she can bring in the crowds like no other."

He longed to ask him why. Why marry such a loose, crass woman, and a diva to boot? But now was not the time. "Is she not in her mid to late thirties? Wouldn't she make a better Rosina than a Susan?"

Sneider visibly shuddered, probably afraid even to ask her.

The time had come. "Tell you what. I'll give you a Klimt painting to fund your project, and I'll throw in a Gaugin if you'll agree to a certain condition."

He glanced up, that glint back. "What is the condition?"

"You know a Gaugin will give you enough money to provide pretty frocks for your wife and the best schools for your son—" He'd said too much. The son had never come up in conversation. Sneider hadn't appeared to notice, so he continued. "Remember that young woman I introduced you to in Amsterdam—Tamar Visser? She'd make a perfect Susan. I'll give you the two paintings if you'll cast Tamar as Susan. Then you can cast your wife as Rosina to bring in the crowds, as you said."

Sneider swallowed and coughed, his voice strained. "I agree that Miss Visser would make a fine Susan. Believe me, I'd love to cast her in one of the leads, but I'm not sure she's interested. As much as I appreciate the offer, you're putting me in a tenuous spot. You know Margot. It would kill her to play a secondary role, not to mention that of an older woman."

His skin was stretching like a tight tarpaulin over his bones. "Those are my terms. Two paintings and you can live in luxury for the rest of your life. Money talks to women like your wife. Tell her about the offer. Talk to Miss Visser. I'll give you twenty-four hours."

Klaus's eyes bulged as the sing-songy voice of his wife sounded from upstairs.

"I'm home. Klaus, are you here?" Footsteps started down the stairs.

"I must go. The offer stands until midnight tomorrow night." Erich spun to leave.

"Wait." Klaus held onto his arm, causing him to bristle against the pain. "I don't even know where she lives."

"Find out," he seethed, wrestled his arm free, and ran out the door.

Chapter Thirteen

"I know that the experiences of our lives, when we let God use them, become the mysterious and perfect preparation for the work he will give us to do."
~ Corrie ten Boom

Daniel's pacing echoed against the old wooden floors as he skirted around stacks of boxes that still needed to be unpacked. "I don't know. The timing is so bad. The burn unit's almost full, and I took off two days for the move to this house. And what about the twins? Just as they're acclimating to their new home, we leave them to go to Paris for who knows how long?"

Tamar massaged her temples. So much upheaval in their lives was causing her head to pound. She put out a hand to keep him in one place. "I know you don't like to miss work, and I admire your loyalty to the hospital, but you haven't had a real break in years. Moving into this house doesn't count. Hadassah has agreed to watch the twins, so they'll be fine. They know her well. And we'll only be in Paris for a few days. Think of it, Daniel—Neelie needs us. All we have to do is find her father so she can have closure." Her hand slightly tightened on his forearm. "And I need closure. Now I bought a map of Paris, and I've circled the address of the gallery, so it shouldn't be hard to find."

His eyes blinked rapidly, a sure sign he was giving in. She hated coercing him into going with them, but they both needed closure. He shrugged. "It's a cold trail. If what Carina Hamel says is true, Neelie's father worked at the gallery over a decade ago. The Nazis occupied Paris just as they occupied the Netherlands, so he's probably not there anymore."

Daniel had a point. It hadn't occurred to her he might not be there. Still— "C'mon, darling. It will be an adventure. And I promise, the moment we find out who owns the painting, I'll let it rest. Then I'll come home and focus on making this house the perfect haven for our family." She peered around at the beautiful wooden beams, the carved banister, and the lovely floors. Sure, they were only renting, but there was so much room, and they were right across from the canal. It was the perfect place to raise their family.

Daniel kissed the side of her head. "Deal." Just then there was a sharp rapping below. "Wonder who'd be at our door at eight o'clock in the evening?" He hurried down the stairs with her at his heels, to the first level where the foyer faced the front of the house. The vague image of a fedora and a raincoat appeared through the beveled glass. Someone tall and thin.

Daniel opened the door. "*Goedenavond.* May I help you?"

The door opened wider to show Klaus Sneider. Had something happened to Karl? To Margot? She hurried to join Daniel at the threshold. "Is something wrong with Karl?" she blurted out. Daniel hadn't seen the man since the Amsterdam audition. "Daniel, you remember Klaus Sneider from the…audition. He is Margot's husband and Karl's father. Come in, Mr. Sneider."

Daniel backed up to let him in, then thrust out his hand. "I'm Daniel, Tamar's husband. Is there something wrong? Does your wife need a doctor?"

He removed his hat but hardly acknowledged Daniel's greeting at first. Something indeed was wrong.

"What is it?" she repeated.

"I'm sorry to come so late, but Margot didn't know that you'd moved. I went by your old apartment, and the concierge wasn't keen on giving me your address, but money finally wore her down."

"That's wrong." She flinched at the rudeness of her tone, but it had never occurred to her that her landlady could be bought.

"I am sorry to come so late, but what I have to discuss with you involves both of you, so Dr. Feldman, I'm glad you are here." He glanced at Tamar. "And Karl and Margot are fine."

"Let's go upstairs, and I'll make some tea." She led the way up the stairs and motioned to the small table in the kitchen. If she'd had more notice, she'd have cleared out some of the boxes in the parlor, but this wasn't a social call. Tamar turned on the kettle, took out cups and saucers, and filled a plate with stroopwafels she'd bought at the market.

Sneider and Daniel had taken seats at opposite sides of the table. Thankfully, the colorful tablecloth covered the scarred wood, and she'd done the dishes. She removed the map of Paris from the table, set the tea tray in the middle, and took a seat next to Daniel, waiting for him to start the conversation. The silence was thick and uncomfortable.

She took the lead. "How are Margot and your son?"

His shoulders seemed to relax. "Fine. Karl misses you and your children. He doesn't understand why you stopped coming."

Daniel answered for her. "Tamar has been busy with the move and other things." His voice was so frosty, Tamar almost shivered.

Sneider's eyes darted to the rooster clock over the sink. "Well, it's late, so I won't keep you long."

The kettle whistled. While Daniel rose to pour the boiling water into the teapot, Sneider removed a handkerchief from his pocket and mopped his forehead. He folded his hands as he waited for Daniel to sit down again. Tamar tried to think of something smart to say, but her mind was as blank as the expression on their guest's face.

Finally, he cleared his throat. "Dr. Feldman, I've been working on getting the Haarlem opera up and running again. Our citizens need something beautiful, something grand to enjoy amidst all the gloom that darkens our city. My hope is to produce three operas this season—happy and fun operas to lift the spirits." He eyed them.

Daniel nodded, as did she. Klaus was right. The city craved culture. She craved culture.

"I have a proposition for you both. Our first opera will be *The Barber of Seville*, and Tamar, you'd be perfect for the role of Susan."

She cut a sideways glance at her husband's face as the resignation settled there. With the trip to Paris and now this, his tidy home life was imploding. Yet what an honor it would be to sing the lead in her hometown. But what about Margot? How would she react to playing second lead? And how could she do this to Daniel and the twins?

"Now, I know that your time is limited with two children and your husband to take care of, so here is my proposition. To begin with, our budget will limit us to three shows a week, which means we'll only work three or four days weekly, and we'd do a four-week run. Since Margot will play Rosina, perhaps we could hire a babysitter to watch your children and Karl during practices—maybe even performances." He checked his watch and stood. "I know this is an unorthodox proposal, and you'll need time to discuss this, but I will need an answer by tomorrow if that's possible."

"When do rehearsals begin?" Daniel asked. Tamar's eyes flew to her husband's face. Was he even considering this? He read her mind. "Not that we're even to the point of accepting your proposal, but we need to know your timeline."

"We'd begin rehearsals in August, and as I said, the opera would run for a month. A two-month commitment is what I'm asking of you both." He headed to the door. "I'll be in touch late tomorrow afternoon. I hope you'll have reached a decision by then." They followed him down the stairs to the foyer, where he had left his coat and fedora. He stopped at the door and turned to them. "You must understand how unusual this is—to offer you the lead soprano role without even auditioning for it." Sneider tipped his hat and vanished into the dark.

They stood in the foyer staring at each other. Sleep would come late tonight if at all. How was she to process this? Only famous sopranos took on lead roles without auditions. One performance when she stood in for Margot didn't qualify her as a diva. But the twins needed her care. And knowing Daniel, he would give in, but it would rankle him under the surface, and the wall would go up again between them. Was she ready to give up being a full-time mother and wife?

They walked upstairs without words. Tamar took Klaus's full teacup to the sink and dumped it. He hadn't even taken a sip. She washed and Daniel dried, and still they hadn't said a word, but the air was loud between them.

His voice was gravelly when he finally spoke. "I won't stand in your way."

Judging from the way his voice trailed off, she read the opposite. "Do you remember what you said when we sat out on the roof alcove not knowing if we'd ever make it to peaceful times, and you made me promise that we'd always be honest with each other? Well, these are peaceful times, and there are still problems. Please, be honest with me—especially now."

Daniel took her hand and led her to the other staircase, the one that rose to the third floor. Abruptly, he whipped around and plunked down on the third step, patting the place next to him. "Guess we don't have to go out on the roof for privacy now."

"Oh," she said. "I keep forgetting we're alone now except for Peri's ears that seem to light up even when he's snoring." Tamar tucked a curly strand of hair around Daniel's ear. "But I miss going out on the roof." She stood. "Let's go. It's not raining."

He rolled his eyes, but his smile belied the action. "Hope we can still fit through the attic door. We were a lot thinner then." They tiptoed past the twins' room to the short set of stairs that led to the attic level.

The attic always brought back those endless days. The mirror on the right wall reminded her of the secret room behind it where they'd hidden Jewish babies during the war. Someday, the twins would enjoy making a secret hideout in that room, and new memories would erase the bad ones. That was what she and Daniel must do—make new memories to erase the bad ones.

It was harder climbing through the small door to the balcony that overlooked the back alley, especially hard for Daniel whose height made him lower to all fours. Now they could sit on the balcony because they didn't have to worry about passing Nazi soldiers.

"Should we climb up?" she asked, pointing toward the alcove, the flat area between the two roofs that offered a private place just big enough for two people.

"Not tonight. It's too dark to see, and we don't know the condition of the roof. Sometime, though." He sat on the wooden floor and pulled her down next to him. His arm enveloped her shoulders, assuaging any doubts about their love waning over the tumult of issues that faced them of late. "You know, this balcony will be a big temptation for Peri. I can see him throwing his soldiers over the railing, then climbing over it to retrieve them."

A shudder overtook her at the thought. "We'll have to find a way to lock the attic door so he can't get in." She rested her head against his shoulder, feasting on the scent that was his alone—a bit of antiseptic mixed with coffee and cinnamon. Her eyes closed against the gentle summer breeze. How ironic to be back in the very place where they'd fallen in love. How absolutely blessed she was to have Daniel in her life. They'd weathered so much and had overcome it all. Surely, normal family problems were no match for them.

His voice pulled her from her reverie. "I wish we had more than a few hours to make a decision. I'm always suspicious of timed offers like this."

"I agree. It almost seems too good to be trusted. Without me even auditioning, Klaus Sneider is offering me the lead when his wife has been taking voice lesson for months. She isn't going to be happy with him or me, should I take the role."

"Yes, and then he's offered to let you work part-time—"

"And provide childcare. Why me? It doesn't make sense. Something's up…"

"Taken at face value, it's a great opportunity for you." He took her hand and rubbed his thumb over her palm, sending a shiver through her. "It's only two months of our lives. I'll help as much as I can. But what happens in October when it's over? What if the opera is such a big hit Sneider decides to go full-time?"

Daniel was right. This wasn't as simple as it seemed. "Could we pray? I don't want to make a mistake that might hurt our children or…us."

He squeezed her hand, his deep, resonant voice giving her comfort. "Our Father, You've told us not to lean on our own understanding. You have promised to direct out paths if we acknowledge You. In James, You've told us to ask You for wisdom if we lack it, and You will generously give it. We bring You this offer that seems too good to be true. Mr. Sneider wants an answer by tomorrow afternoon. Tamar and I will do whatever You tell us to do. In the name of Yeshua Hamashiach."

They sat there waiting for a thunderbolt, but more likely, there would be a gentle answer at the eleventh hour.

After a multitude of minutes, Daniel stood. "Well, I have an early morning. Let's go to bed." He helped her up, pulled her to his chest, and pressed his lips against her cheek, her temple, and then their lips met, and they stayed locked together until the chimes of St Bavo's pulled them apart.

Erich slapped the doorjamb of the entry into Sneider's ersatz dry cleaner. "What do you mean Tamar didn't give you an answer? How could she turn down the role of a lifetime?" The faded, starched collar burrowed into the tender skin of Erich's neck. He fought against the nausea that erupted whenever he stood too long. The medication had run out. The paltry pills he'd taken from the Sneiders' medicine chest when they were out weren't working. He needed stronger analgesics—the kind they doled out in the hospital.

Klaus looked as uncomfortable as Erich felt. "I tried. Made them an offer no self-respecting producer should ever make, and she looked interested. Even her husband perked up. But when I went back the next day, they said they weren't prepared to give an answer in such a short time." His palms faced the ceiling. "They brought God into it. You know how Jews are. Cagey."

"How in the world could they bring God into it?" If he could get a few minutes alone with Tamar…but nothing was easy for the taking anymore.

Klaus shook his head. "Her husband said they'd prayed and couldn't make a decision until they received an answer. What do they expect? To hear voices in their head or something? Anyway, they're going on a short trip, and they said they'd meet with me when they return. So that's better than an all-out no."

A trip? He didn't know how much more of the attic he could take. "Where are they going? When will they be back?"

Klaus shrugged, but the smirk on his lips showed he knew more than he was saying. "They didn't say and I didn't ask, but…"

So this was a game. He hated games. "But?"

Klaus's eyebrows lifted. "Well, I did see a map of Paris opened on their table. Noticed a few places circled and an address written on its edge."

The man was enjoying himself way too much, as if he held the cards. As soon as this farce was over and his art was moved to a safe, hidden spot, there would be no more cards. Klaus Sneider knew too much. "And what was the address?"

"I only saw it for a moment before Tamar removed it, but I think it said 20 Rue Royale."

Paris. Tamar and the doctor were going to Paris. He'd shadow them there, but first he needed more information. "By the way, where did you meet with them?"

"Nice house. I should have studied medicine instead of business. They just moved in. There were boxes stacked in every corner. One of the big houses on the canal."

The Visser house? No, it couldn't be. That woman—Neelie Visser—had to be dead now. But it made sense. Tamar was her niece. He remembered the house well. There were a lot of hiding places in that old house. *Hiding places.*

Erich made a quick exit out the dry-cleaner entrance, the way he'd come in. He told Sneider to keep him informed. Then he circled around to the back and used the key hidden behind the brick to open the back door. Didn't every burglar know to check behind the outlined brick near the door? If his face didn't hurt so bad, he'd laugh out loud as he crept like a cat up the stairs. The occupation years had taught him to be a wily cat, so quiet nobody knew he was listening, so light on his feet he could easily slip past the residents.

A full-blown plan hatched in his head. It was time to move out. Take up residence in a new attic. He'd need some fast money to follow Tamar to Paris, so he'd have to make a quick sale of one of the paintings. A trip to a bar and a grease of a palm, as they said in America, and he'd have enough for a few changes of clothes and a month in Paris if need be. Anything could be bought at a bar for cash—including painkillers.

As he slipped through the hall, he shuddered at the careless way the art—*his* art—was stacked in piles. Didn't they understand even the slightest damage would reduce the value of a painting by thousands? He wouldn't think about that now. Better to proceed with the plan.

Tonight he'd head to a nearby bar on the canal, where people didn't worry about their next drink. Once he'd sold a painting—perhaps a Utrillo or a Gauguin—off market, of course—he'd buy what he needed, then case the Visser house. Make sure it was the right one, but how could it not? There would be a brick. There always was.

Should he take her right away? It would be so easy, so fortuitous. Though he was tempted, the time wasn't right. The paintings weren't in his possession, and he hadn't regained his strength. If the Reich had taught him anything, it had drilled into his skin two things. One, choosing the right moment was paramount. One second early was too soon for success. And, two, the Reich had taught him to keep perfect records. Erich knew the location of each painting, each candlestick, each jewel. He also knew which treasures Sneider's wife had pawned. And he also knew which painting his Tamar had stolen. Even angels had their dark sides. It just made her more intriguing…and more vulnerable to his proposition.

Chapter Fourteen

"The first step on the way to victory is to recognize the enemy."
~ Corrie ten Boom

Tamar's stomach was a glass cage of butterflies as she rushed from one room to the next, packing suitcases for the twins, Daniel, and herself. In her hurry to unpack the boxes, she had no idea where she'd laid the passports or how she was going to get the painting over the Belgian and French borders.

The scrape of furniture sounded from the attic above for the second time that day. It was probably just a squirrel. At least, that's what she told herself. Attics had always given her the shivers. As a child, Tamar made excuses not to go to the attic because of the shadows that seemed to move. The passports were probably in one of the unopened boxes up there. Daniel would be working late since he was taking the week off, so she couldn't persuade him to do it for her. It was time to be a big girl.

After hurrying down the stairs to the parlor, she made sure the twins were occupied. They lay fast asleep on the sofa, their arms wrapped around each other. Hopefully, she'd be back by the time they woke up. As she climbed the last set of stairs, she chanted, "Squirrels don't hurt. Squirrels don't bite." Unless they had rabies.

The door creaked opened, just as they did in those detective novels she used to read when she was a teenager. Now was not the time to think about such things. There were ten to twelve boxes to go through. She hoped the rodent was long gone.

Little light came through the door's window at the other end of the room, so she yanked on the light string. Most of Neelie's belongings were stacked against three walls and took up about two-thirds of the room. Tamar had asked Daniel to stack their boxes along the wall on the right.

A shiver whooshed through her at the sight of something moving, but it was just the reflection of herself in the mirror. The mirror. It would be a long time before she'd push the button at the top of it and step inside the room behind it. The cribs had probably been cleared out.

Time to get to work. With any luck, the passports would be in one of the first boxes. Tamar propped the attic door open so she could hear the twins.

The first two boxes contained baby clothes she'd saved just in case. The third was so heavy, she could hardly haul it away from the wall. Medical books, most likely. She opened it just to be sure. The musty smell of old tomes hit her in the face. She started on the fourth box, which was, thankfully, lighter.

Opening the lid, she uttered a happy sigh to see folders. Tamar sat cross-legged on the floor and carefully leafed through each one. Humming some songs from shul that always calmed her down, she made quick work of old bank statements, Daniel's CV, leases from their old apartment…and there they were. Yes! She opened the passports. Double yes! They were good for five years. The trip was still on.

As she was putting the files back in the box, her hand froze in midair. A rustle, then a thump—so close she could reach out and touch the one who made it. Then a scratching, like the sound of fingernails on a table. She froze. The only things moving were her heart, pounding, and her eyes, darting around the room. Maybe it was that pesky squirrel. And Neelie always said old houses made all kinds of noise as they settled. It was something to do with being built on the less-than-stable foundations so close to the canals. That's why they leaned. Whatever it was, she wouldn't waste another moment in this place. Tamar bolted to her feet and hurried to the door, almost bowling over the twins.

"What's wrong, Mam? You look scared." Zari's little eyebrows furrowed together.

Tamar pressed her hand against her chest. "I just didn't expect to see you two. You scared me. What are you doing up here?"

"Peri said you and Abba were leaving tonight on your trip." Her lip trembled. "We don't want you to go."

She knelt down and tucked her arms around the kids, drawing them close. "We're not leaving tonight, okay? We're leaving tomorrow morning. You always have a good time with Tante Hadassah and Uncle Seth, don't you? She'll take you to the park, and you'll see some of your friends from the apartment. And the time will go really fast because we'll only be gone three days at the most."

"Will you bring us something?" Peri rubbed his cheek against her shoulder.

"Of course, we will. Now, let's get out of this dusty room." She peered over her shoulder and slammed the door shut harder than she intended.

He flinched at the slam of the door, which seemed to shake the foundations of this little room. It had taken him all of five minutes to find the secret button that opened the mirror. Brilliant job of creating this hiding place for the cribs, but not as brilliant as he. So this was where Mrs. Visser had hidden the orphans. If his love hadn't blinded him to Tamar's faults, he would have spent more time up here and found them. Resistance members didn't stray too far from the design.

Touché, Neelie Visser. But there'd be justice. He now knew their schedule and their destination. With his dapper new suit and wire glasses, he'd be unrecognizable. The good doctor hadn't even been able to identify him close-up.

Erich tapped the passport in his pocket. A Dutch name—Dedrich Smit from Amsterdam. A slight man about ten years his senior. It had cost him a jeweled brooch, but it was worth the ticket to Paris.

Chapter Fifteen

"When a *train* goes through a tunnel and it gets dark, you don't throw away the ticket and jump off. You sit still and trust the engineer."
~ Corrie ten Boom

All the anxious feelings Tamar had experienced during the war flooded back when the conductor approached them to check their tickets. Especially anxiety-provoking, that time they'd held fake identification cards on the barge that took them to England. A glance at the vein pulsing on Daniel's neck showed he was sharing her memory.

Fortunately, they needn't have worried. The conductor gave them a cursory look, then he walked on by. She clasped Daniel's fist and gave it a squeeze. It was time to relax and enjoy this adventure. "Just think. In three-and-a-half hours, we'll be in Paris. The City of Lights. Tante, what do you want to see while we're there?"

Neelie peered up from her Bible. She blinked, her veiled hat tilted jauntily on her short blondish gray curls. "Why, I don't know. We're only there for three days. Guess we'll follow the provenance of the painting and hope it leads to my father. First, we'll go to that address on Rue Royale, and Jan suggested we pay a visit to the woman named Isabelle LeClair who works at the Jeu de Paume Museum. Apparently, she's an expert on art stolen by the Nazis, and she may know where my father lives or works. If he's even still alive."

Tamar rested a hand on hers. "You're not that old, Neelie. Your father would be…what? Mid-seventies?"

"But the Nazis occupied Paris. You know what they thought of modern art. They probably killed the artists."

"Don't think that way. We'll find your father, and he'll be delighted to see you. And he'll tell us about this painting," Tamar patted the portfolio. "But don't you want to do something fun? See the Eiffel Tower, Notre Dame Cathedral, the Louvre?"

"What do you want to do, Tamar?"

"Oh, so many things. Stroll along the Champs Elysées, sit for hours at the Café aux Deux Magots, sip an espresso and watch the people walk by, and have my picture sketched at Montmartre. What about you, Daniel? You haven't had a vacation since you were a child."

He folded his newspaper and set it on the seat. "Three days is not that long and finding the owner of this painting and Neelie's father may eat up the time."

Neelie leaned forward. "But if we have time, we should do some fun things. You've both been through so much, and as my son is going to be moving here, I'd like to see if this town is as wild as they say."

Daniel tapped his finger on the little indentation on his chin. "Hm, I've always wanted to try steak frites, a bowl of cheesy onion soup, and crème brûlée. And I wouldn't mind a trip to the Eiffel Tower. I've heard you can see all the way to Belgium from the third level."

Tamar elbowed him. "You sound hungry. I don't see why we can't check at least a few things off our list. But our priority is finding Neelie's father. What was your maiden name?"

"Haan. My father's name was…is Willem Haan. You know what would be a real treat for me? I would love to have a cup of hot chocolate and a pastry at Angelina's. I used to dream about it when we were shivering at Vught, and all we had was that ragged old blanket that couldn't have been thinner."

"And the list grows. We can start right after we check in to our hotel," Daniel said. "I made us reservations at a place close to Rue Royale. Hotel Cambon. The price is moderate, so I booked two rooms. One for us and one for you, Neelie. I reserved rooms on the second floor so we won't have to climb many steps."

"My feet thank you. How will we get to the hotel from the train station?" Neelie took off her glasses, then rolled her eyes. "I'm sorry to bother you about details, but since Frans died, I'm used to planning ahead. I should not worry."

Daniel opened a well-folded map. "Let's see. This train takes us to Gard du Nord. Looks as though we can take two metro trains to Concorde, and then it's a short walk. Or we could walk the whole way—about four kilometers. But if you want, we could splurge and take a taxi." He waggled his eyebrows. "This is a vacation."

"Jan said a lot of the métro lines closed during the war and haven't opened up yet." Neelie massaged her ankle and winced. "I'd rather save my feet for later. How about we ask someone in the train station?"

Tamar piped up. "I agree with Neelie. If we can't take the subway, let's take a taxi to the hotel. Then we won't be worn out when we set out to find Neelie's father. Plus, I don't want to have to carry this painting and a suitcase. Don't you wish they'd invent little carts with wheels for suitcases so people didn't have to lug them around?"

Daniel waved a dismissive hand. "It'll never happen. That would put a lot of porters out of business." He folded the wrinkled map in two. "Looks like we're coming into the city." He pointed at a distant white basilica on a hill. "That's Sacré Coeur. If we have time, we should go visit it. The hill it sits on is called Montmartre. A lot of famous artists lived in the shadow of that church, including our own Van Gogh."

Neelie's eyes lit up. "Maybe my father lives there. Or maybe there are artists that would know where we might find him."

"Hopefully, we'll find your father at the gallery at Rue Royale, but if not, I think we should take Jan's advice and make an appointment with that woman at the art museum—what was its name?" Tamar looked at Daniel, who was poring over the map again.

He pointed at a spot circled with Zari's orange crayon. "It's called Jeu de Paume. Our hotel is just a few blocks away. We can stop by to make an appointment on our way back from Rue Royale." He folded the map and put it in his jacket pocket. "On with our trip, *trois mousquetaires*!"

Erich lowered his newspaper and cut a sideways glimpse out the window. Trains were so handy for eavesdropping. With his back to their compartment, he could hear everything they said. His fedora and newspaper concealed his face. Not only did he know the name of the hotel now, but he also knew the floor they were staying on. He'd take a taxi to reach the hotel before they did, and after he checked in, he'd sit in the lobby until they left to find Visser's father.

This whole ordeal would be more seamless if Tamar came down by herself, then he'd find a way to start a conversation. This time, he'd be sure to hide any trace of his low German accent. He hated mistakes. With proper strategy and a logical mind, he'd carry out his plan to reclaim the painting and the woman carrying it.

Chapter Sixteen

"If God has shown us bad times ahead, it's enough for me that He knows about them. That's why He sometimes shows us things, you know—to tell us that this, too, is in His hands."
~ Betsie ten Boom

Tamar had to force herself to close her mouth. The beauty of the city, its elegance and its history, made her giddy with anticipation. She tucked her arm inside Daniel's after stumbling over a furrow in the sidewalk. All around her were regal cream-colored buildings fronted by balconies and wide, tree-lined sidewalks.

Noting her darting eyes, Daniel said, "I learned in college about the architect who redesigned Paris. Napoleon the Third commissioned Baron Haussmann in the last century to tear down most of the central medieval buildings to make way for wide sidewalks for pedestrians and broad streets for automobiles."

Neelie shielded her eyes against the brilliant sun. "It's always sad that history has to yield to progress, but the view is spectacular. Everything about this place—the ambiance, the cafés, the cacophony of voices and traffic sounds—even the cigarette smoke—fill me with…what do they say? *Joie de vivre*. How I wish Frans were here by my side."

"*Oui*, the joy of living." Tamar hugged her husband's arm. "I understand now. My mother used to tell me of her trips to Paris with my grandmother. They were from Belgium, you know. Ecma said there was something in the air. You had to experience it for yourself. *Je t'adore*, Paris," she shouted, then covered her mouth and giggled.

She glanced down. "Oh, Tante, I love your sneakers. They look so comfortable."

"These old Quicks? I wear them to and from the center but put on my pumps at work."

"Smart woman, this one." Daniel motioned with his head. "By the way, we're two blocks away from Rue Royale." They hurried across the street to avoid a truck honking at them. The driver thrust his arms into the air and said a phrase Tamar hadn't learned from her mother.

"Touché," Neelie said with an uncharacteristic flip of her hand to the vehicle. "Come to Amsterdam, and our cyclists will match your words."

They turned onto Rue Royale, and the air turned even more rich and elegant, if that were even possible. Well-known parfumeries such as Guerlain, Lancôme, and Dior competed for the biggest banner. Tamar closed her eyes and sniffed. Her mother's *Je Reviens* hinted near her nose. Interspersed among the fashion and perfume shops were small galleries—some with closed signs. Neelie pointed at the small twenty on a weathered grayish-blue door.

The name *Danvers* appeared in large letters over the door, and the same name was written on the left display window over the address, XX Rue Royale, Paris. A glimpse in the window showed a few paintings leaning against the wall on the left. Two elegant vases sat in the display windows on either side of the door. The dark room had an abandoned appearance. There was no *ouverte* or *fermé* sign on the door, and Daniel's tug didn't open it.

"Even the two streetlamps look as though they haven't been used in a while." Daniel peeked in the door's window, then backed up, shielded his eyes, and peered at the floors above.

Tamar joined him and followed his gaze. Two awninged windows stared down from the second floor. "It looks abandoned. Wonder if anyone lives up there?" Just as her family had lived above their jewelry store, she imagined the owner—Monsieur Danvers— must live behind those windows. The curtain on the left fluttered, or was that her imagination? "Did you see that?"

Neelie drew close and looked up. "See what?"

"That curtain on the left moved a little bit, I think."

Daniel peered up a second time. "Someone lives up there, and that someone might know what became of your father. Or maybe it is your father." He glanced at his wristwatch, then looked up again. "It's almost five. The businesses around here are going to be closing. How about we ask the neighbors what they know about the gallery?"

On the left side was a jewelry store—Georges Fouquet. It looked pretentious, as did the woman in a fur stole who bustled in with her pink poodle.

Daniel's face scrunched up. "I don't think they'd welcome our questions."

"And I left my fur at home," Neelie said, sashaying in a circle with her nose in the air.

"Stop, Aunt Neelie, or I'll start snorting, and they'll make us leave the neighborhood."

Daniel ambled to the business on the left. "Molinard Parfumerie. This place doesn't look any more inviting." As with the jewelry store, the salespeople were thin, dressed in impeccable dark-blue suits, but didn't appear in the least bit inviting.

"How about that place?" Neelie pointed across the street.

"Dior?" Tamar followed Neelie's gaze.

"No, next to it. Looks like a busy bar or restaurant. Surely, if my father worked here, he would have gone there to eat lunch. Someone might know where he is."

They crossed the street and shielded their eyes to look in the window. The sign read *Weber Brewery*, and patrons filled the tall tables, drinking beer and chatting. A layer of smoke hovered in the air.

"Why don't you go in, Daniel? I don't see any women in there. Maybe it's a gentlemen's club. We can wait out here."

"All right, but what should I ask?"

Tamar shrugged. "Just ask them about the gallery across the street—whether it's closed for good. Who owns it. If anyone live upstairs. Ask if there's someone we can contact—"

Neelie interrupted. "Ask them if they know my father—Willem Haan. Tell them he's Dutch."

Daniel nodded but stuffed his hands into his pockets and remained where he was.

Tamar gently clasped his arm. "What's wrong?"

"You forget I don't speak French that well. How am I going to ask all those questions?"

"I forgot about that. I'll come with you." Tamar glanced over her shoulder. "Coming, Neelie?"

With a brush of her skirt, her tante nodded.

The moment they walked in the door, smoke enveloped Tamar, causing her to wipe her eyes at the sting in the air. Resisting the urge to cover her nose, she focused on the array of art that covered the walls, most of which looked like parodies of famous masterpieces. In one, Mona Lisa rode on a bike and waved. In another, Venus de Milo wore a pink-and-white swimming suit. A pianist wearing a fedora played Gershwin on a beat-up upright piano. The only other female in the place propped her chin on her fists, staring adoringly at the cigar-smoking pianist.

Neelie waved a hand in front of her nose. "Wish they'd open a window. That's what we do at the center. It helps when our residents play cards."

Daniel whispered close to Tamar's ear, "Who would be the best person to talk to?"

"How about the bartender? There are two. Let's head to the older one. You can order us drinks, and we can ask him."

He took her hand, Neelie following close behind. Daniel looked back. "What would you like? How about an Orangina?"

"Yes, please. Ever since I saw the poster on the kiosk, I've wanted to try one." Once they reached the bar, Tamar read his uneasy eyes. "Say, 'trois Oranginas, s'il vous plaît.'" He nodded, then practiced what she said until the bartender walked up and put three napkins in front of them.

Then the man whose sparse gray hair and bushy mustache matched his orange plaid vest placed two meaty hands on the bar. "*Vous désirez, Monsieur?*"

"Trois…Oranginas, s'il—"

"Yes, sir. Right away." The man bent down, then popped up with three orange-shaped bottles. Daniel almost looked disappointed when the man answered in English. Tamar giggled and squeezed his arm, then moved away so Neelie could stand close to the bar. The man placed three glasses next to the bottles and stuck a tall spoon in each.

"Sir?" Neelie cleared her throat and spoke louder. "Sir, would you answer a few questions for me…us?"

The man looked up, three parallel lines forming above his bushy brows. "What's that accent?

"Nederlanders, we are," Tamar said. Although the war was but a bad memory now, people still didn't trust. "And we're wondering if you know of a Dutch man, an artist—"

"My father," Neelie interrupted. "Willem Haan. I'm trying to find my father. Last time I saw him was over thirty years ago." Her hands fidgeted.

The bartender slung a dishtowel over his shoulder. "And why do you think I would know this man?"

Daniel placed his hands on the edge of the bar and leaned forward, stopping every sentence or so for Tamar to translate. "We received word that Mr. Haan may have worked at the Danvers Gallery across the street. He was perhaps an artist there or worked as an art broker back in the early thirties? The gallery looks as though it's out of business now."

The man's lines softened. "Yes, the war wasn't kind to the art world in Paris, especially the galleries around here. It's been almost four years, and many have yet to reopen. But that one across the street? It opens from time to time. I've only worked here the last couple years, but I've heard tell this bar was full of artists and poets sharing a glass and a tale. Old man Danvers across the street was our best customer back then—or so I've heard—but he's been dead for years."

"Oh," was all Neelie said, but her sagging shoulders and solemn face showed her dejection.

Tamar gave her a side-armed hug. "We'll find him, Tante. It's just going to take some time."

The barkeep must have noticed the change in her countenance because he pointed at the far corner. "See that man sitting at the back table all by himself? That's one of the originals from before the Great War, even. He was a close friend of Danvers and his wife, and he might be able to give you more information than I can. His name is Emile Savard."

Daniel removed his wallet to pay, but the man held up a hand. "On the house, Monsieur. Don't like people to walk out of here unhappy."

"Thank you. You've been very helpful." Daniel left a few francs on the bar, then took Tamar's elbow.

"Neelie, do you want to go talk to the man?"

She nodded and turned, lifting her chin. "While we're here, we have to follow every lead." They headed to the back, circling tables full of boisterous revelers. A soccer team took up the most space and obviously had won their game by the number of glasses raised and clinked.

The back of the bar was for the serious drinkers, Neelie noted. The noise level and the lights dimmed. One man held onto his drink while he slept. Two friends huddled close. At another table, a woman whose head bobbed appeared to be falling asleep as well. One good thing—it was quieter back here.

The man in the corner came into view—white hair, dressed in a proper black suit. He nodded and swilled his drink in time to the music. A closer view showed a wrinkled suit, an unshaven face, and a sardonic expression.

He didn't seem surprised by the three of them approaching his table. In fact, a smile spread across his face. *"C'est un plaisir."* He removed his foot from a chair and waved an arm toward Neelie. "Madame?" Then he stood to grab a chair from the adjacent table.

Daniel motioned for Neelie to sit in the chair closest to the man, pulled out a seat for Tamar, then took one for himself.

Good. It was hard enough to understand French without all the noise intruding. And Tamar would be close to translate. Fatigue from a long day of travel brought a yawn from Neelie, yet excitement filled her. This man might know her father, and despite a plethora of unsettling feelings for the man, she longed to see her papa.

Elbows propped on the tables, both she and Tamar leaned close to introduce themselves and tell him why they were in Paris.

The man's words slurred when he introduced himself. "Name's Emile Savard. Yes, I've known Willem for decades." He drew on a cigarette and tapped its ashes into a filled ashtray while Tamar translated into Dutch and introduced them, telling him that Neelie was Willem's daughter. His eyes widened at the last bit of information.

"Met him back in 1913. We'd arrived in town within weeks of each other, me from Geneva, him from the Netherlands. Don't know what we were thinking, but we both left everything to break into the art scene here, and the scene was hot." When he glanced up, he must have realized his *faux pas* at the sight of Neelie's crestfallen eyes. "Sorry, Madame. I didn't mean it the way it sounded."

Neelie shook her head. "It was a long time ago. Please continue."

He took another swig of his drink. "As a matter of fact, we met right here." He pointed a gnarly finger at the barstools. "Old man Danvers, who owned the gallery across the street, liked to give stray cats like me and your father a chance. He hired us to do reproductions of the masters—caricatures, really." He pointed at the framed pictures around the room.

Neelie longed to ask him if any belonged to her father, but she needed information more.

"They sold like umbrellas in a deluge. After work, we'd meet over here, hobnobbing with philosophers, authors, artists—anyone with an opinion. It was a good life until the Great War." He stopped and motioned to a server to bring them each a drink.

Tamar translated what he'd said, and they each shook their heads at the offer.

Neelie couldn't contain her excitement. She blurted out, "Is he…is he still alive?"

The man didn't answer, busy focusing on rolling another cigarette—his second since they'd joined him.

Neelie inclined her head toward the two of them. "We're lucky to have found him. I just wish he'd answer my question." She nodded for Tamar to translate her question again.

He glanced up, then licked the edges of the tobacco paper.

Once the server had brought Emile a drink, Daniel paid the bill. The old man nodded his thanks.

"Anyway, during the war, nobody was interested in art or hanging out to talk about it. Your father had a conscience—that was for sure. Talked about his daughter a lot—I assume he was talking about you—and his wife, but he said he'd made his bed. We all had. During the war, your father vanished for a few years. Figured he went back home."

Neelie shook her head. "No, I never saw him again. Is he—"

"Well, I found out later, he'd gone to one of them big castles on the Loire—Chenonceau, I think he said when he came back. Wasn't he a doctor or something back in the Netherlands?"

"No, he was a pharmacist, but he knew a lot about remedies."

"Ah. Yeah, he helped me through a bout of pneumonia or something. Well, that conscience of his made him up and take care of injured soldiers. They'd set up a makeshift hospital of sorts in the castle. Since we weren't French, we couldn't enlist, but that was his way, I guess. His way of doing penance for..."

That sounded like her father. Neighbors used to come to their house at all hours seeking medical help from him. He even delivered a baby. It made her proud—a foreign feeling, since she'd quashed the goodness of the man from her heart.

"Came back a different man. Didn't talk as much or laugh as much, but he had a new-found determination to create art. Sometimes worked all night on his paintings, then he threw them in the fireplace when they didn't meet his standard."

All this was interesting, but she wanted to know what her father was doing now. Where did he live? Was he the one who had moved the curtain? But she wouldn't rush this man. He was the only connection they had, and who knew how much time they had left?

Emile blew a smoke ring that meandered upward, changed to a more amorphous shape, then slowly vanished. "After the war, Old Man Danvers died, leaving his wife to run the gallery. They'd been like parents to a lot of us young artists. Your father moved into a room above the gallery and assisted her in running the place. Madame Danvers appreciated what he did because she was getting on herself, and I think it helped Willem deal with the guilt he felt about leaving his family back home."

"Does he live there now?" Indeed, if her father was this close, she needed to go to him. Was this urgency from God or because of that picture? Emile was busy waving down the server for another drink but didn't ask if they wanted one this time.

"The gallery was a big success. This whole quarter became a center of art and culture in the twenties and into the thirties, so I don't think it was due to Willem's great business skills. It was just a good time for art all over Paris—the post-Impressionists, the Cubists, the Fauvists—everyone sold their art, and they all showed up here at this bar. Willem didn't drink a lot, though he'd come over for his dinner most nights. Madame Danvers died in the mid-thirties, leaving the business to your father."

Hmph. Neelie should be happy her father attained his dream in life, but how could she? Her mother died without her husband beside her, and he'd missed all the important moments in her own life. Her graduation, her marriage, Jan. *Weren't they good enough for him? No, stop thinking such things, or bitterness will take residence in my heart and turn me into a wrinkled prune of a woman.*

Tamar squeezed her hand under the table. She understood. Instead of drowning in bad feelings, Neelie lifted her chin and said, "Continue, please."

"Not much more to tell. The Nazis moved in, and the art world plummeted." He waved his hand toward the distant street. "Just look around. So many empty galleries. Hitler didn't appreciate modern art. Called it 'degenerate.'" He *tsk*ed. "Imagine Matisse and Van Gogh being degenerate. So most artists went into hiding during those years."

Tamar leaned forward. "So what happened to Neelie's father?"

Emile leaned back and twirled his empty glass. "That man—" His head wagged back and forth. "Carried the guilt on his shoulders like an anvil. Willem couldn't sit still or retreat when the Nazis showed up. See that corner over there?" He pointed with his chin at a table hidden from view by a supporting column. "Willem used to meet there with Isabelle LeClair."

Neelie's eyes darted to Daniel and Tamar. "The art expert who works at the Jeu de Paume?"

He upturned the glass, then motioned for a refill. "One and the same. During the war, that woman saved millions of francs worth of masterpieces by moving them out of the city. Right under the Nazis' noses. Ha!" The server came with a drink and took the empty glasses.

Why had her father been meeting with Isabelle LeClair? Was it more than a business relationship? Her shackles were rising.

Emile blew out a line of smoke, and his head wobbled as he took a drink. "Your father had a death wish. He wanted to do his part, but he was too old to join the Resistance. So he closed up the studio across the street and helped Isabelle move the art out of Paris to some chateau on the Loire south of here—not the same one he'd worked at during the other war. This time, I think it was Chambord.

Anyway, he and a bunch of others transported art from the Louvre and other museums via flower trucks, hearses, ambulances—you name it. If he'd have been caught, it would have been the firing squad. But Willem was like one of those cats with nine lives, you know? Used 'em all and probably borrowed a few."

It did her heart good to know her father was still a hero, even if he'd abandoned the family. Difficult times brought out the bad or the good in people. It was time to end this visit. She motioned to Daniel, who pushed to his feet, took out his wallet, and left a ten-franc note on the table. In strained French, Daniel thanked the man and asked point-blank where they could find her father.

"Why, he's become a recluse of sorts." He stood and motioned with his forehead toward the street. "Still lives above the gallery. Madame Danvers left it to him in her will. We never see him. He could be long gone, for all I know." His eyes widened when he realized what he said, and he hurriedly began rolling another cigarette.

So it *was* her father at the window. Had he recognized her? How could he after thirty plus-years? Neelie pressed to her feet. He probably had put himself on self-imposed isolation out of guilt. Nederlanders always did that—straining under a guilty load for what happened during the war. She saw it every day at the rehab center. "How do we get past the door? It's locked, and he didn't answer when we knocked."

He lifted a shoulder. "Throw a rock at the window? Better yet, you could meet with Isabelle LeClair. Heard she was in town again after spending years in Germany tracking down stolen art."

Neelie couldn't prevent the frown from forming. Why would that woman have a better chance of convincing him to open the door than his own daughter? Still, it had been decades, and her mother had been dead for years. The irony that her son would be working with Isabelle LeClair was not lost on her.

Emile interrupted her thoughts. "Try the window first. If that doesn't work, maybe Madame LeClair can draw him out. At least it's legal. If those don't work, you could go to the police and have them break in, or you could break into the gallery yourselves."

So close and so far away. Neelie lifted her eyebrows and sighed. She turned toward Daniel. "How's your pitching arm?"

He laughed, shook the man's hand, and asked Tamar to say

thank you for all the information Emile had given them.

As they turned to leave, Emile touched Neelie's arm. "Your father is a wonderful man and a very good artist. I hope your reunion with him is everything you want it to be."

As they left the bar, Neelie swiped her hand over her clothes to rid them of the ashtray smell, then she stared at the window on the second floor. "What do you think we should do?"

Tamar linked arms with her. "I think we should forego throwing a rock and breaking your father's window and head to that restaurant in Les Halles where the onion soup is supposed to be the best in town—loaded with cheese and French bread. It's too late to go to the Jeu de Paume today, but tomorrow morning, we can bring the painting with us and meet with Isabelle LeClair at the museum. As my uncle from New York used to say, 'kill two birds with a stone'— though I never understood such violence." She turned to Daniel. "What's the name of the restaurant?"

"Au Pied de Cochon." He scoffed, his nose crinkled. "Pig's foot. No self-respecting Jew should step foot in it. But if the soup is good—"

Neelie cut one more glance at the room above the abandoned studio. While they'd been in the bar, nighttime had fallen, streetlights had come on, and the stars twinkled above. But the room that belong to her father was as dark as the shadows behind her.

The power of money was universal, wasn't it? Whether deutschmark or franc, a few slipped between the fingers could get a man whatever he wanted, especially if the man was hungry for good cigarettes and wine. A mere ten had bought Erich the name of the man across the street. Willem Haan. A pack of Gitanes had brought him the information that the doctor and two woman were after. Visser's father. But what his money couldn't purchase was why they'd brought the painting to Paris.

Chapter Seventeen

"Oh yes, Corrie! Terribly! I've felt for him [the Nazi informant]
ever since I knew—
and pray for him whenever his name comes into my mind."
~ Betsie ten Boom

The aroma of baked bread and coffee greeted Tamar when she threw open the balcony doors to a new dawn kissing the trees bordering the sidewalk. Dishes and silverware clinked below. Now that they were here, she didn't want to waste a moment.

"Wake up, darling," she said. When Daniel didn't respond, she playfully bounced on the end of the bed. Daniel mumbled something and covered his head with a pillow. She leaned close, lifted up a corner of the pillow, and blew in his ear. He slapped at the pillow. "C'mon. I'm starving."

He turned over and pulled her close. "How can you be hungry after that dinner last night? They replaced the bread basket three times." Daniel grinned and ran a hand through his disheveled hair. "All right. How can I resist those dimples? While I take a quick shower, why don't you go next door and jump on Neelie's bed?"

"*D'accord, mon amour.*" She pranced over to the door connecting the adjoining room and lightly tapped. "Neelie? Are you up?"

Moments later, Neelie, her hair still in curlers, opened the door while tying the sash around her robe. "Good morning. Isn't it a lovely day?" She glanced at Tamar's dress and shoes. "I love your polka-dotted frock. Is that new?"

Tamar twirled around. "Hadassah lent it to me. I like the way it swings, and I have the cutest hat to go with it. How long do you need before we can go down to breakfast?"

Neelie checked her watch. "It's already nine-thirty. Yesterday must have tired us out. I've already showered and done my devotions, so I can be ready in ten minutes."

"Sounds good. Daniel's in the shower. Think I'll go down for a coffee. Meet me down in the cafe." Tamar stopped at the bathroom door. A bad Dutch version of *"La Vie en Rose"* blended with the shower water. He'd never hear her over that. She scribbled a note on the hotel stationery, leaving it by his wallet. After climbing in the elevator, she remembered the painting. The whole reason they were here. Tamar darted out before the elevator door closed but ran into a well-dressed man wearing a fedora coming in. "Pardon, Monsieur."

The man nodded, and the door closed between them.

She dug in her dress pocket for the hotel key. Oh no, she'd left it on the table. This day wasn't starting out well, but it was due to her own carelessness. Daniel would never hear her knock through his rendition of Edith Piaf. She pushed the elevator button once again.

It immediately opened, revealing the same man reading a newspaper. She apologized and scooted to the corner of the cubicle. They both faced the door, their eyes focused on the ticking floor number above it. He looked familiar—at least, the cut of his suit did. Her gaze darted to his hands. Angular, manicured nails—hands that had never suffered a callus.

He must have noticed because he made a comment about the weather. Safe. The man slapped the newspaper against his palm.

"Ja, ik hou van de zomer," she responded.

He nodded, checked his watch, and the elevator door opened. But wait—They'd just spoken in Dutch. The thought so unnerved her, she almost ran into a server carrying a tray of coffee cups. Tamar jumped back into the elevator. "I'm sorry. I mean, *pardon.*"

The woman smiled. "It's quite all right, Madame." Then she continued to the café seats outside.

If there had been a tall plant nearby, Tamar would have scurried behind it. This place was so elegant. Had she been in the company of toddlers for so long that she'd forgotten the simple graces of society?

Tamar headed toward the canopied café tables outside the lobby. What she really wanted was to experience what her Belgian French mother had told her about a proper French breakfast. A *petit pain* or a croissant with fresh butter and French jam. And of course, a *café crème*. Once outside the lobby, she sniffed the breakfast scents of coffee and pastries, enjoyed the chatter of nearby birds, and allowed herself a few seconds to close her eyes to feel the summer breeze.

"Madame? Would you like breakfast?"

Her eyes flew open. A man with a pencil-thin mustache stood waiting for her response. "Oui, merci. Une table pour…trois, s'il vous plaît."

"*Bon*, Madame. Follow me." He led her to a small round table with three chairs positioned in the same direction, facing the sidewalk. How very French. Once the server left with her order of a *café au lait*, she allowed herself a breath. How many times had she dreamed of this? Ever since her mother had described Parisian life in a Jewish neighborhood called Le Marais where her mother had spent summers as a teenager with a French aunt, Tamar had wanted to visit this city.

The server returned with a basket of various types of croissant, brioche, and petit pain. He placed before her a knife, tiny spoon, and the smallest cup of coffee she'd ever seen. She slowly lifted the cup, her baby finger straightened, and took a sip. Oh, this was strong. So strong that the cream didn't help.

"It takes getting used to," a familiar voice said next to her. She glanced sideways. The man in the elevator, a Nederlander, obviously. "I prefer a good cup of Dutch coffee."

Tamar offered a weak smile. "I will get used to it." She ripped off a small bit of petit pain as her mother had taught her and used her knife to spread a bit of butter and jam from a small glass jar that read, *Confiture au Bleuet.* The bread tasted just the way she'd imagined it. Crunchy on the outside, soft on the inside.

"So what's a pretty Nederlander doing in a Paris café?"

Her gaze sprang up from her plate, her lips tightening at the low growl of the voice. Clipped. Underhanded. She didn't dare look or answer. No, she'd pretend she hadn't heard. If she hadn't been so eager to start the day, Daniel and Neelie would be with her. Where were they? She stirred her coffee more than it required and checked her watch.

"I'm sorry. That was forward of me. Forgive me. It's just that there are so few of our people here. May I ask where you are from?"

Tamar sipped her coffee and replaced the cup. "I'm from Haarlem. And you?" She managed a clumsy smile.

"Amsterdam." He leaned over and offered a hand. "Dedrich Smit, art dealer, at your service."

Art dealer? She swallowed, hesitant to shake the man's hand, but not doing so would be…uncomfortable. Tamar offered her hand, then quickly busied herself cutting another piece of bread. Was this a God thing? How fortuitous that a Dutch art dealer would be sitting next to her in a French café. Perhaps he knew Mr. Danvers' art gallery, or better yet, Neelie's father, since he was from the Netherlands. Sometimes it was hard to tell a coincidence from God's interventions. "I can't imagine a better place to do art business than Paris," she said, with a glance at the café entrance.

"I agree. Is this your first visit to the City of Lights?" He casually lit a cigarette.

"Yes, although my mother was from Belgium and used to tell us so many stories about her summers here that everything seems familiar to me." She felt herself relaxing. "Sadly, we'll only be here for a few days, so I…we have to pack a lot into a short time."

"May I suggest the Louvre, a stroll along the Seine, and of course, the Eiffel Tower for the view? The Louvre is quite large— ten kilometers, I've been told—but it's worth it." He tapped his cigarette against the ashtray at a fast clip.

Nervous energy. It reminded her of someone. He wasn't as old as her parents or even Neelie but definitely ten years her senior. Perhaps a friend of her brother's. She gave a start. The man was waiting for an answer. "Yes, all those things sound lovely. In fact, we're on the way to visit the Jeu de Paume. Do you know it?"

"Of course. Modern art." His lip curled down. A memory flashed through her of another curled lip that made the person look as if they were sneering. And then he smiled. "Yes, there are a lot of art museums and galleries in this town. It is my second home, so to speak." He set down his spoon and leaned on one elbow. "Tell me, why—?"

Just then, Neelie breezed toward her table, followed by Daniel, his curly locks wet under his hat. The portfolio was slung over his shoulder.

"Sorry it took so long. I couldn't find my passport. Can you imagine? It was in my makeup kit." She took the proffered seat. "I can't wait to try brioche and a cup of tea. Hopefully, Isabelle LeClair will be at the Jeu de Paume today."

Daniel leaned over and kissed Tamar on the cheek and handed her the camera. "You forgot this." Then he took a seat next to her and cut himself off a piece of bread. "What a gorgeous day. Do you think we can parse out some time to visit the Eiffel Tower? Maybe take one of those excursion boats called *Bateaux Mouches* down the Seine?"

She put the strap holding the camera around her neck. "Let's hope we complete our business quickly." It warmed her heart to see her old Daniel sans worry lines and tightened jaw. They needed this time away more than she'd imagined. She cut a sideways glance at the man sitting at the next table. Did she dare introduce him to Daniel and Neelie? Maybe he could open some gallery doors for them. He was now poring over a *Paris Match*, but his position had changed so his back was partially turned toward them.

When Daniel's coffee arrived, his lips pursed at the size of the demi-tasse, but he maneuvered his long fingers through the tiny porcelain handle and brought the cup to his lips. All she saw was his eyes, which were as round as the cup's circumference. "Strong enough to put hair on my chest—not that any more is needed."

She laughed. "You get used to it. Add more cream."

"Don't need any cream in the tea. It's not as good as Dutch tea, but the croissants are amazing, and this jam—I'm going to collect all these little jars and bring them home with me." Neelie patted the portfolio leaning against the wall. "We've brought the painting, so we can leave from here if you have everything, Tamar."

"I do, yes. Let's go to the museum first." She glanced again at the man at the next table. Should she bother him? That inherent shyness of hers always presented an obstacle.

After they'd finished, Daniel left a few franc notes on the table, pulled Tamar up, then retrieved the portfolio from the wall. He handed Tamar a rudimentary map sketched on a piece of hotel stationery. "You're the navigator."

"Lucky me." She grimaced "Nothing worse than reading a map

written in a doctor's penmanship." The art dealer's face was buried in the newspaper, so she didn't say goodbye.

They made their way down the Rue de Rivoli past fancy hotels and chic boutiques. Neelie stopped in front of a shop. "This is the place I was telling you about. Angelina's—the place with the best hot chocolate ever. We must stop here on the way back, okay?"

"Sure, but I'm too full of bread and jam right now." Tamar cupped her hands around her eyes to see inside. So many frocks and jaunty hats. Mostly women filled the restaurant, but there were a handful of men.

Daniel pulled her away. "Where do we go next?"

She squinted at the scrawled print on the map "It appears this road will turn into Place de La Concorde. And then we just look for the museum."

"Easy enough," Neelie said.

They walked four blocks, peering in display windows full of jewelry, cosmetics, or perfume. They didn't dare window shop at Dior or Chanel as a woman and man in stylish suits stood outside the store as if to shoo away the riffraff.

They came to the corner and stopped. "Whoa," they said in unison. Ahead of them was an enormous traffic circle with what seemed like a dozen traffic lanes circling a tall monument.

"That's a Luxor obelisk." Daniel pointed at the tall granite needle in the center of the street. Even from a distance, the hieroglyphics on it were visible. "Less dangerous than its predecessor."

"Don't keep us in suspense." Neelie's eyes lit up.

"It stands in the same place as a certain guillotine that beheaded—"

"King Louis and Marie Antoinette." Tamar sliced at her neck. "'Let them eat cake.'"

"Not just royalty. Lavoisier, the father of chemistry, died there as well."

Neelie shook her head slowly. "Can't even imagine having my head chopped off in front of the crowds, but so many French people died of starvation to fund Marie Antoinette's lavish parties at Versailles. Hmph."

"Well, everything looks like a postcard." She aimed the camera hanging from a strap around her neck and took a flurry of pictures.

Daniel chuckled. "Whoa, girl. You know how much it's going to cost to have them developed?" He glanced at the map and then peered up. "I think the museum is over there near the park—see those iron gates?"

Neelie held a hand up in protest. "No way am I going to cross all those lanes with speeding cars. Look, they don't even have lines on the road."

"Okay, we'll walk around. I don't want to die either," Daniel laughed.

Once in the park, they passed a lovely pond where dozens of miniature sailboats floated as children jumped up and down and pointed at theirs.

Tamar's arms circled her chest. Daniel gave her a knowing look and placed an arm around her shoulders. "I know what you're thinking. It's only been one day."

She nodded. "I just wish the twins were here to play in this park. Peri would love to float his own little sailboat. We should buy him one while we're here. At least we have a bathtub."

Neelie chuckled. "That's one way to make him take a bath." They circled a Greek building with arched windows, looking for the door or a sign as to its identity. "Of course, we'd walk around the whole building," Neelie groused, when they finally arrived at the entrance to the Jeu de Paume.

A man in a uniform opened the door for them. "May I help you?" he said in French.

Daniel eyed Neelie and Tamar, then answered for them. "We would like to meet with Madame LeClair. Is she in today?"

Three lines formed between the guard's peppered eyebrows. Tamar expected them. If this woman was as important to the art world as Neelie had said, why would she meet with three strangers from the Netherlands? Neelie must have had the same thought. She touched Daniel's arm.

"Monsieur, tell Madame LeClair that Willem Haan's daughter wishes to speak with her." The man's furrows remained implanted on his face. "Please, sir. It is important."

His lips pursed, and he eyed the three of them. Tamar said a quick prayer, and she assumed the others added theirs because he eventually nodded, went to a nearby phone, and turned his back to them.

Neelie looked at Tamar and steepled her hands. This *was* important. Important for both of them. It struck her like a thunderbolt—this trip was not about justice. It was all about forgiveness. The picture was the conduit. For Tamar, it was the Nazis in general, and Margot and Klaus Sneider in particular. Even if Officer Bergman wasn't alive, she still needed to forgive him. For Neelie, it was a father who had abandoned her. But how did one forgive someone *and* forget?

The man returned to their group, and this time, the lines had vanished. He hailed a young woman working at a desk to take his place and motioned for them to follow him. After they walked through the main hall and entered the next room, Tamar's lower jaw dropped. The sign next to the arched door read, *Salle Monet.* Benches sat in the middle of the large room. Framed paintings lined all four walls. Every single one looked familiar. Paintings of water lilies, poppies, the St. Lazare Station. "We have to come back here, Daniel. Can you believe this?"

Daniel pointed at a sign beside the door on the left wall. *Salle Dégas.* Another room stood before them, but the sign was too far away to read.

The guard gestured for them to follow him to the right. A glimpse over his shoulder, and he must have noticed their awe-struck faces. "Yes, this is part of the Louvre collection of Impressionist works." He pointed to the door ahead of them. "That leads to the Salle Cézanne. These were some of the paintings recovered by Madame LeClair, but that is her story to tell, if she wishes. Follow me, please."

They left the grandeur of the gallery and entered a dark, dusty corridor filled with boxes. He stopped at the third office on the right and peeked in. "Madame, the three visitors are here. Would you like them to wait out here?"

"No, send them in," the husky, unaccented voice from within said. "*Merci*, Jean-Paul."

Tamar glanced at Neelie, then Daniel. This was it.

The woman behind the desk removed her glasses and stood to her full height. The sight of her took Neelie aback. The picture she'd painted in her mind of Isabelle LeClair couldn't have been further from the truth. The one word that came to mind was *austere.* This woman standing before her who knew her father well enough to allow them an impromptu meeting, this woman who would be working with Jan for the next few months or years, was no beauty. Tall and thin, gray-streaked hair pulled away from her face in a tight bun, a blousy, colorless dress, a long nose, close-set eyes, and lips that curled down at the corners. She looked more like a spinster aunt than a national heroine.

How rude of her. God didn't approve of her judging by appearance. Neelie stepped forward and extended a hand, then nodded to Tamar to translate her Dutch into French. "Thank you, Madame, for allowing us to meet with you with no notice. My name is Neelie Visser, and you have met my father, Willem Haan, or so I've been told. My son, Jan Visser, will be moving from our country, the Netherlands, to intern here in Paris. He will be working as a legal intern on art reclamation legal cases."

The woman held her hand for a few moments, smiling when Neelie mentioned her father's name, and her eyes widened at the name of her son. "*Enchantée*, Madame. Call me Isabelle. I have known your father for many years. The art community in Paris is grand, but it is also *proche*, very close." She peered at the others.

Neelie's hand went to her lips. "I'm sorry. Let me introduce my niece and her husband. *Je vous présente* Tamar and her husband, Dr. Daniel Feldman. My French is not so good."

Isabelle approached Tamar and Daniel and shook their hands, then leaned against her desk. Though Neelie was tall, Isabelle towered over her by at least three inches, yet there was something graceful about the way she moved. She pushed away from the desk and strode out of the room without a word, returning moments later with a stack of three chairs. "Here. I don't usually have guests in this office. Please, make yourselves comfortable." They each took a chair, positioned it by the desk, and sat.

Neelie looked at the others. Their wide eyes met hers. When did the curator start speaking in perfect Dutch?

Isabelle returned to her chair, sat, and must have noticed their surprise. "God didn't give me looks, but he gave me a photographic memory and the ability to pick up languages easily."

Neelie sat forward. "I'd say God gave you better things." Then she caught her breath, realizing what she'd just said.

An easy smile spread over Isabelle's face. "You are so much like your father. Always so concerned about others' feelings. Now, tell me why you are here, but I don't have much time before I have to head to a meeting."

Neelie looked to the others to gather strength. This was her time to make amends with her father, and it was not a time for reticence. But where to start? She summoned a breath. "The last time I saw my father was thirty-five years ago. He told my mother he'd return in a year if he couldn't make it as an artist. As far as I know, she never heard from him again." Her lower lip quivered, and she was hard-pressed to stop it. They were looking at her. She gestured for the portfolio.

Daniel held it out for her. As she pulled the painting out, she peered up at Tamar. "Would you tell Madame LeClair about this picture?" Neelie needed time to collect her thoughts and her emotions.

"Gladly." Tamar took the picture from Neelie and turned it around so it was facing the curator. "The first time I saw this painting was at a gallery in Haarlem when I was eleven years old. I used to stop and look at it on my way home from school. The second time I saw it was in a concentration camp where the three of us were held prisoners."

Isabelle's eyes met Tamar's, then those of the others, at this piece of information. "I had no idea." She shook her head slowly. "I can't imagine what you went through. But what was this painting doing in a concentration camp?"

Tamar's chin quivered, then lifted. "I was asked—no, forced— to sing for the Führer's birthday. There were celebrations everywhere, I was told. Held for officers and their wives." She swallowed visibly. "It hung in the hall where I performed. The third time I saw it was in my bedroom earlier this year. My childhood bedroom, when I broke into my family's home. The house was seized by the Nazis during the war, and…and my parents were taken away—"

Daniel clasped her arm. "Tamar, you don't have to—"

She pulled her arm away. "No, I'm okay. This is why we are here." Her chin lifted again. "My former house is full of art, jewelry, vases—it's a virtual warehouse of treasures. I'm not proud of the fact that I took the painting, but I knew that the occupants of the house didn't own it either. The Hamels owned the gallery in Haarlem where the painting was displayed, and the gallery was taken away from them also."

Isabelle pushed away from the desk. "So you want to know who owns the painting." Her face softened. "Believe me, I don't mean to diminish what you have gone through, but your story is a universal one. It's been the story of my life for the last decade. Now if you'd like—"

Neelie interrupted. "Madame, I know you're in a hurry, but there's a bit more to this story. The girl in that painting is me, and the painter was my father. So that is why we are here. Tamar needs justice, and I need closure. My father has to be in his seventies, and I need to talk to him, find out why he left, and then I must forgive him. My Lord requires that of me."

Isabelle stared at Neelie for a long moment, then held her hand out toward the painting. "May I?"

Tamar handed it to her.

Neelie could feel a frown form. Why wasn't the woman responding to her plea? Didn't she understand how difficult coming to Paris, coming to this office, was? Art types. They were so involved with pictures they didn't understand flesh-and-blood people.

A quiet titter interrupted her thoughts.

The curator's knuckles covered her lips, and her shoulders were shaking. She peered up and must have seen Neelie's expression. "My apologies. I haven't seen this picture in decades, but your father would show it to anyone who crossed his path. He'd say, 'That's my little girl. She's going to be a famous violinist one day.' Yes, Madame, there's no doubt that Willem painted this picture. Is that why you're here? To determine the provenance of the painting?"

Okay, her father was proud of his daughter, but not enough to be a part of her life. No, she had to forgive him and not dwell on such thoughts. Neelie smoothed the wrinkles from her dress. "Don't you see the Lord's hand in this? That this painting has brought me here to you?" She waved a hand and worked hard to avoid any rancor in her voice. "I'm not interested in what your relationship with my father was, but would you be able to connect me with him?

We are only here for a few days, and it is important for me to meet him—to clear things between us before it's too late."

The woman put the painting down, and her arms pressed tightly across her thin chest, but a gentle smile curved her lips. "If you're implying that your father and I were romantically involved, you couldn't be further from the truth. The art community here in Paris, especially between the wars, was small and close-knit. We looked out for one another. Since I worked at the Louvre, then the Jeu de Paume, I did what I could to help further the local artists' careers if I saw potential. So you see, Madame, our 'relationship,' as you call it, was purely platonic."

Neelie's head lowered, wincing at the fact that she couldn't hide her feelings. How she hoped her jealous assumptions hadn't put Jan's internship in jeopardy.

"Madame," Daniel said. "We received a tip that her father lives above a gallery on Rue Royale, so we went to the place yesterday, but it appeared to be out of business, and no one answered our knock."

"You went to the right place. Willem has become somewhat of a recluse. Oh, you should have seen him during the war. He worked day and night moving paintings from the Louvre to a safe place in the Loire. If it weren't for his herculean efforts, we would have lost irreplaceable masterpieces of Matisse, Van Gogh, Degas, Manet, and so many others. But since the war ended, the art world here in Paris has been slow to recover, and the gallery he promised to run for Madame Danvers has struggled. It might do your father a lot of good to see you. Willem has talked of you and your mother so often, and I'm sure just seeing you would do more than you know to help him. He is not a well man."

Neelie was about to ask what was wrong with him when Isabelle looked at her watch.

"Oh, I must dash." The curator stood. "Meet me in front of the gallery on Rue Royale at six this evening, and I'll see if I can beg entrance from him." She circled her desk, rummaged for a file, and dashed out the door before anybody could say a word.

Neelie looked at the others for their thoughts. Somehow this meeting had taken a turn she hadn't expected, and she didn't know what to think. Tamar nodded, her eyes reassuring.

Daniel leaned over and enveloped Neelie in a warm hug. "It's good, Tante. Today you'll meet your father—"

Tamar interrupted. "And one of the top art experts in the world verified that the painter was Willem Haan. Now we just have to figure out if someone bought it from him. This is the best possible outcome, don't you agree?"

Neelie sniffed and rubbed her nose. "I guess. Don't know what I expected."

Daniel kissed her temple. "It's been an emotional time for you. I'm sure your stomach must be tied up in knots, but you'll have closure tonight."

"One way or another," she mused. "What if he refuses to see me? If it was him in the window last night, maybe that's why he didn't answer the door."

"You're still a young woman, Tante, but you have aged a bit since you were the little girl in that picture." He chuckled. "You know what you always tell us? Don't invite trouble. And think about it. Two people have told us how much your father bragged about you. Does that sound like someone who doesn't want to see his daughter?"

"No. But what if he's dying? Or what if he's—"

Tamar linked arms with Neelie. "Let's go see the Eiffel Tower. What do you think, Daniel?"

"After we enjoy some hot chocolate at Angelina's," he said.

Neelie loved these two. Even though they weren't blood relatives, she couldn't imagine two more devoted friends. "I see what you two are doing and love you both for it. Let's go get ourselves some *chocolat chaud* and a pastry or two—one of those Napoleons or a tarte."

Tamar put the painting in the portfolio and handed it to Neelie, then grabbed her sweater. "Maybe we can come back here to see the paintings? What do you think, Neelie?"

She headed to the door and glanced back at Tamar. "If there's time. Of course, we have to visit the Lou—"

Isabelle LeClair blocked the entrance, her face solemn. "I'm sorry, Madame Visser, but we just received a telephone call from a person who said he is the legal owner of your painting."

Chapter Eighteen

"Worry does not empty tomorrow of its sorrow. It empties today of
its strength."
~ Corrie ten Boom

"What caller?" Tamar seized her husband's arm. "What
do you mean?"

Neelie pressed the portfolio close to her chest. "I don't
understand."

Isabelle LeClair's jawline tightened, and lines framed her lips,
yet Tamar couldn't read her face. "I am sorry, but that's all I know
right now. It is customary when ownership of a painting is
questioned, the museum holds on to it until we can determine its
provenance." She held out her hand, and a small smile appeared.
"Trust me. I believe your story, and I will put this painting in a safe
place, so no one will touch it until we get to the bottom of this
situation."

Tamar's eyes darted from the unreadable face of her husband to
the drooped jawline of her tante, to the tall, thin woman who blocked
the doorway. "But what about our meeting with Neelie's father
tonight? We wanted to return the painting to him."

The curator held up a palm and nodded. "We will take it to him,
but the artist loses his rights to the picture if someone can prove that
they purchased the painting in good faith. My staff and I need to talk
to the caller before I can give it to you." A frown cragged her
forehead. "Doesn't it seem strange that the caller informed us of his
ownership at the same time you were here in the museum? Who

knew you were coming here?"

Tamar shrugged. "No one. We don't know anyone here—"

Neelie interrupted. "Wait. What about the man from the bar across the street from the gallery? What was his name?" She glanced at the two of them.

"Emile Savard," Daniel said.

Isabelle smiled. "Ah, Emile. That naughty man. Too much talent and too much drink, but he has a good heart. He was good friends with the Danvers and your father."

"We spoke to him yesterday," Neelie said. "Said he'd known my father from the early days when they both arrived in Paris as starving artists. He mentioned you and said my father worked with you in secreting art out of Paris."

"Yes, he did. Maybe in some way, I can repay your father for his help during the war by orchestrating a meeting between you and him. We'll still meet on Rue Royale, and I'll bring the painting since your father may be able to fill in the missing pieces of ownership, at least while it was in Paris." She looked at her watch, then motioned for the portfolio. "I'll put this in a safe place until we meet at six."

Somehow the afternoon passed with a gray pallor, not due to the weather because the sky couldn't be any bluer. But someone had tailed them, knew about the painting, and wanted to rip it from their hands. But who could it be?

Yes, the chocolat chaud at Angelina's was richer than any drink Tamar had ever tasted—almost like drinking liquid fudge. Well-dressed patrons filled the restaurant, chattering while enjoying tarts and eclairs and ice cream and little sandwiches. The gilded décor suggested the surrounding of a gigantic golden birdcage.

Tamar's appetite had vanished at the Jeu de Paume. They'd gone over every possible person who could have called the museum—even Neelie's father and Margot's husband. But Daniel had pointed out that Mr. Sneider didn't know about the painting, and he certainly didn't know about the Jeu de Paume. And they hadn't taken the painting with them to the bar, so neither Monsieur Savard nor her father could have known about it. That left Madame LeClair who appeared to be telling the truth, but maybe she wanted the painting for herself. All this convoluted talking was giving Tamar a headache.

Finally, Neelie had waved a dismissive hand and said God would work out the details.

To walk off their desserts, they'd strolled through the Tuileries Gardens but stopped to enjoy the giggles and gasps of children as they watched the puppet, Guignol, pound his wife with a limp stick in the puppet theater.

The Eiffel Tower hadn't lifted Tamar's spirits. They'd headed up its steep staircase, so narrow that only one person could fit sideways—dozens of people ahead, dozens behind. It wasn't long before claustrophobia set in the small space devoid of fresh air. When they finally emerged from the stairs to the third level, she inhaled deeply, only to see her husband bent over a trashcan. The view of the city, however, was breathtaking, and the clear sky allowed them to see forever—even Belgium in the distance. They bought a few souvenirs for the twins and postcards for Jan and Hadassah.

Neelie leaned against a wall away from the crowds that hovered over the railings to take pictures or looked through the tower viewers at Sacré Coeur. Tamar noticed and joined her. "Are you okay?"

She nodded. "My feet hurt a bit. Would it be okay if we returned to the hotel, maybe took a nap? I feel as if I can't keep my eyes open."

"Of course. I would also benefit from some quiet time."

Daniel, looking green, leaned against the wall, and agreed that they'd done enough sightseeing for the day.

At six o'clock sharp, they were waiting in front of the Rue Royale gallery—still locked, still forlorn-looking—when Isabelle LeClair alit from a taxicab, carrying the portfolio.

After paying the driver, she joined them by the door, giving them each two air kisses near their cheeks. "See? I brought the painting. Now let's go see your father." She motioned toward the parfumerie next door. "They share the same hall upstairs. I know the owner."

The saleswoman peered at them with a raised eyebrow when they entered until she saw Isabelle, then smiled and greeted her in a flurry of French that strained Neelie's ability to comprehend. The two women chatted for a minute. Willem Haan was the only name Neelie understood in the slew of words. Then the woman handed the curator a keyring.

Isabelle indicated with a beckoning finger that they should follow her through a door behind the counter into a narrow room of organized shelves to a staircase. They climbed the dark stairs to a locked door. Isabelle tried the keys until she found the one that unlocked the door. She turned to face Neelie. "Are you ready for this? I haven't seen your father in months, as I have been away on business."

Neelie swallowed, then nodded. The door opened into a nondescript hallway with a dozen closed doors on either side. They headed to the next door on the left.

Isabelle tapped gently on the door and waited for a few long moments. When no response came, she tapped again, this time saying, "Willem, it's Isabelle LeClair. Please open up." A third, louder knock brought no response, so she inserted a key into the lock and pushed the door open.

Neelie didn't know what to expect, but she gripped Daniel's arm, seeking its comfort and strength. The first impression was the smell. Musty, stale, like an attic where the sun has baked the dust onto storage boxes. The small room they entered resembled a dark studio, an easel with a towel-covered canvas as its focal point. Palettes and newspapers and paintbrushes were strewn over the floor, and a tower of food containers balanced on a coffee table. Her mother wouldn't have approved of the clutter.

A rustling came from a door off the main room, followed by a bout of coughing. Neelie met Tamar's eyes. Was it possible that in mere moments, she would see her long-lost father?

Isabelle signaled them to wait while she went to the door. "Willem? It's Isabelle. May I come in?"

Another cough, then a strained, mucous-filled voice answered. "I'm not ready for visitors. Could you come back some other time?"

"I have someone with me you will want to see. May I come in?"

Another round of coughing. "It's not a good time," the plaintive voice said.

Isabelle held up a hand toward them, then entered. Whispers came from the room.

Neelie couldn't wait any longer. She inched through the door.

A bed with sheets and blankets awry and a shock of white hair were the first things she saw. Isabelle was bent over the man, pulling up the covers, then she stepped aside as she saw Neelie, who moved toward the foot of the bed.

Her father—sallow, sunken cheeks above an unruly beard—was staring at Isabelle. "Not now. I'm in no condition to accept visitors."

"Let me fluff your pillow." She gently lifted his head, and for the first time, he noticed Neelie standing at the foot of the bed.

"Who is this?"

Tears streamed from her eyes, unbidden. She swiped at them and sniffed, but more brimmed and slid down. "I'm Neelie, Papa. Your daughter."

Her father squinted at her—her dapper papa who'd waltz her around the living room, then grab her mother, who'd bat at his arm, telling him she had to make supper. Now he lay, a shriveled shell of his former self. She remembered those intense, dark-blue eyes—almost royal in hue— that now contrasted with his pallid skin. Tears slid down and stained his pillow.

"My Neelie, my Neelie," he repeated time and again. Slowly, he lifted an emaciated arm to her.

She looked to Isabelle, who nodded, bringing clenched hands to her mouth, then stepped back. Neelie filled the space where'd she stood and knelt down at the side of his bed, took his hand, and enveloped it in her own. All her mixed-up emotions ebbed away. *Thank you, Lord.*

"God has answered my prayers, Neelie, you are all grown up, and you look so much like your mother." He took a labored breath. "How I have prayed to see you at least once more, and now you're here."

"Yes, Papa, I'm here." She removed a handkerchief from her pocket and dabbed at her nose and eyes. Then she flipped over the same cloth and gently wiped his face. "What's wrong, Papa?"

He shrugged against the pillow, taking her hand in mid-air. "Leukemia. Hardly *leuk*, don't you agree?" A sparkle crept into his eyes—that same glint she'd see when he'd sneak up on her and give her a kiss or pretend to take a coin from behind her ear.

She laughed in spite of herself at the play on words—*leuk* meaning 'nice' in their language.

Isabelle circled to the other side of the bed and sat at its edge. "Oh, Willem, why didn't you let anyone know?"

He smiled at her. "It's good to see you. How was your time in Berlin?"

"Productive, but let's talk about you. What does your doctor say?"

"Later. What's important is, my daughter is here. How did you two meet?" His voice wavered with tears.

Isabelle patted his hand. "Neelie found me. In fact, she brought this." She bent over, unfastened the portfolio, and lifted the painting out. "Remember this?"

His eyes widened, and he let out whoosh of air. "My little girl." His eyes dissolved in tears once again. "I can't believe it's here. Where did you find it, Neelie?"

She smiled through watery eyes. "It's a long story, but first, I want to hear about you. I feel…I feel—"

"I wasn't there for you, child. Or your mother. The biggest mistake I ever made." He closed his eyes and said nothing more for a moment. Neelie leaned forward. Was he asleep? Or worse? Without opening his eyes, he continued, "Your mother warned me that I was letting art take over my life. At the time, I thought she was trying to hold me back. How wrong I was!"

Neelie's voice came out in an unfamiliar croak. "Then why didn't you come back?"

A gasp came out and he cringed, his hands ripping from hers and grabbing his chest. He took deep breaths, holding up his palm to stay her. "It's just a…it will pass in a minute."

Neelie locked eyes with Isabelle, then turned for the first time to find Tamar and Daniel leaning against the door. Gratitude for their support, for their suggestion to come to Paris, filled her. She whispered, "thank you." When she turned around, her father was staring at her, a smile slowly spreading across his thin cheeks.

"You deserve to know, my darling. At first, Anna and I wrote letters, and what little money I had, I sent to her and always enclosed a card for you—a postcard, a little sketch of something I'd seen.

She'd tell me about her day and you, and I'd tell her about mine. But over time, the letters became less frequent. A week would go by, then a month between letters. And then they dried up. It was as if we'd drifted apart, never to find one another again."

What? She'd never received a card or sketch. Was he lying?

He'd noticed her frown. "You didn't receive the cards?"

She swiped a hand across her eye and shook her head. No, she wouldn't believe her mother had withheld something so precious.

"I hurt your mother so much. We loved each other, but we couldn't have been more different. If I could do one thing before I go to God, I would hug you two and never let you go. And please accept my pithy apology. Words can't make up for what I didn't do for you and your mother." His eyes begged her, so vulnerable, so full of pain.

She leaned over and kissed him on the cheek. How could she not forgive him? He wrapped his arms around her, his shoulder quaking, audibly sobbing as if his heart was breaking. Neelie remained in his arms, her breath coming in shudders. Finally, she backed away.

He used the bedsheet to wipe his eyes. "I planned to come home, I did. Then the war broke out, and the borders closed. So seldom was I asked to do anything bigger than myself. These were my thoughts back then—if I could do something to make you, to make your mother, proud, then after the war, I'd return to Haarlem and win your love again—before it was too late. As I couldn't join the French forces, I moved to Chenonceau, to the castle where they'd set up an infirmary for wounded soldiers."

"Like a penance," Neelie whispered.

"Yes." His eyes took on a faraway look, and the corners of his lips curled up. "I was just a pharmacist, but they weren't picky. Learned how to do surgery on the spot. Watched one, assisted with one, then performed my own. Slowly, that guilty fog that followed me everywhere seemed to clear, although I longed to be with you and Anna." He patted her hand and closed his eyes.

No, he couldn't go to sleep yet. "What happened after the war?" She didn't ask the question on her tongue—why he didn't return to Haarlem if he longed so much for them.

He opened one eye. "Well, Madame Danvers, the wife of my mentor, was near eighty and couldn't run the gallery by herself. I owed it to her late husband, who'd taken me in and given me a job, to help manage the gallery. I'd already made a mess of my family. Now I was given a chance to do the right thing—" He held up a shaky palm. "I know. Another bad choice—putting someone else ahead of you. Still, you and your mother were strong—much stronger than I ever was.

"After Madame Danvers passed away, I was ready to sell the gallery which had been left to me. That's when I sent that painting"—he motioned toward the foot of the bed where it lay—"I sent it on consignment to a Haarlem gallery on the Barteljorisstraat, hoping you'd see it, to remember me. Also, the Nazis were encroaching on Paris, already having destroyed works of art in Germany. I decided the painting would be safer in Nederland. Did you see it?"

"No, not until a few weeks ago." Neelie beckoned for Daniel and Tamar to join her. "Father, this is Tamar and Daniel Feldman. Tamar and I worked together at the opera, and our story goes on from there. But Tamar saw the painting at the Hamels' gallery when she was a young girl."

Tamar stepped forward, her hands fidgeting. "Yes, sir, I did. I always loved that painting. It showed up years later twice, but I never knew the painting was of my Tante Neelie."

"Tante?" He frowned and smiled at the same time.

"Not related by blood but by spirit." Neelie linked arms with her. "When you are stronger, I'll tell you our story, but suffice it to say, God brought the picture to me through Tamar, and now we are here to…to—" Words escaped her.

Isabelle piped in. "To follow the provenance, Willem."

A coughing fit took over. Isabelle grabbed a cloth from the nightstand and brought it to his lips. Neelie rubbed a hand over his leg. Was this it? Had she found her father just to have him die? *Lord, give me a chance to ask for his forgiveness.*

His head lolled back, and he gasped for breaths.

Daniel moved forward and ran a hand over her father's forehead. "Tamar, would you bring me some water and another cloth? He's burning up." Circling to the other side of the bed, he turned on the light and quickly checked each prescription bottle that sat on the nightstand, then shook a few pills onto his palm. "I don't know when he last took his medications. I'll give him a dose now."

Tamar returned with a glass of water and a few rags. "This is all I could find."

"Thanks, go check in the other room to see if there are any pain relievers."

Daniel lifted the old man's head. "I'm a doctor. We're going to try to bring your fever down. Swallow these. It looks as though you haven't been taking your medications."

He nodded and closed his eyes. "I didn't see the point, but now—" His lips curved up slightly.

Daniel spilled some of the water onto a rag and wiped the man's brow, then moved out of the way and handed the rag to Neelie.

With a gentle hand, she dabbed at his forehead. "Papa, we have a lot to catch up on, so you have to keep trying now that I've found you. I have a lot to tell you, but first, I want to ask for your forgiveness." Somehow, she knew the prompt had come from God.

His eyes flew open. "No, I need to ask for your forgiveness. Oh, Neelie, I've made such a mess of things. I've been so selfish. Irresponsible. I've caused your mother and you so much suffering. How do I even ask for such a thing after all this time?"

"Papa, I forgive you. Please don't give up because we have so much to talk about."

He raised a hand to touch her cheek. "God has brought you here. I had given up. Didn't think I had anything to live for. But why would you ask for my forgiveness? You didn't do anything wrong."

"My thoughts were wrong. I blamed you for abandoning me and Mam. She never talked about you, and I knew I couldn't ask questions."

"I know. She was a wonderful woman and did the best she could under the circumstances." He struggled to raise his head. "But I can do one thing for you right now. Isabelle, would you bring me a piece of paper and a pen?"

"Certainly." Isabelle rummaged through her bag and pulled out a pad of paper and a pen. "Would you like me to write for you?"

"Please. *To whom it may concern: I, Willem Haan, bequeath the painting of Neelie to my only daughter, Cornelia Haan*...Neelie, what is your last name?"

"Visser. It's Cornelia Visser. Yes, Papa, I married a wonderful man who is with the Lord now, Frans Visser, and I have a son, Jan. He'll be moving to Paris next month. You will get to meet your grandson. Jan is a kind, young man. He's studying to be a lawyer. He will want to meet you, so you must work hard to regain your strength."

Willem lay back, and a satisfied smile covered his face. "Visser. Fisher in Dutch." He reached for Isabelle's hand. "What else do I need to write to ensure this painting becomes Neelie's property?"

She handed it to him. "Sign it and date it. I don't know if it will hold up in court. There is a claim of ownership on it, but this document should help. We assume that it was stolen from the gallery when it was raided by the Nazis, and you were the owner on record at the time. If it were purchased at an auction, then the courts will decide on its ownership."

"Okay," he said. "We'll leave it in your and the Lord's capable hands. Now, the drugs are taking effect, and I feel I should sleep now. Neelie, would you and your friends come back tomorrow? Perhaps I'll be in better form."

She stood. "Of course." Her heart was so full she needed time to reflect. She bent and kissed her father on the forehead. "I am so grateful to find you, Papa. Get some sleep."

Isabelle placed the painting in the portfolio. "I'll hold onto this until we find out more information about the caller. I will also have our attorneys look over your bequest." She tucked the blanket around his neck. "Get well, Willem. We'll be speaking shortly."

***

Tamar took Daniel's hand as they went into the small living room. "Oh my, I had no idea it was dark out. What time is it, Daniel?"

He glanced at his watch, then walked over to a table lamp. "It's almost nine. It doesn't seem possible we've been here for three hours."

She opened the curtains and stared down at the street, now dark and empty except for a single street lamp and dim lights from the bar across the street. "Three wonderful hours," she said.

So much had happened since they'd arrived yesterday. Neelie had finally reconciled with her father, though why had she apologized? Why did the victim need to say she was sorry? She'd have to ask Neelie about it when she was finished visiting her father.

"*Au revoir*," came from the apartment door. They spun around to see Isabelle leave.

"Au revoir, et merci, Madame," Tamar said, but the door had

already closed. She peered at Daniel who stood next to her. "That woman has been a godsend. She is so busy with her work, and yet she gave up her evening to help Neelie meet her father. Jan is a lucky man to intern with a woman of her caliber."

"Blessed, not lucky." Daniel turned to face her, gently smoothing tendrils that had worked their way loose from her chignon. "I should go down and stand with her until the taxi comes. The street's no place for a lone woman."

"Good idea. I'll stay here until Neelie is ready to go." She kissed his nose. "Thank you for coming with us to Paris. I'm so glad you were here to help Willem."

"I'll be back as soon as I can. Then let's go find a café to have dinner. I'm starved."

The door clicked and his footsteps became fainter. She turned toward the window. The tall woman stood at the curb below with the portfolio leaning against her leg. Daniel was right. The street was devoid of light now that the shops were closed. Was Emile sitting at the same table across the street, nursing a drink and smoking one cigarette after another?

Headlights appeared a block away and drove slowly toward Isabelle. The lights on the roof of the car indicated it was a taxi. Good. Her stomach growled. A *croque monsieur* sounded good, or steak frites. Her mother had made them on busy nights when she and Seth were young—the Jewish version with kosher pastrami without cheese. But secretly, Tamar had always wanted to try one with cheese.

The taxi stopped, and Isabelle opened the back door.

Just then, a dark figure—a man with a fedora and a long coat—appeared out of nowhere. He ran toward Isabelle and snatched the portfolio from her hand. She spun around and grabbed for it, but the man jerked it away, pushed her against the taxi, and ran off. Tamar flung open the window and screamed, but it was too late.

A flurry of movement happened at the same time. Isabelle fell to the street. Daniel appeared out of the parfumerie and ran over to her, helping her onto her feet. The cab driver jumped out and circled the car. French voices mingled. Isabelle pointed toward where the man had run. Daniel took off in that direction.

The painting was gone and so was her husband.

Chapter Nineteen

"The first step on the way to victory is to recognize the enemy."
~ Corrie ten Boom

With a frantic sob, Tamar spun around and dashed to the door. *What have I done? All because I stole the painting, Isabelle's injured and Daniel's going to get killed!*

Neelie rushed into the living room. "What happened? Where are you going?"

"Oh, Neelie, I've ruined everything. I have to go after him." She threw the door open and ran to the next door on the right. Was this even the door? She hadn't been paying attention. The knob didn't work. Tamar raced to the next, which opened. She bounded down the stairs, through a bunch of rooms, and out the door. Isabelle was sitting in the cab, rubbing her leg. "Where did they go?"

Isabelle shook her head. "I'm so sorry. I should have been more alert. It was so quick. I'll call the police."

Tamar didn't hear the rest as she ran toward the corner. Was it just a random theft, or was it an intentional robbery of a defenseless woman? Daniel was a fast runner, but what was he was going to do if he caught up to the thief? What if the man had a gun?

She reached the corner and stopped. To the right, bright marquees lit up the street, and crowds of diners sat at cafés along the sidewalk, chattering, laughing. How dare they? To the left, the street was darker. She headed in that direction. Garbage cans overflowed in volume and odor. A dog sniffed through an upturned one. A chill traveled down her spine. The thief could be lurking in any doorway, ready to leap out at her.

A cat screeched, then skittered in front of her into an alley. Tamar froze, her heart pounding in her chest. *Lord, lead me to Daniel.* She listened. This was not a place for a lone woman. The klaxon of a police vehicle or an ambulance sounded in the distance. Taking a step into the alley, she pasted herself against the wall. A moan came from nearby. "Daniel?"

Another moan. "Over here."

She inched past a construction container toward the voice, but the darkness veiled everything behind it. Something skittered under her feet, causing her to leap sideways and fall against the cold metal container. The smell of rot made her cover her nose and mouth with the collar of her dress. Something sticky on the box stuck to her hair.

"Daniel?" As she stepped away, her heel caught in a furrow and sent her to her knees.

"Tamar? Over here, behind the flats."

She pushed to her feet, feeling warm blood and torn hosiery on her knee. The odor grew stronger as she passed an overturned pile of flats. From beneath them, only a pair of legs were visible.

"Daniel?"

A moan. "Tamar, I'm pinned under this stack. Could you try and pull them off? Just enough for me to get out."

"Of course." Tamar lodged her heel behind the flats to keep herself from slipping, then gripped the top side of the first of two piled on top of her husband. "Here goes." She gritted her teeth and pulled up and back, refusing to think about the sticky goo under her fingers. Then she jumped out of the narrow space so she wouldn't be trapped under it as well. "Okay, that worked. One more to go."

"Be careful, honey," Daniel said.

Once she'd pulled the second flat off of Daniel, she scooted into the narrow, dark space and squatted beside him. "What happened? Do you think something's broken?"

"I'm not bleeding. It's just my head." He rubbed it. "The guy pushed me against the stack, which caused them to fall on top of me." He winced. "So I have two bumps." He took her hand and guided it toward a sizable knot on the back of his skull and one on his temple.

"You might have a concussion. Do you feel dizzy? Should I go get help?"

"No." He sighed. "I'm sorry I couldn't catch the guy. I was so stupid to follow him into this alley. He outsmarted me."

"You're not stupid. You're my mighty warrior. C'mon. Let me help you up. Neelie must be out of her mind with worry." It wasn't easy due to the lack of space and the sheer darkness, and she stepped on his foot more than once. "Slowly."

Daniel brushed off his pants and picked at the detritus clinging to his beard. "I need a shower. Can we forego dinner and go back to the room?"

She linked her arm around his elbow. "Let's take a cab home this time." Once out of the alley, they headed to the corner and crossed the street, back to lights, back to safety. "Who do you think the man was? Did you get close enough to see him?"

He sidestepped a divot in the sidewalk and winced. "No, he was wearing a trench coat and a hat. The guy wasn't tall but quick on his feet. I don't think he was a common thief, but I don't know why. He seemed to know what he was doing. You'd think all that Resistance work would have made me more street smart. Now Neelie's picture is gone."

"Don't beat yourself up. As you said, he knew what he was doing. The man was waiting for Isabelle when she came out. It was probably the person who called claiming ownership."

They finally reached Neelie and Isabelle standing in the dim light of the jewelry store.

Neelie frowned when she saw Daniel's soiled clothes and Tamar's bleeding knee. "What happened?"

"Sorry, I couldn't catch him." Daniel rubbed his head. "He outsmarted me, and I ended up under a bunch of flats—"

Isabelle broke in. "Daniel, he had a sizable lead on you. No one could have caught him. Neelie thinks he may be the caller at the museum. What do you think?"

"We thought the same," Tamar said. "The fact he knew we were here means he was following us. I wonder what it is about that picture that makes it worth stealing? It doesn't make sense." She lifted her palm. "Not that it's not a wonderful painting."

Neelie lifted her own hand. "No offense taken. I'm as baffled as you. It has value to me because it was Papa who painted it. And for you, Tamar, it's the mystery of it all—why this picture from your childhood has shown up in Westerbork, and then of all places, your bedroom."

Daniel nodded, then winced and massaged his head. "And it's also something deeper to Tamar. It's a symbol of all she's lost and what others have lost. She took it from the house so she could return it to the owner. And there's that God thing again."

"What is a God thing?" Isabelle's voice drew their eyes toward her.

Did she even know God? Tamar understood the question. Until she'd met Daniel and Neelie, she'd never heard about God referred to in such a familiar way.

Neelie answered, "It's what many people might call a coincidence, but with God, nothing is a coincidence. The fact the painting Tamar took from her bedroom turned out to be a picture of me is an example of the wonderful things God does for us. Think about it, Isabelle. Because of that painting, I got to see my father, who may not have much time. Do you see how the events are more than random occurrences?"

She offered a polite smile. "Whatever it is, I apologize for being so careless. I should have waited until we were all together, but this has never been a dangerous neighborhood. Before the war, the streets were full of artists and philosophers and writers. You should have seen Rue Royale. By the way, the *gendarme* is on their way."

Tamar surveyed the whole street, finding it hard to imagine this dark, lonely place as the center of culture. A rather square car rounded the corner and stopped in front of them. A police officer stepped out, his tallish hat making him almost reach Daniel's height.

Isabelle took over and described what happened in faster French than Tamar could understand. The officer seemed underwhelmed, at best. He took a few notes, nodded a few times, and couldn't get out of there quick enough.

Isabelle pushed away from the wall. "Well, that was a waste of time. He said there's nothing they can do, but at least we did our duty." She tilted her head. "There's a phone booth on the corner. It doesn't look as though any cabs are forthcoming, so I'll call for one."

"Would you share your cab with us? Daniel has an egg on his head from his fall," Tamar said.

She turned. "Of course. And tomorrow, I'll speak with the caller, if he'll even answer. We'll get to the bottom of this."

Tamar caught up with her long strides toward the phone booth. "How? How do you get to the bottom of a thief?"

Isabelle stopped, and a cryptic smile played on her lips. "That's what the boys and I do. Think of us as ferrets. How do you suppose we were able to outsmart Hermann Göring?" She stepped up her pace.

Ferret, indeed. That animal had come to mind when Tamar first laid eyes on the art curator. Tamar headed back to Daniel and Neelie, who sat on the small ledge of the display window. Neelie's feet must be hurting.

Daniel was a sight to see under the lone streetlight. A dark stain of something covered his left cheek, his pants were rumpled and torn, and his hair seemed to have a mind of its own. How she loved him, running after the thief in a foreign town. Her ramshackle hero. Tamar sat down next to him. "How are you feeling? Is your head aching?"

"Not too bad, but I'd like to cut this evening short. What a day of highs and lows. As Charles Dickens said, 'it was the best of times; it was the worst of times.'"

"We'll get the picture back." She leaned against him, a whiff of something akin to turnips emanating from his sleeve.

Neelie took off a shoe and rubbed her foot. "From your lips to God's ears. What is driving that bravado of yours?"

"Isabelle. She seems to think they'll be able to catch the thief because that's what they do. According to her, it's all about connections."

"Well, we certainly don't have connections here in Paris except for Isabelle." Neelie brushed off her skirt and put on her shoe. "Ah, here comes the taxi."

It had stopped to pick up Isabelle at the corner and slowly rolled toward them. Neelie and Tamar joined Isabelle in the back, and Daniel sat in the front. The remnants of the alley were stronger to the nostrils in this closed space.

Tamar tried to ignore the odor. "Neelie, when are you going to see your father again?" It was better to concentrate on the bright spots of the day.

"Hopefully, tomorrow. I wonder if we could find a wheelchair somewhere. I'd like him to get some fresh air. He's been isolated in that apartment far too long."

Isabelle leaned forward. "We have some wheelchairs at the museum. Stop in and pick one up on your way tomorrow. How long are you planning to be in Paris?"

Tamar glanced at Neelie, then at the back of Daniel's head. "We haven't really discussed it, but at least one of our goals has been met. And an important one." She squeezed Neelie's hand.

Daniel shifted to look back at Isabelle. "I need to get back to work, and we don't want to presume on Hadassah's generosity for agreeing to take care of Peri and Zari, our twins." His eyes moved from Neelie to Tamar. "So how about we leave the day after tomorrow?"

He was right. Tamar nodded. Her sister-in-law had rearranged her work schedule so she could watch the twins, and had they not accomplished what they'd set out to do—finding Neelie's father and returning the painting to its rightful owner? Well, the painting wasn't returned in physical form, but Neelie was the rightful owner, and that paper her father signed proved it.

Neelie was chewing on a cuticle, something Tamar had seen her do when she was distressed.

"Tante, I imagine you don't want to leave that soon, now that you've met your father. What do you think?"

She breathed in and nodded. "We have decades to catch up on, and he's so sick. I need to return to work as well, but what if he doesn't make it until I can come back?"

"Jan will be moving here in mere weeks. Maybe you can stay with him so you won't have to stay in a hotel."

Neelie studied her nails. "I've been thinking a bit since we met Papa. The way everything has interwoven shows God's hand—the timing, the disparate events, you, me, Jan. I have a sense that once I'm back in Amsterdam, I should make plans to move here while my father is still with us. For as long as he has. If I don't, I know I'll regret it."

"You could always bring him back to the Netherlands."

"Papa probably doesn't want to return, and even if he does, I only have one bedroom. It's too small for two people."

A pang of guilt filtered through Tamar. Neelie had given up her large house for them. Wouldn't she rather be in a comfortable house on the canal? "What about moving back to Haarlem? Your father would love to see where you spent your adult life, and there's the canal and the park—"

Neelie held up a hand. "Absolutely not. The place is too big for my father and me. And there are too many memories of Frans and everything that happened during the war. Don't even think about moving out!"

Tamar started to object, but Neelie patted her hand.

"I have a strong feeling God wants me here. My father needs healing, not only in his body but in his spirit as well. Plus, with Jan here, it will be a good time for the three of us. Who knows? Maybe I'll learn how to speak French." Neelie waggled her eyebrows.

Isabelle broke in. "That smile on Willem's face when he recognized you was the first sign of happiness I've seen in the man in decades. He's been mourning his choices—your mother and you—for as long as I've known him. Willem just didn't know how to bridge the gap that he caused. Whether it's your God or a coincidence, your presence will help him."

"Thank you, Isabelle. As you can probably tell, I need to do some healing as well. My God, as you called him, doesn't want me to hold onto bitter feelings. That's why I came. To clear the air between us. And you know what? It was easy—so easy. Perhaps if he'd been pompous or successful, it would have been tougher. We all make unwise decisions at times. Fortunately, our God has a lot of patience. How could I not do the same for my father?"

The taxi pulled up in front of the Jeu de Paume, or as close as it could get to it. A lot of activity—lights, voices, the pounding of hammers—came from the park behind the museum.

"What is going on?" Daniel turned to Isabelle as she opened the back door.

"Oh, I forgot. They're putting up kiosks for the annual art festival this weekend. It's always a lot of fun. Neelie, you should bring Willem. And don't forget to come by and pick up a wheelchair. The boys and I will get to work on finding that dirty thief. *Bonne nuit*, everyone."

Chapter Twenty

"There are no 'ifs' in God's world and no places that are safer than
other places.
The center of His will is our only safety."
~ Corrie ten Boom

Tamar yawned and scratched the back of her head. She'd
lost the battle of sleeping when the alarm clock read three, and by
five, she was already dressed and sitting on the balcony. Daniel's
light, regular breathing indicated he'd suffered no such battle, so she
tiptoed around and read the Tanakh in the bathroom. Now it was six,
and she could hear the voices of servers and the clatter of plates and
tableware from the café below. What she wouldn't do for a coffee—
no, an espresso, and more than a demi-tasse. If this was to be their
last day in Paris, she wanted to be alert.

Grabbing her purse, she sidestepped the desk chair that held
Daniel's clothes for the day, then tiptoed out the door. There was
something refreshing about the world before everyone woke up. The
hum of the elevator was the only sound. The door opened to an
empty lobby except for the mustached man behind the check-in
desk, who was putting what she assumed were bills in the rows of
numbered slots. He nodded to her and said, "Bonjour, Madame."

"Bonjour, Monsieur." She grabbed a newspaper off the desk
and headed to the café outside the main door. A man in a vested suit
handed her a one page menu and led her to a table for two against
the wall that looked out on the street.

"Un café, Madame?"

"Un café express, s'il vous plaît."

In minutes, the server set down a tiny cup and saucer filled to the brim with steaming, very dark coffee. A miniature spoon rested on the saucer. Tamar added a bit of cream, just enough to soften the strength of the brew and cool it down. This would be stronger than any coffee she'd ever drunk, but she intended to be alert to every nuance of what may be her last day in the City of Lights.

A sip of the hot drink caused her eyes to water. How could people drink this? She concentrated on reading the front page of *Paris Match*—something about the Vichy government and a picture of General de Gaulle. Another article about a strike of bus drivers. Her limited knowledge of French made it impossible to grasp anything more than the basic facts. Her mother wouldn't be pleased.

"Goedemorgen, Mevrouw. It's a beautiful day today, is it not?" Dutch.

She shifted her glance to the man beside her. Dedrich Smit. The art dealer from the day before. So much had happened since then, yesterday's breakfast seemed a distant memory. Now he sat at the small table next to hers, and she'd been so intent on translating, she hadn't heard him sit down. Like a wily fox, he was. She responded to his greeting and returned to her newspaper, not wanting to encourage conversation.

"How was your day in Paris yesterday? Did you enjoy the Jeu de Paume?"

"Yes, it was quite nice." She didn't add that she hadn't actually visited the art in the Jeu de Paume. "And we climbed to the third level of the Eiffel Tower."

He tapped his cigarette against the rim of the ashtray. "Then perhaps you'll visit the Louvre today."

She shook her head. "I'm afraid we won't be able to. We'll be contending with a wheelchair today, and if the museum is as large as you said, it might be too much to handle. And it's a shame to waste our last day in Paris indoors when it's such a pretty day." Surely, Daniel had woken up by now, although after what he'd encountered the night before, she wouldn't bet on him rising early.

"So this is your last day?" He almost looked disappointed, then his eyes lit up. "I have the perfect suggestion, then. The art festival starts today in the Jardin des Tuileries. It's huge. Artists from all over Europe come to display their works. That's one of the reasons I'm here. There are some rare finds at fair prices. It's close to the Louvre as well. In fact, it used to be the hunting grounds of the king who lived in the Louvre when it was his palace. And there are sidewalks which won't make it difficult to wheel your husband around."

Why did he think it was her husband who needed the wheelchair? She started to correct him, but the server came with her bill. She paid for her coffee, then stood and faced the man. "*Dank u wel*, Mr. Smit, for the suggestion. It sounds like the perfect solution."

"What a glorious day." Neelie marveled at the dappled light filtering through the broad-leafed oak trees that lined the sidewalks. She sniffed deeply of the delicious aromas emanating from a patisserie on the other side of the street. "May we stop at that bakery? I'd like to take back some macarons to the staff at the rehab center. And maybe pick up a brioche for myself. We forgot about breakfast."

"You're right. And we didn't eat dinner last night. No wonder it smells so good," Daniel sniffed then winced and touched the bump on his head. "Ouch. The simplest actions send jolts of pain to my head."

Tamar gently touched the bruise on his cheek. "Maybe we should go back to the room."

"No, I don't want to miss today. I'll be fine." He smiled and nodded, then cringed. "We should buy some goodies for the twins and Hadassah."

Tamar's gaze stayed on him. "Okay, but if it gets to be too much, we'll go back to the hotel. Let's take our breakfast to the park by the Jeu de Paume since we're close. There's an art festival today. Remember? They were setting up last night when the cab dropped Isabelle off. Mr. Smit—he's a fellow Nederlander and an art dealer I spoke with this morning—said we should visit the festival. That we could find some good deals there. And, Neelie, your father might really enjoy it."

"Perhaps." They waited for a car to pass before they crossed the two-lane street. Neelie eyed the rows of beautifully decorated pastries—Napoleons, tarts, eclairs, crème puffs—all works of art. How she loved this town. "First, I have to convince Papa to leave the confines of his flat, then to be wheeled around. Doctor, can you add some medical persuasion to my request when he turns me down?"

"Of course." He stepped back while she and Tamar entered the patisserie. "Fresh air is always good for the body as well as the soul."

They stood in a short line, waiting for the sparrow-like woman behind the counter to finish her conversation with a local. How was it possible to work in this place and remain so thin? When it was Neelie's turn, her appetite and the pretty designs coerced her to buy more than she needed, but while in Paris....

They found a cluster of chairs at the edge of the park within sight of the art museum. Neelie enjoyed every morsel of the chocolate-filled, flaky pastry. Jan was going to gain so much weight living here, but he could stand to add more than a few kilograms with that lanky body of his.

Daniel passed around his éclair filled with vanilla custard, but Tamar's snowman filled with coffee mousse dripping with chocolate ganache won the contest for best pastry of the morning.

As they were preparing to leave to find a water fountain, an elderly woman clad in a long dress and apron approached and held out her hand.

"*Ca fait trente centimes*, s'il vous plait," she said.

Neelie glanced at Tamar. "What is she asking for?"

Tamar spoke to the woman, their conversation whipping back and forth. Then Tamar fumbled in her pocket and took out some change. The woman stuffed it into her apron, nodded, and shuffled to another bench.

"What was that all about?" Daniel cocked his head in the woman's direction.

"The fee for sitting in the green chairs. My mother had told me about them when I was young, but I forgot. These are called *senat* chairs. They are more comfortable and better situated than the benches, which are covered with bird droppings. So the government allows widows to collect money for the chairs' upkeep, but we can sit on all the benches we want for free."

"Ah, good for the widows, then. Shall we be on our way?"

Daniel offered an elbow to Neelie. "We should be at the museum before it gets too busy."

"Good thinking." Neelie linked her arm with Daniel's. "Should we just ask for a wheelchair or should we speak with Isabelle?"

Daniel's brow furrowed. "Hm, we don't want to bother her unless we have to."

"I agree," Neelie said, and Tamar nodded.

The same man from the day before—the man Isabelle had called Jean-Paul—was at the door of the museum directing people to the ticket window or answering questions. When it was their turn, his salt-and-pepper eyebrows lifted, and his eyes lit up. "Ah, the friends of our Madame LeClair. How may I help you today?"

Tamar spoke to him in French, having to act out the word for wheelchair. The man was clearly confused about their purpose, his eyes darting over the three of them to determine who was injured and why they'd need to take the wheelchair outside of the museum. Finally, Tamar asked to speak with Isabelle.

"I will see if Madame is available." He strode to his desk.

Tamar turned to the other two and grimaced. "I hate to bother her."

"Maybe she'll have some news about our missing painting," Daniel said. "This may be the last time we're able to see her."

The man returned and told them she'd be out in a few minutes, then he went back to his post.

"My father may tire quickly, and if that's the case, after we drop him off at his place, we could perhaps visit this museum's collections when we return the wheelchair." Neelie glanced from one to the other.

Tamar rubbed her arm. "I'm still amazed at how easily you reconciled with him. You didn't even tell him how much he hurt you and your mother. I was sure you'd try to get some justice for the loss of your father during your childhood, your teen years—and he missed Jan's childhood completely."

Neelie sighed. "And it's his loss. I understand what you're trying to say, and I did want to tell him off when I first went into that room. Please don't take this the wrong way. Justice is a virtue, but forgiveness is divine."

Tamar's face scrunched into a frown. "What do you mean by divine?"

"Well, we need justice—to make things right—maybe even put things back the way they were. But we can't forgive on our own. It takes God to help us forgive—that's why it's divine."

She seemed to ponder Neelie's words, then whispered, "You spend as much time as you need with your father. In fact, if you'd like some privacy, Daniel and I could go find something to do in order to give you some time—"

Isabelle LeClair appeared, pushing a wheelchair. "Good morning, my new friends. I'm sorry Monsieur Beaujolais didn't understand your purpose. I should have forewarned him, but a meeting took my time this morning."

Neelie extended her hand. "Thank you so much for all you have done. It's because of you that I reunited with my father. We will take good care of this wheelchair." She longed to ask if there was any news but lost her nerve. They had imposed enough.

Isabelle seemed to read her mind. "It is too early for me to know anything yet about your painting, but I have two of my associates calling all their contacts to be on the lookout for the girl with the violin."

This was good news. Mere weeks ago, Neelie had forgotten all about the painting, but now it prevailed in her thoughts—somehow intertwined with finding her father and recapturing what had been lost. It was too early to announce to Isabelle her plans to move here until she'd talked to her father and Jan, but she'd written her address and phone number at work on a piece of hotel stationery in case there was news. She handed Isabelle the information.

Isabelle read it, her lips curved up, and a girlish prettiness overtook her normally stern countenance. "We'll be in touch. And if I don't see you before you leave, have a safe trip back to the Netherlands."

The atmosphere outside the museum had changed from peaceful to clamorous during their short time inside. People streamed through the gates of the park in packs. Accordion music mingled with the chatter of the crowds and the giggles and shouts of children. Her father was going to love this festive gathering, and so was she.

Daniel insisted on pushing Neelie in the wheelchair—to save her feet, he countered when she refused. "You are the injured one in our party. I should push you." He waved her off with a *tsk* and a hand.

Tamar had been quiet all morning. Neelie didn't want to intrude, but she did, anyway. "Tamar, did you sleep well last night?"

"Not really," she said. "It was dark when I woke up, and I sat on the balcony for a while, then went down for some strong coffee to stop yawning."

Was that all? Doubtful. "So what's on your mind?"

She lifted her shoulder. "I don't know. The man sitting next to me—his name was Smit—Dedrich Smit. He's an art dealer from our country. Mr. Smit is the one who told me about the art festival."

"Looks as though he gave you good advice. So what's wrong?"

Her arms tightened around her chest. "I don't know. Just a feeling. I've been thinking back to who might have known where we were going yesterday. Remember, you and Daniel met me in the café yesterday morning? You brought the picture—"

Daniel interrupted. "It was in the portfolio, though. And I don't think we mentioned the name of the picture or even that it had a painting in it."

"Yeah, I've been racking my brain to recall what was said in his presence. I know we mentioned the Jeu de Paume. Did we say Isabelle LeClair's name?"

Neelie nodded. "We were wondering if she'd be at the museum."

"Well, I hate to say it," Daniel said, "but you might be onto something. If the man's an art dealer, he probably knows who Isabelle is. We were so busy concentrating on Neelie's father, we weren't paying attention to our surroundings—if someone was following us. What did the guy look like, Tamar? I don't remember him at all."

"He was well-dressed, maybe ten years my senior, and thin. Now that I think of it, I've been bumping into him often. We rode the elevator together yesterday from the second floor to the lobby. He sat next to me in the café, and there were a lot of empty tables he could have chosen, but today he sat next to me. Again."

"What did you talk about?" Neelie asked.

"You know, he actually spoke to me in Dutch. I didn't notice it at first. How did he know I was Dutch?"

"Maybe he heard us speaking in Dutch." Daniel shrugged.

"Could be. We talked about the weather, and that Paris was his second home." She shook her head. "If he's an art dealer, and we mentioned Isabelle's name, he could have realized the portfolio had a painting in it, and since Isabelle is a well-known curator, the painting must have some value—"

Neelie finished her thought. "So he followed us to Jeu de Paume and called the museum claiming the painting was his."

Daniel frowned—that same look of worry he'd shown when she talked of breaking into her former house. "But he must have named the painting when he called, claiming it was his. How would he have known which painting it was? We need to call Isabelle and ask her what the man on the phone actually said."

Neelie cast a glance over her shoulder at the museum. "Why don't we just return to the museum and tell her in person? We're this close."

Tamar grabbed the wheelchair handles. "Hop in, Tante."

They returned to the Jeu de Paume at a fast clip, and Neelie had to admit it felt good to get off her feet. People lined up outside the door. Patience had never been her forte, but they took their place at the end of the queue. They'd presumed enough on Isabelle's time.

Twenty minutes later, they'd reached the guard who took one look at them and headed to his desk. Moments later, he returned. "Madame LeClair is just going into a meeting, so she doesn't have time to come out here, but she's waiting to talk to you on the phone." He led them to his desk and handed Daniel the black receiver, which he in turn handed to Neelie.

She took it. "Hello, this is Neelie Visser."

"I'm sorry I don't have more time to give you. How can I help you?"

At least Isabelle spoke her language. "Thank you. I'll be quick. Tamar mentioned a man who sat next to her in the hotel café both yesterday and today. His name was Dedrich Smit. Does the name sound familiar to you? He said he was an art dealer."

"No, I've never heard the name. Is he Dutch or German?"

"Tamar said he's Dutch. He may have heard us mention your name and the Jeu de Paume, and we were carrying the portfolio at the time. Could it be that he's the one who called you? And another question—did the man who phoned yesterday call the picture by name? Because if he did, Mr. Smit can't be the one who took it."

A long pause ensued at the other end of the line until Isabelle spoke. "As you know, I didn't take the call, but I can question the person who did. You three need to be careful today. If the robber is Monsieur Smit, he may be following you again."

"We will. Thank you for all you've done." Neelie hadn't thought of the man following them again, but why would he, if he already had the painting?

Tamar couldn't help but giggle at the children's shrieks as Guignol chased his wife with a bat around the puppet stage. Unlike the day before, the children squeezed into every millimeter of the benches, and many sat cross-legged on the ground. What appeared to be grandparents and nannies stood back in a horseshoe to allow all the kids to see the puppet show. The children's parents were probably using the puppet show as a babysitter while they browsed the rows and rows of art kiosks.

Daniel whispered in her ear, "You miss the twins, don't you?"

Her arms hugged her chest. "Yeah, Peri would love this. Zari would think it's too violent." She smiled up at her husband, whose warm breath tickled the top of her head. "It's such a lovely day, and I'm so glad Neelie gets to spend it with her father. I'm going to miss her when she moves here."

He kissed her head. "Well, now you'll have a reason to visit. We should go find them." Tamar took his hand and let him lead her back to the aisles swarming with people.

This was more than just paintings. She breathed in the scent of crepes emanating from a man in a chef's hat who stood wide-legged over an outdoor stove, deftly whipping his spatula over bubbling batter, smoothing and folding it, then shaking powdered sugar onto it. He handed it to an adolescent with a long black braid. An audience stood around him, clamoring for his attention.

A woman wearing a lab coat and a beret signed books for the people who queued before her. Artisans displayed their crafts— tablecloths, wall hangings, wooden toys, homemade stationery. Tamar linked arms with Daniel. "I'd like to come back here later to buy wooden souvenirs for the kids."

"*Small* wooden things because we don't have much room in our bags." He chuckled. They'd caught up to Neelie, who stood behind the wheelchair as her father carried on a conversation with a man with a Dali mustache.

"I found her," Daniel said. "Should've known she'd stop to watch the puppets."

Neelie reached out and squeezed Tamar's hand. "You'll be home in no time." Her eyes went to her father. She cupped her hand on the side of her mouth. "He seems to know everyone here."

"Then he must be enjoying himself." Tamar gave a soft chuckle.

Neelie nodded. "There are a dozen lanes of art, and we've made it halfway down this one in almost an hour. At this rate—"

"Neelie? I'd like you to meet an old friend from back in the days before the Great War. Meet Albert Dauphin. We roomed together in Montmartre. Who didn't room in that apartment back then?" He slapped his knee. "We should have worn nametags, there were so many artists in and out." He looked up at Neelie with adoring eyes. "This is my beautiful daughter, Neelie. What a blessed surprise it was when she and her friends showed up with Isabelle LeClair yesterday. I'd given up on ever seeing Neelie again—" A coughing spell doubled him over.

Neelie patted his back. "Papa? You okay?"

He held up a hand and nodded between breaths.

Neelie turned to the slight man with a beret perched on his head, the quintessential picture of a French gent. "I'm happy to meet you, Monsieur, and these are my friends, Tamar and Daniel Feldman."

He twisted one end of his mustache between his thumb and forefinger. "There wasn't a day gone by that your papa didn't speak about you and your mother. I'm astonished, really, that he didn't hightail it back to Holland after the war."

She nodded, her lips pressed together.

Yes, Neelie had forgiven her father, but the feelings were still raw. That was the same way Tamar felt about Margot and even Captain Bergman, the one who'd betrayed them all, just because she wouldn't go out with him again. She could intend to forgive them, but then the memories came crashing back, and all those painful recollections created more bad feelings inside.

"Did you hear that, Tamar?" Neelie tapped her upper arm.

"What? I'm sorry—I was lost in my thoughts."

"Papa was just telling his friend about the painting that was stolen, and Monsieur Dauphin thinks he saw it in one of the kiosks."

Hope sprang within her. If only it were that easy. Of course, they'd have to buy the painting, but the prices seemed to be reasonable. She searched the paintings on the walls of Monsieur Dauphin's display for a price, but there were none. "Where did he see it? Which row? Daniel and I can go find it."

"He can't remember, but he said he thinks it wasn't too far from a booth where they were offering samples of wine."

Tamar glanced up at Daniel, who nodded at her. "We could ask someone to steer us in the right direction." Her eyes narrowed. "But how does he know which painting it was?"

"Why don't you ask him?" Daniel said.

She waited for a pause in the two men's conversation, then she asked in French what he remembered about the painting. Was it hanging on a wall? How big was the painting? Why did he remember that particular one out of all the artwork at this festival?

The man's eyes crinkled when he laughed. "*Autant de questions*. You'll remember that I lived with this man when he was bemoaning the separation from his family. That painting was never far from him. I've seen it dozens of times."

She smiled at the man. He looked like a poster for French art, even down to the black-and-white striped shirt under his black jacket. Turning toward Neelie, she moved close to her ear. "Will you be okay if we run ahead to find it?"

"Of course, dear. I'm having the time of my life being here with my father. Look how the color has come back in his cheeks. Take your time."

Daniel grabbed her hand, and they hurried to the end of the row. "You look on the right side, and I'll take the left side."

"And if I see someone in charge, I'll ask for directions to the wine kiosk." From what she could determine, this row was somewhere in the middle. Her sense of order told her to take a left at the end and start at the first row, but then there appeared a whole other section of rows running perpendicular. "This is like a maze. I wouldn't want to get lost in here."

When they reached the end, Daniel blew out a loud breath. "Art is big in Paris. I'm just amazed that they could set this up so quickly."

"Yeah, I wish we could take our time and enjoy this festival.

This is better than the Louvre or the Eiffel Tower. It's real life. The smells, the chatter, the different shades of people." She spotted a man in a suit who wore a nametag talking to a woman. "That man over there might know where the wine is." She hurried over to the pair, waiting for them to finish their conversation. A word here and there were familiar, but they seemed to be speaking an unfamiliar dialect—perhaps from Normandy or Brittany.

Daniel stood behind her, resting both arms on her shoulders. She reached for one his hands for courage. It wasn't easy to speak to foreign men, especially when they didn't speak her language. Finally, the gentleman turned to her. A quick glimpse of the nametag read *Claude DeBoe*. Tamar gulped and said, "Bonjour, Monsieur. We're looking for the wine kiosk. Do you know where it is?"

"Oui, Madame."

Whenever she spoke in French to the housekeeping attendant, the waiter, or the receptionist in the hotel lobby, they responded in English. Not this man. A fountain of French flowed so quickly from his lips, she couldn't keep up. Finally, she just said, "merci," and they left.

"Well?" Daniel hurried to catch up to her. "What did he say?"

"I don't know. I couldn't understand his French. Seth used to say, 'If you don't use it, you lose it.' Guess I'm not fluent anymore."

"I think he'd had a bit too much wine. He probably can't remember where it is. How about we start with row one? It shouldn't take us too long if we walk fast and keep our eyes open."

She interlocked her elbow with his. "And don't forget. We need to find something for the twins and Hadassah."

"Let's step up our pace and find that picture before it's sold."

They flew past kiosks that she would've wanted to browse through. Past Cubist and Dadaist art. Past more traditional still-lifes and landscapes. The Saturday morning *markt* in Haarlem's St Bavo's square was one of her favorite destinations of the weekend, although it featured less art and more food and clothing than this one. So many things drew her eyes, she had trouble keeping up with Daniel's long strides, and she almost tripped over a young child pushing a buggy.

The first and second aisles yielded no wine kiosk or painting of Neelie. Tamar pulled back to force Daniel to slow down. "Maybe Monsieur Dauphin was mistaken. Sometimes people say things but don't really mean them."

Daniel complied by taking smaller steps. "Well, these are the cards that were dealt us, so we have to play them. We'd regret returning home when there's a chance we can find the painting. And I'm enjoying this place, aren't you?"

She patted their joined hands with her free one. "Oh yes. I see so many things I want. It's probably a good idea we don't slow down. But I would like to buy some memento of this trip just for us. You realize this is the first time we've had a vacation since we were married."

"Since we met, you mean." He chuckled. "And yes, if you see something you want, we'll buy it." The third and the fourth aisles revealed nothing, but they did pass the wooden toy kiosk.

"Daniel, I want to stop to buy a wooden car for Peri and a marionette for Zari. If I don't buy them now, I won't be able to find this place again."

"Okay." He shoved a hand in his pocket and brought a few bills. "Here are enough francs to cover the cost. I'm going to see what else is down this aisle, so we can move on." After kissing her temple, he headed straight on, and she returned to the toy kiosk.

More than a few parents had the same idea as she. One man's son wearing a sailor's suit sat on his shoulders pointing at a sailboat, then a Jeep, then a truck, saying, "I want that one. And that one." She had to laugh. Peri would be just like him. The sailor boy was about Peri's age, so she should pay attention to what appealed to him.

The young boy finally decided on the sailboat. Tamar waited while the salesman placed it in a white box and taped the sides.

"Ca fait vingt francs, Monsieur."

Twenty francs? That was more than a week's worth of groceries. Could she justify paying that much? And she still had to buy presents for Zari and Hadassah. She counted the bills in her hand and checked her pockets for any centimes she'd gathered in the last few days. Almost fifty francs.

Just then, she felt a yank on her sweater. She looked down to see a young girl, perhaps six or seven years old with long blond hair that needed a good brushing. A small bow dangled halfway down a strand that had once been a braid. A faded white dress many sizes too big hung on her like a tent. Her dirty feet were devoid of shoes.

"*Un message, Madame.*" Grimy fingers handed her a small notecard folded a few times.

"What is this?" she said in Dutch, then remembered where she was.

The gamin foisted it at her. "Take it."

Tamar peered up to locate Daniel, but the crowd blocked her view. "Who gave you this?"

"The man." A frown puckered her forehead. "Take it now. I have to go."

Tamar unfolded the paper and stared at slanted, unfamiliar handwriting. *Your painting is on display. Madeleine will take you to it.* The girl was shifting from foot to foot as if she were stepping on hot coals. Tamar bent to her level. "One more question. Was the man who gave you this the artist at the kiosk? Did he have a mustache?"

"*Oui, Madame. C'est un artiste. Suivez-moi.*" The girl whipped around and dashed away.

Should she follow? If she didn't, the girl would be out of sight in moments. At least the girl was heading in Daniel's direction. Obviously, Monsieur Dauphin couldn't leave his post, so he sent Madeleine, but how did the girl know who Tamar was?

Tamar dashed off as best she could in her stiff oxfords. If she ever came back, she'd buy more accommodating footwear. As she dodged browsers, small children, and a wheelchair, she kept a lookout for her husband and finally saw him just ahead, leaning over a table lining the front of an art kiosk, peering at a paper. The man on the other side of the table was pointing at something on the paper. Probably a map or a historical document of some sort. She glanced ahead. The girl was veering to the left.

"Daniel?" she yelled as loud as she could as running took her breath. He didn't turn around. "Daniel!" she screamed, not caring if anyone looked her way. "I found the painting." She'd reached Daniel and started toward him, but the girl had vanished around the corner. "Daniel, follow me."

Tamar stepped up her pace, glancing once over her shoulder. The man in the kiosk was pointing in her direction. Good, Daniel knew. It seemed odd that Monsieur Dauphin would send such an unkempt little girl to her, but perhaps she was an orphan who earned centimes by running errands.

Once she reached the end of the aisle, Tamar slowed but didn't stop. The milling crowds made it difficult to see the small girl, but she kept her eyes pasted on the ecru-colored dress.

These were aisles they'd already gone down, so perhaps the girl was conning her. Then about a Haarlem block away, she spied bare feet veering to the right between two kiosks. This was an area they hadn't yet checked out.

Tamar glanced behind her. No Daniel. Should she go back? But what if she lost the girl? She set her mind on the girl and sped as fast as her shoes would let her. Off the well-maintained park path onto the grass she went, slipping between kiosks, one of whose hosts stared at her with narrowed eyebrows. She slowed and backed up. "Did you see a little girl run past?" Which came out in the wrong order and tense.

The man gave a quick shake of the head. Did he not understand or was he lying? Huffing a mixture of discontent and breathlessness, she hurried past the kiosk, then stopped and circled slowly.

The girl had vanished, and now she stood in the middle of what appeared to be the backyards of rows of contiguous kiosks. Only a few young fellows sat on the grass smoking and cajoling each other, their backs resting against the curtained wall of a booth.

Before she could talk herself out of it, she strode toward them. "Did you see a little girl running through here?"

They glanced at each other and shrugged. What, was there a club or something they all belonged to? Tamar suppressed the words on her tongue and flounced away. She might as well go back and find Daniel. He was probably wondering where she went. She was going to receive such a lecture.

Rounding the corner between the two kiosks that led back to the festival, she blew out a breath. How frustrating. Now they'd have to go back to the original plan.

Just then, her head was jerked back. Someone pulled on her shoulder. Daniel? Was he trying to scare her? Well, he'd succeeded. "Daniel, stop it. You're scaring me." She tried to whip around, but an arm circled her neck from behind. Not Daniel. Maybe one of those boys? She grabbed the arm that was tightening around her throat. "Stop." She tried to scream, but her voice didn't work.

A sting on the back of her neck. A bee? No, bigger. She slapped at it, or tried to. Warm breath on her neck. Her fingers dug into the hand that surrounded her throat, but the more she dug, the more her windpipe was closed off. She couldn't breathe. The sting burned like a hot tool pressed against her skin. Spots gave way to a gray curtain that closed to nothing.

Chapter Twenty-one

"Worry is an old man with bended head, carrying a load of feathers
which he thinks are lead."
~ Corrie ten Boom

Where was she? Daniel couldn't believe Tamar had gone off without telling him. The gray-haired clerk with a bowtie at the toy kiosk remembered a short blonde waiting behind a man who bought a sailboat. Tamar probably became impatient, but why would she leave?

Daniel retraced his steps to the man with the map, stopping to ask everyone he passed if they'd seen a blond woman with a polka-dot dress. This was not like Tamar at all.

"Monsieur?" A voice spoke behind him. Daniel turned to see the old man from the toy booth shuffling toward him with a pained look on his face. "I remember something else," he said once he'd caught his breath. "Let's walk back. I can't leave my kiosk unattended."

"What do you remember?" Something akin to fear touched his heart. He wasn't ready to give into it yet. There had to be some logical explanation.

"A young girl. Small. I don't know ages, but she looked like one of the little beggars that steals from all of us when our backs are turned. She was talking to your wife. I wasn't paying attention because I was waiting on a customer, but I recall the girl giving your wife something—a paper, I think. Maybe she was trying to sell her a postcard. They do that all the time."

"But you didn't see her leave with the girl?"

"No, I'd gone to the back of the booth to grab another boat for the customer. When I returned to the counter, she was gone. I figured she was tired of waiting. People do that all the time. No patience these days." His eyes met Daniel's. "I'm sorry. Don't know why I said that. But if you can find the girl, she may be able to help you."

Daniel couldn't get away fast enough. Who would send his wife a note? They didn't know anyone here—except for Neelie, her father, and that artist. This wasn't like Tamar to leave without telling him. Not at all. Okay, logically, the only one who would have sent a note was Neelie. And the man at the toy booth had said the little girl was a regular, so Monsieur Dauphin may have given her a coin to relay the message. But how would she know who Tamar was? Clothes. Neelie would have given a description of what Tamar was wearing.

Daniel started back to Monsieur Dauphin's booth, but by this time, surely, Neelie and Willem would have moved on. Still, it was a place to start.

As he passed the booth where he'd been poring over a map of the area, the proprietor called out to him, "Monsieur, over here. What is wrong?"

"My wife is missing." He searched for the word. "*Perdue*. I don't know where she is." Tears brimmed, borne of frustration or worry—he didn't know.

The man stood to his full height, which fell short of Tamar's stature. "*Est-elle blonde*? I saw a woman running. I think she called for you."

"When?" Why would she be running? Why didn't he hear her? Why didn't the man tell him?

"While we looking at the map. I saw lady look over…" He patted his shoulder. "At you. But you were talking, so I didn't interrupt."

Daniel summoned his breath to calm down. "Okay, did you see what direction she was going?"

The man's eyes scanned the ceiling. "Lots of people. Let me think." He closed his eyes. "Oui, she went to *le bout*…the end…and turned *à gauche*." He pointed to the left. "Maybe fifteen minutes, maybe less."

"Thank you, sir. I wish I would have known, but…" What Daniel needed to do was pray, not cast blame, while he tried to track her down. If it was an innocent thing, Tamar wouldn't have run. And she'd tried to grab his attention. *Lord, you know where she is. Lead me to her, and keep her safe until I reach her.* He didn't say *amen*. It was too final, and he needed to be in constant contact with the only one who could help him at this point.

He headed to the end of the lane. People milled around. Mothers browsed through patterned quilts and dishtowels. Men chatted with the shopkeepers, clearly uninterested in spending any more money. A group of pre-teens tagged each other and darted away, their shrieks and yells filling the air. Daniel sniffed. Roasting meat—maybe chicken or sausage. Normal things, but his life at the moment was anything but.

A blonde browsed at a booth the length of two blocks ahead. Daniel raced to catch up with her before she disappeared. "Tamar? Wait for me!" She must not be able to hear him over the din of the crowd. "Tamar?" His feet ate up the distance between them, and he clasped her arm and turned her around with more force than he meant to.

"Oui?"

His heart sank. He apologized. Said he was looking for his wife, who wore her blond hair the same way. She smiled and said something he didn't understand.

Backtracking, he kept his eyes alert to all directions. It was time to call the police. But they wouldn't do anything. How could they? People got lost in crowded places all the time.

But then there was the little girl. What could that have meant? Tamar must have followed her and had to run to keep up. No matter how he looked at the facts, he didn't foresee a happy ending. That little girl had possibly led his wife into a trap. Maybe the best thing was to find Neelie—even call Isabelle. He needed someone who spoke French, and someone who spoke God's language.

His eyes darted from left to right and back. Anybody who saw him would think he'd lost someone or something, but no one offered to help. If he were leading someone into a trap, he'd lead them away from the crowds. Daniel took a closer look in between the booths to the area behind them. That's where he'd go if he wanted to—then he saw it. The size of a file card on the ground—the kind he'd used to study definitions in medical school. It was surprising he'd even been able to see it as it lay between two kiosks about three or four meters away from the path.

He hurried to pick it up—a ragged, folded, dirty paper. *Please, Lord, may it be a clue.* He opened it. *Your painting is on d—. Mad— will take you to it.* The paper was wrinkled, and moisture had damaged part of the words. His wife had held this paper. She'd dropped it on purpose to create a trail.

Tamar was in danger!

His heart shuddered and he fought the desire to sob. That wouldn't help bring her back. *Come on, Resistance Boy, you've made it through two concentration camps. Buck it up.*

First, he'd pray and then he'd do the next logical thing. With his lip quivering like a leaf in the wind, he implored God for her return, for her safety, as if imploring would make a difference. God loved Tamar more than humanly possible. Daniel sucked in a shaky breath and prayed less hysterically for a clear mind to make split-second decisions, acute eyes to see past the normal, and help from others to expand his territory. *Keep her safe, Lord. She's in your hands. Nothing can happen to her without your permission.*

The logical next thing to do was to ask the man in the closest kiosk if he'd seen her. It would be odd to see a woman running between the booths, so he should remember. Daniel returned to the kiosk on his right, the one closest to where he found the note. The kiosk appeared to be unattended, until he approached. A wizened old man, thin as a reed, sat slumped in a lawn chair toward the back. Had the old man been sitting there fifteen minutes ago, he might not have noticed Tamar.

He summoned every word of French he could remember and asked God for more. "*Monsieur, vous parlez anglais?*"

The man shook his head but said nothing.

"*Ma femme—elle est blonde—*she ran past here." Daniel acted out running with hand motions. He held up his hands in desperation. "I don't know *où elle est.* Help me?"

The man shook his head again, struggled to his feet, and limped to the counter's edge, stopping for a breath along the way. A fit of coughing took him over, and he leaned over the counter. "*Je regrette, monsieur.* I...did not...see...her." Ragged inhalations sliced the sentence into pieces.

Show him the note.

Right. Daniel held out the note to the man. "Do you know this name? *Mad?*"

The man's head swiveled a third time, and he used a shaky hand to swipe his hair back. "It ees dirty, *n'est-ce pas?*" He felt for his glasses in his shirt pocket, then held the paper as far as he could away from his eyes. "Mad...there ees *une petite fille*, Madeleine, and she is…how you say… *un petit escroc*." He waved the palm of his hand.

"*Escroc? Je ne comprends pas.*" Daniel frowned.

The old man made a grabbing motion with his hand and almost lost his balance. "*Elle est voleuse.*"

A thief. He knew what it meant even if he didn't speak French. Daniel thanked him and moved away. If it had just been a theft, Tamar would have found him. No, this was more than a theft. Time to find Neelie and the nearest gendarme.

It shouldn't have been that easy. The muses were looking down at him with favor, although of course, they didn't exist. Now he'd possessed the two things he wanted most with very little effort. Something he'd learn from the Third Reich—a rule of human nature, really. People were so busy tending to their own interests, they didn't notice what was going on around them. How true it was today. Here Erich was in the midst of thousands of '*flaneurs*,' as browsers were called in French, and they didn't see him abduct a woman.

Another thing he'd learned from the Reich was to think ahead of all possible outcomes. And the muses had helped him once more. He'd chosen the area behind the kiosk because of the wheelchair sitting behind it. A perfect way to transport the "sleeping" Tamar back to the hotel room without attracting suspicious eyes. Of course, he'd done his homework and determined how to enter the hotel without having to traverse the lobby. He and his sleeping beauty simply waited until the housekeeping entrance was devoid of females, slipped into the service elevator, and were in his room in no time.

He couldn't take his eyes off her. So serene even in sleep, so lovely. Lips that begged for tender kisses. His finger traced a meandering stream down her soft, supple cheek. Tamar deserved to be loved with all the passion and depth of devotion he'd held for her since the moment he'd heard her singing five years ago.

In time, she'd learn to forget the doctor. He didn't appreciate her. Tamar's restlessness was obvious to Erich. She wanted out of the relationship. Fine china needed to be treated with gentleness—revered, even worshipped. Erich was a patient man. But it would take a while to convince her they belonged together. That only with him and through him would she be able to realize the heights to which he'd take her.

He ran a finger down her nose. Felt the tip. "Darling, people from all over the world will flock to hear you sing. Think of it. Milan. Florence. Berlin. Leningrad. Wherever you go, you'll be a star. That will be my gift to you." He bent down and kissed her lips.

Of course, he wasn't stupid. There'd be resistance. She'd put up a fight at first. Gently, methodically, he'd show her how fulfilled her life would be with him. Until she appreciated what he'd done for her, he'd keep her sedated with the drug he'd sold a copy of a Klimt for, until the widow Visser and the doctor had returned to the Netherlands. It was about planning for every outcome.

Chapter Twenty-two

"You can never learn that Christ is all you need, until Christ is all you have."
~ Corrie ten Boom

Dashing from one lane to another where every kiosk looked like the previous one, Daniel finally spotted Neelie fanning herself under the shade of a lofty elm. Her father's head lolled to the side, rising and falling with each of slumber's breaths. Daniel hurried to her, his lips disobeying his command to stop quivering. Losing his composure would accomplish nothing, and time was running out.

Neelie bolted from her seat, alarm showing on her face. "What's wrong? Where is Tamar? Is she hurt?"

Between breaths, he blurted out, "She's vanished. I can't find her anywhere. I'm afraid she's been abducted or something." He dug for the note in his pocket and thrust it at her. "Did you write this? Did the artist your father was talking to write it? Why can't I remember his name?"

Before she read it, Neelie took ahold of both of his arms. "Sit down now. You're as pale as a sheet. You look as if you're going to faint." Neelie circled him around and pushed him into the seat. Then she opened the note and read. "No, I didn't write this. Neither did Mr. Dauphin, at least when we were with him." She removed her glasses. "Now tell me what this is all about."

His heart had stopped thrumming, and the panic that had overtaken him abated at least a bit. The words tumbled out of him, then the tears sprang despite his efforts to control them. "I don't know what to do." He bit his lower lip. "Since the war's been over, I've become soft. It's as though my mind's frozen."

Tender arms circled his neck. "Take a deep breath. We need to pray. God knows where she is. We will pray for Him to lead us to her, and until then, we'll trust God to keep her safe." Neelie's head rested against his, and she prayed verses he'd learned as a child—promises about comfort and safety. Then she straightened up and brushed away his tears. "All right. So what do you think happened?"

He let out a shuddering sigh. "Someone used a child to deliver this message, and that someone knew about the painting we're hunting for. That's why I thought Monsieur Dauphin wrote it. Who else could it be? I found the note between two kiosks at the edge of this festival. Behind the kiosks is nothing but a grassy area. The child lured her to that area away from onlookers, and Tamar fell into some kind of trap. She dropped the note so I would find it."

"It's time to go to the police." Neelie tapped on her father's arm. His glassy eyes opened, and he blinked several times at their serious expressions.

"What happened?" He shook his head as if to loosen the cobwebs.

Neelie explained and showed him the note. "Does this handwriting look like Mr. Dauphin's? How do we contact the police?"

He took the note and read it. "What? I don't recognize this handwriting. As for the police, they're usually standing by the park entrance. Might even be a few walking around here." The old man held his fist high like a standard. "Let's go find that wife of yours."

Daniel helped him off the bench and into the wheelchair. He hadn't stopped praying. Where was she? What were they doing to her? Was she targeted or was this random? Panic and desolation gripped his throat like a vise. What could the police do? They'd probably say he was overacting; that she'd made a new acquaintance and lost track of the time. "We'll need your help talking to them, Mr. Haan."

"Of course," he said. "I'm no expert, but it's plain to see that the theft of the painting is somehow linked to Tamar's disappearance. What do you think, Daniel? Neelie?"

Daniel took control of the wheelchair and headed toward the exit. "I agree, sir, but I don't understand why anyone would be interested in that painting. No offense, but it's not a Rembrandt. Could there be something hidden in the frame?" The speed of his gait accelerated, matching the pounding of his heart, but he couldn't slow down.

Neelie tried to keep up. "The only one who knew about that picture here in France was whoever called Isabelle at the museum. Why don't we head to the museum since it's adjacent to this park? Isabelle might be able to help us more than anyone else. And Daniel? Could you slow down, please?"

"Sorry." He lowered his head but complied. "It's just…the more time she's gone, the less chance we'll have of finding her." Tears brimmed again, spilled, and flowed down his cheeks. "I've never been so much at a loss." He swiped at his eyes with his knuckles.

Neelie ran her hand down his arm. "Oh, sweetie, it's okay. God knows where she is. Tamar's strong. Whoever took her doesn't know the army he's dealing with. We'll find her."

Two gendarmes stood by the tall exit gate chatting. The three of them hurried over to them and waited for a pause in their conversation. One of the two took off his high-brimmed hat and scratched his head, then waved at his friend and left. They approached the remaining police officer, who noticed them for the first time and stepped forward to greet them.

Neelie's father handled the conversation, which Daniel couldn't follow except for the names. The officer nodded, looked their way, then asked where they were staying. He also asked to see a picture of Tamar. Daniel took out his wallet and pulled out the only photo he had of her, the one where he'd caught her unawares, daydreaming on a checkered blanket where they'd enjoyed a picnic with the twins in the park. Swallowing past the lump in his throat, he reluctantly handed the photograph to the gendarme. The lack of expression on the man's face as he glanced at the photo indicated that he wasn't on Daniel's side.

With a twitch of his black mustache, he handed the picture back. "Sorry, Monsieur, one sees so many ladies in the park on these days of the festival. She'll show up, I promise you. When she does, you can give her good talking-to, eh, Monsieur?" He nudged Daniel with his elbow. "Do not fret. She probably was side-tracked. You know how women are."

Daniel stuffed his fist into his pocket. He couldn't help Tamar if he ended up in a French jail. "Merci." He took hold of the wheelchair handles and strode away before he said something he'd regret. When they were an adequate distance away, he stopped. "I…don't…know where to go from here." Never had he felt so ill-equipped…not in the Resistance…not in Vught…not even when he and Tamar escaped past the guards to the woods and ran for their lives.

Neelie grasped his arm. She probably longed to tell him to get a grip but was too polite to do so. In her calm, resolute voice, she said, "We will go and see Isabelle, and she will tell us what to do. She knows people. We don't. But we know God."

He sniffed and nodded, flushing over the fact that he was falling apart.

Without a word, they headed to the Jeu de Paume. The guard took one look at them and called, no questions asked this time. He nodded, then beckoned for them to follow him to Isabelle's office.

Her back was to them as she fingered through files in a cabinet. Daniel helped Willem into a chair, and he and Neelie stood near the door. She spun around and smiled at them.

"I called the guard who'd taken the message, but there was no name. All he could say was it was a man's voice, and he said that Mrs. Feldman's painting was not hers but his, and he'd be in touch. Not a lot to go on, although the guard did say the man had an accent." Isabelle's eyes grew owlish. "Dr. Feldman, you have no color in your face. Where is Tamar?"

Neelie, thankfully, intervened. "Tamar's missing, and we don't know what to do. I found this." Daniel handed her the note, now in worse shape than ever, having been handled so much.

Daniel spoke past the raspy crack in his voice. He explained everything that had happened up to this point. "We were hoping you'd have the name of the man who called so we could follow up on that lead. Who else would know about the painting other than the man who took it from you?"

Isabelle nodded, working her lips as she dropped into her chair. Then she straightened. "Whenever I face a dilemma like this, I take out a paper and write down in logical order what I do know, so let's do that." She grabbed a pen. "So what do we know?"

Neelie started. "There is a man—a thin man with an accent who claims to own the painting, who must have followed us to my father's house, ripped the painting from your grip, and is probably the same man who wrote this note and paid a little girl to give it to Tamar. Am I inferring too much?" She peered at their faces. "Now who is this man?"

Daniel spoke next. "It has to be the man whom Tamar met at the hotel café both mornings. He said he was an art dealer from the Netherlands, so he'd have an accent. He heard us say we were coming to meet with you, so he could have followed us and—" He gasped. "I just remembered something Tamar told us. She said the man was on the elevator with her that first day. Remember? Tamar was surprised to hear someone say 'good morning' in Dutch. How did he know she was Dutch?"

Neelie covered her mouth. "And we're on the second floor, and didn't she say he got on the elevator on the second floor? That would mean his room is on the same floor as ours."

"Sounds a little too coincidental to me," Isabelle took off her glasses. "What if he followed you from Haarlem? What if this was all a plan?"

"That would make sense if it was the people who are now living in Tamar's house. I wouldn't put it past Margot. She's not a nice person at all—used to scare us all with her tantrums at the opera house." Neelie pretended to spit over her shoulder. "And her husband is probably just as bad. What's his name?"

"Klaus Sneider. If he discovered Tamar took the painting..." Daniel frowned. "But if he already had the painting, why abduct Tamar? The only man who'd ever do that is—" With a quick intake of breath, he locked eyes with Neelie.

"Bergman," they said at the same time.

"But how could a Nazi remain in our country? Was Tamar right all along?" He slapped a palm against his forehead. "What an utter fool I've been. I should have listened to my wife, should have noticed the plastic surgery. I was so busy examining the burns, it didn't occur to me to look deeper."

"You're certainly not a fool, Daniel."

Yes, he was. She'd tried to tell him the man at the hospital was Bergman, but no, he knew better. And now she was gone. Ouch. A slap on his back. He twisted around to see Neelie's frown and her arms across her chest like an imperious general. "What did you do that for?"

"There's no time now for self-incrimination. You did nothing wrong, but we have to come up with a plan. *Now!*"

"You're right. So what should we do?" He eyed his three compatriots in the tiny office. An army of one senior, two middle-aged women, and a weakling.

Isabelle picked up the phone on her desk and told someone she'd be out of the office for the next few days. "There." she replaced the receiver. "I'm all in. It will go better for you if you have a French-speaking person with you." She picked up her pen. "So who's this Bergman?"

Neelie quickly told Isabelle and her father about the Nazi officer who was obsessed with Tamar's singing and her beauty. How during the war, she had pretended to be Neelie's niece to conceal her Judaism. Bergman kept asking her out, and she kept declining. In an act of vengeance, Bergman accused Neelie of hiding Jews, turned their house upside down, and had them sent to Westerbork.

Willem spoke up. "But after the war ended, how could Bergman remain in Amsterdam?"

"Plastic surgery," Daniel said. "He was one of my burn patients. An ambulance brought him to the Gasthuis when I wasn't at work. The patient was comatose. We were told he was in a warehouse fire. He never spoke a word until Tamar came to sing for the patients. She recognized his voice, but I told her she was mistaken. When we finally took the bandages off weeks later, he didn't look anything like the man he'd been, but I never suspected plastic surgery. Big mistake. Anyway, he escaped, and we never saw him again—"

Neelie interrupted. "So he was probably working with Sneider and Margot in stashing the art at Tamar's old house. Maybe Bergman was hiding out there after he escaped and saw Tamar take the painting."

Isabelle stood and leaned on the desk. "Far-fetched, but it would explain why he followed you to Paris. We should call the police right now."

"They won't do anything," Willem smirked. "I think you should go talk to the hotel personnel. Find out who's staying on your floor. He may already have checked out, although it would be a perfect place to keep her hidden. Time isn't on our side."

Chapter Twenty-three

"Faith is like radar that sees through the fog—the reality of things
at a distance that the human eye cannot see."
~ Corrie ten Boom

Her mind was as thick as porridge. It took more than the usual effort to open even one eye. *Where am I?* Tamar tried to lift a hand to wipe the grit from her eyes, but it wouldn't budge. Something was pinning it down, as was her other hand. Was she still sleeping? The smell of starch and cigarettes combined into an unpleasant odor. Blinking her eyes to remove the gauzy film, she stopped when each blink evoked a throb to her temple. This was not her room, though the same picture hung on the wall. The same-shaped mirror hung over the bureau. The same lamp. "Daniel?" her voice came out in a croak.

The rustle of fabric. Muted footsteps as if on a rug. A face moved into the sphere of her vision, moving in and out of focus. Her heart leapt, then… Not Daniel. Not Neelie. Where was she? Her breath sped up. "Who are you? Why am I here?"

The face moved closer, inches away. The smell of ashtrays and something else. Something antiseptic. The man from the café leaned over her. She twisted away as best she could, squeezing her eyes shut.

"Ah, my beautiful lady is finally awake. Now I have both beauties back." He smiled a satisfied grin past stained teeth, his eyes too bright for this room.

"Who are you?" She licked her dry lips, looking around.

"Where are my husband and my aunt?"

He backed away, opened a small gold case, and took out a cigarette, tapping it against the edge of the container. "All your questions will be answered in good time. But now your job is to sleep. Think about it. When was the last time you had a really good sleep?" Again, she heard a trace of an accent.

Tamar tried to sit up, but the room spun, sending a wave of nausea through her. She closed her eyes and lay back down. "You're the man from the café. The art dealer. Why have you brought me here against my will? I want my husband."

He chuckled a bit too much. "You are a saucy girl. In a few words, I came to reclaim what is mine."

"Reclaim?" The pain in her head made her squint. "You don't own me. I don't even know you."

He shifted sideways to gaze at her. His suit hung on his thin frame. It was as if she was looking at a mask. "Then you're not looking close enough." He lowered himself onto the bed so that his face was centimeters from hers. "What do my eyes tell you?"

She turned away from him. He grabbed her chin and forced her to face him. "I don't know. I just want to see my husband." Tears trickled down her temples to her ears. "What do you want from me?" Her thoughts traveled to what seemed like a long time ago when she'd raced after that ragged girl at the festival. How foolish she'd been not to stop and tell Daniel. He must be so worried. If she could somehow bargain with this man, maybe he'd let her go.

He took a puff of his cigarette, the smoke wisping up in a spiral to the ceiling. "Do you remember 'Bambino Caro'? That was the first time I heard that splendid voice—that heavenly voice that took me to paradise."

So it was him. Revulsion filled her. No, she wouldn't give him the satisfaction of saying his name. "Your face has changed. You were in my husband's hospital. I knew it was you, but nobody believed me."

He set his cigarette in the ashtray on the bedside table, lowered his head to her hand that was taut against the bed, and rested his lips against it. Her breakfast welled up inside her, and she tightened her lips to stave off the acid that brimmed at the surface. She couldn't even wipe her mouth. Swallowing, she managed one word. "Why?"

He glanced up at her, and she looked away. "Why? Because I

haven't stopped thinking about you since that first day in your aunt's foyer." He chuckled. "Of course, we both know Neelie Visser is not your aunt. Still, I have to say your blond hair and striking blue eyes fooled me, and I quite dislike being fooled." He sat up and traced a finger along her cheek. "But all that's in the past. You know, I saw you stealing that picture from the Sneiders' house—" Bergman started laughing and slapped his knee. "I mean, *your* house. Oh, the irony. And I thought, 'that girl has guts,' as they say in America. Hubris. Good for you, sweet pet, but that painting happens to belong to me, as does all the art in that…your former house." He lowered to kiss her nose.

She squirmed against the bonds that held her down.

He stood and relit his cigarette. "So how did I know it was your former house?" Bergman pivoted to face her, his face now a collage of Picasso parts. "Oh, don't worry. Sneider doesn't know. That witch of a wife doesn't know, either, and I won't tell. It will be our little secret." He touched his lips, then moved toward the bed and bent to touch hers.

She pursed her lips and turned her head away from him.

"As I recuperated after my stay at the Gasthuis, I spent more than a few days in the attic, and there in the piles of disorder, my eyes landed on a box containing family photos along with a menorah. And there you were in the center of almost all of them." Bergman shifted to grab the familiar portfolio and carefully removed the painting.

Tears rolled down her face, and there wasn't a thing she could do to stop them. There was the girl with the violin   the girl that had spurred her to embark on this journey of what—justice?

"Now, now. Quiet those tears." His finger trailed down her cheek once again. "I know why you stole this painting. It was the girl—she looks just like you in those early photographs. Just think. As long as we're together, I'll let you keep it. We can hang it in our parlor or bedroom. Wherever you like."

"It doesn't belong to you." The raspy words slipped out. She hadn't wanted to say anything. "That girl is Neelie, and her father painted it. Her father bequeathed it to her until you ripped it from Madame LeClair's hands."

"That is unfortunate. It seems everyone wants a piece of this picture. Yet we all know that possession is nine-tenths of the law, and I acquired it legally. And now it will be yours as well." He placed it back in the portfolio and put it in the closet. "I need to go out for a bit. Until I can trust you, I'll have to keep you sedated."

She turned her head and squeezed her eyes shut at the prick of the needle to her neck.

A middle-aged couple with a poodle moved out of their way as Daniel barreled into the hotel lobby, followed by Isabelle and Neelie. They'd lost countless minutes having to drop Neelie's father back at his apartment, then more lost minutes taking the wheelchair back to the museum. They weren't just dealing with a criminal—they were pitted against a mastermind trained by the Nazis. With German precision, Bergman would have planned every detail, every possible outcome. It almost seemed impossible that the man would have brought Tamar back to the hotel, much less to a room on the second floor. But they had to take each step as they found it, one at a time.

With a sharp intake of breath, Daniel held the ladies back. The hotel manager would be more willing to help them if they didn't accost him with panic on their faces. The women seemed to understand without him saying a word. They approached the desk where the man stood sorting through letters, his polished black hair reflecting the blue light of the overhead chandelier.

He tapped his fingers on the counter, then glanced up with a polite smile. "May I help you? Monsieur Feldman, isn't it?"

Where to start? "My wife is missing. I believe she's been abducted." Maybe too much information, judging by the dubious expression on the man's face.

"Abducted? Why would you say that?" He leaned forward as if to keep the conversation from traveling to passersby. "I just saw Madame Feldman this morning."

Daniel peered sideways at the women. His lack of French was not helping his case, so he turned to Isabelle. "This is Madame Isabelle LeClaire. She is curator at the Jeu de Paume. Her French is better than mine."

Isabelle detailed in hurried French what had transpired that afternoon.

"You have called the police, non?" the man said, his eyebrows meeting in the center.

"Not yet. We believe the man responsible is staying on our floor—" Daniel stopped, searching for more words, then Isabelle took over. He caught the word *Nazi* and knew she was telling the man that it would be in the hotel's best interest if the police were not called until he gave them the information they sought.

The color in the hotel manager's face vanished. "So you want to know the identity of the guests on the second floor? It's against hotel policy to give out that information." His lips formed a single line.

"Well, then," Neelie broke in, her chin held high and her nostrils flaring. "We will call the police, and they'll arrive with sirens blaring."

Isabelle patted her hand. "These are unusual circumstances, and time is not on our side. Please"—she read his nametag—"Monsieur Dureil, it would be better not to make a commotion. Think what it would do to the reputation of this hotel. Look at the list, sir, for the name of a single man—a man who claims to be an art dealer—thin, in his forties, well-dressed, Dutch accent. He takes his breakfast at your café. Perhaps your waiter would remember this man. Although I assume he's registered under a false name."

Daniel thanked the Lord for this woman who had championed their cause and prayed for a change of mind. The man was wavering. Small beads of moisture spotted his forehead. His eyes darted from one of them to the other. He ran a finger under his collar.

"Very well. I recall the man you're talking about. I agree it would be better for all concerned if we checked out his room before the authorities are called." He opened the ledger and flipped back a few pages, then his finger slid down a list of signatures and stopped at one. "I believe the man's name is—" He leaned forward and squinted. "It's hard to read, but I think it says, *Georges Dufour*. A French name. Perhaps you are mistaken."

Neelie inclined her head. "Non, Monsieur. As we said, he wouldn't use his real name."

With pursed lips, the hotel manager turned to the cubbyholes behind him and took a key, then placed a phone call for someone to take his place at the desk. "If you'll accompany me, we will make short work of this."

The slow elevator ride was uncomfortably silent except for the groan of the pulleys laboring to lift them up. The four of them stood shoulder to shoulder in the small space, facing the same direction. The moment the door squeaked open, Daniel spilled out, but Monsieur Dureil held up an arm to block him.

"You must stay back and not cause a scene." The man huffed, spun around, and headed down the hall, stopping at the third door from the elevator. He knocked, then when no one answered, he put his ear to the door and knocked again.

Just then, the elevator door opened, and a man stepped out into the hall, carrying a bag. His gaze lifted at the sight of a crowd around his door. He strode past Daniel, his eyes on the hotel manager. "What is this all about?"

Daniel hid his fists behind his back. Tamar had been right. It was the man from the hospital, the man who'd vanished, the man Tamar believed was Bergman. It took everything he had to keep from grabbing the guy by the collar and hanging him from one of the hall light fixtures, demanding to know what he had done with his wife.

Isabelle must have sensed his anger and squeezed his arm.

The hotel manager's face reddened, and he blustered out a flow of words that Daniel couldn't understand, but Isabelle did. She held him back and stepped forward.

"We…uh…heard some sounds coming from this room. Like someone crying."

The man shook his head. "C'est impossible." He removed a key from his pocket, opened the door, and stepped back to let them enter. "See for yourself."

They piled in. Except for a newspaper and a closed suitcase on the bed, there was nothing to see. Even the bed was made.

"Obviously, you were mistaken. I was just preparing to check out." He set his bag down and gestured toward the bathroom. "Would you like to check in the shower?" The slight man's lips pursed. He seemed to be enjoying himself.

Daniel could constrain himself no longer. He shoved the man against the wall and lifted him up by the throat. "What have you done with my wife, Bergman?"

The man's eyes widened. "I don't know what you're talking

about. I don't even know who your wife is. Put me down or I'll call the police."

The manager yanked Daniel's arm from behind. "Are you insane? Put him down!"

Had he made a mistake? No, this was the same man who'd been in the burn ward—the same man from whom he'd removed the bandages that covered his face. "I see your scars are healing nicely. Excellent plastic surgery, but nothing that can't be undone." He tightened his hold around his neck, then set him forcefully on his feet. "Call the police, Nazi Officer Bergman." He enunciated every word.

The man's eyes smoldered as he smoothed his sleeves. "I don't know what you're talking about, but what I do know is that you accosted me in my room. Now I do recall having met your lovely wife down in the café, but as you can clearly see, she is not nor has she ever stepped foot in this room."

The manager bustled between Daniel and Bergman. "Now, there's no need to make a scene and upset the other guests. I'm sure, Mr. Feldman, that an apology will appease Mr. Dufour."

The yellow-bellied coward continued to sniff and strut as if he was the victim. "Monsieur Dufour, or whoever you're pretending to be, I don't know where you've taken my wife, but I assure you, I will find her, and when I do, the Nuremberg trials would be a tea party compared to—"

Neelie grabbed one arm, Isabelle the other, and they pulled Daniel toward the door.

When they were back in his own, Daniel paced the small space. Neelie sat on the bed, pulled off a shoe, and rubbed her foot, and Isabelle sat at the desk, staring out the window.

"I have to do something." He stepped out on the balcony and leaned over the railing, as if Tamar would come strolling up the sidewalk. Tears of frustration threatened, but he returned to the room.

Isabelle spoke up, running her fingers through her hair. "She wasn't under the bed or in the closet. I checked while you were otherwise engaged."

Neelie spoke for the first time, her voice just above a whisper. "Bergman's a smart man. Do you really think, if he'd abducted Tamar, that he'd keep her in a room so close to ours? Would you if you were him?"

He spun to face her. "No, I guess not. But what can I do? I've got to find her."

Isabelle shifted in her seat. "One thing, Neelie. Did you notice the bag he was carrying?"

She shook her head. "Not really."

"Well, while Daniel was *distracting* the men, I caught a glimpse of what was inside. Croque-monsieurs and two frites."

"So he's really hungry." Daniel sniffed.

"That thin of a man? Think about it. He came on this floor with a bag of sandwiches and french fries."

Daniel's jaw dropped. "You're brilliant, Isabelle." He strode to the desk and hugged her but backed up when she startled. "Sorry. So that means she's in this building. What are we waiting for? Should we call the police? We don't want him to move her someplace elsewhere." He glanced at his wristwatch. "Oh no, we've already lost a half an hour. We have to find him."

Neelie put on her shoes, stood, and patted his back. "Slow down. We have to do this right. Okay, think."

His gaze darted toward the door. "She's on this floor. That's where he got off the elevator. But she wasn't in that room, so she's in another, but how do we find out?"

Isabelle picked up the phone. "We need reinforcements. I'm going to call the security detail at the museum and ask them to come here. If we do find Bergman, he's not going to lie down easily."

Neelie went to the door. "Do you think there's a service elevator? Tamar wouldn't have come willingly with him, so he must have drugged her." She darted down the hall but came back minutes later. "There's one at the end of the hall around the corner. I counted twenty-six guestrooms, ten of which have the *Do not disturb* sign on the doorknob. If I had to guess, it would be one of those ten and the one closest to the service elevator."

Her eyes opened to the dark. Where was Daniel? She tried to move her hand, but it wouldn't budge, pins and needles in her fingertips the only response. It all came back. Bergman's enunciated words, his overly bright eyes, the tic of his lower lip that no plastic surgery could eradicate, those threats. She peered around. Was he in the room? Did she dare let him know she was awake again? Because if he knew—she didn't want to think of what could happen to her. It was easier to pretend to be asleep.

She listened for any sound, all her senses on alert. The rustle of a fabric. The odor of a cigarette. Nothing. What time was it? It had been hours since she'd used the restroom. Surely, Bergman wouldn't want her to have an accident. "Hello? Is anyone here?"

No answer. Was he toying with her?

She squirmed. "Hello? I need to use the bathroom." She tried to move her feet and realized they were tied down as well, the twine digging into her ankles. Lifting her head, she saw the outline of a rope around her chest that was holding her tight to the bed. At least he hadn't stuffed her mouth with a cloth.

In the fog that swirled in her head, in the dizziness, she hadn't thought to pray. Now she would and she would do it out loud. "'Lord, God of heaven, all power rests in Your hands.'" Verses she'd memorized edged away the haze. "'He will cover me with His feathers, and I will find refuge under His wings. His faithfulness will be my protective shield. I will not fear the terror of the night, the…'" Words failed her, but songs took their place.

Songs from shul. Songs she'd learned at camp. Hymns from the congregation Daniel and she attended whenever he didn't have to work. Songs she'd taught the twins. At first, her voice was tight, and indeed, she longed for a drink of water. But despite the bindings around her chest, she was able to pull in deep breaths, and her voice came out strong. As loud as she could, she bellowed out one tune after another. Oh, that someone would hear. Someone would call the desk. Someone would complain.

Tamar tried to concentrate on the words—the promises of her God, her Redeemer. They were all she could cling to now. But thoughts of Bergman hearing her made her lower her voice until she focused on the promises again. She had to believe that because this room looked almost identical to their room, she was in the hotel somewhere. Maybe on the same floor.

Wake up, Daniel. Wake up, Neelie. Find me before he comes back.

Daniel couldn't sleep, though Neelie had urged him to. The police had been notified after the hotel manager had refused to allow entrance to the guards from the Jeu de Paume. But the officer who'd shown up was as dubious of Daniel's claim of a Nazi having kidnapped his wife as the hotel manager had been. Daniel had to admit, it sounded far-fetched.

He stared at the ceiling. Every time he closed his eyes, horrific images of what that monster was doing to his wife kept sleep at bay. Even with Isabelle taking the first hour of watch, he couldn't just lie here doing nothing. Enough. He sat up, grabbed his shoes, and slipped out the door.

Quiet met him in the cloying, floral hall as he passed the elevator. The dim lights lent a sinister feel where crime seemed to wait to pounce from every door. Even the air was as stilted and heavy as a funeral parlor's. He stopped at the third door, leaning his ear close. Nothing. Bergman was probably with Tamar right now. Daniel summoned a shuddering breath, continued to the end of the hall, and rounded the corner.

Isabelle leaned against the wall at the end of the hall, her head bobbing. He'd let her sleep. It had been a long day for all of them. He glanced at his watch—two in the morning. Pivoting, he made his way to the other end of the U-shaped hall, past their door—his and Tamar's. A lump formed and tears welled.

Rounding the corner, a slight sound reached his ears. A voice. Female. Muffled. He stepped up his pace, breaking into a run at the familiar song. Hebrew. That voice he'd know anywhere. Two doors from the service elevator, he stopped. Listened, just to be sure.

"Thank you, Lord," he breathed.

Daniel backed up to kick the door open, but reason made him stop mid-stride. He had no weapon—only the rage that would lead him nowhere. Time to call the police. Yet he didn't want to break the tenuous connection. What if Bergman took her somewhere while he was making the call? He noted the room number and ran to alert Isabelle and Neelie.

In minutes, they stood facing the front desk. The night

manager—a man with thick black eyebrows and a dour expression—was even less agreeable than his predecessor. Neelie stood in robe and slippers, her fierce, alert eyes belying her apparel. Isabelle demanded he call the police immediately in a flurry of French that left Daniel nodding but understanding nothing.

"Tell him to hurry. If Tamar was singing, that might mean she's alone in the room—"

"Or he's making her sing," Neelie interrupted. "I don't think he'd do that if someone might hear."

The manager made the call, although Daniel caught the roll of his eyes. When the man set the receiver back, Daniel beckoned the women toward the elevator, then called over his shoulder to the man, "Room 166, Monsieur."

Once the elevator door closed, Daniel said, "We don't want to let Bergman know we're onto to him, or he might hurt her. He won't have anything to lose at this point."

"So what should we do?" Isabelle smoothed back a strand of hair that had escaped her chignon.

Neelie posted her hands on her hips. "Why, we pray for God's rescue. He doesn't wage war the way we do. We need to do things His way. Let's go to your room, Daniel."

That was the last thing Daniel wanted to do, but Neelie was a tower of strength when it came to faith. Bergman wouldn't have a prayer.

Like the walls of Jericho, the unfolding events came tumbling down quickly—too fast for Daniel to do anything but leap out of the way. Two gendarmes and the manager knocked on their door ten minutes after they'd started praying. "A slow night," the officer said. He slowly took out a pad of paper and asked for an account of what had happened.

Couldn't they do this later? Every second away from Tamar was crucial. Daniel gave a quick narrative, drumming his fingers on the desk as Isabelle translated and the officer scribbled what she said.

Finally, he stood, telling them to stay in the room and let him and his partner handle it. That wasn't going to happen. They followed the manager and the police officers to the room near the service elevator. Each officer stood on either side of the door, their guns at the ready. One officer motioned to the manager to knock, which he did.

"Daniel?" Tamar's faint voice.

Daniel rushed to the door and rested his cheek against it. "Tamar?"

The manager fumbled through a ring of keys until he found the one that opened the door. He put the key in, turned it, and—

The service elevator whirred. Bergman?

The police officers opened the door and waved them all into the room, whispering for them to be quiet, then silently shut the door. A desk lamp provided light.

"Everyone find a hiding place. He may have a gun," one of the police officers whispered. His gestures to hide were easier to follow than his words.

The manager, Neelie, and Isabelle hurried into the bathroom. The police officers hid behind the closet door, their guns at the ready. A gasp from the far corner. Tamar. Daniel rushed to the bed by the window. "Tamar?" He dropped to the side of the bed. Saw the rope binding her legs and arms. "What did he do to you?"

She lifted her hands as far as she could. "Daniel?"

The sound of the key in the lock. "Shh." Daniel put his finger to his lips, then lay prone in the space between the bed and the wall. Bergman was too smart to be duped. If the police didn't apprehend him immediately, taking advantage of the element of surprise, he'd get away—or worse. And Tamar was so vulnerable lying there. An easy target for a madman.

Tamar's dry lips tightened. So close to safety. So close but so far. Bergman would win in the end. He always did. The evil in his heart made him invincible. She'd not give away the hiding place of the police officers by looking at the closet where they hid. In fact, she'd close her eyes when he looked her way. Better for her if he thought she was sleeping.

Bergman walked in. She could actually hear him sniff as if he smelled something in the air. His key fell to the desk, making her start. He grabbed his key again, then whipped around at the squeak of the closet door. The two police officers walked toward him, revolvers trained on him, leaving no room for him to flee.

One of the police officers pulled out his badge. "Erich Bergman, you're under arrest."

Did Bergman have a gun? He wouldn't give up easily. Tamar's eyes were wide open as she watched the movie unfold.

A knowing, smirky smile covered Bergman's face as he backed up, stuffing his hand into his pocket.

"Hands up. Now," said one of the officers, training his revolver on her captor.

Bergman's eyes lingered sideways on Tamar, always in control, always with that smile. He raised one hand, the other swiped a fistful of something from the desk, stuffing it between his lips, then joining his other hand in the air. His gaze never left her as the officer cuffed his hands behind his back and pushed him into the chair. Still, he sat watching her. He didn't even flinch when Daniel stood and Neelie came out of the bathroom and hurried over to her.

Daniel sat on the edge of the bed, leaned over, and kissed her forehead, nose, and lips, then took his Swiss army knife out of his pocket and cut the bindings that held her. Tamar sat up slowly, swallowing past the nausea and the dizziness. She rubbed the life back into her numb fingers, then gently circled the red welts on her wrists.

"For what crime am I being held?" Bergman's first words were low and slow but a bit garbled, his eyes never leaving her.

"Kidnapping, for one," said one of the officers.

"Theft of art." Isabelle held up the portfolio. "I found this in the closet."

"War crimes," Neelie almost shouted.

Bergman rolled his eyes. "Good luck with that." His head bobbed a bit, and his eyes blinked as if he was trying to rouse himself. Yet that smile remained.

Tamar narrowed her eyes at him. "If you want a confession, you'd better hurry." She lifted her chin.

Just then, Neelie's words came back to her. *Justice is a virtue, but forgiveness is divine.* It would take all of God's help to forgive this man. She swallowed against a dry throat. "You're a coward, Officer Bergman. Taking your life like your predecessor." Her words hit their mark because his brows furrowed into a *V*. "But I…forgive you," she said under her breath. "It doesn't make it right what you did, but I don't want to carry this bitterness another second. I can't."

He continued to stare at her, a single tear sprouting and rolling down his cheek. That controlled smile vanished, replaced by a series of tics, and for the first time, she saw the man behind the mask. His head drooped, bobbed twice, and rested.

A police officer rushed over and checked his pulse. "He's fading."

Instead of relief, tears filled her eyes. Her arms circled Daniel's neck, and he rocked her gently back and forth as he did Peri when he'd fallen.

"Not exactly how I wanted to spend my last day in Paris," she said, sniffing and peering up at him through the tears.

A weak smile played on Daniel's lips. "I heard your singing."

She laughed. "This voice of mine is a blessing and a curse."

Blockheaded fools. Appearances made it easy to deceive. The plastic surgery had taught him that. The cocktail of drugs that mimicked hypothermia was having its effect. Thought Tamar could be trusted. Big mistake. Love had made him careless. Well, the doctor won the battle, but the war was his to be won. People didn't pay attention to the dead. Next time…there'd be no…survivors.

Epilogue

"Now, Mr. Oppenheimer, keep your hands to yourself." Tamar skirted another of his grasps and rolled her eyes. "I'm here to sing. Don't you want to hear me?"

The old man pointed at his lips. "Just one little kiss on my smacker."

Neelie walked up behind his wheelchair. "Are you giving Miss Tamar a hard time? She won't come back and sing if you don't behave." She patted the old man's moth-eaten cardigan that he refused to throw away. "You know she comes all the way from Haarlem to sing for us." Bending down beside him, she wiped the drool from his chin. He was already nodding off.

"He's harmless," Tamar said, low enough not to wake him up. "When I first started coming to the rehab center, all he did was stare straight ahead. I'd say flirting with me is a step in the right direction." She winked at her tante.

Neelie stood and took hold of the handles. "All the residents are in the common room waiting for you. Of course, the twins are entertaining them."

"Oh no, what are they doing now?" She spun around and headed toward the common room with Neelie on her heels.

"Don't worry about them. Zari's standing on a chair behind the podium pretending to read a book to them, and Peri's making funny faces. The children are a big hit. They remind the residents of happier times."

At least two dozen men and women sat in chairs or wheelchairs in a semicircle facing the piano and the podium. Before going to the microphone, Tamar called the twins to her side and greeted each guest with a handshake or a hug. Some of them seemed so frail, the labor camps having aged them by decades. Dear people with so many scars. Her hand went to her face. Had she aged decades as well?

Tamar returned to the makeshift stage, checking the microphone with a tap of her finger. She nodded to the pianist and opened with a familiar Yiddish song. Although a few of the residents stared at nothing or slept, most nodded to the rhythm or swayed or sang along. The children danced and twirled uninhibited in the space between the podium and the audience. Amazing, how therapeutic her twins' antics were for this group—just by being themselves.

After singing a few songs, she thanked them and joined Neelie, who stood against the back wall as the attendants entered to accompany the residents to the dining room for lunch. "It seems more of the people are participating now."

"Your singing is a balm for them, Tamar. It calls them back to the times before the war. Now if we could just persuade that husband of yours to join you and the kids," Neelie said.

She pressed her arms against her chest. "I know. After our trip to Paris, I thought he would agree to come for counseling, but he's back to working too many hours."

"In God's time, Tamar. In God's time, he'll come around."

Tamar pushed herself away from the wall. "Well, I should grab the kids before Peri breaks something."

"He's a good boy." Neelie ran a hand up and down Tamar's sleeve. "I know this isn't the opera, but your time will come."

"Now that Sneider and Margot have been arrested, the opera won't be opening any time soon, but I'm okay. The twins need me right now, and Daniel does too. And you know what? Now that Bergman's dead, I'm not afraid of my shadow anymore. I don't need justice anymore. I couldn't be happier than with where I am right now." She looked at her aunt. "And you? Any more news on when you'll be moving to Paris?"

Neelie lifted a shoulder. "It isn't easy finding a replacement here, but I'm planning to go for a long weekend once Jan gets settled in his new apartment." She enveloped Tamar in a hug. "I'm so happy that you're happy. Will we see you next Thursday?"

"Of course, and maybe we could plan a picnic with the twins." Tamar gathered the children's jackets and found them sitting at a table with some white-haired women, who were letting them nibble on their sandwiches. With an apologetic shake of her head, she said, "C'mon, kids. We need to hurry to catch the train home. It's a long walk back to the station, and I'm not going to carry you."

She lifted the rucksack over a shoulder and took the twins by the hands. The minute she opened the door, a warm blast of sun met her. "Such a pretty day. Maybe we can go to the park at home and—"

"Papa!" Peri clamored down the stairs and threw his arms around his father's legs.

"What are you doing here?" she said. Something must be wrong. His face said it all.

Daniel bent down and picked Peri up. "I have some bad news." He kissed her temple and ruffled Zari's hair.

"What happened?" What could be so bad that he'd leave work to come all the way to Amsterdam? "Why didn't you come into the rehab center?"

He shook his head as if the very thought was repugnant. "I received a call from Isabelle LeClair. She said Neelie's father passed away last night. Isabelle thought it best that we tell her in person. That's why I'm here."

"Oh," was all she could say. Daniel pulled her down onto a step, sat next to her, and posted the twins on each of his knees. "To have just met him and then to lose him, and he didn't get to meet Jan."

"He was a very sick man." Daniel rested his lips against his daughter's hair. "I guess there's comfort in knowing she had two days with him, at least."

"There's that, but it will still be tough on Neelie. Losing her son to Paris and now this. Should I bring her out here, or should we go in?"

He swallowed and shifted to stare up at the tall brick building with a transom over the black door. "I guess it would be best to go inside. But there's something else." His gaze was solemn as he locked eyes on her.

"What is it?" Why did troubles come all at once? She was hardly over Bergman, and now there was more?

"It's good news, really. Your brother and Hadassah have received word that they'll be able to make Aliyah this month."

"Oh, so they'll be moving to Israel." Was everyone being torn away from her? Moving to Zion had been their hearts' desire ever since the war ended. But she would miss them so much—even her brother's constant barbs. "Well, let's throw them the best going-away party we can!" She cut a glance at his profile when he didn't respond in kind. "There's more?" She grabbed Peri as he leaped from the fifth step. "Enough, Peri." She placed him next to his father.

Daniel blew Zari's hair away from his face as she wrapped his tie around her wrist. "Nothing, really. It's just, everyone seems to be moving forward but me. You remember when we said we wanted to tell the world about what happened behind the barbed wire? They'd believe us because we'd been there? Well, you and Neelie are here using the gifts God gave you to help the survivors. Seth and Hadassah are going to help establish Israel. That's huge. And Jan and Isabelle have dedicated their lives to returning stolen art—"

"Stop it, Daniel. You're using your medical expertise to heal burn victims. That's huge too."

"I was this close to Bergman's face, and I wasn't astute enough to recognize plastic surgery, even when you insisted it was him. I'm so sorry I didn't listen to you. I let a Nazi slip through my hands, and I almost lost you." He chewed on his lower lip. Suddenly, he stood, lifted Zari to sit on his shoulders, and helped Tamar to her feet. "Well, I'm done living in limbo. You and I and these little ones are going to do what we set out to do." He turned to face the building, seized Peri's hand, and took a step up. "And it starts here."

The End

Dear Readers.

I hope this book blessed your heart in some way. It and its predecessor, *A Song for Her Enemies*, may be the most significant books I'll ever write. It would mean so much to me to chat with you, answer any questions you may have, even pray with you. Listed here are the different conduits to reach me. Please consider writing an honest review on Amazon, Goodreads, or any site that you use. We writers need reviews and people to read our books.

Thank you,

Sherri Stewart

Newsletter Facebook Twitter Instagram Website

Sherri Stewart is woman of faith who loves all things foreign and different—whether it's food, culture, or language. A former French teacher, principal, attorney, and flight attendant, her passion is traveling to the settings of her books, sampling the food, and visiting the sites. She savored boterkoeken in Amsterdam for *A Song for Her Enemies*, and crème brûlée in Paris for its sequel, *What Hides behind the Walls*. A widow, Sherri lives in the Orlando area with her dog, Lily, and her son, Joshua, who always has to fix her computer. As an author, editor, blogger, speaker, and Bible teacher, she hopes her books will entertain and challenge readers to live large and connect with their Savior. Join, chat, and share with her on social media. Newsletter Facebook Twitter Instagram Website

9 781956 654790